WE DARE NOT
WHISPER

WE DARE NOT WHISPER

Jan Netolicky

BRICK MANTEL BOOKS
BLOOMINGTON, INDIANA

Published by Brick Mantel Books, USA

Brick Mantel
BOOKS
www.BrickMantelBooks.com
info@BrickMantelBooks.com

An imprint of Pen & Publish, Inc.
www.PenandPublish.com
Bloomington, Indiana
(314) 827-6567

Print ISBN: 978-1-941799-15-4
eBook ISBN: 978-1-941799-16-1

Cover Design: Jennifer Geist

For Rick

TABLE OF CONTENTS

Prologue...7

PART ONE: Before...9

PART TWO: After... 179

PART THREE: Now...249

Acknowledgments 255

Discussion Questions for *We Dare Not Whisper* 257

Remembering.

All those mornings I ran the shower, hot and long, until the bathroom mirror wept steam, clouding my reflection. I did not want to see evidence of Mother's handiwork, see my eyes bruised from lack of sleep, see the lines that creased my forehead and etched parentheses of sorrow around my mouth. Bracing my arms on either side of the basin, I practiced what I would say to her if I could, snarling essays of anger composed and endlessly revised through the brutal night hours, never finding an attack cruel enough to match my pain.

My brown eyes blackened with the darkness of my rage. "How could you? What gives you the right?" Silent screams echoed in my head. "You bitch. You selfish bitch."

Hollow words. Empty now. But then? Then, to give voice to those words would have been a relief. To fill my lungs with air, to feel my chest rise in righteous anger, to shriek the assault on my mother—surely, that would stop the bleeding, would salve the wound. Maybe, then, a scar might form, pink and puckered, a reminder I'd done battle and survived.

Everyone would see, of course. My scars rise in thick, ropy relief, marking each indignity I've ever suffered like a soldier's medals worn to commemorate bravery. There's the now-smoothed ridge from sixth grade when Debbie Halloran buckled my locked knees from behind. I fell awkwardly—as I do everything—slashing my right knee in an asymmetrical Z. Or the vestiges from the gym class volleyball game where I slammed my head against the wooden floor. My memory convinces me I made a spectacular dig in response to a vicious spike, and the ensuing split lip and bloodied eyebrow were a fair exchange for the save. Others may have a different recollection, one in which my slow and clumsy feet tangle themselves in a comic pratfall, but they are my scars and I may attribute them to heroics if I choose.

The sad truth? I am no hero and silencing pain is not an act of valor. Silence is simply a lie we dare not whisper, and it doesn't matter if we lie to save face or to hide the truth or to protect the ones we love. I will not be silent anymore. Not just for Mother and Dad, but for Jonny. And for my son.

It isn't fair, you know, that Trey idolizes Jonny. My brother isn't here. I am. But it doesn't matter. Absent or not, Jonny is his hero. From the time he could walk, Trey mimicked Jonny's every mannerism, perfecting the imitation until you could swear he was Jonny in miniature. Even now, when Trey pushes his hair back from his eyes or pulls up his T-shirt, exposing his belly so that he might wipe sweat from his eyes with the relatively clean underside of the fabric, I draw an involuntary breath and squint to make sure Jonny has not suddenly been shrunk to Trey's three-foot-four frame. I see Jonny when Trey concentrates with single-minded ferocity, crinkling his brow, chewing his fingernail. I see Jonny when Trey sets his shoulders and crosses his arms in a rare show of defiance. And when Trey reluctantly succumbs to exhaustion after a day of chasing frogs and building stone towers in the garden, he channels Jonny's characteristic stretch, lacing his fingers behind his neck and flexing his bent elbows back. Seeing him so posed, I could almost believe his arms have become angels' wings.

Does Jonny wear angels' wings? Had he earned that right in his twenty short years? Or is the cross where he died nothing more than an asterisk footnoting the epicenter of our family's despair?

PART ONE:
BEFORE

ONE

Jonny was born on Valentine's Day, one of the snowiest on record in our southeastern Wisconsin community. Being so near Lake Michigan, spectacular storms courtesy of the lake effect are routine but rarely are we Midwesterners stymied by the weather. Hardships shape our character, we proudly maintain, and if we sometimes bow our heads against a stiff wind, we convince ourselves that we are simply giving thanks at the altar of our resiliency. Even for the heartiest of us, this was a snowstorm for the record books.

The storm began innocuously enough late in the afternoon on the thirteenth of February. Although forecasters had been predicting up to a foot of snow by morning, the sky had seemed benign during the day. But as dusk approached, silent clouds of rosy-gray flannel crowded the heavens and big fluffy flakes fell endlessly, straight down, like a stage curtain dropped from a vast proscenium. By the time Dad had placed boiled hot dogs and his signature jalapeño mac and cheese on the table, snow had covered the bottom step leading up to the back porch which wrapped around two sides of our house.

"Go on and eat now, Luce," he said. "You can get another bottle of ketchup out of the pantry if there's not enough here. I'm going to check on your mother." He disappeared into their bedroom just around the corner from the kitchen. I heard him murmur, "What can I do for you, Bets?"

On doctor's orders, Mother had been confined to her bed for the last month. She insisted she was *not* going to the Aurora Women's Pavilion in West Allis to wait for the delivery of this child, world-class obstetrics and NICU notwithstanding, no matter what Dr. Bennet said. Yes, she was spotting occasionally, and no, the baby didn't seem to kick as frequently as I had in the last trimester, but Mother was not an alarmist. "Dr. Bennet is worse than a little old lady. I'm fine. I'm perfectly fine," she insisted. "Besides, I have plenty of labor to manage here at home. I'd go crazy at Aurora, just twiddling my thumbs and waiting."

Even though she was swollen and uncomfortable, she was resolute in her belief this child would arrive with far less drama than that which accompanied my birth. On the matter of a precautionary hospital stay, Dad tended to side with Dr. Bennet, but—as in most disputes with Mother—her will prevailed. And so she settled in at home to wait. Dad and I engaged in a delicate ballet of being present but unobtrusive until we were called upon to perform some menial task. After school, I usually started a load of laundry and set the table, sorted the mail and fed Gunner, our yellow Lab. Occasionally, I might even dust around the lamps and groupings of pillar candles my mother favored or run the vacuum cleaner while my father fixed dinner. The arrangement worked because of Dad's job which, in other circumstances, gave rise to Mother's biting indictment of his "spectacular underachievement." The feed mill he managed was on property adjacent to our farmhouse in rural Waukesha County, so he was never too far from my mother's side.

I know why Dad worried. He remembered my birth eleven years earlier, just three days before Thanksgiving. I was a huge baby, all nine pounds, fourteen ounces of me, and Mother endured excruciating back labor for nearly twenty-three hours. She once admitted in a moment of weakness that she screamed obscenities at anyone who recklessly ventured into the delivery room during the last seven hours. Coincidentally, news of the Jonestown Massacre had dominated the airwaves in the days just prior to my birth, and Mother supposedly requested a Kool-Aid cocktail from one of the delivery nurses. "I hated you before you were born," she told me, "for the hellish labor you put me through. And I haven't quite forgiven you yet." This last was admitted with a conspiratorial laugh, as though her weak attempt at humor would soften the truth of her confession.

I can say with certainty that my birth was just the first of many trials I inflicted upon my mother. Not only did I ignore her inflexible timetable with my delayed entrance upon her stage, I caused her uncommon pain in the process. I had also proven to be an inadequate substitute for the child who was stillborn just three months after her marriage to my father.

Her punishment began with my name. Dad wanted to call me Jeannette after Mother's favorite great aunt. "No, Nolan," Mother insisted. This one reminds me more of your side of the family. Your mother." I never knew if Mother referred to Grandmother's and my physical similarities—large-boned frame, mousy brown hair, dark eyes, and olive-tinged complexion—or to our dispositions. I suppose, in the end, it really didn't matter. On my mother's balance sheet, neither of us quite tallied approval. And so I was named for Grandmother Lucinda Evelyn, mercifully shortened to Luce by my father.

As I grew older, I suspected that, for Mother, Luce was short for Lucifer since she reminded me constantly I was the devil incarnate. At times, Luce might also be a clever homonym for *loose,* an adjective my mother would apply to my tongue, my morals, and the clothing she insisted most appropriately camouflaged my size 16 frame. "Girls your size shouldn't wear revealing skirts," she would admonish. "That skimpy T-shirt is simply too tight. Change it. No one wants to see those rolls around your middle."

Our battles pitted her rules against my rebellion, her disapproval against my disregard. She usually won and I retreated, bloodied by vicious swipes of her razor tongue.

A little before three in the morning on that Valentine's Day, fluttering pain signaled the onset of Mother's labor. Dad fired up the tractor and cleared our long drive out to the highway, only to discover there was no highway to find. He would not, as he had planned, have time to shuttle me to Grandmother Lucinda's before driving Mother to the hospital. Even as her contractions intensified, Mother stubbornly insisted we could safely navigate to his mother's home and then trek to the hospital. Whether she was truly concerned for my comfort during her delivery or she simply wanted me conveniently absent, I can't say. In retrospect, those last long months of her pregnancy must have thrown Mother off her game not to factor in errant February weather, stranded snowplows, and a rising wind which created blinding whiteouts.

For once, Dad overruled her. He ushered us both to the Explorer, engaged the four-wheel drive, and drove as fast as caution and visibility would allow. With uncharacteristic forcefulness, he had the final word. "Luce can curl up on a couch in the waiting room. I'll have Mom come to get her as soon as the roads are cleared. We need to get you to the doctor."

As it turned out, I didn't need to curl up anywhere. Jonathan Ian Garrison was born exactly eleven minutes after we arrived at the emergency room, our shoulders tight with the urgency of our mission. Mother couldn't have been happier. She had no time for an epidural or episiotomy. Jonny had been considerately prompt, perfectly proportioned, serene in the midst of a hurried delivery, and the boy she had always wanted. Mother's fierce love affair with her son began, auspiciously, on the day of hearts. Dad and I were witnesses to this grand affair, but not participants.

Two

I **first saw Jonny through the** expansive glass separating the new-born nursery from the visitors' viewing hallway. Dad lifted me in his arms so I could see, unimpeded by the presence of other baby-gazers. Jonny was tightly swaddled in a white blanket, his head covered by a tiny stocking cap adorned with delicate red hearts, handiwork courtesy of the Aurora Hospital Ladies' Auxiliary. In our haste to get Mother to the hospital I had forgotten my glasses. Even though I squinted, the little valentines on his cap looked like droplets of blood on a snowy field.

Three

When I was a child, my favorite pastime involved dragging a tall stool to my mother's closet where she kept her cache of family photo albums and high school yearbooks. On the shelf above the rod which held her cotton camp shirts and serviceable Levis she had stacked boxes of photos and leather-bound diaries, the contents of each one labeled by year in bold black Magic Marker. I was always careful to replace the boxes exactly as I had found them. I imagined if I inadvertently rearranged the contents, I would somehow rewrite the events of her life before she met and married my father.

Pictures of her in her infancy were my favorite, perhaps because as a baby she did not yet manifest the bitterness of the woman she became. Maybe the signs were there, but I was simply unobservant. Mother certainly maintained as much through most of my childhood. I remember an elementary school lesson on growth and human development in which our teachers posted pictures of themselves as babies and invited students to match the photos with their adult counterparts. I was miserably inept at the game, somehow oblivious to clues such as Mrs. McPherson's widow's peak or Mr. Tilly's sharp nose.

No, I could not envision Mother's plump cheeks would become gaunt, her perfect rosebud mouth would eventually thin into a desperate little line, her unusually light eyes would darken, either with rage or resignation. My mother was a beautiful child.

My mother's parents, Aldrich and Elnora Pennick, doted on her. She was an enchanting little thing, yes, but she was also a miracle baby of sorts. According to family lore, told *ad nauseum* at every holiday gathering, after several vain attempts at becoming pregnant, a despairing Elnora broke down at a Fourth of July picnic. Sure she was destined never to give birth to a child, she sobbed over a plate of potato salad and grilled brats and announced she and Aldrich were initiating adoption. She believed she was infertile and needed to move on by enlisting her father's law firm in the search for an infant. Caucasian. A girl, certainly. With luck, the offspring of handsome parents who would be bright enough to understand that giving their child to Elnora and Aldrich would be the ultimate act of selflessness. To celebrate her future magnanimity, Elnora drank Vodka gimlets all afternoon. That evening, she conceived Elizabeth Claire Pennick, forever known as Bets. Beloved, beautiful Bets, photographed more often than Marilyn Monroe. Her albums chronicle her childhood, each moment labeled with date, event, and—occasionally—editorial comment.

Elnora and Bets, 2 hours old! Mother, already eschewing standard issue hospital garb, robed in delicate pink knit. Grammy Elnora, flushed and jubilant.

Bets, 13 months. Big girl! Mother taking her first solo steps, belly and elbows forward, arms posed as though performing some funky dance rhythm.

"Queen" Bets on her throne, 27 months. Mother, naked, perched on the potty chair.

Bets, 3ʳᵈ birthday. Yum! Princess Cake from Sendik's! Mother, in rhinestone tiara and white satin dress adorned with layers of tulle ruffles, surrounded by opened gifts and elaborately wrapped presents.

Bets, first day at school w/ Miss Nelson, kindergarten teacher. Mother clutching Cinderella backpack. Miss Nelson, kneeling.

Bets visited by Tooth Fairy, age 6. Mother, gap-toothed, brandishing a five-dollar bill.

Bets, recital, age 7. Cutest of the 101 Dalmatians! Mother in white leotard with black spots, performing with similarly clad dancing Dalmatians. Is she out of step, or are they?

Bets playing with Plantation Belle Barbie.
Bets turning cartwheels on the lawn.
Bets riding a carousel pony.
Bets chasing the family's Wheaten terrier.
Bets with commencement medals.
Bets laughing with boys. Lots of boys.
Bets. Endless Bets, always smiling. Always.

Perched on the stool in her closet, I used to imagine my own image superimposed upon my mother's face in those photographs. I imitated her confident poses, the saucy set of her shoulders, the way she grinned just so for the camera. Who could not want to be my mother?

Now, though, I often wonder if those photos documented Mother's enchanted life or Grammy Elnora's ruthless culling of ugly reality.

FOUR

Fifteen years into their marriage, my parents were vastly different people than they had been when they first met. This is not idle conjecture on my part. Her diaries offer beguiling proof that once she loved him.

Mother met my father during her last year at Marquette. Following the traditional Pennick family career path, she was studying law—her specialty was to be corporate patents, but she failed to earn her degree. In my presence, at least, she never blamed Dad for changing her life and ending the Pennick legacy of family lawyers, but one of her later diary entries confesses her bitterness.

> *One semester. That's it. One stinking semester short. That, the bar exam . . . a LIFE. STUPID. FUCKING STUPID.*

Had things been different and Jonny were still alive, I doubt she would worry her lost career. She'd be too busy interfering in his life to bother with briefs and court dates.

When she and my father met, she was engaged to a classmate who hailed from Racine. Antony's family was Italian; he was exotically handsome and fiercely Roman Catholic. The Pennick clan had little time for religion, but Mother accompanied her fiancé to weekly masses and agreed to become a member of his parish to demonstrate her commitment to him. She once joked she was willing to accept his religious devotion if he was willing to let her drive his MG.

Turns out, the joke wasn't so funny. When Antony was vacationing with his family in Rome, supposedly making arrangements for his extended Italian clan to attend the nuptials, he left the MG with Mother. She drove that little red convertible to a patent seminar sponsored by a Milwaukee law firm for which she was interning. The seminar was held at the Convention Center, coincidentally the site of a regional agricultural expo. In what would be described as a "meet cute" in film parlance, she and my father literally bumped into one another. I should say that my mother accidentally dented the passenger side rocker panel of my father's Chevy Cavalier with the rear end of Antony's MG as she was exiting her parking space.

They exchanged insurance cards and phone numbers. One thing led to another, and by the time Antony returned from the old country, my mother had returned his MG, restored to its original finish, and her engagement ring. She and Nolan James Garrison were now officially an item.

I'm not exactly sure what possessed my mother to abandon Antony, who seemed to be her perfectly scripted life partner. Although he didn't possess Antony's European flair, my father was a good-looking young man . . . a bit under six feet, slender but with a muscular build from his job at the feed mill. His light brown hair sported steaks of sun-bleached gold, and there was an appealing earnestness in his wide-set brown eyes.

Looks aside, he'd probably languish untapped on today's e-dating websites. According to Mother's diary, my father wasn't much for parties or big crowds. He didn't go to bars, avoided live theater and museums, and fine dining meant any place where he waited less than ten minutes for a table on Saturday night. But at the time, at least, Mother seemed to find these departures from her own lifestyle "charming" and "sweet." She gushed about his sincerity, about his ability to win the unwavering devotion of the few people he allowed to get close, about the way she just knew anything he told her was the God-honest truth. I suppose in her circles, she had never encountered someone so *real* as my father before. Too, Mother was always used to being pursued, and I don't think my father was ever a hunter. Is indifference a powerful aphrodisiac?

Once she had sighted my father in her crosshairs, her diaries reveal a rather calculated, systematic approach to winning his affections. My mother, who could not to this day define a walk-off homerun or a squeeze bunt, shamelessly feigned interest in my father's one true passion: baseball. He had been a lifelong Cubs fan, heretical thinking in Milwaukee. To those few willing to listen, he could cite batting averages and on-base percentages, recall with uncanny detail lore from the franchise's storied history, and make nonchalant reference to Ernie Banks or Ron Santo or Fergie Jenkins as though they had been his childhood chums. Frankly, even when OSHA required Dad to recertify in CPR for his job at the mill, he resuscitated the dummy with chest compressions to the beat of "Tinker to Evers to Chance . . . push; Tinker to Evers to Chance . . . push." Who knew that the Cubs' fabled double play combination would win games AND save lives?

Mother was no fool. Wanting to avoid awkward silences in the earliest days of their courtship, she coyly introduced the Home Run Game. It became a familiar constant, and they played it every time they went anywhere in my father's Cavalier. The rules were simple: Mother would name the starting location, a compass point direction, and a number between one and ten (perhaps the Blatz Brewery Complex on Broadway / southwest / four). Then she would decide upon an arbitrary time limit, anything falling within thirty-minute parameters. As soon as the clock started running, Dad would drive in the designated direction, attempting to score "runs" based upon his luck or his skill at navigating through intersections. Red lights meant an automatic out. If he logged three outs before the allotted time had expired, Dad lost the game. For every green traffic signal they sailed through, Dad was given a "hit" in Mother's score book. No extra bases here, only singles. Consequently, it took four "hits" to score a run. In the case of yellow lights, Mother was the umpire, and her rulings were never overturned.

I gather that if my father managed to score runs equal to or greater than the target number Mother had named, the rewards were sexual. Perhaps, at first, a kiss or maybe a fleeting brush of his hand against her breast. Later, the stakes were higher. Knowing my mother, I would venture the runs needed to *score*, initially, were impossible to achieve. Brilliant, really. And if he knew Mother was blatantly manipulative, Dad seemed eager to play by her rules, a pattern that never varied even long after they abandoned the Home Run Game.

Cliché though it may seem, Mother became pregnant only a few months after they begin dating. By design? I don't know. But if their relationship truly mirrored America's Favorite Sport, Mother's post season priority wasn't her unborn child. On the day her test results were confirmed, Mother's diary hardly mentions my father and the fact that they would forever be linked by the baby growing inside her. Rather, her entries all focus on Grammy Elnora's sense of urgency in booking the Wisconsin Club for a December wedding reception. Mother's baby bump notwithstanding, my grandparents were determined to spring for an outlandishly expensive wedding—the kind my mother certainly would have staged had Antony been standing at the end of the aisle.

Mother's wedding pictures are beautiful, and many. Thankfully, Mother and Dad did not fall prey to the styles embraced by most seventies-era couples. For them, no groomsmen in ruffled shirts, cream tuxedos, and bow ties to match the pastel gowns of the bridesmaids. Dad and company were impeccable in crisp, black one-button tuxes, tailored shirts with French cuffs and pearl studs. The bridesmaids wore simple but elegant tea-length sheaths in emerald green, and Mother, as always, took center stage in an elaborate gown with beaded bodice and gossamer sleeves. Although Grammy Elnora hired (according to one diary entry) the "best photographer in Milwaukee" to masterfully frame each picture and perhaps camouflage for future generations Mother's pregnancy, I doubt whether anyone at the affair was fooled by the A-line silhouette of her wedding dress.

Pictures in the wedding album, like those of Mother's childhood, artfully document the high points of the event. Pre-ceremony shots find Mother and Grammy Elnora adjusting the folds of the gown and posing in almost-embrace. There's one of Mother in soft focus, eyes cast demurely on her bouquet of crimson roses, and another of her gazing at the spectacular stained glass window in the sanctuary. Others capture Granddad Aldrich cradling Mother's chin, bridesmaids cementing their elaborate up-dos with Helene Curtis hairspray, and groomsmen wearing Cubs hats, baseball bats resting casually on their shoulders. The album also includes an endless number of composed groupings, all the possible permutations of relatives and wedding party bookending the newly wedded couple who, by the way, appear nearly as plastic and perfect as the miniature bride and groom adorning the wedding cake.

Without benefit of flash bulbs, the shots taken during the exchange of vows have an unreal, almost peachy cast to them. Snapped from the choir's balcony at the rear of the church, the pictures look down upon Mother and Dad as they perform the expected, traditional rites: lighting the unity candle, bowing heads in prayer, giving and receiving rings. And, of course, the kiss. Only one shot in that rose-tinted series is slightly out of focus, the one of Mother and Dad facing each other, hands joined, while Reverend Marshall blesses the union.

Once the ceremony was over, the photos depict a far more relaxed mood. There are Mother and Dad emerging from the church in a shower of rice; the two of them climbing into a limousine; their triumphant entrance through the doors of the third-floor ballroom, Mother lifting her bouquet over her head as though it were a trophy; the wedding party gathered in various poses around the Victorian-themed Christmas tree by the Wisconsin Club's grand staircase; Mother and Dad's clasped hands hovering just above her bouquet, her engagement and wedding rings sparkling impressively.

The most gimmicky shot taken that day by the photographer was a favorite of Mother's, one of the few wedding pictures she framed to hang on the stairwell. Dad's broad back is to the camera and Mother's arms are wrapped possessively around his neck. She grins broadly and winks knowingly. In her right hand is the marriage license, signed in bold script.

FIVE

The nursery could not have been more charming. Dad has never denied Mother much of anything, but as a matter of pride he insisted that when decorating the baby's room she stay within a budget he could afford. Although acquiescence was out of character for Mother, she seemed eager to comply. Perhaps pulling off a low-cost renovation offered an unfamiliar challenge, or maybe it gave her permission to ignore Grammy Elnora's insistence on a frilly bassinet and designer linens. Whatever the reason, for a young woman of privilege Mother proved to be incredibly resourceful in furnishing the baby's room.

Not knowing the baby's gender, she decided upon a safe palette of greens and yellows and a woodland theme. She covered the worn hardwood planks with a deep-piled, forest-green carpet remnant from a local discount flooring outlet. Buttercream yellow softened the rough plaster walls and hid unsightly cracks. She found pictures of whimsical forest animals in a *Highlights* magazine, painstakingly transferred the images to a graph paper grid and recreated them, enlarged to scale, on the walls of the nursery. Here, a bushy-tailed squirrel nibbled on an acorn; there, a floppy-eared rabbit nosed through a ferny glen. Higher up on the walls fanciful ladybugs and graceful dragonflies hovered near the crib and changing table which had been rescued from Grammy Elnora's attic. Next to the yellow rocking chair sat a basket of books, the corner cozily bathed in light from a flea market floor lamp with fabric shade. A padded bench beneath the window sheltered plush animals—masked raccoon, white-tailed deer, flat-faced monkey—motionless with anticipation.

As she readied the room, surprisingly, Mother also seemed to ready herself. She wanted to be a mother. A good mother.

The weeks ticked by and Mother searched baby books for names, writing endless combinations in her diary. She kept notebooks documenting each day of her pregnancy, what she ate, how she felt, when the baby kicked most spectacularly. Lists of questions for her doctor fill line after line.

How much weight should I gain? Are there foods I shouldn't eat? Will it hurt to take aspirin for my headache? What is the best exercise to prepare for delivery? If I strain when I go to the bathroom, does that hurt the baby? I toasted Nolan's promotion to mill manager last week. Just one little sip . . . that shouldn't affect the baby, right?

Dr. Spock's *Baby and Child Care* was her bible during those early months, the spine separated from the text, the pages taped in place. She kept dozens of articles from magazines, advice columns carefully cataloged with important points underlined or starred (sometimes both), everything from preventing diaper rash to breast feeding to the importance of sleep schedules for the newborn. I doubt generals staging the invasion of Normandy had invested as much time as my mother did in preparation for this child.

She and my father were giddy. They joked about all the tests to determine the sex of the unborn baby. My father wanted a girl; Mother seemed sure the baby would be a boy. They laughingly tied Mother's wedding ring from a string and suspended it over her swollen belly, but neither of them could remember which motion—a circle or pendulum swing—signified which sex. Mother's law school friends were certain she was carrying a boy. Grammy Elnora knowingly declared her darling Bets would have a girl. "You're carrying her just like I carried you . . . up high. And you're thick all the way around." Until the birth, my parents agreed to call the baby Chris, a gender neutral name infinitely preferable to "It."

Mother's diary reflects the serenity and quiet joy of late night conversations, the ones in which they imagine calling Chris to dinner (my father: Chris-tiiina; my mother: Chris-topherrrr, oh Chriiis), what they would do if a bully antagonized their little one, how they would always present a unified front and disagree about parental matters in private, themes for birthday parties, rules for sleepovers, the importance of always reading before bedtime. Mother welcomed my father's nurturing. His consideration for her was gentle and constant, and she delighted in his awe at each new development.

From Mother's diary, 1977

Thursday, Jan. 27

Nolan and I were awake most of the night. Chris was so active, we think he has invented an imaginary friend and they were sparring. Twins?

Monday, Feb. 7

Flowers arrived today. Nolan said it's "just because" and that "Christina" and I should get used to them. I pretended to be mad at him for such extravagance, but they do look so pretty on the dining table.

Wednesday, Feb. 16

Nolan is the most patient man. EVERYTHING made me cry today, and I don't know why. When I told him about the sheets getting caught in the agitator and the washing machine stopping mid-cycle, he didn't say anything. His silence made me furious, so I started to cry about THAT. Then he looked at me very seriously and told me I have a known medical condition that has no cure. He assures me it's not fatal, but I'll have to deal with it my entire life: I carry my bladder between my eyes. He's even starting a support group, and he's naming himself CEO. I LOVE that man! Reminder: washer repairman scheduled for Friday morning between 8–12.

Saturday, Feb. 26

I never have a camera when I need one, but I'll always keep this image in my mind: Nolan cupped his hands around my huge middle today. He kissed just below my belly button and said, "I love you already, Christina, almost as much as I love your mother."

They were a family, Mother, Dad, and Chris. True, Mother shared an exclusive bond with the child in her womb, a secret *knowing*, a marriage of melody and harmony between two beings so in concert that nothing more is required. But for a time, Dad danced to their music.

Six

From Mother's diary, March 1977:
Thursday.

Nolan is taking off early from the mill for our 3:30 appointment. I need to remember to grab some more thank you notes while we're out. Heather sent the softest white blanket for Chris, and I want to send her a special little card. I wish the drug store sold energy too. I'm just so TIRED all the time.

Friday.

Yesterday's appointment went well. Dr. Schroeder says Chris is probably about five pounds by now, maybe more. I complained about peeing every hour on the hour and heartburn like there's no tomorrow. I used to inhale stuffed jalapeños. This too shall pass, as they say. We'll have a couple more tests to do at my next appointment. I need to think about packing for the hospital! So much to do these last few weeks, just need some gumption to get at it all.

Saturday.

I'm as big as a barn—Nolan says a lovely barn. Can't see my toes. I waddle. Such heavy pressure on my back! I told Nolan "Mr. Chris better be worth this." He said, "She will be."

Sunday.

Week 36! Trouble sleeping . . . hard to get comfortable at night. Smells from the mill making me sick? I haven't felt like throwing up since the first trimester. MISERABLE!

Monday.

Nolan said particulates from the mill are actually lower than usual. Maybe the flu? Bedtime for Bets.

Tuesday.

Fever and muscle ache. I feel so stiff. Nurse at Schroeder's office said to force liquids and call if anything changes. She asked about spotting. Nothing. A good sign?

Wednesday.

Chris isn't moving. Meeting Schroeder before office hours. O God O God please let everything be OK

The dated entries stop for several weeks. Empty white pages from Mother's diary reflect light from the bare bulb of her closet, and there is so much white. White that expands, balloons, feeds upon itself. White that swallows the small space where I sit, suffocating me.

Then, stark and wrenching and outrageously inadequate, this:

Christopher Nolan Garrison was delivered to the loving arms of his mother and father and then to the arms of his Heavenly Father on Thursday, March 17, 1977. He is survived by his parents, Nolan and Elizabeth Garrison of Waukesha; grandparents Aldrich and Elnora Pennick of Mequon, and Lucinda Garrison of Wauwatosa; an uncle, Kurt Garrison and wife Heather of Ralston, NE. He was preceded in death by his paternal grandfather, Robert James Garrison.

Randle-Dable Funeral Home in Waukesha is handling the arrangements for a private family service. Charitable contributions to the Baby's Breath Foundation for Stillbirth or condolences for the family may be forwarded to the funeral home.

SEVEN

According to Grandmother Lucinda, the ceremony was simple. My Pennick grandparents were rock solid, arranging flights for Uncle Kurt and Aunt Heather from Omaha, calling a caterer to serve a light luncheon after the service, and ensuring the mound of freshly turned earth was softened by huge bouquets of bright gerbera daisies. Throughout that interminable day, Grandfather Aldrich hovered around the mourners, silently offering in vain a mantle of protection against the crushing weight of their grief.

In his eulogy, Reverend Marshall promised a long life well-lived in heaven for Christopher. Aunt Heather, a high school English teacher, sobbed through one of her favorite works.

> *It is not growing like a tree*
> *In bulk, doth make Man better be;*
> *Or standing long an oak, three hundred year,*
> *To fall a log at last, dry, bald, and sere:*
> *A lily of a day*
> *Is fairer far in May,*
> *Although it fall and die that night—*
> *It was the plant and flower of Light*
> *In small proportions we just beauties see;*
> *And in short measures life may perfect be.*

At the conclusion of the service, my father stood to read a letter he had written to my brother. Several halting words later, he simply shook his head and walked to stand behind my mother, his hand on her shoulder. Father Marshall gently took the paper from my father and with solemn dignity burned it in the flame of an altar candle. "Christopher knows what is in your heart. That is all that matters."

My mother, according to Grandmother Lucinda, was as hard as the marble marker engraved with Christopher's name and the date of his death. "But I understood," she told me. "It is not possible to put a child in the ground and not bury a part of yourself at the same time."

Eight

Mother's compulsion to confide in her diary, cruelly suspended as it was, eventually returned, so I have seen a copy of the death certificate. *Listeriosis* sounds so clinical and tidy, like a refreshing mouthwash and not the deadly infection which claimed my older brother. Had mother's symptoms been less acute, a quicker response and massive doses of antibiotics might have prevented Christopher's death. Had he lived, the odds are great that he would have had neurological damage.

No other mention of Christopher's name appears anywhere in Mother's diaries. In fact, other than the obituary and a copy of the death certificate, she did not log another entry for the rest of that entire year. Not, at least, until New Year's Eve, when she penned her one and only resolution for 1978.

I will unlock the nursery tomorrow.

NINE

On more than one occasion, Mother has reminded me babies come with a birth certificate but not a warranty. Before she brought me home from the hospital in November of 1978, she took precautions, implementing a fail-safe plan in case this pregnancy ended the way Christopher's had. She painted over the creamy yellow walls of the nursery in favor of an impersonal pale gray. One might imagine the woodland creatures of Christopher's time simply faded into an impenetrable mist. Likewise, the green carpet which had once suggested a dappled forest floor was discarded in favor of bare hardwood. Instead of refinishing the old oak planks, she scoured them with vinegar and water, still her preferred cleaning solution, leaving them lusterless and smelling sourly antiseptic.

The trauma of my lengthy delivery gave her plenty of material for her daily entries, and for weeks after installing me into the new nursery, Mother complained about every facet of my care. Apparently, I was a fussy baby for the first three months, wailing my colicky indignation at her through all hours of the day and night. Despite the help of a lactation consultant hired by Grammy Elnora I refused to nurse, so Mother was also saddled with preparing formula and sterilizing bottles. At one point she had tried breast pumping, but her diary noted the tenderness and time investment *"is NOT, absolutely NOT worth the trouble."* Before her milk dried up, she spiked a fever from severe mastitis, a further inconvenience that did nothing to endear me to her.

Many of the entries surrounding my childhood detail illnesses and accidents, carelessness and clumsiness. Dad has joked that he should have leased my own room at the hospital, given all the time I spent in emergency rooms and the children's wing. Apparently, I developed the pattern early. There is a picture of me at ten months, encased in an oxygen tent of heavy plastic, where I suffered through a particularly nasty bout of whooping cough.

When I was three, I fell from the seat of a shopping cart onto the concrete floor at the Warehouse Market, one of those behemoth stores which sells tires three aisles removed from the frozen foods. I blacked out momentarily. When I came to, a lump the size of a lemon had formed behind my right ear. Mother reports leaving her cart half loaded near the display of rotisserie chickens and whisking me away to the emergency room for overnight observation. I would be more moved by the concern implied in this detail if not for the equally lengthy description of her distaste in scrubbing my vomit from the upholstery and floor mats of her car.

The year I learned to ride a bicycle I fell and slid on sandy pavement, peeling a layer of skin from my forearm. For most kids a little Bactine and a gauze bandage would have taken care of the injury. Instead, my arm festered from a raging infection impervious to several rounds of penicillin. Three days of IVs and multiple blood tests later, my severe anemia was diagnosed. *What are we going to do with this child?* Mother worried. *She needs to live in a bubble.*

A few months before my seventh birthday, I was treated to an end-of-the-summer trip to the State Fair Grounds for Barnum and Bailey's *Greatest Show on Earth.* I thrilled to all the acts, but none could trump the aerial ballet of the trapeze artists. At home, I tried to recreate their gracefulness by flying from the top of our picnic table to the T-bar clothesline pole in the back yard. Emboldened by my first successful leap and grab, I moved the picnic table farther from the pole. The very next attempt found me sprawled flat on my face, my nose resembling that of an inept boxer and my left elbow twisted exactly opposite its proper direction.

Dr. Schroeder could do little for my nose except yank it back in place. Save the swelling and bruising and a deviated septum which required surgery much, much later, the slight hook in my nose was of little consequence to me. Restoration of my arm, however, garnered the very best kind of attention possible. Dad allowed me to choose a bright-blue cast, jaunty and eye-catching for the beginning of second grade. An instant conversation starter, it was the perfect canvas for classmates' uneven signatures and it earned me the undeniable distinction of Coolest Girl at School.

Mother hated it. In the humid days of late Wisconsin summer, the dye from the cast bled onto my shirts and shorts, and—to Mother's dismay—her sheets, bath towels, best tablecloth, and anything else I happened to touch.

Nolan must be out of his mind. What on earth was he thinking? Luce would have picked lime green with purple polka dots if it had been possible. I might as well be raising two children.

Were all her memories of me so harshly impatient? Honestly, no. Moments of lightheartedness and affection punctuate her diary.

Wednesday, July 22, 1981

Nolan is buried with work at the mill—trying to do so much, short-staffed as he is. Momma and Daddy treated Luce and me today. Luce got a trip to the zoo and I got some time for myself. She talked about the "ragoo-tang" nonstop. Daddy bought her an engineer's cap and they rode the train around the park until Momma said she needed some Dramamine.

Saturday Sept. 4, 1982

Woke Luce early this morning and didn't tell her we were on our way to Gurnee. First trip to Great America! Her favorite ride? The carousel right inside the entrance gate. We barely saw much else in the park. She fell asleep on the way home, and when we put her to bed she asked Nolan if we could go again tomorrow! Oh, and she couldn't get enough cotton candy!

Friday, Feb. 10, 1984

First graders performed their annual circus for the parents. Luce played a clown—full whiteface, curly wig, big shoes and all. She stole the show. Nolan and I laughed so hard. Daddy recorded it on videotape. Maybe we'll show it at her graduation open house someday . . . unless she can come up with enough cash to persuade us otherwise!

One entry recalls an event crisp in my memory. In an effort to curtail my clumsiness, Grammy Elnora persuaded (blackmailed?) Mother to enroll me in tap classes which met every Tuesday and Friday after school:

Momma says it will give Luce confidence and some coordination! Nolan said it can't hurt, so we'll give it a go.

When I first tried on my black practice leotard, my chubby thighs and lack of poise didn't seem to matter because I would be dancing in a recital as Mother once had. I *loved* the lessons. Mother, encouraged, noted that I could execute the clumsiest *toe-heel, toe-heel, step, ball change, step, ball change* and still tap out a syncopated rhythm that caused my dance instructor, Miss Pennington, to straighten her shoulders ever so slightly. After months of lessons, Miss P decided our Tuesday-Friday group would perform a patriotic number to the resonant strains of a Sousa march. Our venue would be a dance platform erected at the fairgrounds during Summerfest.

Mother said on the evening of the recital, I spent more than a few moments admiring my red satin leotard with broad bands of blue and white sequins across the bodice. My fellow dancers and I were to carry little American flags and stand in smart columns on either side of the stage apron while the senior girls did their Rockette-inspired routine. As the older girls danced, we were to smile, wave our flags, and march in time to the music. When the senior class exited the stage, the Tuesday-Friday group would tap our way to glory. At least, this was my expectation.

I had not accounted for the bright white heat of the stage lights nor the epic stage fright which settled itself just below my breastbone. The most damaging oversight, however, was that neither my well-meaning instructor nor my mother had offered even the slightest instructions about not locking my knees when having to stand for extended periods of time.

Mercifully, I don't recall much. Grandmother Lucinda said everyone knew something was horribly wrong almost from the beginning of our number. Mother wrote with a flourish:

> *A few bars into the chorus, Luce turned an ALARMING shade of green (it clashed with the red white and blue! ☺). She started swaying (I'll give her this—it was in time with the music—her dance lessons are not entirely for nothing) before her eyes rolled back. She crumpled into the first row of seats, upstaging the senior girls. Nolan told her she stopped the show—literally—and then we were off to the ER—AGAIN.*

> *Nolan and I agree. No more lessons—not Tuesday, Friday, or any other day of the week. Luce's "confidence and coordination" are going to break the bank.*

TEN

Mother's entries about the medical mishaps and mounting bills which accompanied each visit to the doctor may have sounded glib, but the government policies of the late seventies and early eighties sent farmland values in the tank and family farmers into foreclosure, directly affecting output at the mill.

Many nights I heard Mother and Dad doing verbal battle in exaggerated stage whispers, their arguments often ending with a door slamming or, worse, deadly silence. Dad spent lots of time sorting and resorting papers into piles at the dining room table, but whenever I'd ask what he was doing, he'd reply, "Solving a puzzle, sweetie," so I was blissfully unaware of their troubles until I was much older and found the ledger books documenting our finances and those of the mill. Mother had even included in her accounting books a newspaper clipping about an Iowa man in a place called Hills who shot his banker, his wife, his neighbor, and himself after he lost the farm which had been in his family for generations.

Closer to home, there was gossip about child abuse on the rise and divorce rates keeping pace with foreclosures. Even Mother's friends were not immune:

> *Roger made a horrible scene at the Piggly Wiggly yesterday. He actually threw a bag of decaf coffee at Leslie when she said their regular brew is keeping her up at night. He kicked over a display in the produce aisle and threatened to burn the place down if anyone got in his way.*

> *Nolan is beside himself. He was the first one Roger called after he calmed down. Roger's so ashamed, apologizing all over himself, but he's still in jail. Leslie has a horrible bruise on her left cheek and a cut inside her mouth. What will they do? Nolan wanted to post bail, but I told him we just don't have the money.*

On the same day I began second grade, Mother accepted a position as a part-time legal aide at a small firm in Waukesha. I can say with some conviction her employment was not truly necessary, even given the dire economy. After all, my Pennick grandparents would have carried Mother and Dad through any crisis—financial or otherwise, but I'm sure Mother wanted to work as much as Dad wanted to maintain our family's independence.

During the school year, Mother dropped me off by 8:45 and picked me up when the day ended at 3:30. On in-service or early dismissal days and every week day during the summer, Dad let me play on the sales floor at the mill with him. Even as the crisis abated, Mother continued to work. *It's not my own practice, but at least I can get out of the house and talk to ADULTS.* The arrangement seemed to work for all of us.

The original feed mill had actually been restricted to grinding and mixing raw product to specifications from the farmers. Under Dad's management and with hefty investments from the mill's owner through the years, the operation expanded significantly. Suppliers still delivered raw material to the elevators, but before the hammer mill ground the material into smaller pieces suitable for the mixer, we ran the product past magnetic plates to eliminate ferrous impurities. Next, a twenty-five horsepower electric motor turned the mixture, Dad's own special formula: a protein source such as soybean or cottonseed meal, a grain source—usually corn, and the vitamins and minerals needed to promote growth and maintain health. From there, the feed was pushed into the conditioner which injected steam, the moisture and extreme heat softening and sanitizing the mash before it went to the pelleter. Workers set the appropriate die plates for each specific type of feed and as the die plate rotated, stationary knives cut the pellets to a pre-set length. In one of the final steps before bagging, the feed moved through the cooler to reduce the heat generated by the pelleting.

We produced bulk feed for almost any domestic animal imaginable: cattle, horse, rabbit, goat, sheep, hog, chicken, and even specialty feed for deer and bison. Although we could have turned out about 1,000 pounds per minute, we often ran at 60–75% of that rate because we had so little storage space for the bagged feed. Handlers loaded between ten to twelve truckloads every day, a job tolerable only during the winter months when the heat from the injector warmed the mill to almost tropical temperatures. Work done in the summer months, my father often said, was practice for living in hell.

Except for the smell, to which I never became immune, the mill was a perfect playground. I was not allowed to go near the pellet machinery, nor did I want to. The noise of the grinder and heat were off-putting enough, but the drying process emitted a stench that fouled the air. Dad called it his "elixir," sarcastically describing it as a wine steward might a fine Bordeaux: "Undertones of rotting eggs with a hint of cabbage, and a smooth finish of garlic-infused beer." Sometimes before heading to the mill, I would smear Vick's VapoRub under my nose to mitigate the reek, but on humid days, even that trick didn't work.

In the open expanse of the storage and sale room, Dad gave me free reign. If there were no buyers on the sales floor, I imagined myself to be a fearless mountain climber scaling the fifty-pound bags of feed stacked eight or ten deep on wooden pallets. The bags formed stair steps that gave slightly, allowing my little feet to gain purchase. When I lost my footing (and I often did), that same resiliency broke my fall and precluded trips to the emergency room.

Occasionally bags of feed would break open or the string stitching loosen, spilling hard little pellets that crunched into satisfying grains on the concrete floor. Dad even allowed me to do fancy pirouettes on the balls of my feet, the crumbling feed enabling me to rotate like a top. My record was just over four complete spins, by the way, and I attributed this feat to residual talent fostered by my dance lessons. Dad was adamant, however, that I clean up the floor after every performance. He complimented me endlessly for the way I wielded a broom and dust pan.

In all circumstances, my father was a consummate manager. As easily as he applauded my janitorial stints, he motivated workers whose jobs were dirty and dangerous, making each one feel solely responsible for the success of the operation. When our local paper ran an article spotlighting the history of our mill and Dad's continued success in manufacturing an excellent product at a competitive price, Dad wouldn't pose for a picture unless the entire staff was included. The same unyielding integrity and straightforward manner which had first impressed my college-educated mother served Dad equally well with the mill workers who were characterized more by their brawn than their brains.

Even with the mill's owners, Dad commanded respect. His boss, Mr. Hanby Matthews, conveniently oversaw his multiple mills, trucking firm, and several livestock farms from his posh, sprawling estate in Kohler, far from the protests of those offended by the smells associated with his agricultural empire. When the stench at the mill became a point of contention for developers encroaching on the wide fields surrounding our little operation, they threatened legal action. Dad drove to Kohler, unannounced, and in a single day won approval from Mr. Matthews to authorize purchase of a $200,000 air scrubber which significantly reduced the offensive emissions. In private, Mr. Matthews complained to my father about the extravagance of such a purchase, but he had no reservations about publicly accepting an award from an environmental group touting his concern for air quality. Dad's special gift was the ability to make Mr. Matthews believe the air scrubber had been his idea all along.

My mother alone could remain indifferent to Dad's guileless charm for any length of time. Rarely do I remember her laughing at one of his tentative overtures—a joke or goofy play on words (he was always mixing up movie titles or mangling names of stars), an attempt to tickle her behind her knee, or a spontaneous gift of wildflowers plucked from the ditch adjacent to the highway. After Christopher's death, silent withdrawal spawned by grief morphed into self-imposed isolation. Simultaneously, she was the prisoner within a fortress of indifference and the jailer who zealously guarded the point of entry to her private cell for nearly eleven years.

She had staying power, I'll give her that. I'm not sure if she simply willed herself not to care about those of us who had outlived Christopher, or if the Prozac she took with increasing frequency and prescription strength allowed the numbness to become her norm. How she ever became pregnant with Jonny is a true mystery of the universe. Grandmother Lucinda, in snarky candor, vows the only way my father could have ever gotten close enough to "have his manly fun" would be if my mother were stone-cold drunk or "boopshooby psycho" on drugs.

But become pregnant she did, and on that snowy February day when Jonny was born, Mother was resurrected from her apathy.

ELEVEN

A **nyone would understand if I** harbored jealous resentment of the attention Mother gave to Jonny. But I didn't, honestly. I loved Jonny as much as she did, maybe more in my own way. Jonny was easy to love.

That first week at home, Dad could occasionally pry him from Mother and place him, swaddled in a downy receiving blanket, into my waiting arms. "She'll be just fine, Bets," my father would murmur. "I'm right here. Nothing can happen." Mother might snort her disapproval, but Dad insisted. I *did* long to hold him, but just beneath my wonder at his tiny perfection lurked a far more powerful emotion—fear that I would break him and then Mother would hate me—and Dad—forever.

Whether aware of my trepidation or not, Jonny would cuddle in sweet contentment, turning his face to rest against my chest. In the following weeks I learned to support his neck and head with my left hand and cradle his bottom with my right so as to lift him upright against me. Mother would grudgingly allow me to burp him after a feeding, and I would lie back against the cushions on the couch, alternately rubbing soothing circles or gently patting him on the back. Propped against me in this way, his head snug beneath my chin, we might have resembled a rare two-headed creature—one vigilant, the other restful. Silently I counted each warm breath he exhaled into the hollow of my neck. His breathing was slow, almost thoughtful, and I could feel his chest compress with each tiny whoosh. I often gauged my own breathing to keep time with his and then, it seemed, our hearts beat in rhythm as well. If allowed, I could have sat with him like that for hours.

Mother, of course, chose not to return to her job at the law firm. Jonny's arrival ended any further need for diversions from the tedium of home. She ministered to his every need, anticipating his wants even before he could formulate them, I'm sure.

He was her first thought in the morning, her every consideration throughout the day, her final prayer each night. She embraced the routine of bottles and baby formula, diapers and disinfectant; she expected the rest of us to follow suit. When she introduced solid food into Jonny's diet, only bland meats and vegetables which could be suitably pureed graced our menus. If Jonny were napping and Dad happened to thoughtlessly slam the screen on his return from the mill, his next entrance would be blocked by a latch on the door and a note of reproof Scotch-taped to the frame. Once, when she ran out of baby wash at bath time, Mother sent Dad to the convenience store just off the highway. He had the sad misfortune to return with the wrong brand (no matter it was the only brand the store carried) and suffered two days of her silence for his negligence.

I wonder still why Dad tolerated her draconian ways. He might have altered what was to come if he had confronted her, told her to quit being such an ass about every little detail, reminded her there were more than two people living under the Garrison roof. He has always said life is a series of trade-offs and things have a way of balancing themselves out. Where was the balance for him? What justified his silence in the face of her demands? Did her decision to flush the Prozac down the toilet tip the scales? Did her overprotective outbursts and pure passion for Jonny act as counterweight to the indifference following Christopher's death and the resignation following my birth? Or did simply surrendering, thereby cutting his losses, seem more tenable than going to war when loss was inevitable? And so he stood by whenever Mother intervened on Jonny's behalf.

Jonny's delicate skin could only be soothed a thick, pricey lanolin cream, not the baby lotion which had seemed perfectly suitable for me. He couldn't be expected to eat over-processed canned vegetables; only fresh would do. T-shirts from Wal-Mart were too cheesy for her son. Instead, Mother would wait for a sale at the Boston Store in New Berlin or drive for an hour to the affluent neighborhoods in Cedarburg to paw through name-brand castoffs at rummage sales. Summers found Jonny slathered in sunscreen; in winter, he was enveloped in goose-down-filled jackets and expensive thermal boots which lasted only one season before he outgrew them. I remember with horror when she lengthened my jeans, camouflaging the old hem line by sewing decorative fabric tape to the crease. Jonny never suffered such wardrobe indignities.

Despite tight budgets, Mother found funds enough to enroll Jonny in a musical rhythms class for toddlers and, later, a tumbling class which lasted no more than the first session. When the instructor positioned her charges in a coiled crouch so they could "leap like frogs from lily pad to pond," Mother pulled the plug. "Those children were all over the place. Someone was bound to get hurt," she explained to Dad.

She screened preschools and worried over applications, unwilling to sabotage his early childhood with sub-par experiences at the sand tables of inferior institutions. A trip to the store always meant an extra treat for Jonny, whether it be a Hershey's bar or a Masters of the Universe action figure.

No matter the attention Mother lavished on him, Jonny never became one of those spoiled children, sure of his entitlement. He didn't refuse Mother's extravagance, sure. What kid would? But I've never seen anyone *appreciate* like Jonny. His gratitude was genuine and spontaneous. It was like granting the giver permission to overdo. I have vowed, should I ever have another child, that I will not show favoritism, that I will not minimize one child in order to lift up the other. Yet, as Jonny's sister, I begrudged him nothing. His exuberance, his curiosity, his innate joy, his earnest compassion more than made up for Mother's niggling criticisms of everything not-Jonny.

Some experts will say small children can think only of themselves first. If that's universally true, then Jonny would be the exception to prove the rule. So many times he would do or say something to put others at ease despite any discomfort or inconvenience to himself.

My first year at Creighton, I traveled to Waukesha for a short visit. There had been some trouble with my FAFSA application and my tuition funds were being withheld until we ironed out the difficulties. Arriving mid-afternoon, I saw Jonny at the kitchen table, his spoon poised over a bowl of cereal. He was a fiend for cereal, Jonny was, and his favorite was a combination of Kix, corn flakes, and Rice Chex. If left to his own devices, he'd forgo our everyday stoneware dishes in favor of one of the Pyrex mixing bowls from Mother's cabinet. The red one was his favorite; the little blue one was too small, the yellow one too big, the green one just right by Jonny's standards but still too large for Mother's radar. With the precision of a scientist, he'd pour in generous helpings of all three kinds of cereal, layered evenly in crispy, golden strata to be followed by a river of icy whole milk. A purist, he wanted no fruit or additional sugar. If Mother would have allowed it, he'd eat cereal for every meal. As it was, Jonny managed to satisfy his cereal addiction twice a day—once at breakfast and as a mid- afternoon snack.

On this particular day, Jonny was not chasing little balls and flakes and squares around the red mixing bowl with his usual passion for scarfing down the cereal before it went limp in the milk. Instead, he sat with his head tilted dejectedly, his cheek resting on the heel of his left hand. With his right hand, he held the spoon handle with two fingers, much as a wealthy matron might hold a tiny silver bell used to summon her butler. He glanced up at me before returning his attention to the bowl.

"Whatsamatter? Not hungry?" I asked.

He shook his head.

"You better eat up. At the rate you're going, you'll be finishing that cereal when Mother is serving tonight's stew. Come on. Don't let it go to waste."

"It's awful," he countered.

"Did it go stale in the box?" I asked. "Fat chance of that, the way you go through it."

"No."

"Well, what then?"

"It isn't any good with orange juice."

For some unexplained reason, his bowl was filled with orange juice gone syrupy from Kix/flakes/Chex now softened into a whitish paste.

"Why on earth did you put orange juice on your cereal?" I demanded. Dish duty was my responsibility. Having to flush that mush conjured an image of the last time I draped myself over the toilet bowl, heaving from a vile stomach flu. Just the thought made me gag. "So. What gives? Why did you do something so stupid?"

"Because the only milk left is Dad's two percent. If I took it, he wouldn't have any for breakfast in the morning. He likes cereal as much as me. So I used orange juice." He sighed. "I don't think I like orange juice anymore."

He was eight at the time, too young to realize the rarity of his gesture, the selfless grace in his gift. But this was Jonny.

TWELVE

Eleven years separated Jonny from me. In some families, I suppose, that distance would be enough to render siblings strangers. One could not separate so easily from Jonny, however. It took work.

Do not be mistaken. Jonny was no angel. Like all little boys, he threw his share of tantrums, blurted innocent truths at inopportune times, and embarrassed Dad and me (never Mother, in my memory) in ways unexpected and inventive. But he was guileless in his transgressions, sincerely apologetic when he realized that his actions had somehow resulted in hurt feelings, and utterly forgivable when he slipped his arms around our necks and hiccupped his sorrow. I once screamed at him for taking beads from a broken necklace I meant to repair and placing them in the bottom of the bowl inhabited by his pet turtle. By the time I had cooled down, I felt I was the guilty party, not Jonny. Whatever hurt I inflicted upon him in my anger, I suffered a thousand times more long after he had forgiven my impatience.

Mother rarely allowed Jonny enough space to get into serious trouble, self-imposed or otherwise. Her umbilical cord was incredibly resilient, lengthy, and sinuous, securing her connection to her son long past his toddler years. To be sure, it was easier to maintain the tie when Jonny was an infant. She placed him at her elbow when he was in his swing or wore him cradled next to her heart in a papoose-like wrap of complicated folds and tucks. His bassinet stood in the corner of her bedroom even after Mother reluctantly moved Jonny to the nursery. "Just in case, Nolan," she assured my father. She never stipulated in case of *what*.

When he first learned to crawl, his mobility presented problems for Mother. Jonny would rest most of his weight on his left forearm and pull himself forward with his right hand, his legs pumping behind for added propulsion. Slipping across our wooden floors, he was able to cover lots of ground in a short period of time. Mother found her daily chores constantly interrupted as she rose to pull him closer to her, grabbing onto his feet and sliding him gently backward as she laughed each time, "Not so fast, my little man." Initially, Jonny must have thought this a delightful game. His first word, if you can call it that, sounded like "Nahso," his permutation of Mother's cautionary phrase. In time, however, he would howl his reluctance and Mother had to find other ways to keep him near.

He learned to walk when he was thirteen months old which sorely tested the Mother/Jonny tether. She asked Dad to fashion a contraption that was part step stool, part cage so that Jonny could stand safely beside her when she cooked. At Mother's insistence, Dad also designed a clever pressure-secured barrier with a latching gate which could swing both ways to block stairs leading to the second floor. Perhaps because of his limitations inside the house, Jonny loved the outdoors. His favorite activity involved walking the length of our driveway to the mailbox by the highway. Of course, Mother was always there to hold his hand.

On those rare occasions when Mother allowed Jonny to wait outside by himself in the front yard for the mail truck to pass by, she kept constant vigil out the living room window to monitor his movements. One windy September day—he was four, I think—Mother heard a crash from Jonny's bedroom. Evidently a powerful gust had knocked over and shattered a crystal-framed picture of Jonny that sat on the wide windowsill. She rushed upstairs, checked to see Jonny examining something crawling in the grass, and hurriedly picked up the broken shards. When she returned to the kitchen for broom and dustpan, she made another circuit to the living room to assure herself of Jonny's safety. He was nowhere to be seen. She bolted for the door, frantically yelling his name as she circled the house. Agonizing minutes later, Jonny strutted proudly down the driveway, a hefty stack of envelopes in hand.

When she told my father about the incident at dinner, Jonny safely in his chair directly to Mother's right, she was still close to tears. Her lip quivering, she explained that Jonny heard the mail truck and had run to the road in hopes of saying hello to Miss Gwen, our postal carrier. He either did not hear Mother's anguished cries or chose to ignore them. As she dropped to her knees to gather him in her arms, she demanded—half fearful, half angry, "Jonathan Ian Garrison, don't you know you're not supposed to leave my sight?"

"Apparently not," Jonny replied.

Of course, the story eventually became legend for Mother, an anecdote retold proudly as evidence of her son's wry sense of humor and impressive vocabulary, unique for one so young.

Truly, Jonny's antics most often elicited laughter. One afternoon, he served "tea" to Mother's college roommates, a cold beverage he scooped from the toilet because he couldn't reach the sink. He painted Dad's truck with mud after a spring downpour turned the front yard into oozy muck. Mother, of course, insisted his artwork be preserved for nearly two weeks. She didn't want to stifle his creativity, she said. And when a couple of Seventh Day Adventists trekked to the front door to witness for their faith, Jonny stuck his thumbs into his diaper and winsomely begged, "Off. Off." That summer, we found an unusually large number of religious pamphlets left in our door or secured beneath the windshield wipers of the Explorer.

Memories of less happy times with Jonny are more painful because of the contrast. The worst of those began with such promise. It ended in ugly self-recrimination. It was the first crack, the rock chip in our family windshield that eventually fractured beyond repair.

THIRTEEN

At **Jonny's birth, Grammy and** Granddad Pennick purchased a portrait package from Campbell Photography which allowed ten sittings over a five-year period. A high-end family-owned operation, the studio specialized in artful, one-of-a-kind keepsake portraits. As a result, lovely full-color matte 8x10s of Jonny from infancy to toddler years graced the stairwell of our farmhouse. In one of the earliest, three-month-old Jonny, unable to sit up on his own, is nestled in Mother's hands. The photographer steadied the camera on Mother's left shoulder, a second head with a Cyclopean eye to capture Jonny's expression straight on. Mother propped his head forward with her left hand, her thumb resting near his right ear and the tip of her little finger just visible on the left side of his neck. Scrunched as he is, his little chin rests on his chest, plumping his cheeks to Rubinesque proportions. Despite the discomfort he must have felt in this staged pose, he sports his characteristic Jonny-smile—mouth open wide, dimples a punctuation mark of joy.

The same trademark grin is evidenced in all the portraits, each one some family member's favorite. Grammy Elnora claims the one of Jonny in a plaid sunsuit, one strap securely in place, the other just off his shoulder. He sits on a little wooden stool, his hands demurely placed in his lap. His knees appear to be fused together, a hinge securing his legs from the knees down. His feet are spread apart, the heels lifted and facing outward with only his curled toes touching the platform on which his stool rests. Grammy cannot help but pause before this particular picture whenever she visits, cooing, "Those toes. I could just kiss those toes."

I was always taken with the one of Jonny at nine months where he sports nothing but a snowy white diaper, fur-lined boots, and a miniature Santa cap of vivid red. He is seated with chubby legs splayed and his torso leaning in slightly toward the camera, arms outstretched as though reaching for a present just beyond his grasp. In fact, he was reaching for me.

Mother's choice is the one commemorating Jonny's third birthday. He is wearing a red long-sleeved dress shirt, black pants, black-and-gray striped vest, and a black fedora with a jaunty red hat band. Sitting on a curved staircase embellished with mahogany banister and wrought iron spindles, he cradles his chin with both hands, a debonair three-year-old Romeo with a bouquet of roses at his feet. One could imagine him waiting wistfully outside the door of his Valentine, ready to declare his undying love to one lucky lady.

At any rate, we were nearing the end of the contract period with the studio and Mother, in a surprising mood of inclusiveness, decided Jonny and I should pose together for the last portrait. He had just turned five and Mother arranged to have the picture taken outside. Conveniently, the weather had collaborated with Mother's timetable and provided a heavy, wet blanket of new snowfall deep enough for Dad to fashion a narrow wall of snow as a staging prop. He suggested a more conventional snowman, one Jonny and I could build together as the photographer captured candid shots of our fun. As usual, he was overruled by Mother, who—supposedly out of my hearing—noted I could better hide my own snowman-shaped silhouette behind a fortress of snow. Besides, she added, the wall would allow Jonny to sit at a level nearer to my own height and provide a wealth of creative shot opportunities. She had gathered a bright red plastic saucer sled, a vintage toboggan Dad had used as a child, a pair of her figure skates tied together by their laces, and a couple of snow shovels, one from our garage and the other a plastic child's toy. She even spent nearly an hour the morning of the photo shoot sketching possible compositions of people and props in her diary.

By midafternoon the photographer, a thirty-something woman named Alice, arrived. She secured her tripod and gaily announced, "Let's get started. Where is the *talent* for this little venture?" Instantly, Mother took charge, her tone authoritative and insistent.

"Luce, stand behind the fort. Now lift Jonny up and let his legs straddle the wall. No, move a little more behind Jonny's shoulder."

"Why don't you hold the saucer up and let Jonny kneel in front of you? He'll look so adorable if he's framed by that red saucer."

"Turn the toboggan on its side. Now, Luce, crouch down behind it and let Jonny sit on the edge. Hold on to him."

"Try a close-up of Jonny blowing a handful of snow into Luce's face. Be sure to get this one from the shoulders up, Alice."

Hard as she tried to conceal her impatience, Alice finally stood, silent, her forearm resting on the top of the camera as she waited for Mother to position us in each new tableau. I can't say how many pictures she took, nor how many she was contracted to take, but thirty minutes into the session she curtly announced, "One more pose, Mrs. Garrison."

"We haven't used the shovels yet." Mother turned deferentially to Alice. "What do you think Jonny and Luce could do with them?"

"Shovel snow?" Alice's thinly veiled sarcasm was completely wasted on Mother. "All right, you two," the photographer said. "Grab those shovels and let's get this last shot."

Jonny palmed his little yellow-handled plastic number and I reached for the well-used shovel Dad had produced from the garage. "Okay, kids. Fill your shovels. Get a big scoop, Jonny," Mother admonished. "No, bigger. Now throw the snow toward the camera. This will be *so* cute," she gushed. Grudgingly, I hefted a load of packed, wet snow, its weight nearly toppling me forward. I tucked my head and rocked my arms back and forth like a clock's pendulum to gain sufficient momentum to toss the snow. "Ready, set . . ." On *"go,"* I straightened my back and thrust the shovel forward.

Life suddenly became the final scene in a movie, played out in excruciating slow-motion. Frame by frame, I saw Jonny twist toward me and bend slightly at the waist. Saw the concrete-scuffed edge of my shovel rise toward his head. Saw the impact that slashed his right eyebrow. Saw the jagged cross-hatch of flesh against stark white bone. And then blood. Blood flowing endlessly, thin and red.

Jonny raised his hand to his forehead, not yet overcome by the pain and shock that followed. He seemed confused when his hand brushed not white, cold snow from his eyes but sticky red rivulets. He examined his mitten with a kind of detached fascination, looking toward me for an explanation I was powerless to give. Suddenly, real time returned. Like the comically evil German in the climax of *Raiders of the Lost Ark,* the right side of Jonny's face began to sag, almost as though it were made of melting wax. His eyelid drooped, the corner of his mouth relaxed and curved downward.

Did the snow muffle all sound? Mother must have screamed, but I didn't hear her. My ears seemed full, as though I were swimming underwater. Alice pantomimed a startled "O" as she brought her hand upward to shield her eyes from the carnage. In the confusion, she knocked over the tripod and her camera thunked heavily against the handle of the snow shovel I had dropped on impact. Almost simultaneously, Jonny fell backward as though he had been shot. Mother reached him first, but it was Dad who scooped him up. He tore off Jonny's stocking cap, filled it with snow and pressed the fuzzy compress against the wound.

Mother hovered beside Dad as he trudged through the deep snow toward the house. Her wailing pierced the air, "My baby. My baby. Oh, God, please. . ." She turned momentarily to me, snarling and vicious. "What did you do? What were you thinking?" I stared blankly after her. *What had I done?*

"Hush, Bets. We'll sort all this out later. Get my keys. Call the hospital and tell them we're on our way." His calm decisiveness seemed automatic and comforting. Dad knew what to do. Dad would make everything okay.

He gently buckled Jonny into the back seat while Mother found clean towels to replace the makeshift compress. She placed them on Jonny's forehead and climbed into the seat beside him for the ride into town. Standing by the passenger's front door, I whimpered my sorrow. Mother ignored me as Dad navigated the drive in reverse, wasting no time attempting to jockey around the photographer's van. As soon as he reached the highway, he shifted and fishtailed out of sight.

"Luce, do you need me to call someone? Someone who can be with you until your parents come back?" Alice asked. When I didn't reply, she pressed, "Luce, will you be all right?"

I don't really remember, but I must have indicated she could pack her equipment and go, for I found myself suddenly alone and cold. Unbelievably cold. It seemed to have taken on a life of its own, an icy alien who, after researching all the potential vessels in which to reside, had chosen me to possess. I did not think to go into the house to warm up. I did not think I would ever warm up.

My fingers and toes ached in their bitter numbness as I shoveled scoop after scoop of snow over the bloody evidence of my carelessness. Then I sat on the porch to wait for Mother and Dad and Jonny to come home.

What had I done?

FOURTEEN

Nearly three hours later, the Explorer turned into the driveway. The headlights pinned me to the front porch where I sat waiting for their return. Mother opened the back door before the vehicle stopped and hurried around to the driver's side. Dad left the Explorer's lights on to illuminate the path to the front door. He didn't want to stumble as he carried a sleeping Jonny up the steps and into the house.

Jonny's cheek rested on Dad's shoulder and his arms hung limply. Except for his injuries, startling in the glare of the headlights, he would have appeared to be merely an exhausted little boy. Although his stocking cap once again covered his unruly dark hair, it did not camouflage the heavy bandage over his right eye. The white surgical tape darkened the bruises that pooled beneath his eye and snaked across the bridge of his nose.

"Is he . . . ?" I faltered. "Is he going to be . . . ?"

Without ever looking at me Mother sniped, "At least you didn't blind him."

Dad, far kinder, murmured, "Let us get him into bed, Luce. Then we'll talk."

I heard them upstairs in Jonny's room. They were speaking in low tones, soothing and quiet. The toilet flushed, water ran in the sink, muffled footsteps crisscrossed the floor. A chair scraped and then Dad came down the stairs, alone.

He looked terrible, gaunt and exhausted, but he tried to rearrange his features when he saw me hunched over the kitchen table.

"Luce, Jonny's going to be okay. Really. He looks worse than he is." I couldn't meet his eyes. "Look at me, Luce. He's okay." When I didn't raise my head, Dad pulled another chair beside me and rested his hand on my shoulder. "Can you tell me what happened?"

"He just . . . I was . . . he turned . . ."

Dad lifted my chin. "Luce. Listen to me. Don't beat yourself up. It was an accident. It could have been much worse. The doctors cleaned the wound and stitched him up. I'm telling you, it could have been worse."

"How many stitches?" I asked.

"Twelve, but Jonny was a trooper. It took a while because the cut was kind of jagged and the doctors wanted to take their time. In a few months, you probably won't know anything ever happened. Maybe a little ridge through his eyebrow, that's it."

I could barely see him through tear-swollen eyes. Snot coated my upper lip. "Can he ever forgive me?" I sobbed.

"I don't think you have to worry about *Jonny*," he intoned wryly. "If I know Jonny, he'll thank you someday. Women like their men rugged." Dad's lip curled up into a crooked little grin. And I knew he was right. Tomorrow Jonny would get out of bed and smile his dimpled Jonny smile and wear his bandage like a medal of honor.

Between us, there would be only my guilt and Mother.

FIFTEEN

No **8x10 commemorating that afternoon,** glossy or otherwise, ever joined the rest of the collection of framed portraits on our stairwell. The spot near the landing on the second floor remained accusingly bare, indicting me in its absence. I believe Alice sent a catalog of proofs to Mother and Dad, and there were dozens of shots prior to the accident that would have been suitable. Sometimes I imagined those photos bound together in a macabre flip book like the cartoonish ones I used to draw in fourth grade. Each picture, only slightly different from the one before, would unfold into a story. If I simply thumbed through them backwards, I could reverse the outcome.

After Mother glanced through the book of proofs, she carried them to her bedroom closet. I know her gesture was not to protect the fragile shell hiding my remorse. Perhaps Mother was as adept as Grammy Elnora at winnowing the chaff of family disappointments.

SIXTEEN

Jonny looked as though he had been targeted by a vicious mugger. The shovel had severed muscles and destroyed tissue. Once the bruising faded and the swelling had subsided, the damage was more prominent than the doctors had hoped. Because Jonny inherited the same gene for ropy scars which plagued me, the tear bisecting his eyebrow never receded into a faint white line. Instead, a puckered ridge of flesh forever branded him.

My scars were entirely hidden but no less disfiguring.

Life changed at the Garrison household. Our last name seemed an apt label for the way Mother and I interacted with one another. We were passive antagonists, each of us walled behind our particular fortress, each of us practicing our own brand of détente. Dad and Jonny played the ambassadors of good will, well-intentioned but powerless to change long-standing resentments. Strained summits were held around the dinner table; negotiations stalled over pot roast and potatoes.

Even weeks after the accident, Mother rarely spoke to me nor I to her. We found avoiding one another a far more substantial affront than any direct accusation. She could inflict more damage with silence than with sarcasm. Trust me, the easiest way to destroy someone is to make her invisible.

I suppose, in my sixteen-year-old arrogance, I thought I could outlast her anger. I thought her fury would fade with Jonny's bruises. I was wrong. We could not repair a relationship that had never really existed in the first place. And so I removed myself from her.

It began with quiet subversion, a campaign to keep Mother uninformed about all things Luce-related. I did not share with her school newsletters or open house schedules. I volunteered neither details of assignments nor report cards. More than once, I intercepted letters from school or erased messages left on the answering machine. When pushed by school authorities, I forged her signature on requests for parent conferences, making it clear that Elizabeth Garrison could not be scheduled into any of the available time slots. And I took a perverse pleasure in telling my teachers that my mother was simply "too busy" to bother herself with my education. If Mother took notice of this information embargo, she never mentioned it to me.

So I escalated the war.

The laundry room, of all places, became a battlefield. I left a Post-It note stuck to the box of Tide telling her I'd wash my own clothes. *Anything of mine you find in the basket, don't bother. I'll get it later.* If Mother couldn't be inconvenienced with me, certainly she couldn't stand to handle my sweaters and jeans and T-shirts and underwear. Lord knows I wouldn't want to *contaminate* anything.

I chose not to ride in the car with her unless the entire family went somewhere together. If I needed materials for a school project, I either waited until Dad came along on a weekend afternoon or I went without. I would rather go to class unprepared or borrow supplies from a lab partner than ask Mother to take me to Wal-Mart. Even if she were willing to take Jonny and me to buy spring clothes, I refused. Had baby Christopher lived to become my older brother, I trust he would have asked me if I were out of my freaking mind. I imagined his exasperated admonishment. *Are you nuts? Take whatever Mom is willing to give you and keep your trap shut.*

I launched other offensives in the dining room. At first, I'd sit at the table with the rest of them, picking at whatever Mother had prepared for dinner. Even if I were starving, I wasn't going to give her the satisfaction of eating anything she made. Occasionally, Dad would comment upon my lagging appetite. I would shrug noncommittally, say I wasn't really hungry or I had snacked before dinner or my stomach was upset. Ostensibly in support, Mother might then intervene with a saccharine observation to Dad, never me, about my long-overdue commitment to losing weight. In retaliation, I would sneak money from her purse to buy packages of powdered donuts or bags of chips from vending machines at school and stash them in my backpack or the drawer of my nightstand.

I did worse than take money from her purse. There are dozens of ways to make someone suspicious and paranoid, and I was particularly inventive. Subtle. Stealthy. That was my plan. I wanted to *disturb* as much as *destroy*. If I could, just once every day, upset her normal routines, slow her down with unexpected vexations, make her second guess herself, it was a day well spent. It became almost a game. Could I tamper with every one of her senses? I wanted to get inside her head. I even wanted to mess with her by *not* messing with her.

My most malicious acts took place in her closet, that inner sanctum of treasured diaries and photo albums. Those would have been the obvious targets, so I ignored them. Instead, armed with a razor blade, I cut her clothes. Nothing overt—maybe a slit in the seam of her favorite chinos, a tiny rip in a new dress, or a shirt collar prematurely frayed with several scrapes from the blade. I nicked several strands of threads on the waistband buttons of her pants, hoping they would stay fastened until she was out running some errand or other. I even stripped aglets, those little plastic cases on the tips of her shoelaces, from her Reeboks and pulled the laces free from the eyelets. Wet tea bags have superior staining power on light fabrics, I discovered, and I was practically a Picasso with my Q-tip dipped in bleach.

In her bedroom I tangled the chain of her gold necklace and dropped one of her favorite earrings into the deep pile of the carpet. A few drops of vinegar in her bottle of *L'Air du Temps*? Easy. Sally Hansen's *Hard as Nails*? Not so hard when thinned with polish remover. Mascara dries and clumps if the wand isn't screwed on tightly, and a compact of pressed powder cracks into unusable chunks if "accidentally" dropped on the floor.

The kitchen afforded endless opportunities. She usually baked brownies or chocolate-chunk cookies, Jonny's favorite, on Friday mornings. My Thursday mission might center around a midnight raid of the pantry, nearly emptying the canister of sugar or throwing out the half-full bottle of vanilla extract. Sometimes, after breakfast, I would prick the plastic gallon of milk with a safety pin. Returning home from school I would find her on her knees sponging milk from the shelves as she vowed revenge on some hapless stock boy at Piggly Wiggly. The safety pin worked wonders on her Playtex gloves, too. Once, I experimented with a small rip in the garbage can liner. That little enterprise reaped huge rewards days later when a bulging sack spilled soggy coffee grounds and rotting banana peels all over the linoleum. Funny enough, she had apparently "forgotten" to replace the vacuum bag on her electric broom when she tried to clean the mess.

Little chores such as mending a hem became far more tedious when the eye of her sewing needle had been treated with a drop of Krazy Glue. If she happened to find a needle she could thread, the earpiece of her reading glasses was bent ever so slightly and the lenses smudged with greasy fingerprints. I interrupted her almost obsessive need to be on time by turning back the hands on her watch or advancing the dial on the digital clock radio. For good measure, I might crank up the volume, too. I changed her preset buttons on the car radio; when she was expecting golden oldies, she might get alternative punk. Instead of NPR, she got the Catholic Hour.

Although Mother never accused me—how could she; she didn't speak to me—I was getting to her. Her voice grew increasingly shrill. She wasn't sleeping well. Dad had always been a target when she vented her displeasure, but she even became edgy and impatient with Jonny.

The strain weighed on Dad, an unwanted but inevitable casualty of war. He had always managed to find middle ground by appealing to reason, by counting on the presumption that embattled parties wanted to cooperate in order to coexist. His approach worked when land developers had complained about the mill's stench and in countless other disputes between management and employees. Entrenched as we were, neither Mother nor I bought into Dad's philosophy. We didn't want to cooperate. We didn't even want to coexist, really.

When I think of those weeks and months after the accident, I picture Dad as a blob of salt-water taffy. We are relentless, Mother and I, twin pairs of gyrating arms that pull and stretch him, twist him around our tireless machinations. Ever in motion but never touching, we circle each other in our familiar, cyclic pattern, each striving to pull Dad in just as the other pushes him away.

Of course my grades plummeted. Had I devoted half the time to my homework as I did to being a *saboteur extraordinaire*, I could have held the number-one GPA ranking in my class. My "homework" consumed me to the point of exhaustion. Lying awake each night, I plotted new torments for Mother until I became a victim of my own ambition, immolated as surely as a moth drawn to flame.

Any excuse to be away formed easily on my lips. I sought to ingratiate myself with anyone who would include me in her circle, knowing all the while my presence was tolerated only because everybody looks better when standing next to the fat friend. Such shallow friendships were usurious. The interest I paid for the investment of my time far outweighed any dividends. I knew I was wasting my time and maybe my chance for college. I did. But I had charted my battle plans and there would be no retreat.

Ironically, my academic achievement was the one legitimate thing Mother used to brag about. I sacrificed my accomplishments on the funeral pyre of our mutual fury, but I'm sure I felt the loss more than Mother. It was easy for me to know how to be successful at school. The rules were clear, the procedures locked in place. Early on, I had figured out how to be better than my classmates at something. No dates for after-game mixers. No invitations from classmates for a trip to the mall or weekend sleepovers. No skipping class. No fun . . . at least, not the kind most kids have. I had plenty of time to read and complete assignments and study for exams and write research papers and make elaborate displays on tri-fold boards with impressive lettering.

As a seventh grader, I had been invited to take the PSAT with juniors by virtue of my standardized test scores in reading and math. I performed well enough to be invited to a luncheon in Madison to receive a scholarship for one university course of my choice. For once, Mother left infant Jonny with Grammy Elnora and Dad took a day off from the mill. They snagged seats in the sixth row of the auditorium, and they clapped and whistled when the governor shook my hand. At home, Mother secured my certificate to the refrigerator with an oversized "GOOD JOB" magnet. Even then, I didn't mind that my certificate did not warrant a frame on the stairwell. It was Whirlpool-worthy, and that was enough.

Before the accident that day in the snow, I garnered honors in History Day competitions and had been named a finalist in the regional Modern Woodmen speech contest. My teachers invited me to participate in Junior Great Books discussions and I took part in Mock Trial, opportunities offered only to advanced students. After the accident, I seemed eligible only for the competition pitting Mother's will against mine. No judges could objectively score our respective performances. No impartial panel could determine who bested the other. And because a winner could not be named, a champion crowned, we seemed destined to engage in emotional gridlock until one or the other yielded.

By the end of my sophomore year, I was failing AP European History, Biology, and Phys Ed. I was keeping my head above water in Advanced Algebra and Human Geography, barely. With only three weeks of school remaining, my counselor, Mrs. Streit, pulled me out of English, the one class I could afford to miss. She didn't sugarcoat her concerns.

"Luce, explain these grades. I have 'In Danger' notices from five of your teachers. FIVE. What's going on? You make the Honor Roll your freshman year and the first two trimesters this year. You are on track for advanced placement honors and you're building an impressive résumé for college apps. You could write your ticket to any school of your choice. Then you fall on your face. I've sent messages home and I hear nothing . . . NOTHING from your folks. Your records show they attended midterm conferences in October, so I know they care. What is going on? If I didn't know better, I'd say you were into drugs, missy."

"I just got behind this term, that's all."

"Don't pull that with me. I've been around the block, and this kind of thing doesn't just *happen*," she said. "I'm not messing around here, Luce. Either you tell me what's going on or we're both getting into my car and I'm driving out to your house to speak with your folks. You think I'm going to let you throw away your talent and your future? Think again."

"You can't fix this, Mrs. Streit. No one can."

"Maybe not. But I sure can't fix it if I don't know what's broken. Come on, Luce. Come clean."

Counselors must take a college course entitled *Wait Time 103*. Mrs. Streit sat at her desk, not moving. She looked at me square on and she didn't blink. Her stare said *I'm not going anywhere. Neither are you.* Like Mother, she was stony and unbending, but her silence anticipated. It didn't dismiss.

Once I opened my mouth, I couldn't stop. I started with the failing grades that precipitated Mrs. Streit's concern and worked my way backward. I left nothing out: the accident with Jonny, the guilt, the silence, the sneaking and lying, the cruel pranks. I might as well have been a troubled patient on the psychiatrist's couch, painfully recounting all the injustices I'd ever withstood and all the ways I had retaliated. Mrs. Streit listened to everything, never interrupting until I was spent. I was absolutely empty, but there was no lightness in my revelation.

Mrs. Streit's shoulders sagged with the weight of my burden. "Clearly, Luce, we have a problem bigger than either one of us can handle. Have you talked to anyone about this?"

"It's not exactly something you want plastered all over," I said. "Family disintegrates. Film at eleven."

"I'm not talking about broadcasting your troubles, Luce. But let's be honest. What you're doing now isn't exactly working, is it? Your family needs help. If you keep doing the same things, you're going to get the same results. I'm no doctor, but this seems pretty destructive—for everyone involved."

"So what do I do?"

"What do you *want* to do?"

I wanted to flip the pages of my life's book backwards, all the way back to before Jonny was born. And I hated myself for the depth of my wanting.

SEVENTEEN

Once our situation went public, everyone—the school psychologist, my teachers, Mrs. Streit, my grandparents—agreed Mother and I needed an "attitude adjustment." Our situation was toxic. Our actions, individually and collectively, were poisoning the well of our family's future.

Two weeks after school ended, Dad and I loaded the Explorer with my clothes, books, and a manila folder thick with school assignments. Together, we made the nine-hour drive to Ralston, Nebraska, a suburb of Omaha and home to Uncle Kurt and Aunt Heather.

At first, Dad had resisted, had dug in his heels with uncharacteristic force. "How can we *heal* as a family if we don't *live together* as a family?" But even he had to admit that we weren't exactly living together as a family anyway. Aunt Heather, who had spoken so eloquently at Christopher's funeral, was equally moving in her entreaties to my father. Not surprisingly, Mother needed no convincing.

In her litany, Aunt Heather barely drew a breath. She had taught English at Ralston High for eighteen years. She'd dealt with all kinds of kids with all kinds of family issues; childless though she was, she knew a thing or two about teenagers:

> *Luce is vulnerable. Her grades are suffering. She looks haunted, absolutely haunted. Nolan, Bets, do think this can go on indefinitely? Where on earth could Luce go if not home with Kurt and me to Ralston? Could anyone better care for her than blood relatives? Do the two of you realize residential treatment is expensive—if, in fact a treatment center would take Luce? As much as you think this is an impossible situation, Bets, your daughter is certainly not the most desperate case out there. She could be hooked on drugs. She could be violent. She could be a runaway. The waiting list to get into a good program might come too late. Do you really want to take that chance? Thank God you have a*

viable alternative, Nolan. Her last, undeniable salvo: *Do something to help yourselves heal, or by God, I will. This borders on child abuse. Take charge while you have a say in what happens. Make changes that make sense.*

Aunt Heather and Uncle Kurt negotiated a "summer sabbatical." With sponsorship from Mrs. Streit and under Aunt Heather's guidance, I'd complete work to regain my academic footing and be ready for a fresh start, back on track with passing grades by the fall semester. We told Jonny I was going to a special school for the summer. Having just completed his first year in preschool (Tuesdays and Thursdays, 9:00–11:30), he understood "special school." He probably envisioned me clapping to musical rhythms, eating granola bars at snack time, and building towers from oversized Lego blocks. Right up to the moment of our leaving, he acted as though I were off on some great adventure.

He hugged me fiercely before I slid into the passenger's seat. "Bye, Luce. I love you. Do good in school." I pinched the fleshy part between my thumb and index finger to keep from crying.

Mother, of course, couldn't have been happier. She had the moxie to keep her glee to herself, at least, but I had no reservations about where she stood. I would be out of the house and out of her hair for a few blessed, calm months.

EIGHTEEN

Conversation during the long ride across Wisconsin and Iowa was as flat and monotonous as the landscape. While I knew that this exile was probably the best scenario any of us could construct, I could not entirely forgive Dad. I felt like the last kid chosen when teams are picking sides for a game of dodgeball. I had wanted him to be a more compassionate captain. I didn't expect to be a starter, but I still wanted to make the team.

Aunt Heather and Uncle Kurt lived in a modest but comfortable home on State Street in one of the older Ralston neighborhoods. An avid cyclist, she insisted on riding her bike to and from Ralston High—rain or shine—during the fall and spring terms. Snowy Nebraska winters, however, demanded Uncle Kurt drop her at the school before commuting to Offutt Air Force Base, home of the Strategic Air Command and the Fifty-Fifth Wing. He worked as a liaison between the Air Force and civilian electrical contractors, a job rife with stress and frequent, extended trips to military bases around the world. When he wasn't traveling for work or logging late nights on the base, he liked to volunteer his services as a cross-country girls' track coach at the high school where Heather taught. They were as close to a power couple as I knew, and I often wondered why they had not opted for a more ostentatious home or lifestyle. Uncle Kurt, in this regard, was much like Dad. He needed little more than a place to hang his hat, he liked to say.

Rather than spending money on a big house neither he nor Heather wanted to clean or maintain, they preferred to travel during Heather's summer hiatus from school. The year prior to my arrival on their doorstep, they had spent three weeks in Fiji. No five-star hotels for them, however. Villagers used to Aussies *on holiday* were charmed by Kurt and Heather's interest in native customs. My relatives finagled an invitation to the home of Temesia, brother to the chief of Naboutini. They participated with their host and his children Teme, Sammu, and Dukes in the preparation of a numbing brew made from ground Kava root Heather and Kurt had brought as a gift for the honor of their visit.

Two summers before their island vacation, they accompanied a group of ophthalmologists, dentists, and general practitioners on a humanitarian mission to Haiti. This was actually the third time they had made such a trip. The group from Offutt AFB had collected hundreds of pairs of old eyeglasses, cataloged the prescription strength of each, and loaded them—along with vials of vaccine and antibiotics—on their "Heart to Haiti" flight.

Armed with medical supplies and optimism, the doctors and their volunteer entourage flew to the island of Hispaniola to minister to impoverished natives. They opened temporary clinics in churches and schools and welcomed patients suffering with everything from head lice and toothaches to cataracts and cancer. Heather said a single pair of glasses might cost the equivalent of a year's salary for the average Haitian. Routine medical care was nonexistent. Dentistry was unheard of.

Every day at dawn, all those seeking medical attention began to form lines extending the length of the village. Wounds festered, raging fevers weakened malnourished children, eye infections blinded young and old alike, blackened teeth rotted in gums which oozed pus. Patiently, the villagers waited their turns, passing the time with quiet stories, impromptu songs, games with sticks and rocks. I couldn't help but think of the contrast between Haitian families and their northern neighbors, we clock-watching Americans in our climate-controlled waiting rooms impatiently thumbing through *People* or *Popular Mechanics* or *Good Housekeeping*. Post-treatment, patients exited the make-shift clinics inoculated, bandaged, splinted. Teeth were pulled, minor surgeries performed, and vision corrected. Glasses were not fashion statements. Rather, they found their new owners based solely on the relationship between need and availability. Young boys might sport glittery red frames while old grannies preened in their heavily framed bifocals.

Aunt Heather documented the mission. She put together a slide presentation and recorded a tape of her observations. Whenever she spoke at Optimist Club or Shriner gatherings, school assemblies or public library community programs, she was able to secure even more glasses or donations of other supplies to be distributed on the next trip.

I had seen her slides: starving children, their bellies distended from severe malnutrition; mothers squatting outside huts cobbled together from rusty sheets of corrugated metal; families at open-air markets adjacent to runnels of open sewage; barefoot toddlers in ragged thrift-shop T-shirts. The Haitians had no reason to trust doctors and pharmacists and translators, yet they smiled through the vaccinations, withstood stitching of cuts, beamed when presented with a new pair of glasses, gently probed cavities left by the nearly painless removal of dead teeth.

One could not see the pictures without wanting to help. My aunt and uncle seemed able to rally the most recalcitrant; Ebenezer Scrooge himself, even without benefit of ghostly visitations, would have gladly emptied his pockets in support of their causes. For Uncle Kurt and Aunt Heather, the greater the need, the greater their commitment. Perhaps that is why they welcomed me so warmly. It was as though I were one of their Haitian children. They had tested my vision, found me myopic, and fitted me with glasses that brought everything into focus. And for my part, I adjusted to the new frames.

I owe them everything. I was to stay with Aunt Heather and Uncle Kurt for the summer. I didn't go home for ten years.

NINETEEN

By **the middle of July,** I had successfully completed all the work necessary to erase the blemishes of incompletes and failing grades on my transcripts. And for the first time in a long time, I didn't feel incomplete. I didn't consider myself a failure. I had applied for a summer job at Oak Hill on Q Street, a private pool within walking distance of State Street and where Heather and Kurt were members. Afternoons found me checking out towels or stocking concessions. Employees earned free swim privileges, a perk I enjoyed early in the morning before swimming classes started and when the pool was usually deserted. An emerging confidence didn't necessarily carry over to public displays in my bathing suit.

Vanity, in fact, turned out to be a powerful motivator. In the evenings, I began jogging with Uncle Kurt. He ran with the cross-country team when they trained in the fall, and he maintained he needed a head start in order to keep up with girls twenty-plus years his junior. Although I didn't lose a lot of weight, I discovered I actually had a waist and calf muscles.

Dad could see the change in me when he, Mother, and Jonny visited on Labor Day. If I'm being honest, I could see the change in the three of them as well. Several months of separation had been good for all of us. Mother appeared rested and younger looking. I saw her take Dad's arm in flirty schoolgirl fashion. She seemed to have regained a sense of humor, even making jokes at her own expense. Dad laughed often and smiled with an ease I had almost forgotten. Jonny, of course, would have been happy in any circumstance, but the promise of a trip to Omaha's Henry Doorly Zoo sealed the deal.

Looking back, I believe the outcome had already been decided. The Garrison Treaty of the Luce Relocation was hammered out via long-distance phone calls and long, complicated letters between the Waukesha and Ralston factions. To ratify, we simply needed a face-to-face show of good will.

Heather, our Shakespearean expert in residence, added a poignant footnote to our treaty:

> *There is a tide in the affairs of men.*
> *Which, taken at the flood, leads on to fortune;*
> *Omitted, all the voyage of their life*
> *Is bound in shallows and in miseries.*
> *On such a full sea are we now afloat,*
> *And we must take the current when it serves,*
> *Or lose our ventures.*

In the fourth act of *Julius Caesar*, she explained, Brutus knows the civil war with Octavian and Marcus Antonius is in its final stages. He realizes that the ebb and flow of power shifts with time, and he argues to Cassius that the fool who waits to act loses opportunity and risks running aground.

We battle-weary Garrisons had taken a page from Shakespeare's playbook. We had, seemingly, seized an opportunity to right our ship and sail it on waters which no longer swirled in dangerous eddies but moved us forward on gentle currents.

TWENTY

The name of every student attending Ralston High School appears in tiny italic print in the index of the yearbook. If the student is included in a picture—either school portrait or candid shot taken by a yearbook staff member—the page number correlating to each picture is noted as well. Seniors are further honored in a separate index with an exhaustive alphabetical listing of activities and numbers denoting their years of participation.

I did not own the longest list of events in the yearbook, but by no means was mine the shortest. Had I come full circle? I remembered sitting in Mother's closet as a child, a voyeur to her past. Now I had my own collection of memories preserved between stiff covers adorned with the school's mascot, a stylized ram in regal profile looking to the left, the curled horn and neck artfully creating the "R" in Ralston.

Lucinda Evelyn Garrison

> *Circle of Friends 2, 3, 4; Courtesy Club 3, 4;*
> *French Club 3, 4; Library Worker 2, 3, 4;*
> *Newspaper 3, 4; Senior Committee 4;*
> *WordSong 2, 3, 4; transfer from Waukesha 1.*

Circle of Friends met weekly. It was the first group I joined at RHS. Their mission: to befriend students with disabilities and include them in school activities. This one was a natural fit for me. I knew firsthand the importance of inclusion. I was paired with Bella, a Down's syndrome teen who attended classes with a one-on-one associate at her side. Aside from our regular meetings after school, I went to Bella's house every couple of weeks just to hang out. We might listen to a new CD or go to the mall, study, or watch TV. Her parents were amazing. Patient and smart, they looked at Bella's disability as a challenge, not an impairment. As a result, Bella didn't see herself as different. She walked the halls between classes, hive-fiving students she passed and greeting everyone with, "Hey, you. Looking good." She worked as hard at her alternative assignments as I did at my college prep classes. Her goal to live independently after graduation was as highly anticipated as any student's acceptance to a topflight college. Although I graduated the year before Bella, I returned to Ralston for commencement and help serve sandwiches and cake at her open house celebration. In classic Bella fashion, she high-fived every member of the school board as she walked across the stage to receive her diploma and then turned to the audience. "Looking good," she beamed. Right along with every graduating senior, family members, and friends, I stomped my feet and finger-whistled my approval.

For Courtesy Club, I ushered at school performances or played tour guide to the eighth-grade students when they visited campus for spring orientation, all temporary gigs. Library workers, however, showed up two or three days a week opposite gym class. We shelved books, worked at the resource center, wrote out overdue notices and dispatched them to homeroom teachers. Sometimes Mrs. Mitchell trusted us to pull research materials and organize them on carts for special units.

My least favorite activity was Senior Committee, and I have my Humanities teacher to thank for that. Ralston planned a district-wide revamp in language arts and Mrs. Christianson thought I would be the "perfect" student rep to sit in with curriculum coordinators and English teachers from the middle and high school. When I complained about the snail's pace of the process—the unending studies and reporting of findings—Uncle Kurt laughed and commented, "If you want to avoid doing anything meaningful, assign the work to a committee. No better way to kill progress."

WordSong, hands down, was my never-miss club. Ralston administrators believed students would be more engaged, more connected to school if they had the opportunity to create organizations which reflected their interests. To launch such a group, students needed only to draft a proposal and secure a teacher to act as sponsor. Aunt Heather was WordSong's unanimous choice.

Ours was a writers' group, loosely organized except for our commitment to meet weekly to share our creative writing with one another. Prior to our Wednesday afternoon gatherings in Heather's classroom, we could duplicate the pieces we intended to share and hand them over to Heather for distribution at the meeting. No agenda dictated the order of our readings; we simply waited for someone to volunteer. In the beginning, awkward silences filled the space. None of us even made eye contact during these vacant moments. To do so would be to exert undue pressure, a direct violation of our only bylaw. Each of us *wanted* to read, to have a willing audience. Each wanted to hear our fellow WordSongers praise honesty of emotion or inspired word choice. We just didn't want to be the first. Aunt Heather could have been teacherly and called upon one of us to begin, absolving us of taking initiative. No. She simply waited. Then, tentatively, sometimes even comically in unison, a quiet voice or two would begin. Poetry, personal reflections, short stories, lyrics, incomplete drafts, even embittered rants over some perceived offense at home or among friends, these were the subjects of our "word songs."

I loved the diversity of our group. At first our membership was girl-heavy, but a muse whispers in the ears of both genders. Boys had something to say. Understandably, most didn't want to say it in a larger classroom of football players or wrestlers. Barrett Hawkins broke that barrier. A state-qualifier at 138 pounds, he was a charter member of WordSong. The first piece he ever shared had us rolling on the floor. He recalled his earliest experience with wrestling, admitting he went out for the sport because of the "sexy singlets." He wrote that he loved only women who loved cauliflower ears, and his best, most-often used move was "lie on my back and look at the lights." Somehow, perhaps on a dare, he had conned Jesse Nichols to come. A gifted artist, Jesse never read, but he sketched as he listened to the rest of us. Often at the end of a WordSong session he would tear heavy sheets from his pad to present to the author who inspired his drawings. Another member, Matthew Weston, wrote edgy, dark poetry unconventional in rhythms and images. When he read, we listened, transfixed, to the rich cadence of his voice. We felt sophisticated, accomplished, convinced our expressions were fresh, our ideas utterly original.

Then there was Sadie McNutt, Sadie-Lady, the uncontested WordSong queen. While the rest of us were pretenders at the craft of writing, Sadie was the real deal. She was the most outgoing of the group, always laughing the loudest or punctuating her observations with wild gestures. She began every WordSong meeting with personal anecdotes embellished with exaggerations and outlandish details. Enormously overweight, she constantly poked fun at herself. "Why not identify the elephant in the room?" she would say. Then she would turn her head toward her right shoulder, lift her arm in the air and imitate the trumpeting of a bull elephant. We pounded on the desks and hooted our support. We even used her antics to advertise WordSong. "You won't believe what Sadie-Lady did last night. Really, you have to come."

An only child of professional parents, Sadie wanted for nothing. Her mission was to share her good fortune with others, and every scheme was founded in grand, noble gestures. She proposed food drives for the local homeless shelter and a prom night for residents of the Senior Center in nearby Papillion. Although no one could question her good intent, most of her projects died for lack of follow-through. For Sadie, the devil was in the details. Still, her generosity was legend. The summer before her junior year, her parents took her to London. She returned with gifts for everyone in our group, each thoughtfully selected with the recipient in mind. I still have the scarf she gave me, a soft winter muffler resembling a ribbon of liquid marble.

She was also the saddest person I have ever known. Sadie was in most of my classes and—no contest—the smartest girl at RHS, but she struggled to maintain a C average because she missed so much school. If you looked up "depressed" in the dictionary, Sadie's picture would be the definition. As much as I loved her, I learned the hard way never to count on her. I had committed to every cause she championed, had volunteered to contact donors, had scheduled meetings at her request and which she never attended. I made excuses for her and fielded the inevitable complaints when she simply abandoned her own plans midcourse. She was Sadie-Lady, though, my best friend. I just kept pushing the *replay* button on our relationship until that last time when the tape finally broke.

We were partnered in College Prep Composition for a presentation on logical fallacies, and we had spent a full week researching *ad hominem* and *tu quoque*. The grade counted for one-fifth of our midterm score. This was a Big Deal. The night before we were to present, Sadie promised to polish our handouts and have her father duplicate them on the color printer at his office. We practiced for over an hour, working on delivery and inflection, memorizing our script so we wouldn't have to rely on our notecards. Of course, she never showed for class. Never called to let me know I was on my own. Never cared that half of a whole is incomplete, unfulfilled.

That afternoon, when I stormed her house to find her watching reruns of *The Twilight Zone* on cable, her best defense was inimitable Sadie: "You know I'm a head case. Nobody can trust me. Don't feign surprise, sweetie. This is all on you, Luce-Goose."

And, in a way, she was right. Sadie was not the first person I had trusted. She would not be the last. What was the old adage? *Fool me once, shame on you. Fool me twice, shame on me.* My need to believe could not trump her need to escape. I had looked Sadie in the eye and convinced myself that this time she would deliver, knowing as I did that Sadie's only constant was inconstancy. I was through with her and told her so. "Okay, no more surprises, Sadie-Lady. You're a head case. Lesson learned." Outside the classroom, we saw little of each other the rest of our senior year and not at all the summer before college.

The last letter I ever received from her came in the fall of my freshman year at college. Contrite and subdued, she proposed we get together over winter break, but she never called.

One week before the winter term was to begin, Sadie dyed her blonde hair purple, dressed herself in a sequined camisole and black leggings, filled the bathtub with water, and quietly cut her wrists. Her parents found her when they returned home from a business dinner.

After the funeral, several of us gathered at the mausoleum to read our favorite Sadie pieces retrieved from treasured WordSong portfolios. I selected her "Inconsequential Chains," and faltered only once to still the quiver in my voice: *Bind me if you will/Inconsequential chains restrain/ but cannot claim me/cannot save me/Save me.*

Sadie-Lady could not be saved. Lesson learned.

TWENTY-ONE

Living in Ralston was like extracting a decayed tooth after months of suffering. Pull the tooth and the pain goes away, but the tongue, remembering, still searches the hole left behind. To acknowledge absence—even absence of pain—is to accept a void.

Through those first uncertain weeks of summer before my status as houseguest morphed into permanence, I was drugged by an unfamiliar peace. I did not wear my shoulders by my ears as I had after the accident with Jonny. I did not tense involuntarily nor shiver nervously. My mouth did not turn to cotton and my bowels were not liquidy after I ate. I slept deeply and dreamed rarely.

But I could not deny the void. I missed home. I missed them all.

I missed Jonny's end-of-the-world sobs and his unrestrained giggles and the tender spot behind his knee that, when tickled, turned one to the other. I missed his imagination that created entire cities out of shoeboxes and I missed the smell of baby wash Mother still used when she bathed him. I missed his stick figure drawings and the crayons broken in their creation. I missed his hand in mine as we crossed the street and the way he squirmed from my lap to stand and belt out the "Number Nine" song when he watched *Sesame Street*. I missed his insistent "'Scuse me" when he wanted my attention and the gift of his smile when I gave it to him.

I missed Dad's corny, repetitive jokes when he teased Jonny or me, his capable certainty with anything mechanical, the way he could fall asleep in his recliner, his index finger poised on the remote control and the television screen tuned to the last channel he had surfed. I missed the impulsivity at grocery check-out lines that compelled him to buy packages of strawberry Twizzlers and king-sized Snickers bars and the sheepish guilt that made him hide the crumpled wrappers beneath the seat of the Explorer so Mother would not find them. I missed his patient explanations when Jonny endlessly asked "Why, Daddy?" and his infallible courtesy as he waved another driver ahead of him during the snarl of rush-hour traffic.

I even missed Mother. More accurately, I missed the idea of Mother.

More than I can say, I wanted them to miss me, too. I never stopped wanting them to miss me.

I wanted them to sympathize when I didn't get the part of Mrs. Day in the fall production of *Life With Father*. I wanted to hear good-natured complaining about the clothes I ruined during Ralston's Homecoming Week Mud Bowl. I wanted them to buy more tickets than they could use for the French Club's ham dinner fundraiser and to sponsor Marie, the foreign exchange student from Rennes whose father worked at the Citroen plant there. I wanted them to read the feature stories I wrote for the school paper and praise my editorial on high school drinking. I wanted them to confirm Bennett Eidemiller was a jerk for leaving me at the Winter Festival and taking Cecily Nihart home instead. I wanted them in the audience on Senior Night when I was named a Merit Semi-Finalist and I wanted them to help me pick out graduation announcements and choose their favorite proofs from my folio of senior pictures. I wanted them to celebrate my acceptance to Creighton and applaud my dollar-stretching prudence for living in Ralston rather than on campus. I wanted them to meet the only two men I dated seriously in college and I wanted them to cry with me when the relationships ended badly.

I wanted them to be my family. Despite everything Heather and Kurt did for me, I wanted Dad and Mother and Jonny to be my family. I could have learned about loss without leaving them.

TWENTY-TWO

Throughout high school and college, Mother, Dad, and Jonny either came to Ralston or Heather, Kurt, and I traveled to Waukesha for holidays or long weekends. I anticipated with dread the forced togetherness of that first Thanksgiving and Christmas. Luckily, we never foundered in awkward silences for long. Since childhood, Kurt's ease with Dad had never changed, and I was eternally grateful for Heather's ability to conjure topics of conversation from the deadest of airspace. Still, this kind of blended family was a new paradigm for all of us and it took a while to figure out how to execute it with grace.

One thing we could all agree upon? We managed best when we kept busy. In Waukesha, we borrowed snow shoes or cross-country skis and explored the trails of Minooka Park. Heather always requested a side trip to Cedarburg, a picturesque little hamlet north of Milwaukee where we splurged on gourmet caramel apples and attended winter festivals with Christmas-themed parades and ice-sculpting by local artisans.

If we observed holidays in Ralston, Uncle Kurt and Aunt Heather usually arranged for us to help serve turkey dinner at a homeless shelter in Omaha or work at the food pantry. Even Jonny liked to help stock shelves or bag bulk foods like pasta and dried beans. We baked cookies, caroled, filled and delivered gift baskets to needy families. There were family-friendly films at discount rates in the local theater or the Tree of Lights celebration to attend.

One snowy Christmas when Jonny was eleven we attended early-morning service and lingered over a brunch of Heather's famous Denver omelet and homemade cinnamon rolls. We had barely scraped the plates and loaded them into the dishwasher before Uncle Kurt impatiently hustled us into our warmest winter gear.

"What gives?" Dad asked.

"You are about to experience a long-standing Ralston ritual," Kurt explained. "You'll love it. Everybody, make sure you have your insulated gloves. Does anyone need a stocking cap?" He stopped briefly at the garage service door, disappeared for a moment and emerged dragging a long wooden toboggan.

We followed Kurt and Heather one block over to Maywood, one of the steepest hills in the city. Members of the Ralston police force had set up barricades at the top and bottom of Maywood from S Seventy-Fifth to S Seventy-Sixty and stacked plastic saucers and sleds from the parks and recreation department near the summit. Dozens of neighborhood families had already gathered to spend the day speeding down Maywood without fear of out-of-control sliders playing roulette with traffic at the bottom of the hill. In glorious small-town wisdom, the people had implemented their own variation of the "fence at the cliff" parable rather than "the ambulance in the valley."

Kurt and Heather greeted friends as we took our places at the top of the hill. Among the dozens gathered were Doris and Ed Hauser with sons Dan, James, and Robbie. Parents, young children, teens in pairs or large groups: we were all thrill seekers. A student of Heather's, Mary Jo Federson, squealed with delight as she and her younger sister Bernice shoved off on a huge silver saucer. We watched them coast safely to the bottom, stand, and wave enthusiastically to those of us waiting our turn.

Everyone knew the routine. The entire width of the street was reserved for sledding runs. Spectators could stand along the east side and hill climbers stayed to the west. In our down-filled jackets, we probably resembled puffy, colorful army ants swarming from a single source down predetermined paths only to return to our home base dragging the wooden and plastic spoils of our efforts behind us.

Kurt claimed the first run was "adults only." He was a Maywood Mayhem veteran, one of a group of hard-core sledders who had fashioned a ramp about a third of the way down the hill for the daredevils who insisted on pushing the envelope of safety. Although the ramp wasn't especially steep, toboggans and snow saucers were launched with surprising distance and speed.

He situated himself at the front of the toboggan and directed Heather, Mother, and Dad to follow suit. Before clambering on, Dad bellowed and gave the narrow sled a massive shove. The four of them screamed like little girls as the toboggan picked up speed and careened down the hill. Kurt guided the toboggan over the center of the ramp and yelled with blood-pumping adrenaline as the group went airborne. They landed cleanly and, as one, raised their arms in celebration.

When they had trudged back up to the top, breathless with laughter and exertion, Kurt challenged, "Just try to beat that run. An Olympic ten all the way."

Although Kurt was just being Kurt, Dan, James, and Robbie Hauser seemed ready and willing to take a dare.

"Olympic ten if you're a senior citizen," Dan laughed. "Do you old people get a higher handicap on the scorecards?"

"Let's show 'em how it's done," James urged. He took his place and motioned for Dan and Ritchie to climb on the toboggan. "We need a fourth," Robbie said. "Luce, come on. You can be our token girl. Sit between Dan and me."

"Fat chance," I said. "Like I'd let you talk me into being the filling for a Hauser sandwich."

"Okay. Your loss," Dan said. "Jonny. You're our man. Climb on."

Jonny sat at the end of the toboggan, struggling to wrap his short legs around Robbie Hauser.

"Do we need to put you up front?" James asked Jonny. "We can switch. No problem."

"I'm good. I can hold on."

"Okay, then," Dan said. "You better, 'cause we're not taking any prisoners. Everybody ready?"

Jonny scooted forward and glued himself to Robbie's back. "Are we talking or are we sledding?" He made a final adjustment, squeezing his knees against Robbie's hips. "Let's do this."

Crouching slightly like runners on starting blocks, Dad and Kurt placed their hands midway up Jonny's back. "On three," Kurt signaled. "One . . . two . . . three . . . " They dug in, powered forward and stumbled, their arms comically outstretched as if, in a moment of indecision, they might be grasping to pull the toboggan back rather than send it hurtling down the hill.

Jonny's high-pitched whoop mingled with the lower voices of the older boys in a raucous symphony of exhilaration. Then, suddenly, they were in trouble, their approach to the ramp off the mark. They intended to hit it dead on; that was clear, but we could tell right away they were going too fast to make the necessary corrections in time. We watched as James leaned hard to his left, trying desperately to stiff-arm the toboggan back on course. Like a row of ring-tailed lemurs clinging to each other on a slender branch, Dan, Robbie, and Jonny—chests to backs, groins to buttocks—leaned too. Robbie managed to untangle his left leg from beneath Dan's arm and dig his heel into the snowpack, a maneuver which slowed the toboggan only slightly but succeeded in unseating Jonny just as the sled hit the ramp.

Had we been watching a cartoon, we would have laughed to see the hapless rider at the rear of the toboggan fly backwards and to his left, execute a neat sidewinding three-quarter somersault and land flat on his back, his head bouncing twice, his arms and legs splayed in a pose reminiscent of Da Vinci's Vitruvian man.

But this was no cartoon and Jonny was no pen and ink drawing. He lay on the snowy toboggan run, motionless, his eyes closed.

Kurt and Dad reached him first, Mother, Heather, and I only a step behind. Unlike the bystanders who gathered close to huddle over Jonny, their faces frozen in tragic masks, my first reaction was an audible sigh of relief. I had expected, had steeled myself, to find a halo of blood beneath his head. *He could not have hit that hard without splitting his skull. He couldn't.*

Mary Jo Federson offered to call 9-1-1; someone else cautioned against moving him in case his neck was broken. At this, Mother screamed. Wordless. Agonized. A keening wail more frightening than seeing Jonny, motionless and pale as the snow beneath him.

An older gentleman who identified himself as Dr. Lyons intervened. "Hang on. Let's not get ahead of ourselves." As if on cue, Jonny opened his eyes and mouth simultaneously. I expected him to cry, but he didn't. He struggled to rise, to draw a breath, to suck air into his paralyzed lungs. Robbie Hauser's face reflected the fear we all carried knotted in our bowels.

"Easy. Easy, now," Dr. Lyons soothed. I couldn't be sure if he addressed Jonny or the rest of us who waited in awful anticipation. "You've had the wind knocked out of you. Raise your arms like this. Now relax. Try to take some slow, deep breaths. In and out of your mouth. Slow, son. That's right. Don't panic, now. You're going to be fine."

And, within a few minutes, Jonny was fine—fine enough to breathe, raggedly. Fine enough to be embarrassed by all the fawning attention from complete strangers. Fine enough to be humiliated by Mother's insistent hovering and harpy accusations.

"Jonny, Jonny. My God. You scared me half to death. Why weren't you holding on? You have to be more careful. Do you know what could have happened here? Jonny, baby, you drive me insane with worry. Are you listening to me? " Mother insisted.

Cataloguing each careless move Jonny ever made, every anxious moment she spent worrying about his safety, she squeezed him dry with her tearful tirade. *Did he care so little for her that he would deliberately put himself in harm's way? Shouldn't he be old enough to think about her for a change? What would she do if anything happened to him?* Jonny was sitting up now, his chin against his chest, silent, but trembling. Whether from the cold or cold fury, I didn't know. He rubbed snot from his nose with the back of his jacket sleeve.

"Bets, listen to yourself," Dad attempted to stem the flow of her vitriol. "This isn't helping."

"How dare you speak to me?" she spat at him. "If you hadn't pushed him so hard, this wouldn't have happened. Are you proud of yourself and your precious sledding contest?"

She turned back to her son. "Jonny, can you walk? Do you need us to carry you home?" In that moment, my brother suffered more from Mother's ministrations than any punishment on the toboggan run. His eyes pooled with tears and he turned away from her fluttering hands. With an almost imperceptible set of his shoulders, he stood with difficulty, still gasping occasionally to regulate his breathing.

"I want to go home, Dad," he wheezed.

Dr. Lyons fingered the back of Jonny's head and checked the symmetry and size of his pupils. "I think you can take him home, but do watch for signs of concussion. If he exhibits confusion, slurred speech, headaches, nausea or vomiting, contact your family physician right away. He might evidence signs of sleepiness or dizziness, too. Remember," he cautioned, "concussive symptoms can last days, even weeks, so be vigilant."

We all trudged home. In the lead, Mother and Dad flanked Jonny, steadying him as they headed between houses and through back yards on the way to State Street. Kurt had to turn back to retrieve the toboggan, momentarily forgotten in our haste to leave the accident behind us. Or, perhaps, a calculated move to distance himself from Mother's ugliness?

From my vantage I watched Dad walk straight ahead, never making eye contact with Mother. For her part, Mother was engaged in a pantomime of desperate entreaties countered by Jonny's stiff posture of indifference.

TWENTY-THREE

Despite protests from everyone, Mother slept on the floor beside Jonny's bed that night. In the morning, she gathered and boxed Christmas gifts, stripped sheets from the bed, wiped down the guest bathroom, and stacked tightly zippered luggage and a duffel bag of dirty clothes next to the front door. Her industriousness was the most crystalline of indictments.

She would not hear of troubling Heather for breakfast. "We'll just pick up something on the road." Offering perfunctory good-byes, she marched to the car and planted herself in the passenger seat, fastening her seatbelt with a derisive click. She waited there until Dad and Jonny reluctantly followed her.

Theirs would be a long trip home to Waukesha.

TWENTY-FOUR

When I was growing up in Waukesha, partisanship defined our family politics. If I wanted to see a movie with a friend who hadn't made Mother's short list of approved associates for her teenage daughter, Mother was the last person I would ask. Instead, I would approach Dad and plead with him to "talk to her for me." He consulted with her, argued my case, and delivered her verdict. Decisions momentous or insignificant were often made without my ever speaking to her. Nor was I privy to the rationale behind the pronouncements she funneled to me through Dad.

Heather and Kurt didn't operate that way, but it took me awhile to realize some families actually talked *to* one another rather than *about* one another. If I crossed the line with Heather, Heather let me know it. When I wanted to be a team manager for Kurt's cross-country girls and hinted that Heather might "put in a good word," she refused out of hand. "I don't want to be the manager," she laughed. "Ask him yourself." So when Mother, Dad, and Jonny made their awkward exit that morning, Heather and Kurt did not whisper their reactions in private conversations behind closed doors. To hide their disapproval of my parents would have been disingenuous. I had seen everything they had seen. My voice was as valid, and valuable, to them as their own.

"I feel so badly for Jonny," Heather began. "And I don't get your brother, Kurt. I know Bets can be difficult, but we're talking about Jonny's welfare here. Why doesn't Nolan do something about her?"

"Dad picks his battles," I offered. "They'd be at it constantly if he crossed Mother on everything."

"We only see the tip of the iceberg," Kurt noted. "Nolan told me last night that Jonny's about had it with his mother. Evidently they had a big blow up just before Christmas break because Bets still insists on walking him to the end of their driveway to catch the school bus. For Pete's sake, the kid is in fifth grade. Can you imagine the kind of flak he must take? She's nuts."

Heather shook her head. "I guess Jonny almost didn't go out for flag football last fall because Bets wouldn't sign the permission form. She told me there was no point to it because he wouldn't be playing in high school. She cited some article about the rise in football injuries for high school kids."

"Yeah, Nolan shared that one with me, too," Kurt said. "He signed the form without Bets knowing it and she wouldn't talk to him for days. I guess once the deed was done, she stayed for every practice and made a point of talking to the coach about his being overly aggressive with the kids right in front of all Jonny's teammates."

"Your mother needs some help," Heather nodded to me. "Every parent worries, but she's over the top."

"I used to be jealous of Jonny," I admitted. "Not anymore."

"Was she always this bad?" Heather asked.

I didn't really know how to answer that. "Jonny is everything to her. She's frantic about him, but she's killing him."

Had she always been this way? Was she always crippled by her fear that Jonny, like Christopher, might be taken from her? Had Dad's compassion and sympathy for her loss become the scaffolding which supported her outrageous rules and restrictions?

"Mother told me yesterday that unless she goes with him, Jonny won't be going door-to-door selling magazines for the annual school fundraiser this spring because of all the *sicko predators*—her words—out there. She tries to protect him from everything."

"Someone needs to protect Jonny from her," Kurt snorted.

Just who that someone would be, we hadn't a clue.

TWENTY-FIVE

The tidal wave of Mother's anger washed over her relationship with my aunt and uncle for some time. Dad and Jonny were caught in the undertow. I stood on the shore and watched.

In her skewed version of the events on that Christmas afternoon, Heather and Kurt were complicit in Jonny's accident and in his subsequent, *unreasonable* anger over her concern for him. Kurt had suggested the outing. He had set the stage for a senseless competition. He had helped push the toboggan off course. And Heather? Hers was the guilt of omission. She had done nothing stop Kurt.

For the next two years, Mother manufactured entirely plausible reasons why holidays or extended weekends would not be spent in one another's company. Weather forecasters need only mention the possibility of snow or a wintry mix and travel plans were summarily canceled. She heard Dad worry over some unnamed trouble at the mill and they'd just have to see what panned out. Jonny's annual checkups or her mammograms were guaranteed to fall in the middle of spring break. The skies were unsafe after 9/11. Old college friends called at the last minute for impromptu visits. A migraine headache left her unable to stand. Her bedroom desperately needed a new coat of paint. The washing machine was thunking and she was at the mercy of the repairman. Grammy Elnora's arthritis was acting up and how could she leave her mother in the lurch? Each excuse offered with sorrowful regrets. Each followed by promises to reschedule soon.

We marveled at Mother's ability to lie on the fly. She must have posted a master list of ready excuses indexed and cross referenced by season, occasion, and persons involved. No doubt each fabrication was accompanied by a corresponding scale to indicate the appropriate level of alarm with which to infuse her voice.

After a while, Heather and Kurt made a game of one-upsmanship, inventing ever more fantastic deceptions Mother might add to her repertoire.

"She needs to redrill her bowling ball."

"Her shoelaces need pressing."

"The military contacted her for a covert mission."

"She's working on a pilot for a new sitcom."

Eventually, whenever they anticipated Mother might be calling to beg off some family function, they were emboldened enough to answer with, "Let me guess, Bets. Something's come up. Perhaps . . ." and they would try out one of their outlandish excuses on her just to hear her respond in righteous indignation the *real* reason why the Waukesha Garrisons would not be traveling to Ralston for the Fourth of July or why Heather, Kurt, and I would need to cancel Thanksgiving plans in Wisconsin.

Mother's vagaries played havoc with my work schedule. In the beginning, my boss at the coffee shop just off the Creighton campus was amenable to my requests for changing shifts or switching weekends with a coworker. She became less understanding after the third or fourth time I retracted the request following one of Mother's apologetic phone calls.

I worried Linda might regret her decision to hire me, for reasons unfathomable at the time, over the other viable applicant, Karis Monroe, a willowy blonde majoring in theater arts. Had the decision been mine to make, I would have wanted Karis behind the brew counter. She more than I would invite return visits from the male students and faculty who frequented *Java, the Hut* early in the morning, throughout the day, and during cram sessions or frenzied grading marathons extending well into the night. I like to think I interviewed more impressively than Karis. Realistically, her rigid rehearsal schedules probably limited her availability during evening and weekend hours, the hardest slots to fill. I didn't mind employment by default as long as I could collect a regular paycheck.

I would never have been able to afford tuition at Creighton if I had to live on campus. Staying with Heather and Kurt saved thousands on room and board. Between that, the funds from Dad, FAFSA money, my academic scholarships, and wages from *Java*, I managed to avoid burying myself under crushing debt and still garner a top-notch education. Even so, before I could even think about graduate school, I needed to bankroll a boatload of cash. Linda came through for me with full-time hours and managerial duties whenever she had to be gone.

If I'm being honest, working at *Java, the Hut* was more than a job. Linda, the owner, had capitalized on the wildly popular *Star Wars* franchise when she opened her themed coffee house. I'm not sure how she circumvented copyright infringement, but Linda cleverly incorporated character names from the movie trilogy into the beverage and pastry selections, much to the delight of her customers. The most popular offerings? Millennium Mocha, Darth Dutch Coffee, X-Wing Espresso, Leia Latte, Calrissian Cappuccino, Skywalker Scones.

Java was also one of the first houses in the area to offer freshly brewed coffee by the cup as opposed to a bank of self-serve carafes. The precision of the brew process appealed to me: weighing the beans and grinding them to a sandy consistency, nestling the coffee filter into the cone and rinsing it with hot water to rid the paper of its cottony taste, cradling the cone and moistened filter in a measuring cup, blooming the coffee for a full minute to saturate the grounds, pouring water over the center of the cone in a slow and steady stream and then waiting for the brew to filter, savoring the customer's appreciation as I handed the warm ceramic mug across the counter. I could engage the regulars in easy conversation as I served their favorite orders, remembered via association with the pet nicknames I ascribed to each customer.

Gray the Flavor Guy was one of the first to consistently join the queue at my station. A soft-spoken man in his mid-forties, he always requested one of the specialty flavored brews which changed daily. He might scan the white board of selections, pulling thoughtfully at his beard before deciding on a hazelnut cream or chocolate macadamia. Self-deprecating in demeanor, Gray craved conversation more than his hazelnut cream. More often than not, he shared extremely personal information—intimate, not necessarily inappropriate, details—about his children or the ex-wife he so obviously missed. He worked on campus, and if I spotted him from a distance, I usually took pains to avoid running into him. A face-to-face would ensure a protracted monologue from which I could not gracefully extricate myself, and I would invariably be late to class. At *Java,* he paid for my undivided attention along with his coffee.

The most colorful of my customers was Crazy Texas Ted, a circus of disruption whenever he frequented the coffee house. Of indeterminate age, Crazy Texas was tall with black, wildly disheveled hair, horrible teeth, and a face pitted either from childhood acne or disfiguring pox. He claimed to have served in The War (which war was anyone's guess) and to live in an apartment adjacent to *Java* where he swore he kept a live fish in his bathtub. Afflicted by Tourette's, for which he took medication only sporadically, he stomped and grunted his way to the brewing station, peppering his order with expletives and spittle.

Linda called Flavor Gray, Texas Ted, and several others my "peeps" because they consistently bypassed shorter lines with far less wait time to stand at my brewing station. She intimated with a strange mixture of derision and respect that I, more than any other barista, tolerated relationships with the oddball customers. And why not? I was the poster child for tolerance of oddballs.

Flavor Gray and Texas Ted were, in fact, far more predictable than my own mother. I knew what they wanted and I knew how to deliver. I could read their thoughts as plainly as text on a teleprompter, and I never divined hidden meanings behind offhand observations. They were exactly who they appeared to be. Always transparent. Sometimes pathetic, yes, but also sympathetic. Mother could take a lesson or two.

During those years of on-again, off-again plans which never materialized, Mother's weak duplicities actually infuriated me far more than her desire to separate me from her, Jonny, and Dad. It was bad enough she wanted no contact with me. She also assumed I was stupid enough not to *know* she wanted no contact with me.

Eventually, she stopped calling with excuses. She stopped calling altogether.

And then Dad stepped up, usually phoning early on Sunday nights. Our exchanges, stilted at first, hovered around safe topics. The weather. Business at the mill. A new Mexican restaurant on the river walk in downtown Waukesha.

His voice, raspy with the effort of pretending normalcy, asked questions absent the rising inflection which might invite a response. It was as if every question had already been answered and the answer was *no*.

Finally, when I could depend upon the regularity of his calls and I no longer wrestled with the *what if* of disappointment, our one-liners morphed into actual conversation. Over the course of several months I learned that attrition at the mill meant he assumed more hands-on work during the day. His evenings were spent at the kitchen table balancing ledgers, verifying orders, documenting compliance measures for federal emissions regulations, and checking off any other administrative task which otherwise could not be squeezed into his day.

The drudgery of the work week lessened somewhat during spring and summer when Jonny's and Dad's passion for baseball in general and the

Cubs in particular afforded my father a much-needed distraction. None of us was surprised that Jonny's loyalty to Chicago's North Side nine mirrored Dad's. His most-prized possession was a 1990 Ryne Sandberg error card misidentifying the future Hall of Fame second baseman as a *third* baseman. Grandmother Lucinda found the card encased in acrylic armor at a flea market in Racine, plunked down her fifteen dollars, and handed it over to an ecstatic Jonny who promptly enshrined the card on the nightstand in his room.

Whenever possible, Dad and Jonny either watched the broadcasts on television or tuned into WGN 720 to hear the play-by-play. For Jonny's thirteenth birthday, Dad had gifted my brother (and himself) with a pair of bleacher seats in the Friendly Confines for the June fifteenth game against the White Sox. Early on game day the two of them caught the Amtrak Hiawatha Service out of Milwaukee. They ate stadium dogs and nachos and Jonny cheered for his hero, third baseman Bill Mueller who went two for four and scored a run, inspiring my brother to ratchet up his own performance on his AAU team back in Waukesha.

Dad couldn't say enough about Jonny's fielding prowess. He had proved to be a natural at third base, handling the hot corner with fluid grace and powerful, accurate throws to first. He was only a mediocre hitter, however, which rankled Jonny. He had always batted in the bottom of the order, but he dreamed of being a lead-off man. To that end, Dad shopped second-hand sporting goods stores until he found a used but serviceable SoloHitter, a marvel of simple engineering guaranteed to improve a hitter's power.

As soon as winter weather softened to spring and Jonny could shed bulky overcoats, he was at the SoloHitter, swatting ball after ball, finding balance in his stance, honing his hand-eye coordination, building strength and muscle memory. Over the course of the season, Jonny improved his batting average, impressed his coach, and subsequently moved up in the batting order.

"It's an obsession with him, Luce," Dad would laugh with pride. He gets in a hundred swings a day, double that before a game. And if he doesn't connect well in the batter's box, if he isn't sharp at the plate, then as soon as he comes home he's out there past dark, hitting, hitting, hitting. The more upset he is, the more swings he takes. I swear, Luce, I can't keep him in balls. They're rags on a string when he's finished with them."

Only occasionally did Dad mention Mother, and then only when I asked point blank. Although he never provided details, I gathered she was increasingly unpredictable and volatile. I could not tell if his reticence had more to do with his shame over her behavior or his inability to deal with it. I do know he tried to time his phone calls when she was out of the house because our conversations ended abruptly whenever a slamming door and a theatrical "Jonny baby, Nolan, I'm home," announced her presence. Her voice chafed, prickly and imperious, as though nothing carried any significance until her arrival. Even over the phone, five hundred miles was not distance enough to dull the hot points of anger that exploded behind my eyes and burned in my ears.

I suspect I was not the only Garrison child to react so viscerally to Mother's presence. Often, just before Dad's hurried good-bye and promise to call the following Sunday, I would hear another door slam as Jonny made his exit to pound relentlessly on his SoloHitter, his bat attacking the ball tethered to its frame.

TWENTY-SIX

The phone rang earlier than usual on that Sunday afternoon in September, but a quick glance at caller ID confirmed Waukesha's 414 area code.

"Dad, hi. You're early today."

"It's not your father. It's Bets. Your mother."

I probably would have laughed at Mother's apparent need to qualify her identity had the surprise of hearing her voice not rendered me silent.

"Lucinda. Did you hear me?"

"Why are you calling? Is Dad okay?" If Dad hadn't called, it was because he couldn't. I swallowed bile.

"Yes, he's fine. Don't always expect the worst. I'm calling because of Lucinda."

I have read about those people who, near death, experience an out-of-body sensation, an ethereal floating above oneself, removed but still witness to the corporeal. Had something tragic befallen some other Lucinda, my shadowy doppelganger, and God in His cruel humor had chosen my mother to deliver the news?

My confused silence must have confirmed Mother's low opinion of my inability to grasp the obvious.

"Lucinda, your grandmother. I'm calling about your grandmother. She has had . . . an *accident*."

"Tell me what happened."

"I'm trying. We're still piecing together the details, but apparently her stubbornness has landed her in the hospital."

Mother must have enjoyed this stage, the prolonged suspense, the anticipation with which her audience waited for the drama to unfold as she, a Greek chorus of one, narrated the heroine's downfall.

"We think it happened Friday afternoon or evening. She was trying to reach something in the top cabinet in the bathroom but instead of pulling her step stool in from the kitchen, she decided to stand on the toilet lid, of all things." How easily Mother slid into the glib patter of an amusing anecdote told at a cocktail party. "Well, of course she fell."

"Oh my God, Mother. You say this happened Friday? Why am I just being told now? How is she? Was she hurt very badly?"

Now the voice of dispassionate reporter: "She broke her hip, cracked two ribs, and suffered a concussion. We didn't know ourselves until this afternoon. She didn't show up for brunch at the Senior Center earlier today so some of the ladies she meets there started to worry. They called her house. When they couldn't reach her, they called your father. He found her on the bathroom floor. As soon as she is stable, the surgeons will operate."

"What do you mean, *stable*?"

"Because she was on the floor for so long, she's extremely dehydrated and her blood pressure dropped dangerously low. Surgery would be too risky right now. Basically they're medicating her and watching vitals. She seems very confused about it all, Lucinda. Your father suggested you and Kurt might want to come back to Waukesha."

He *suggested*. We *might* want to come back. For all the sense of urgency she evinced, she might have been listing ingredients in a recipe.

"We'll be there. As soon as I get off the phone I'll square things with Kurt and Heather. Tell Dad I'll call him. Give Grandmother my love."

And then, almost as an afterthought, Mother added, "By the way, you'll be staying at Lucinda's while she's in the hospital."

Mother had spent her entire life imprinting upon me the role of docile daughter and yet that single sentence, delivered so blithely, dissolved every inhibition that had ever muzzled me.

"Really, Mother? Really? Are you fucking kidding me? You're worried about sleeping arrangements while Grandmother is lying in the hospital? Well, forget about it. We wouldn't think of putting you out."

"Honestly, Lucinda. You jump to such irrational conclusions. I simply meant that she wouldn't worry about her place so much if someone were there to look after it. I'm just trying to put her at ease."

"Of course you are, Mother. You're a goddammed saint."

The click on her end of the line was like a check mark, a duty done.

TWENTY-SEVEN

Grandmother Lucinda was never the same. Lying on the bathroom floor, unable to move through the agony, fearful she would
not be found, she drained whatever reservoir of strength she ever possessed. Once feisty and unconventional, sure to scandalize even perfect
strangers with off-color humor or unvarnished observations, she shrank
into herself. I barely recognized her.

Long before my exile to Ralston, it had been Grandmother Lucinda
who picked me up from school for mid-day dentist appointments or acted
as my personal chauffeur when I overslept and missed the bus. Although
grateful to her, I remember slouching down so my classmates would not
see me in the passenger seat as she nosed her tank-like Buick through
milling students making their way across campus, sometimes yelling out
the window to "Move it or lose it" when they didn't open ranks to clear a
path.

If I needed a ride home after a Mock Trial practice or speech competition, the car radio was always tuned to Rush Limbaugh's program.
A staunch straight-ticket Republican herself, Grandmother might agree
with his politics but never his posturing. "You know, Luce, he's full of
shit."

No one could be sure what might trigger an outburst. Once I went
with her to the drug store to pick up a refill for her cholesterol medication. When the pharmacist's assistant totaled her order, Grandmother
Lucinda demanded to know why the price had nearly tripled.

"There is now a generic brand for this medication that is far less expensive, Mrs. Garrison," the tech explained patiently. "Your insurance
won't cover the brand-name drug anymore. If you don't want the generic,
you'll have to pay the difference. I'm sorry, but there's nothing I can do."

I backpedaled behind the aisle of cold remedies and pain relievers
as Grandmother Lucinda railed against health insurance carriers, mon-
ey-grubbing pharmaceutical companies, and franchised drug stores that
no longer cared about personal service and the loyalty of customers who

had been buying enemas and aspirin there for over twenty years and yes, she'd take the generic medication now and take her business elsewhere the next time she wanted anything from a box of Band-Aids to a blood pressure cuff which she would surely need if she so much as drove past their store again.

This was the same woman who, outside a theater in New Berlin, confronted a group of giggly middle school girls and the pimply-faced boys trying to impress them. When one of them flipped her off as we were looking for a parking spot, she stopped the car in the middle of the street and glared at him. He grinned, pointed at her, and pantomimed crude hump-pumps. She rolled down the window, pointed back, and sweetly intoned, "I once had a mongrel dog who did that. I had him neutered."

Following surgery for her broken hip, she rehabbed at a nursing home in West Allis. A sprawling one-story red brick with white colonnades and groomed, gated grounds, it aspired to homey ambience. Once inside the building, however, nothing could camouflage the institutional feel nor mask the assault of medicine and urine and fungicide as tangible as a slap in the face.

Visitors buzzed for admission into the wide foyer decorated with floral wallpaper and potted peace lilies. In the large open lounge to the right, stripes of sunlight fell across mute residents, some diminutive as dolls in their overstuffed wingbacks, some made fragile by the metal framework of wheelchairs and the fleece throws draped over shoulders or across laps despite the superheated air. For the ambulant, meals were taken at round dining tables meant, I am sure, to foster community and conversation. In reality, the seating arrangement served only to underscore each resident's infirmities as measured against those of her dining partners.

Attendants and medical staff alike wore artificially cheery pastel scrubs more believable in a nursery than a nursing home. Assuming a familiarity they had not earned, they addressed residents by their first names or, even more demeaning, with the collective *we*.

"Eileen, we need to put more weight on that leg."

"Come on, now Dorothy. We won't be able to get out of our wheelchair if we don't do five more repetitions today."

"Lucinda, dear, have we had a bowel movement today?"

The facility's director, as if the statistic were a personal achievement, noted that seventy percent of the residents would be able to go home after an intense rehab program. Unstated, of course, was reference to the remaining thirty percent who would die there.

Months later, I would question the director's calculations. What percentage of the care center's population returned home only *then* to discover they were already dead?

TWENTY-EIGHT

Grandmother **was released from the** care facility after nearly three months, her hip mended, her spirit broken. She had regained limited range of motion and flexibility but had lost weight, strength, muscle tone, and any interest in getting better.

In addition to the injuries suffered when she fell, a series of ministrokes left her both addled and easily agitated. She traded her driver's license for a walker, handed over medical and legal power of attorney to my father with Kurt as successor agent, and bitterly relinquished her independence to the whims of a live-in caregiver.

It didn't matter to Grandmother Lucinda that I left Ralston, left my job at *Java* and my plans for grad school at Creighton, left the certain sameness of my home with Heather and Kurt, left everything stable and sure and predictable and safe to move in with her.

She was an unwilling agent of change . . . hers, and my own.

TWENTY-NINE

Dad and Kurt agreed. Taking care of Grandmother Lucinda should be a paid position funded by her annuities and a long-term care policy she had purchased shortly after her husband, my grandfather Robert, passed away more than thirty years before. Perhaps to assuage their guilt over the need for me to postpone grad school, Dad and Kurt insisted I accept the going rate charged by professionals. I refused.

"We'd be getting a bargain, Luce. You'll take care of Mom with more love and compassion than any stranger. She sure as hell will be better with you in the house than somebody she doesn't know or trust. We won't have to worry, and we can't put a price on that."

If my presence made Grandmother "better," I cannot imagine how unmanageable she would have been for an ever-changing slate of caregivers arriving for day and evening shifts, alternating weekends and holidays. Even with me she was suspicious and mistrustful, questioning everything I did and challenging my answers.

For a while, she refused to take her meds without a battle. The pills, she said, stuck in her throat and made her choke. "Are you trying to kill me? I can't swallow these horse tablets." If I cut the larger pills in half, she complained about the bitter chalkiness. With marginal success, I tried smearing them in butter or sometimes dipping them in Hershey's chocolate and serving them to her on a spoon.

She accused me of keeping secrets from her because I separated the mail into three stacks and gave her access to only one of them. Offers for pre-approved credit cards, supplemental insurance (for just pennies a day!), or other junk mail was tossed immediately, a practice that grew from her attempt to activate a two-year account for a pricey Wine of the Month club. Dad picked up the second stack—bills, financial correspondence, medical statements, appeals for charitable donations—once or twice a week. Grandmother could only be trusted with the innocuous: *People* and *Better Homes and Gardens,* glossy catalogs selling everything from specialty coffees to walk-in bathtubs (from which I tore out the order forms before giving them over), and the occasional piece of personal mail which arrived with decreasing frequency.

Dementia settled in, a fog hazing her every thought, shrouding her in a forgetfulness often burdensome to those around her and, in those rare moments of crystal lucidity, embarrassing and frightening to her. I ached to see the empty vacancy of confusion lift from her eyes because it preceded a brief but irrefutable understanding: she knew enough to know she wasn't *right*.

Childlike, she would whisper, "Luce, who am I? What is happening to me?"

Timing was crucial then, fleeting and fickle. I would recall every shared experience I could think of, every funny story Dad had ever recounted about her, every place she'd ever traveled, every friend she'd ever mentioned. I had never been more desperate. Desperate to grab a piece of her and hold it in my palms for her inspection, desperate for her to see what she had been and what she was, still, to me before the memories sieved through my fingers and were lost.

As she deteriorated, she became more docile but infinitely more dangerous to herself. One night I woke to pee and then tiptoed to her room to check on her. She was neither in the bed nor in the closet, a favorite destination when Sundowner's Syndrome kept her awake at night and impossible to rouse during the day. I screamed her name, but she did not answer. The 9-1-1 dispatcher sent a patrol car, but by the time officers arrived I had located her in the garage, fumbling to start the car with a shoehorn.

"Where are you headed? Can I take you somewhere?"

"I need to get to the mall. Take me to the mall. Luce will be six tomorrow and I forgot to buy a gift. She won't understand if I don't bring a gift to the party. She likes purple. Maybe I could find her a purple dress."

I led her back to her room. "The stores are closing now, but I'll take you tomorrow. I'm sure we'll find the perfect gift. We'll wrap it up and take it to the party and sing happy birthday and eat cake."

First thing in the morning, I called a locksmith. Two days later, padlocks secured every door, and I wore the key on a chain around my neck.

THIRTY

Kurt and Heather called weekly and visited every six weeks or so. In an attempt to keep connected, they sent pictures of themselves and penned long letters I read to Grandmother who would stop me frequently to ask, "Now, who is Heather?"

Dad drove to Tosa every third or fourth day, more often if emergencies arose. He wanted to check on Grandmother, but he also wanted to provide some relief for me. Even though I was always exhausted, I made a point of getting out of the house to browse the bookshelves at Barnes and Noble, wander through Marshall's, rent movies I could watch when Grandmother was napping, scope out gallery night in the Third Ward, and—if I were feeling particularly indulgent—treat myself to a massage and facial. One hour with Lisa at *Table for One* left me nearly boneless.

Mother was conspicuously absent. I preferred it that way.

Sometimes, usually on weekends, Dad would bring Jonny. At first we were like twin magnets of similar polarity separated from one another by an unseen but undeniable force. After so many years apart, we were feeling our way, struggling to erase empty years, to make new memories.

Jonny had the good fortune to avoid customary teenaged gawkiness. At fifteen, he was nearly as tall as my father with the same muscular build and the fluid grace of a natural athlete. Like Dad, his fair skin tanned to a golden bronze, but the resemblance ended there. He had inherited Mother's dark hair and robin's egg eyes; except for the gnarly scar bisecting his right eyebrow, he could have been a successful model.

Long after the fact during one of our at-home movie nights, Dad revealed that Jonny actually had been something of a local celebrity. When he was six, he had appeared in a print ad hawking produce for a regional grocery chain and was featured in a thirty-second television spot for a sporting goods store in which he and a six-foot-eight Marquette basketball alum played a game of horse. Once Jonny made the winning shot (of course!), the announcer solemnly intoned "Bentley Sports, Where Every Athlete Small to Tall Shops." Invariably, Jonny echoed the commercial's tag line before falling over in mock death throes and kicking his legs in jerky spasms. "If you *ever* show that tape to anyone, I will kill myself, I swear," he laughed.

Dad often sorted through old photos or home movies shot on 8mm film that Grandmother Lucinda and my grandfather had taken on every occasion possible. She was probably the only person in the free world who still owned the reel-to-reel projector needed to view those grainy images, faded to a uniform rose color, playing out on a portable roll-up screen. Transfixed, Grandmother would narrate over the clack of the film, laughing about the rainstorm that blew away their tent at Jackson Hole camp grounds or mirroring twelve-year-old Kurt's gestures as he pointed in succession to the stony presidential faces on Mt. Rushmore.

The flickering light reanimated her to the grandmother of my memory, a woman of quicksilver temperament and generous heart. Sometimes her lucidity lasted a few brief moments, less than a single reel of film. Other times she would sit through several showings and then extend the viewing by asking Dad to replay the films in reverse.

In one, Kurt and Dad retreat counterclockwise on carousel ponies, dismount, and race walk backwards from the amusement ride. In another, Grandmother purposefully dismantles a flawless apple pie, unlacing the lattice crust and levitating chunky fruit filling from the pie shell into the mixing bowl, each step in the process more fantastic than the last. And then, the stunning finale in which she seamlessly fuses a thin continuous band of peel over the white flesh of an apple, restoring it to an unblemished whole.

The most riveting scene finds a geyser of water sucked back to placidity just as Grandmother Lucinda in skirted black swim dress rises from the spray like some uncertain sea nymph, thumb and index finger pinching her nose, right leg straight and extended slightly forward, left leg bending at the knee as her gracefully arched foot and pointed toes reach back to find the safety of the pool's edge. Without so much as a glance behind her, she nails the landing, gathers her hair—incredibly dry—into a loose bun secured by a print scarf which has floated from the concrete deck into her outstretched hand, and waves self-consciously at the camera.

Her dementia condemned us all to perpetual rewind. Until the day she died, we reached back to the past, reckless in our prayer that she might always nail her landings, grieving all the while because her celluloid self was more alive than the woman who sat beside us.

THIRTY-ONE

The immensity of our mission was no more challenging than that of any family who must watch a loved one deteriorate, but Jonny was equal to the task, often using humor to deal with Grandmother's eccentricities and outbursts.

I remember one evening when I had attended a showing of *Maria Full of Grace* at an indie theater in downtown Milwaukee. Driving back to Tosa, I could not shake the film's depressing aftermath, the lingering images of three young women, terrified drug mules who swallowed heroin-filled rubber pellets and flew from Colombia to New York. Our situations were far different, but I felt an unsettling kinship with the lead character, a young woman whose life had taken a path far different from the one she imagined for herself.

When I walked into the house, no one appeared to be home. As usual, a reel of film was suspended from the projector's feed arm and the screen stood ready. Only the audience was absent.

And then, unobtrusive as the quiet hum of a refrigerator defrosting itself, a rhythmic drone drifted from Grandmother's room upstairs. I took the steps two at a time, expecting the worst. When I entered, however, she was sitting upright on the far side of her brass bed proprietarily clutching her purse in her lap. Jonny was standing just to her left. Both hands were wrapped around the bedpost as though he were choking up on a Louisville Slugger. Periodically he shook the bed, causing Grandmother Lucinda to shimmy slightly. As for the droning? It came from Jonny, sort of an open-mouthed reassuring murmur that, clearly, Grandmother took to be the whine of an engine.

"You are late, dear," Grandmother scolded as soon as she saw me. She gestured vaguely over her shoulder. "Hop in and fasten your seat belt." I lifted my eyebrows slightly and tilted my head in her direction, a non-verbal *What gives?*

"Glad you could make it, Luce. We have decided to do some sightseeing," Dad offered from his place next to Grandmother on the bed.

"Robert, you really need to take this bucket of bolts to the mechanic. It just doesn't have the get-up-and-go it used to," Grandmother complained to my father. At that, Jonny would shake the bedpost vigorously, eliciting a small but satisfied smile from her. "There's life in her yet, though." She reached out to pat an imaginary dashboard and turned to my father. "Well, what are we waiting for?" she demanded. "Let's go."

Dad leaned back slightly behind Grandmother's field of vision, motioned two thumbs-up, and mouthed "Jonny's a genius." He gave my grandmother quick hug before properly aligning his hands in the ten and two positions on a non-existent steering wheel.

They "drove," my father pointing out invisible landmarks while Jonny provided the horsepower and sound effects, until Grandmother succumbed to exhaustion. We took her purse from her, eased her down to her pillow, and covered her with the chenille spread.

"We couldn't calm her down, Luce," Dad explained softly. "I've never seen her so agitated. We just finished watching an old movie of a trip we took to DC when Kurt and I were kids and she didn't make a sound. Then she was yelling she needed to go but couldn't say where and she was making no sense. I kept telling her we couldn't go anywhere but that just set her off even more. All of a sudden Jonny told her to get in the car and we'd take her wherever she wanted to go. He put her in bed and told me to sit beside her. She said she wasn't going anywhere 'til she had her purse with her in case she saw a souvenir. That's when you came in. Jesus, what a night."

Jonny, my handsome brother whose arm should have been draped over the shoulders of a pretty young cheerleader in a darkened theater on this Saturday night, instead whispered hoarsely, "Night, Grandma," and brushed a tender kiss on her forehead. "See ya, Luce. I'll be back next week."

In that instant, I nearly forgave him for a lifetime of being loved too much.

Thirty-Two

I **had often heard Grammy Elnora** comment, with some degree of malice, that Grandmother Lucinda came from hearty stock. "All the women in her family are tough old birds, Luce. They're ornerier than any disease. I think every last one of them outlived their husbands and even some of their children."

Longevity was not Grandmother's friend, however. I have no doubt she would have traded those last, lost years for a sudden, spectacular heart attack in a very public place. A dramatic clutching of the chest. A gasp of pain. A graceful crumpling. The quick summons of paramedics who would valiantly but vainly try to revive her.

If given a vote in the matter, she would not have wanted to pad her survivor's résumé, would have willingly bypassed the forgetfulness and confusion, the depression, the inability to recall a face or name, would have said *Thank you, no,* to the indignity of my wiping her bottom when she messed herself. She would have headed straight for the checkout line, express lane.

In her bewildered state, she could not formulate a coherent thought, could not sequence the words necessary to pray for her release. So I prayed for her. God help me, I prayed she would die, would slip quietly away in her sleep. Failing that, I would settle for something fast and definitive. Aneurysm, stroke—I wasn't picky as long as she didn't suffer.

God was impressed with neither the fervor nor frequency of my pleadings. In answer to my prayer, He did not take Grandmother. Instead, He gave us Harold Meyer Lewis.

THIRTY-THREE

The **photo ID badge clipped** to the collar of his navy polo shirt identified him as Hal, RESPIRATORY TECHNICIAN, and he had arrived to do battle with Grandmother's congestive heart failure.

She had just come home from a hospital stay to treat alarming symptoms: lethargy, labored breathing, swollen legs and ankles, acute fatigue. Doctors proclaimed her *this close to a heart attack,* issued dire warnings about excessive fluid intake, recommended a reduced-sodium diet, and prescribed diuretics, HCTZ, and benazepril. Her oxygen levels remained low enough to warrant concern, so the hospital scheduled home respiratory therapy upon her discharge.

Hal arrived a few minutes early, opted to use the brass knocker as opposed to the doorbell, and stood deferentially waiting for a verbal invitation despite the opened door. Before stepping across the threshold, he introduced himself, pointed to his badge, and asked if I needed further documentation as to his identity.

"The van in the driveway with *Heston's Home Health Care* is good enough for me," I laughed, "unless you're a car thief."

He smiled. "If I'm a car thief, I'm a lousy one. I should aim for inconspicuous, huh?"

"Yeah. Maybe something in a gray sedan. Please, come in. I'm Luce Garrison."

His forehead wrinkled in confusion as he checked the paperwork on his clipboard. "You're Mrs. Garrison? I expected . . ."

"I'm not *that* Garrison. Lucinda is my grandmother. I was named for her. Please, though, call me Luce. I am Grandmother's caregiver."

"Let me just unload the equipment. I'll be right back."

The Perfecto oxygen concentrator looked like a dehumidifier's more sophisticated older sister. Compact and sleek, it fit nicely next to the little oak television stand in the corner of Grandmother's kitchen. With movements both practiced and precise, Hal uncoiled plastic tubing and checked the outlets, assuring us as he did so that we could easily roll the machine to any room in the house. Then he walked me through the operator's manual, showing me how to set and read the flow meter, clean the air inlet filter, change the nasal cannula, and use the back-up system in case of a power failure.

To make us completely mobile, he also set up the HELiOS, a portable system which stored liquid oxygen in a lightweight canister. I learned to fill the unit and clean the connections, crack the oxygen cylinder and attach the regulator, and to always *always* pay attention to the audible alarm system. He then set the flow meter to two liters a minute as per the doctor's order and asked if I had any questions.

"Only a million. How will I remember all this?"

"Relax. You don't have to remember it. Everything is in the manual, and you can call the agency if you need help. My cell number is on the orientation sheet, in the manual, and on this card. Don't hesitate to call, even if it's after hours. Really. Call anytime."

Was Hal simply being the consummate professional, selfless and available to his clients because of their neediness, or could I detect a personal interest? I had been in his company for less than an hour, but I felt an unexpected ease with him. No one would describe him as attractive, but something about him invited scrutiny.

I guessed him to be in his late thirties, maybe forty—hard to say because he was prematurely gray, his thick sideburns framing a broad, flat face as smooth as a teenager's. He was tall, well over six feet, a bit thick-waisted and soft-looking despite lugging respiratory equipment around all day. He spoke too loudly, perhaps because most of his clients were hard-of-hearing or, equally likely, he was used to talking over the drone of the machines he serviced. I liked him instantly.

"Thanks, Hal. You've been so helpful. I hope I don't have to bother you, but I appreciate the safety net."

He reviewed the maintenance schedule, gave me copies of the instructions and safety statement, the brochure outlining the patient's rights and responsibilities, and the patient complaint policy. "I hope you won't have to use this last form," he joked. I signed the required paperwork and insurance claim forms.

He gathered the crumpled plastic packaging and broke down the empty cardboard boxes, told Grandmother Lucinda it had been a pleasure, and shook my hand.

I am sure I blushed.

THIRTY-FOUR

As stipulated in the service contract, Hal returned in a week to check on the concentrator. He declared it in perfect running order, but only two days later, I called the agency, panicked, because the yellow warning light was on and an audible alarm sounded constantly. The machine's sensor automatically checked for oxygen purity every ten minutes, and for some reason the concentration level had fallen below 85%. The instruction manual warned if levels dropped below 73%, the red alarm would flash and the oxygen concentrator would shut down. I had tried to troubleshoot without any luck.

"Not a problem," Hal assured me as he checked the connections and inspected the filter and humidifier. Within minutes, he had the Perfecto humming again. I apologized for the unscheduled stop, but he said that was part of his job. "Makes me feel needed, Miss Garrison. I'm glad you called."

"Luce," I insisted. "Please, just Luce, not 'Miss Garrison.'"

In the following weeks, I harbored a genuine hatred for the reliability of the concentrator. Hal returned for a service call only when Grandmother's doctor increased the flow rate because her breathing became ever more difficult. Even then, his visit wasn't strictly required. By that time, I was comfortable with adjusting the controls and it was simply protocol to inform the agency when the prescribed therapy changed. Had Grandmother needed more than five liters per minute, we would have to upgrade to a more powerful concentrator.

Hal showed up at the end of the day. He was on his way home to Menomonee Falls, he said, and just stopped by as a courtesy. He asked if he could quickly inspect the machine, so I led him to her bedroom. To the Perfecto he gave only cursory attention, but when he looked at Grandmother, a melancholy seemed to settle on him. She was lying on her back, bedspread pulled beneath her chin, her eyes closed, cannula tubing looped over her ears and across waxy cheeks, the oxygen hissing life though tiny prongs in her nose. She seemed to be breathing without much distress.

"You don't need to wake her," he protested.

"Really, it's okay. She needs to get up for her meds anyway." Careful not to startle her, I touched her shoulder and murmured, "Grandmother, Hal is here to see you."

Slowly, she roused enough to open her eyes, but there was no mistaking the vacant stare she turned on Hal. "Who the hell are you? What are you doing here?"

"Grandmother, it's Luce and the man who takes care of your oxygen machine. You remember, he is the one who helps you breathe. His name is Hal. Remember, Grandmother?"

"Get that son-of-a-bitch out of here. Get him OUT. GET OUT. GET OUT." She wheezed with the fury of her demand.

Embarrassed, I turned to offer an apology, a plea for him to forgive her rudeness. "She's not herself . . ." I stammered, but he touched a finger to my lips and wordlessly shook his head.

"Don't. Don't say anything. I'll wait for you in the kitchen."

I worried the prolonged delay. Once agitated, Grandmother wasn't easy to appease, and by the time she was once again resting fitfully, I expected Hal would have *run* to his van, merged with traffic on Watertown Plank, and happily lost himself in the anonymity of rush-hour traffic headed north on 45.

But he was sitting at Grandmother's pine kitchen table, his hands tracing the outline of gaudily bountiful grapes and too-red apples which decorated her vinyl tablecloth. He could have been a restorer of ancient artifacts, so delicately did his thick, capable fingers caress the images.

"I am sorry you had to see that. Even when she was well, she could be a bit rough around the edges, but sometimes I don't even know who she is anymore." I felt compelled to add, softly, "And most of the time she doesn't know me either."

In a breakdown so monumental I was stunned not to see it coming, I blubbered my self-pity. Stupidly. Uncontrollably. I hated my hysteria, the shrieking of a madwoman, the frenzy of anger and awkwardness which recognized no signposts warning *Caution: Reduce Speed Ahead*. I was crying from humiliation and from helplessness, from isolation and desperation, from a longing for something unnamed but tangible for all its absence.

And Hal was there to fill the holes. Into those fissures he shoveled compassion, quiet words of consolation, a whisper of acknowledgment, murmurs of understanding. With infinite gentleness he eased me to his lap and cradled my head beneath his chin. I heard the reassuring, regular thrum of his heart pulsing, pulsing, pulsing. For a while, then and later, I forgot about Grandmother.

Thirty-Five

Hal's log sheet did not record the stops he made in Tosa after hours, the nights we sat on the couch watching old movies on TMC or the late suppers we shared after I had checked on Grandmother. There was no place on his inventory to chart how often I beat him at Scrabble or he buried me at Trivial Pursuit. He did not tally the bottles of wine we uncorked nor keep track of the times I watched him shrug into his work shirt from my vantage on the bed in Grandmother's guest room.

On those mornings after he stayed the night, I watched him as he slept, his mouth open, his chest rising and falling with assuring regularity.

Can gratitude disguise itself as love? If so, when the masquerade is revealed, should we feel cheated or relieved?

THIRTY-SIX

Harold Meyer Lewis, thirty-eight, was unlike other home health care specialists. For him, the job was not a stepping stone to a better career nor a part-time gig to augment income or to pave the way for higher education. No, he felt a calling to attend the Grandmother Lucindas of the world because it was a way of life, because he could ease the end for these elderly sufferers, because it was their time, and most of all because he had not been able to help his wife when she had needed help most. Hal could tend to Grandmother Lucinda because he did not once pretend she would live and he knew with absolute certainty he could make a difference in the quality of life for whatever days she had left.

He spent six years caring for his wife Connie who suffered from breast cancer which had metastasized to the lymph nodes, the spine, the brain. He had been steadfast through the mastectomy and the eight different rounds of chemo, each more devastating than the last, through the nausea that left her trembling, through shower drains clogged with clumps of hair, through radiation that burned her flesh, through clinical trials and holistic healers and diet gurus, through experimental drugs and religious zealots and all of it was for nothing because Connie had died trying to postpone the inevitable and if he had to do it over again he would have traded those six agonizing years of treatments and nausea and hair loss and neuropathy and empty hope for just six months of travel and laughter and there would be no one wearing a white coat or carrying a stethoscope or ordering blood draws or transfusions or chemo drips or PET scans and they would have held hands through the worst of it and he could have said his goodbyes to his wife, to a woman who did not allow cancer to have the last word by condemning her to a morphine-fogged exit, and *that* was the only way she would ever have beaten cancer.

The final indignity had been Connie's desperate wish for children. They found they were pregnant when the cancer diagnosis came, and they terminated the fetus to treat the mother, an unthinkable choice which mocked them in its futility.

The pee stick showed pink, but well before I bought the test kit Hal and I had ended. He had risked much for me already, and *Heston's Home Health Care* van did not belong in our driveway after business hours any more than Hal belonged in my life. He had a contract to care for Grandmother, not me, but I had needed him and I had willingly taken all he had to give. I could not ask him to commit to a child who was not Connie's.

THIRTY-SEVEN

G   **randmother Lucinda died at home** on the sixth of August in 2006. She was as withered as the unwatered plants on the porch steps.

I had not spoken with Hal since he traded patient rotations with another respiratory tech, a young woman named Christy who was studying to be a nurse practitioner. She was efficient but impersonal, just one in a cadre of hospice caregivers who ushered Grandmother through her final days.

Trey's birth, a C-section delivery performed as scheduled, preceded her death by twenty-six hours. Had the baby been a girl, I would have named her for Grandmother, but not Lucinda. Never Lucinda. She would have been Eve, a loving permutation of our middle name, the Eve of a new generation of Garrisons.

Grandmother had not the capability to know of my son's arrival, but I asked Jonny to put the phone to her ear as I whispered from my hospital room, "His name is Robert Trey Garrison." It was the only way to keep the legacy of my Grandfather alive and perhaps honor the man who courted and kept company with Grandmother Lucinda's memories until the end.

THIRTY-EIGHT

We **Garrisons could have been** the subject of a commercial for the Super Bowl, a million dollar piece of advertising fluff garnering rave reviews at water coolers the following morning.

Screwing around with an older man? Check. (Voice over: "In your grandmother's house when she was dying, *for God's sake. What were you thinking?")*

Getting pregnant without getting married? Check.

No permanent job? No insurance? Huge hospital bills? Check. Check. Check.

Moving home with an infant son? You'll pay the price.

Trey was my ticket back to Waukesha, back to my old room on the second floor with the faded gray walls, back to the farmhouse once as familiar as my face in the mirror, back where everything was the same and everything had changed.

No matter my shameful behavior, my utter disregard for propriety, Mother welcomed my little boy with his fuzzy dark hair and sapphire eyes, so like her own Jonny in infancy. Reluctantly, she allowed me along for the ride.

Not that she had much choice. Grandmother's lengthy illness had decimated her estate, and although the house in Tosa brought a fair price, most of that was earmarked—at Kurt's and Dad's insistence—for my hospital bills. After taxes and probate, there were small stipends. For me, the seeds of a trust for my son. For Jonny, the core of a controversy.

Mother had always intended for Jonny to take up the Pennick family business. He would earn his undergraduate degree, enroll in law school at Marquette, pass the bar exam on the first attempt, and land a plum job with Grandfather Aldrich's firm. *Of course, sweet boy, you'll have to earn your way to partnership.*

Jonny had other plans. We were different in many aspects, my brother and I, especially in our take on education. I reveled in the ritual of school. Jonny, far more intellectually curious than I, hated the drudgery of read, regurgitate. An average student, he was most comfortable working with his hands at the mill or tinkering with machinery on the farm. I knew he had dismantled and reassembled the engine on Dad's brush hog, rewired every outlet in the farmhouse kitchen, designed and built a trestle table when the workbench in the machine shed rotted, and replaced flashing on the chimney. He didn't have any formal training, but he was intuitively analytical, able to assess and fix a problem faster than most people could locate the service manual. School was a thing endured, something to be got out of the way. If he could crotch-rocket through his senior year on the back of a repo Honda Superhawk, titanium with silver-painted wheels, he'd never ask for anything else.

Dad sided with Jonny. Mother, as usual, balked.

"The kid is responsible, Bets. He's got his head on straight and he's never done anything to shake our trust. There's enough money to set aside for school, if that's what he wants, and for the bike, too. For God's sake, he's graduating next year. What are you going to do then?"

"Well this isn't next year, is it?" she'd counter.

Jonny didn't leave the matter to Dad. He began a low-tech but pervasive crusade impossible to ignore. I called it the Siege of the Sticky Notes. He must have invested a week's pay from his part-time job working with Dad at the mill to fund his ad campaign. On each square of neon green paper he printed in block letters JONNY WANTS A SUPERHAWK. There were obvious places to post: the refrigerator door, bathroom mirrors, the television screen, inside every cupboard door. The more ingenious finds were plastered on clock faces and watch crystals, glued inside the bottoms of coffee mugs and on dinner plates, clipped to bags of chips or rolled around a sleeve of Ritz crackers, tucked into boxes of Kleenex, slipped between stacks of towels in the linen closet, nestled into every pair of shoes, rubber-banded onto key rings, fixed on the ceilings above our beds, stuck under the lids of both toilet seats. He wallpapered his argument in, on, over, under, and around everything we saw or touched.

To stem the onslaught, Mother told Jonny he could use the Jeep whenever he wanted. Dad had traded the old Escape for a low-mileage but hard-used Grand Cherokee to which Jonny had free access, but chauffeuring friends to Friday night football, Miller Park games when the Cubs were in town, events at Summerfest, or—a huge concession—concerts in Madison didn't compensate. Jonny wanted wheels of his own.

Whether swayed by Jonny's Siege of the Sticky Notes or his own long-overdue defiance of Mother's will, Dad finally acted. Offering no explanation or apology, he inked his name below Jonny's on the title and then followed my brother home as he navigated the city streets and rural back roads to our long driveway, the throaty rumble of the Superhawk's engine announcing their arrival. He ushered Jonny up the porch steps and into the kitchen where Mother waited with stiff spine and stood motionless through her harangue.

And after her rage, after the name-calling and cursing and crying, after she pummeled Dad's chest and slapped him across the face, she lowered her shoulders, placed both hands on his cheeks, and leaned close to his ear as if to ask forgiveness.

"You goddamned son of a bitch, you just signed his death certificate."

THIRTY-NINE

Despite Mother's histrionics, Jonny proved to be a cautious, responsible driver who always wore a helmet, told my parents where he was going and when he'd be home, called if he were late or his plans changed, and—most significantly—pretended he owned the Superhawk because Mother had given her unqualified support. He even sweet-talked her into taking a ride on the back of the cycle. She snuggled behind him and clasped her hands around his waist, her shrieks of mock terror trailing behind them as they disappeared down the drive. When they returned, she was as giddy as a girl on her first date. We could almost believe she *had* approved Jonny's purchase.

Pretense, in fact, ruled our little kingdom. Dad pretended the scene in the kitchen never happened. I pretended not to have witnessed Mother's ugliness. She alone seemed unable or unwilling to distinguish her charade from reality, and because we coddled her delusions, we forfeited our claim to legitimacy. We brokered truth for tranquility, investing every day in Mother's veneer of composure.

But Trey? Trey faked nothing. Not the way he quieted at her lullabies, twisted head and shoulders to follow her every movement, grabbed her extended fingers or kneaded her cheeks when she bent to kiss his nose. There was no counterfeit in his smile, dimpled with what Grammy Elnora called "God's thumbprints." To be honest, neither did he fake curdled burps or liquidy green poops and fiery diaper rash, fountains of pee against the wall and onto the floor the moment his diaper was off, nor howls in the middle of the night. Mother was enchanted by it all.

In his presence Mother was transformed and, in an odd way, he altered my view of her as well. For the first time, I *knew* I was my mother's daughter. I loved my son as obsessively as she loved Jonny, as passionately as she must have loved baby Christopher, and the similarity frightened me. I needed to chart my own map, forge a route far different from the path she had chosen, but didn't we share the same destination? Didn't we both want to shield our children from harm? Didn't we both pray to preserve their innocence? With every breath, didn't we ask for them a lifetime of health and happiness? And because we could not make them invincible, could either of us be faulted for wanting to bubble-wrap them and stow them safely on a shelf?

I remembered the futility of those long-ago days hidden away in Mother's closet when I had wished my face looked back at me from her old photographs. Too much had happened to rekindle that fantasy, but I could at least refocus the harsh lens through which I had examined her. For a time, that was enough.

FORTY

If **there were such an** award, Jonny would have been named Uncle of the Year. From the beginning, he did not struggle with the awkwardness typically ascribed to men caring for infants. Even at the hospital, Jonny cradled Trey so naturally in one arm I could have imagined my brother was a running back and my son a football.

Between school, sports, and his job at the mill, Jonny's time was precious, but when he came home he was a slave to my son. He would scoop Trey him from his swing and dance him across the kitchen floor to an off-key rendition of some Garth Brooks song. He made silly faces, widening his eyes or sticking out his tongue, and beamed when Trey would imitate him. If Trey stretched his arm in Jonny's direction, my brother would engineer a clumsy fist bump complete with explosive sound effects and then be compelled to repeat the act a dozen times to sustain Trey's delight.

Jonny mirrored Trey's every move. During tummy time, he staked out real estate on the baby blanket so he could lie face-to-face with his nephew. If Trey pushed himself up and rolled from front to back, Jonny did likewise, and when Trey began to crawl, Jonny dropped to the floor in a comic impression of his faltering progress.

At Christmas, I gave Jonny a navy long-sleeved tee embroidered with "PINT" in yellow stitching and Trey an identical navy onesie, embellished with "HALF PINT." Jonny loved the idea so much that in the spring he bought Trey a miniature purple graduation mortarboard and T-shirt to match his own cap and gown. Immediately after the ceremonies, a picture of the two of them in commencement finery popped up on North High's web page. The same shot was included in the handbook which was mailed to students early in the summer.

In fact, the photo was responsible for Jonny's meeting Maureen Webster. A year younger than my brother, Maureen had transferred to North High during the last trimester of her junior year. She planned to study journalism after graduation and was looking to include an edgy feature story in her portfolio. If she could impress the paper's advisor, she just might leverage her intent to become a member of the staff even though all the positions had been filled. When she came across the image of a handsome senior hoisting a similarly clad baby, she assumed Jonny was a teen father. She located him, cagily avoided the nature of the interview, and scheduled a time to visit at the farm.

She was disappointed to learn Jonny's story was not the one she had envisioned. She was not disappointed with Jonny.

After the first awkward moments (Mother scowling, offended by the implied stain on Jonny's character, Maureen apologizing, Jonny holding Trey high above his head and singing *Who's your daddy?*) Maureen gathered her notepad and purse to leave.

"What's your hurry?" Jonny asked. "It's a long drive out here, so why don't you stick around? Maybe you could find something else to write about." They wandered off, returned nearly an hour later, and were still sitting on the porch when Dad came in from the mill. By this time, Maureen had become "Mo," and Mother, from her vantage in the kitchen where she could listen without being seen, fumed.

"Shouldn't she be going? It's time for dinner and I'm not setting another place at the table."

"Shhh. If you can hear them, Mother, they can hear you."

"I don't care. It's rude to overstay your welcome."

"Yeah," I snickered, "she's being rude."

A few minutes later, Dad, Jonny, and Mo joined us in the kitchen.

"Bets, I've asked Mo to stay for dinner," Dad began. Mother glared laser beams at him.

"Thanks so much, Mr. Garrison, but I really can't." For a second, the hint of a smile flashed. "I've already overstayed my welcome."

She turned toward me, extending her hand. "So nice to meet you, Luce. I'm sorry about the misunderstanding, but Trey is adorable. If it weren't for him, I wouldn't have met all of you. Good afternoon, Mr. Garrison. Mrs. Garrison. I'll talk to you, later, Jonny."

FORTY-ONE

Mo stood almost three inches taller than my brother, slender and long-limbed, but she never slouched to match his stature. She was fair skinned with sun-darkened freckles sprinkled over her nose and cheeks. Her eyes were nearly as vividly green as Jonny's were blue, and she complained constantly about her long, thin hair so fine it could not be tamed by clip combs or elastic bands. She wore it pulled in a no-fuss ponytail as sensible as she was, and she rarely bothered with anything more than a little mascara to darken her blonde lashes.

Sometimes I found myself wondering how a young woman like Mo managed to be so comfortable around people she had known for such a short time. I watched her, looking for some artifice, a "tell" revealing her true self. No one her age managed such poise unless she was hiding *something*.

If she were acting, her performance was Oscar-worthy.

In many ways Mo reminded me of Aunt Heather. Her forthright confidence was natural and easy, and she had none of the affectations of most high school girls. Her laugh was half-snort, half-giggle, and she laughed often, frequently at her own expense. She didn't mind entertaining us with anecdotes of embarrassing mishaps, thereby endearing herself to me. I could feel at ease with someone who had climbed a step stool to change a light bulb and was knocked cold when rotating fan blades in the ceiling's fixture caught her square on the temple.

Jonny had dated several girls throughout high school, but—go figure—none of them ever wanted to spend much time at the farmhouse. Mo was different. If Jonny had chores to do or a shift at the mill, Mo didn't wait for him to be available. We never knew when she might show up in cut-offs and a tattered T-shirt, ready to hop onto the mower or help weed the garden. One afternoon when Jonny had just begun painting a small chest to store Trey's clothes, she grabbed another brush and did all the drawer fronts.

She and Dad hit it off from their very first meeting that day on the porch. I could tell he liked the way she invited herself on a personally guided tour of the mill, asking thoughtful questions and listening as if the answers mattered to her. She didn't mind the smell or the heat or the height, never hesitating as she navigated the narrow iron stairs and cat-walk adjacent to the conveyor belt high off the mill floor. Dad let her fill in a couple of times on the sales floor when he had to handle a minor crisis or make a run into town, and he always joked his customers didn't mind ever-higher feed prices with a pretty girl at the cash register.

Although I didn't need convincing, she cemented my support with her interest in Trey. She offered to take candid shots of him and burn them to a disc, and when she presented me with the finished product, I was touched by the time and care she had so obviously taken. Close-ups captured the gamut of his expressions. She rendered each photo in artful finishes—black and white, sepia, soft focus, even themed collages. The best shot was of Trey in his cloth diaper and a sheepskin-lined red bom-bardier's cap with outrageously long flaps framing his chubby belly and thighs. When we held it beside the long-ago Christmas portrait of Jonny on the stairwell, Mo and I were both struck by the uncanny resemblance.

Aunt Heather and Uncle Kurt took to her instantly, too. Dad had in-sisted they be invited to Jonny's graduation; since then, an uneasy truce evolved. Although Mother wouldn't go to the mountain, so to speak, Heather and Kurt visited regularly in Waukesha. True, they stayed in a motel rather than with us at the farmhouse. "Too much togetherness, too much risk," Kurt explained to Dad, but whenever Mo was around, they were delighted to spend time in her company.

We sat around the table long after we finished dinner, the dishes ig-nored, and—except for Mother's reticence—the conversation animated as it never was before Mo. She was fascinated by my relatives' exten-sive travel experiences and commitment to humanitarian work. The son of one of her father's business associates had recently returned from a twenty-seven-month stint with the Peace Corps in Madagascar where he helped to introduce alternative fuel sources to villagers. She dreamed of making a similar trip after college and maybe launching a career with a non-profit enterprise. For now, though, she'd settle for a week of ministry through Milwaukee's YouthWorks. Her church group had applied for a mission trip to Standing Rock Reservation on the border between North and South Dakota and they were finalizing their travel arrangements.

"The Lakota people are really hurting," she explained. "You wouldn't believe how many people don't have jobs. They live in the worst conditions. I've seen pictures of their homes and it's so sad."

"What does your group do there?" Kurt asked.

"Some of us will be doing maintenance stuff. Painting, simple repairs, maybe cleaning, hauling junk, that kind of thing. On other mission trips I've taken, volunteers worked with food banks and started community gardens. Lots of times, we don't know where we're needed most 'til we're assigned our jobs. I just hope I get to work with some of the Lakota kids on this trip. Most of them live with only one parent."

"And just how much can you expect to accomplish? I doubt you can make much of a difference if you're only there a week," Mother interjected.

"Well, we're not the only group going on missions. Organizations from all over schedule different times throughout the year. If lots of people contribute even a little, then, yeah, we can make a difference."

"Isn't that nice?" Mother's monotone could not have been more insulting.

Mo's reply could not have been more gracious. "Yes, Mrs. Garrison. It's *very* nice."

In mid-August, Mo left with a group over thirty strong for her mission trip. Even 760 miles away, she was still redefining the Garrison family dynamic. Mo's absence confirmed for Jonny what the rest of us had already suspected—missing her was too painful to become permanent.

He was antsy the entire week she was gone. Classes at Carroll University would be starting in a couple of weeks and he didn't want to squander a second of time that could be spent with Mo. Although he did his best to disguise it, I think he resented her commitment to YouthWorks. He snapped at Dad when my father teased him about it.

"You'll have a better chance with her if you move to a third-world country, son. She's out to change the planet one needy person at a time."

"Yeah? Well then I should be first in line. I come from a long line of needy people." He was instantly sorry, but I saw Dad wince.

Mother was an enigma. Usually so cocksure of her ability to manipulate Jonny, she could only second-guess her insistence that he attend the local college in Waukesha rather than UW in Madison. Her argument had been that Jonny would save money on housing and food and he could still work part time with Dad at the mill. The most compelling reason, her wish to keep him under her thumb, was unspoken but understood.

Mo's insertion into this little vignette changed the game. Having built her claim on "It's best for Jonny," Mother could hardly admit her true motives without exposing herself as a fraud.

Where he once would have tolerated any college just to move away from home, Jonny now had a reason to stay. And although Mother wasn't openly hostile toward Mo, she clearly worried Jonny was too serious too soon. Her dilemma left her with no good options. She knew Jonny's being close meant being close *to Mo*.

Just as her mood had brightened when I left for Ralston, she was practically giddy the week Mo was gone. A demonic energy replaced her usual lethargy; before she had completed one thing, she began another. The kitchen saw a frenzy of activity that week. She treated us to all her specialties—braised short ribs, lasagna, marinated pork chops, fried chicken. She babbled on at the dinner table, a disjointed monologue impossible to follow. Throughout the meals she was frantic, popping up to spoon another helping onto Jonny's plate, refilling Dad's glass of tea, slicing more bread which nobody ate.

Dad worried she wasn't sleeping. He said she came to bed late and was up, showered and dressed, before his alarm buzzed at six. I know a couple of times she had changed Trey's bedding in the middle of the night when he had wet through his diapers and sleeper. If he had cried, I hadn't heard him, but I found the soiled linen in the laundry hamper the next morning. Her reserves seemed inexhaustible. Then Mo came home.

Mother was surly the evening Jonny went with Mr. and Mrs. Webster to meet Mo at the bus station. Despite her insistence, he elected not to eat dinner with us, saying the Websters had plans to pick something up on the way home. Before heading out the door, he tickled Trey, nodded to me, and leaned toward Mother to plant a kiss on her cheek. In pointed rebuke, she turned her face from him. Nor did she acknowledge the forced cheer in his, "See y'all later." Her stony silence lasted throughout the night, and when I put Trey down after his last feeding she was still sitting stiffly in the ladder-back chair at the kitchen table. I assume she remained there until Jonny arrived home, well after midnight.

I could not hear their exchange, nor did I want to, but Mother and I had wrangled on so many occasions I could have written the script. Jonny would begin with a greeting as though nothing were wrong. She would not respond. Frustrated, Jonny would demand to know why she needed to wait up for him. *I am perfectly capable of finding my way home. You treat me like I'm eight, not eighteen.*

Wallowing in the insult of Jonny's words, she would clench her jaw and fold her arms over her chest, a metaphorical breastplate to guard against further wounding. Her posture would be erect, shoulders rigid, thighs pressed tightly together, one leg crossed over the other. The only movement would be the involuntary trembling of her foot, a metronome measuring the intensity of her anger.

Oh, yes. She would be angry. She would be angry because Jonny had chosen to be somewhere other than where she was. She would be angry he did not think of her as he slid into a booth across from Mr. and Mrs. Webster in some quaint little diner to celebrate Mo's homecoming. She would be angry Mo's shoulder brushed his shoulder, angry her hand rested lightly on his thigh. She would be angry when he ordered his favorite, a thick cheeseburger, and she would be angry when he forgot to eat as he watched Mo tuck an errant strand of hair behind her ear, momentarily interrupting her animated retelling of every surprising, tragic, touching, embarrassing moment of her mission trip.

Astonished at his good fortune to be a part of such easy company, he would give not a moment's consideration to the inflexible woman who gathered thoughts as dark as the room where she waited, alone, for him to come home to her. And because of her anger, she would appeal to him, accuse him, wheedle and blame. She would employ guile and guilt, would cry and question. Jonny would have no answers because her questions made no sense.

My brother would turn his back to Mother and climb the stairs only when she had exhausted her arsenal, when her emotional blackmail could not ransom his loyalty, when he could no longer pretend she was the victim and he the villain.

FORTY-TWO

During the fall semester, Jonny grudgingly enrolled in three classes at Carroll: Intro to Statistics, Microeconomics, and Psychology 101. The pragmatist in him realized a business degree meant higher earning power and more opportunity, but that carrot didn't offset his resentment at "jumping through a bunch of hoops" to prove he could do what he'd been doing for years as Dad's second-in-command.

"I don't understand why some fancy piece of paper counts for more than experience on the job. Look at Dad. No one can manage the mill better than he does and he never graduated from college. He knows the operation from the ground up. Hell, he oversees the entire place. He fixes anything that breaks down, he does the books, he hires the guys. They all look up to him, and you can't convince me he'd be a better boss if he'd gotten a degree."

On that point, I couldn't argue. Dad knew how to get the best from the people who worked for him. They liked him, but they respected him more. If some issue with a worker surfaced, Dad asked the guy to join him for a cup of coffee, talked plainly about the problem, and solicited solutions both of them could live with. Even when the infraction was serious, I had never seen anyone storm out of Dad's little office just off the sales floor. Guys who walked through his door left with their dignity intact.

Jonny's logic had merit, but Dad didn't allow himself to become a pawn. While he didn't deny his skill in dealing with people, Dad confessed he knew too little about business law and was slow to catch on to changing technology. "This stuff is critical, Jonny. When I started working at the mill in high school, I didn't have to worry about the things you'll come up against. Half the time, I struggle just to keep one step ahead. Right now, I've got workers with more education than I have, but the time for that has passed. The competition for a job—any job—is fierce, son. Face it, you won't be at the mill forever and you need to be able to market yourself. The more you have to offer a company, the better off you'll be. You can't be too prepared. Stick it out. You won't be sorry."

So on Mondays, Wednesdays, and Fridays, Jonny straddled his Superhawk, strapped on his helmet, slung a backpack over his shoulders, and headed to Carroll. His classes were finished by two in the afternoon, but he often stayed late in Waukesha to spend time with Mo.

"Studying," he explained to Mother when she badgered him. She seemed willing to accept the ruse as long as Mo no longer came to the farmhouse.

I suspect Jonny told Mo about the scene that night she came back from Standing Rock. Either that, or her own demanding schedule kept her away. Regardless, her absence was a balm to Mother. She never asked about Mo and Jonny offered nothing, even biting the inside of his cheek when Mother intoned "I'm glad you're not seeing her as much. That girl is simply not right for you."

In fact, Mo was the most right thing in Jonny's life. I had never seen him happier.

He hated school, but I'm convinced Jonny stayed at Carroll because of her. He had confessed to me he wanted to chuck it all after the first month. *It's not for me, Luce. I'm not cut out to do four years of this. Besides, quitting would really piss Mom off.* True, Dad had made a strong case for business school and his advice was usually gold to Jonny, but I doubt even his arguments could have persuaded my brother to stick with his classes if Mo hadn't been toeing the sidelines cheering him on.

She and I occasionally ran into one another and though our conversations never lasted very long, I could tell she cared deeply for my brother. They were seeing each other as often as they could, but keeping a low profile wasn't easy on either of them. Mo had every right to expect Mother's acknowledgment, if not her approval. No matter how much of a catch Jonny was, not many girls would have been willing to play understudy to Mother's starring role. Mo wasn't any girl.

Invariably, Mo would tell me how much she missed seeing Trey. We talked about finding a "neutral site" for another photo shoot. "I'll bet he changes every day, Luce. It would be so much fun to see him."

She asked about Dad, Heather, and Kurt and—once—even Mother. Her questions, cautiously diplomatic, recognized but did not judge Mother's particular flavor of madness.

"I don't want to make trouble with your mother, Luce. She's not thrilled with me, I know, but I don't think this is about me. It's about Jonny. He says she is just very protective of him, and she's . . . fragile."

"Fragile?" I snorted.

"No, really. I don't blame her. If I had a son like Jonny, I'd want the best for him, too." She paused and tugged at her lower lip with her teeth. "I just wish she didn't think I was some kind of competition. I don't want to take him away from her, but I'd sure like to share him." We both laughed, awkwardly, understanding implicitly that there was nothing funny in her statement.

When I later told Jonny about Mo's comment, his eyes narrowed to angry slits. "God, Luce. Our mother is freaking nuts. What the hell am I going to do?"

"I think you just keep doing what you're doing. See Mo when you can. Avoid any mess with Mother, if that's possible," I offered. "Something's gotta give, but if I were you, I wouldn't be pulling my finger out of the dike until I have to."

"Sometimes I just want to put my fist through her face," Jonny confessed. "How did we ever get to this place? We're all so stinking afraid of setting her off. I'm sick of tiptoeing around her, being so careful about what I do or what I talk about. When is it her turn to give a little? Shit, if she cares so much about me, shouldn't it matter to her what *I* want?"

"I'm the last person to cut her any slack," I reminded him, "but here's the deal. No matter what you say about her, you can't say she doesn't love you. Her problem is she confuses loving you with controlling you."

"That's a load of crap, Luce."

"It's a fine line, Jonny-boy. And, really, we have to take some of the blame, 'cause in a way, we've made her who she is. We give in to her—everybody gives in to her. Admit it. You, me, Dad, and now Mo. We keep thinking *let's just get through this one thing,* but there's never just one thing. Then all of a sudden we want to change the rules because she's a monster, but it's too late. Nobody had the balls to stop her when she could still be stopped."

"By 'nobody' you mean Dad?"

"Hey, I'm not throwing rocks here. I don't know how Dad can handle people at the mill the way he does and then just come home to be her doormat, but she's like quicksand. The harder you try to pull away, the faster she sucks you down. Sometimes it isn't about being right. It's just about surviving."

Jonny paused, nodding. "I can't wait to get out of here."

"Unless she's made a reservation at the psych ward, you don't have much choice but to wait it out. Look, when Trey is just a little older, I'm going to find a place of my own to rent. It's not going to be fancy 'cause I can't afford much, but it'll be mine. Things are going to change for you, too. By the end of this year, Mo will be done with school. She'll be doing something big, and I guarantee it won't be in Waukesha. Don't tell me you won't be trailing after her wherever she goes."

"And where does that leave Dad?" Jonny asked.

"Dad's stuck with her," I joked. "He's the one who married her." Jonny snorted.

"Seriously, he's been with her all these years. In a screwy way, they feed off each other."

"Luce, do you think she'd have been different if Christopher had lived?"

"Honestly, no. Not with me." I laughed then. "But just think. Maybe, with *two* adorable sons, she'd be twice as psychotic but you'd only have to deal with her half the time."

Jonny punched me playfully in the shoulder. "Love you, Luce, but your Mom-math sucks."

FORTY-THREE

Mother might have been crazy, but she wasn't blind and she wasn't deaf. She knew Jonny was still seeing Mo. She would have been surprised by the frequency with which they met and the intensity of their feelings for one another, but she was the master of illusion.

In Mother's world, governed by a perverse logic only she could understand, she saw Jonny's secrecy as a kind of tribute to herself. She confessed as much in her diary: *I know Jonny tries so hard to protect my feelings. He knows how much that girl upsets me. He'll come to his senses soon enough and I'll be there when he needs me.*

She was willing to forgive Jonny his attraction to Mo because she was confident in his attachment to her. One would pass; the other was permanent.

There are times when I wish I had Mother's gift for rearranging reality. I would alter *what is* to fit neatly into *what if*. Surely my truth would be more comfortable than hers. But then I wonder: At what cost? On what scale do we weigh the damage wrought by skewed perceptions?

Mother had already exacted her pound of flesh from each of us, but she had done it with our help. We had allowed Mother her delusions—no, we had actively participated—perhaps at first from pity; later, from self-preservation. We took the stage in her private theater and under her direction we mouthed the lines she wrote for us until they no longer seemed like lies. Every performance was the same—the delivery stale, the gestures meaningless, but who could blame us? Our little drama had been in production so long the rehearsals blurred to reality. We were a comic tragedy come to life, a troupe of weary actors portraying caricatures of ourselves.

Having lately joined our cast of misfits, Mo alone seemed positioned to find a new role.

Forty-Four

When she was named a semi-finalist for the Morehead-Cain scholarship program, we expected Mo would pack her bags and leave us immediately after graduation. The Morehead offered merit scholars four years of fully-funded, unparalleled opportunities beginning the summer before freshman year. She seemed a perfect candidate with impeccable credentials of service and leadership and a cadre of supporters to write glowing letters of recommendation. The interview on North Carolina's campus had gone well, she thought, and she allowed herself the danger of hope.

Jonny was thrilled for her but worried for himself. Would she still be Mo after four years at Chapel Hill? How could she ever be content with Waukesha—with him—after traveling the globe during summer interims?

"She wants this so much, and I want her to be happy. I just don't want to lose her."

Dad tried to offer perspective. "This is tough, son. If you two are supposed to end up together, you will. If not, it's better to find out sooner than later. Easier to walk away before you have too much invested, son."

"Yeah, I know. But . . .," Jonny began.

"But nothing. You have to love her enough to let her be happy. You hold her back, she'll resent it . . . and you."

"So do I pretend I'm perfectly okay with her leaving?" Jonny asked.

"No." The force of his answer surprised them both. "No," he repeated more quietly. "You tell her the truth. All of it."

"She'll think I'm a loser. *Mo, I'm worried if you get the scholarship you won't be with me anymore.* God, *I* think I'm a loser."

"Get over yourself, son. The only reason most people do anything is because they're afraid. When it's 'fight or flight,' fear can make sense. Other times, it's just an excuse to escape. I hope you don't act on the wrong kind of fear, Jonny."

"Fear is fear."

"No. Don't ever believe that. There is noble fear and a coward's fear. I sure as hell wish I had known the difference between them a long time ago."

Whether or not Jonny confessed his apprehensions to Mo, I can't say. By the time the notice of rejection came from Morehead, apologetic in its finality, the point was moot. Devastated, Mo withdrew her application to NC in favor of Emory University in Atlanta. They welcomed her.

"Chapel Hill's sloppy seconds," she pronounced as she tossed the letter of acceptance from Emory on to the counter next to the cash register. Even the possibility of a chance encounter with Mother could not keep her from sharing the news with Jonny at the mill. Wrapped against the early March chill in leggings and a hooded fleece, she had come directly from her home.

I was working on inventory when she came in looking for him. I had never seen her so deflated.

She leaned over the port-a-crib to kiss Trey. "Hey, little man. Where's your Uncle Jonny? Is he here, Luce? I couldn't reach him on his cell."

"No, he's out making a delivery for Dad. If he didn't pick up, he's probably with a customer but he should be back soon." I hesitated. "So it's going to be Emory, huh? Great school. Very selective."

"Yeah. We Morehead rejects are lining up in droves."

"It may not be any of my business, but . . .," I paused, inviting her to agree with me. When she was silent, I finished. "I guess I don't see your problem. Yeah, you didn't earn the Morehead, but NC accepted your application for admission, just like Emory did. You have A-list schools courting you. It may not be a full-ride, but I'm guessing you landed financial aid and merit scholarship offers at Emory. Jeez, Mo, the weather in Atlanta alone is cause enough for celebration. This isn't a bad thing."

"Oh, Luce, I know. I sound like such a baby. It's my own fault for thinking I had a shot. I gotta pull out of this funk."

"Emory will be great. I graduated with a guy from Ralston who studied pre-med there. Loved it. He's an orthopedic surgeon in Chile now."

"Who's chilly?" Jonny said from the doorway.

"Nobody, doofus. I was just congratulating Mo on her acceptance to Emory."

He hesitated for the briefest moment before crossing the sales floor to wrap her in bear hug and swing her around. "That's awesome. I'm happy for you."

When she didn't respond, he pressed. "Are you okay with this?"

She shrugged her shoulders, retrieved the letter from the counter, and held it for him to read. He stood behind her as she sat on a stool, his right arm slung over her shoulder and across her chest, gathering her to him as if she were a drowning victim. They were positioned like that when Mother walked in. Stiffening, Mo fingered Jonny's wrist in a subtle attempt to escape from his embrace. He tightened his grasp.

"I thought I saw a familiar car in the drive. Maureen, I haven't seen you in quite a long time." Her words, though cordial enough, could not mask her displeasure. She stared as though Jonny's arm were an alien appendage grafted to Mo. "What are you doing here?"

"I came to see Jonny, Mrs. Garrison. I wanted to tell him about Emory."

"Emory?" She seemed to be running through a catalog of acquaintances.

"Yes. Emory University in Atlanta. They have accepted my application for admission next fall."

Only then did Mother relax her guard. "Well, isn't that wonderful. When will you be leaving?"

"Now, Mrs. Garrison. I'm leaving now." By dismissing the hypothetical future in Mother's question, Mo exaggerated the insult. And then she devised an insult of her own, a memorable, malicious departure.

Unblinking, she turned full-face to Mother and raised both her hands to Jonny's forearm. She gripped him until her fingers appeared bloodless. Then she stood, spun within his embrace, and kissed my brother, her mouth possessing his until I lowered my eyes in embarrassment. When I looked up again, Mother had made a silent exit.

FORTY-FIVE

We waited at the mill for Dad, behavior classified as cowardly fear, I am sure. When we didn't respond to his greeting, he studied each of us in turn.

"What's up? You three look like it's the end of the world."

Mo explained what had happened. She apologized to Jonny for using him to get at Mother and then she apologized to Dad for whatever awaited at the farmhouse.

"Not exactly my finest hour. I am truly, truly sorry, Mr. Garrison."

"Forget it," Dad said.

Jonny walked Mo to her car, gently closed the door and knuckle-rapped the hood twice. He stood watching her until she disappeared down the drive and then returned to us on the sales floor. Believing there might be safety in numbers, we headed for the house together. Jonny carried Trey like a talisman of luck, but I didn't think any amulet would pacify Mother. I was right.

She had been making rigatoni with meat sauce before Mo's arrival interrupted her preparations. Now the kitchen resembled a crime scene. Tomato sauce thick with chunks of sausage and peppers splattered the walls. The stockpot of pasta had boiled over, infusing the air with an acrid char. Green beans and mushrooms lay on the floor among shards of glass from the shattered Pyrex casserole dish, and Mother had upturned dishes of cottage cheese and canned apricots onto each of our placemats. She had driven the point of a steak knife into the table's surface, and I could imagine her grasping the handle with both hands, lifting it above her head and then chopping down with murderous force until the blade caught and held.

Dad scanned the room, his shoulders sagging with resignation. "You two take Trey. Go into town and get something to eat. I'll take care of this."

"I'll stay," Jonny offered. "This is partly my fault."

"You'll need help, Dad," I added. "We'll both stay."

"No. Go. And take your time."

FORTY-SIX

We **couldn't muster much of** an appetite, even though La Estacion served the best Mexican food in Waukesha. Almost as soon as the waitress set our plates of chiles rellenos and fajitas in front of us, we asked to have them boxed. Jonny was scraping the last of the adobo sauce into a Styrofoam container as I gathered Trey's book and toys to stuff into his diaper bag. Tony Marquez, the owner, stopped by our table.

"Jonny Garrison. I haven't seen you around for a few weeks, amigo."

"Hey, Tony," Jonny said. "I've been kind of busy with school . . . and things. You remember Luce? And Trey?"

"Sure. Hello, Luce." I nodded. "The little guy is growing. How old is he now?"

"Nearly two."

"Cute kid. He'll be a heartbreaker." He looked at our to-go boxes, frowning slightly. "Didn't Elisa just bring your dinner? Is something wrong with the food?"

"No, man. Not a thing, just poor timing. We need to get back home."

"Okay, then. Don't be such a stranger, Jonny. And be sure to bring that girlfriend of yours in the next time." He grinned at me. "Two pretty ladies would class the place up."

"You don't need to flatter me, Tony," I managed a smile. "We've already paid the bill."

"Senorita, cortar mi corazón." He placed both hands over his heart as though to protect it from harm. "Good to see you. Say hello to your parents for me."

On the drive home, Jonny was so distracted he nearly missed our turn. "It's not right, Luce. We shouldn't have left Dad alone. This is on me. I should be the one cleaning up the mess."

"I don't know if there's 'right' in anything anymore. But we're doing exactly what Dad asked. I think he wanted some time alone with Mother anyway," I countered. "And, trust me, there's enough mess to last until we get back."

I am still haunted by the magnitude of *mess* that greeted us.

Nosed right up to the porch steps was a Waukesha County Sheriff's patrol car. Even before we entered the house, we could hear Mother's outraged screams from her bedroom.

"Keep your hands off me, you fucking asshole. Get out of my house."

Dad stood at the threshold, unable to leave, unwilling to enter.

"Mrs. Garrison, you need to calm down. You are going to have to come with me. If you'll just try to relax, this can go a whole lot easier." A stocky, middle-aged officer held Mother's forearms behind her back. She lunged away from him with such force I thought her arms might snap at the shoulder. His partner, probably near my own age, was wiping blood from a scrape across his cheek. "We don't want to put you in restraints, Mrs. Garrison, but we will for your safety and ours."

"Bets, please . . ." Dad's voice was barely audible. "Can't you just please do what the sheriff is asking?"

She whipped her head toward Dad, snarling, then parodied his words in a nasal whine.

"Bets, puhhh-leeeease. Just puhhh-leeease let this asshole handcuff you like some fucking common criminal." She twisted violently against the officer, but when she could not free herself, she turned her head and spit on him.

"That's it, ma'am." He tightened his hold as he signaled to his partner. "Get the vest, Cal." The taller officer hurried to the patrol car. He returned with a lead-weighted smock which he slipped over Mother's head and secured behind her back. It enveloped her from her shoulders to her knees. Almost immediately, she seemed to deflate.

"Nolan, are you going to let these men treat me like this? How can you let this happen?" The fight had left her; she was nothing more than a shell, hollow and pitiful.

"Bets. Bets, please. You need help. You need help, Bets."

"Don't let them take me, Nolan." Dad had pressed his lips tightly together and sucked them between his teeth. He looked ancient. Gray.

"I'll be there, Bets. I'll follow you."

She saw us in the hallway. "Jonny? Jonny, you tell them not to take me." She turned to the shorter officer. "Listen to my son. He'll tell you he needs to have me home. I'm his mother. He needs me here."

My brother stood as if nailed to the floor. He opened his mouth and reached a hand toward her. For a moment I saw him as an infant, latching on to Mother's finger with his chubby fist. Her face lifted, softened with hope.

"Mom, I need . . ." He faltered as bright tears traced the contour of his nose and mapped the curve of his lips. "Mom, I need you to get better."

Forty-Seven

Because no physician had referred Mother, hers was considered an emergency detention. Dad was instructed to gather documentation to present at a probable cause hearing, scheduled to take place within seventy-two hours of her detention. He needed anecdotal evidence corroborated by at least one other witness to bring before the magistrate. In the meantime, hospital personnel told us Mother would be seen by a psychiatrist and, most likely, a social worker to determine the level of her illness and whether or not she was treatable. If she agreed that short term commitment was warranted, no further legal action need be taken after the probable cause hearing. But if she resisted, the process could be wrenching.

Dad contacted my Pennick grandparents, but neither Grammy Elnora nor Grandfather Aldrich could bring themselves to sign the required commitment papers.

"We'll help in any way we can, Nolan. Just not that. Please, don't ask us to do that."

Dad begged them. They would not listen, but they had not seen her that night. They could not imagine her fury, the uncontrollable rage which consumed her. They had not watched her pull curtains from their rods, sweep toiletries from the vanity and throw the broken remnants at Dad's face. They had not stood in horror as she raked pill bottles from the medicine cabinet and fumbled with the safety caps, intent on swallowing every pill in the house. They had not seen my father swat a handful of red and blue capsules from her hand, scattering them like confetti. And they had not heard her promise to kill herself.

Dad needed two signatures. Absent my grandparents' cooperation, the choice was no choice at all. Jonny was not yet twenty-one, so the task fell to me.

Dad was apologetic. The last thing he wanted to do, he said, was to further alienate Mother from me. In thirty-one years, this was his first direct acknowledgment of the barrier separating us. I could not help but despise his timing. Where was his regret when we were stringing those endless miles of barbed wire fencing between us?

I swallowed my rage and I signed the papers. Dad filed them with the court. On the day of the hearing, I accompanied my father to the hospital.

That morning was blustery, the skies heavy with the threat of rain. Just as we pulled into the parking lot, the first fat drops splattered the windshield and Dad apologized for not throwing an umbrella into the Jeep. Lately, he seemed full of remorse for the most incidental of transgressions, but I was not yet generous enough to forgive his guilt on any level.

The charge nurse buzzed us in to the locked facility and ushered us to a small conference room off the main hallway of the psych unit. As we waited for the magistrate and the hospital personnel, we looked through the tempered glass wall out into the common room. If I had anticipated a scene from *One Flew Over the Cuckoo's Nest,* I was disappointed. The hub of the unit was like any waiting area in any public place: a large, carpeted, well-lit gathering spot appointed with couches, chairs, tables, reading material, a flat-screen television tuned to *The View.* Four long rectangular tables stood in two columns near the nurses' station, a glassed-in cubicle offering unobstructed vistas of the entire space.

Five patients sat in the common area. A couple more were at one of the tables playing Uno. It could have been a campus union at any university, but the co-eds were dressed in hospital gowns and pants, the print on the cotton faded by multiple bleachings.

Patients' rooms were adjacent to the common area. Some doors were closed, some slightly ajar, still others wide open. I could not help my curiosity. I admit I stared into the rooms hoping, perhaps, to find evidence of the instability which brought each patient here, some artifact of madness to separate *them* from *us.* And if such relics existed, what would Mother's be?

Suddenly Dad rose, as though this were a formal affair requiring a certain level of decorum. A tall nurse with artificially red, spiky hair preceded Mother into the conference room. She motioned for Dad to sit down. Only when he was once again seated did the nurse escort Mother to a chair on the opposite side of the room. I stifled an uncomfortable laugh. Had this been a boxing arena, my parents would have resembled opposing combatants prior to a title bout, but without the obligatory stare down. They could not look at one another.

The nurse picked up the receiver on the desk phone and punched in four numbers. "Whenever the judge arrives, we're ready to go."

I would have thought the arrival of the judge, psychiatrist, and social worker would escalate the tension in the room, but the opposite was true. Judge Marcia Hakes took her place behind the desk, opened a laptop and sat with her chin resting in her left hand as she slid a wireless mouse with her right. The only sound in the room was each muffled click as she accessed Mother's digital records.

Judge Hakes reviewed the commitment papers we had signed and occasionally asked us to clarify or elaborate on the examples we had included in the filing. Satisfied there were no glaring discrepancies, she moved on to the psychiatrist.

In lay terms, Dr. Renslow said his preliminary examination suggested Bipolar II disorder. "Given her history of depression and her rare hypomanic episodes, I am surprised she has not been diagnosed previously, but she is a viable candidate for treatment on an outpatient basis," he concluded. He had prescribed 300 mg of lithium to stabilize her mood and 2 mg of Risperdal, an antipsychotic.

"Does anyone have anything else?" Judge Hakes scanned the room. "All right, then, folks. Here's what we're going to do." Looking directly at Mother, Judge Hakes stipulated the conditions on the release form, checking each item as Mother nodded in assent.

Mother had waived the need for a final hearing by agreeing to take all her medications in their prescribed dosages, keep her appointments with the treatment staff and case managers, cooperate with recommendations for psychiatric treatment or therapy, advise the treatment staff if her address changed, refrain from taking controlled substances not prescribed for her, promise not to consume alcohol, and to remain in the inpatient treatment facility until she was discharged.

"We're done here. Thank you all." The judge stood, slid her laptop into a leather case, and bobbed her head sympathetically toward Dad, a momentary departure from her professional dispassion. She must have presided over many such cases, equally sad. She knew better than anyone that on the extensive inventory of conditions required for release, the most important item of all was omitted. No one had asked Mother to admit she needed help.

FORTY-EIGHT

Mother stayed in the hospital for another couple of weeks. Because visiting hours were more restrictive in the psych unit than for the rest of the hospital, Dad could not see her at all during his working hours and for only a limited time in the evenings. My Pennick grandparents drove in from Mequon daily and called my father to share their impressions with him after each visit so he "knew what to expect."

She was serene, they assured us, safe. There had been no episodes, no erratic behavior. She was compliant, quiet. In other words, she was no longer Mother.

"Better living through chemistry," Kurt observed over the phone when Dad called Ralston to give a status report. His attempt at humor fell flat.

When Heather asked to speak to me, there was nothing funny in her question.

"Shouldn't you and Trey come back to Ralston? What about that little boy's safety? If Bets can be so violent . . ."

"I know, Aunt Heather, but I don't think you need to worry. She dotes on Trey, and whenever she's around him, she's calmer. Better, really, than when she's on her meds."

"It's not his job to be her Prozac," she insisted.

"When she gets home, we'll see how she is, I promise."

There was no mistaking the message in Heather's silence.

"I will not put him in danger, Aunt Heather. You have to know that. I won't ever leave him alone with her." She huffed her displeasure. "Besides, Dad is a wreck. Trey is good for him, too."

Although he knew Mother had left him no recourse but to call the sheriff's office, Dad could not absolve himself of his guilt for signing the commitment papers. He had not been present at the onset of her final breakdown, but he still felt responsible. I wondered if suppressed emotions accumulated over the years become more powerful—and ultimately more damaging—simply by virtue of delay.

Dad was not the only one to struggle. Jonny resented Mother's obsessions, hated what his life had become because of her, but he was not immune to self-doubt. He balked at Dad's suggestion to visit her.

"Your mother asks why you haven't come. She wants to see you, Jonny."

"I'm the reason she's there. You saw what happened, what she did after . . . after Mo. I don't want to set her off again, Dad. I don't even know what I would say to her."

"I'm in no position to give advice about the way you should deal with your mom, but maybe it's time we just told her the truth. Tell her how you feel about Mo. Tell her why you thought you had to keep that hidden."

"Mo thinks I should write everything down in a letter, but I'd feel like an idiot. What would I do? Just say, 'Here, Mom. Here's a list of all the things you've done in my life that have screwed me up.'" Jonny shook his head. "That would be one hell of a list."

Dad paused, considering. "I won't deny she can't see straight where you're concerned . . . I guess where any of us are concerned. But she's a sick woman."

"So you're suggesting I tell her stuff that might make her blow again?"

Dad shrugged. "I've promised myself I'm going to try and be up front with her. I don't want to sugarcoat things anymore just to keep the peace. Besides, there hasn't been any real peace for a long, long time. I just hope there can be in the future."

"You do what you have to do, Dad," Jonny replied. "I'd rather write her the letter. And never deliver it. Jesus. I'm such a coward."

During her inpatient stay he saw her, once. Before buzzing for admittance into the ward, he had stopped at the hospital flower shop to buy a small bouquet of tulips, flowers which he could not leave with her because no glass receptacles were allowed on the floor. He left the square vase with the charge nurse who placed the arrangement of a half dozen red blossoms, proudly erect on kiwi-colored stems, right next to the tempered glass window so Mother could admire them from a distance.

Jonny said she gave them barely a glance. Instead, she sat across from him at one of the long tables, taking both his hands in hers.

"She promised to be good," he recounted with wonder. "She said she wouldn't be angry anymore, that I could bring Mo to the house and it would be okay with her. Then she asked if I hated her. She said she couldn't bear it if I hated her." He shook his head as if his memory were playing tricks on him. "God, Luce, she was like a little kid."

"What did you say to her?" I asked.

"I told her I didn't hate her, but sometimes I hated what she did."

"That couldn't have been easy."

"Shit, Luce. It was the hardest thing I've ever done. I can't remember ever telling Mom how I really feel about anything. Then I told her I was sorry Mo and I hadn't let her know about us. She started crying and hanging on to me. She said she'd never do it again. She said she was taking her medications and her doctors said she could get better. Then she hugged me and wouldn't let go." He raked his hands through his hair and then laced his fingers behind his neck. "She's messed up. I felt sorry for her, Luce. But you know what else? All the time she was holding on to me, I just wanted get away."

FORTY-NINE

Mother came home the Thursday before Easter. From that first afternoon, she seemed determined to keep her promise to "be good." She wanted us to act like a family again, she said. I winced at "again." When had we ever acted like a family?

She took her pills faithfully, loudly announcing each dosing and even inviting us to look in her mouth to assure ourselves she had swallowed the meds. In her diary she color-coded her upcoming appointments: blue for the counselor, green for the psychiatrist, and red for the blood draw to test her thyroid levels.

Grammy Elnora offered to come to the house to be with her, but she immediately declined. "Nolan checks on me. Lucinda and Trey are here with me all day." I thought it odd she had not named Jonny in her cadre of caregivers. "Really," she told Grammy Elnora. "We'll be fine."

I don't know that Mother and I were ever *fine,* but her tolerance, manufactured and maintained with mood-altering drugs, marked the longest stretch of civility we two had ever known. On the calendar that hung next to the refrigerator we crossed off a series of Xs to document our courtesy toward one another. Uneventful days were days to celebrate, "holidays" sacrosanct in their sameness.

And so, as mothers and daughters do, we colored eggs for Trey's basket. We shopped the Waukesha farmer's market for seedling tomatoes, hot house peppers, onion sets, and sweet basil. We took Trey to story hour at the library or, occasionally, splurged on a trip to Betty Brinn or the zoo. We made dinners and cleared dishes and attacked spring cleaning with resignation.

Granted, there were times when the tenuous fabric of her serenity seemed ready to unravel. She would stop in the middle of making sandwiches or pruning the shrubs, fix a stare on nothing in particular, and stand motionless. Only her lips moved in this inner dialogue, sometimes lasting for nearly a minute, before she returned to her task.

After watching her slide into several of these zombie states, I worked up enough courage to ask her what she was doing, what she was repeating to herself. She seemed surprised I had noticed, smiled sheepishly, and confessed she was "compartmentalizing." When I asked her to explain, she said her therapist told her she was allowed only thirty minutes a day to worry. She was to designate a finite window of time into which she would package all her anxieties, her depression, her self-pity. If she found herself stressing out, she was to repeat to herself, "It's not time yet. It's not time yet."

"You're kidding me," I said. "It works?"

"Not always. It wouldn't without the lithium, but it helps me feel like I have some control."

That we could even joke about "worry time" seemed to be a watershed. Laughter had never been a staple in our household so we were anxious to stockpile it.

Jonny was still skittish with Mother. He had found ways to be absent much of the time, choosing to work extra shifts at the mill or to spend time at Mo's after school. He was comfortable being in the same room with Mother only if Trey were present. Then we would all laugh as Jonny played "bombs away," pelting Trey with pillows from the couch or watching him navigate the tunnels of elaborate forts Jonny constructed from card tables and old blankets.

I would watch Mother watching Jonny. She battled her inclination to sit next to him, to touch his cheek, to draw him near with a spontaneous hug. Her reservation with him was disquieting because, for the first time in my memory, she seemed afraid of being rejected. I had never seen her so vulnerable.

In late April, Jonny told Mother he would be escorting Mo to her senior prom. There was an awkward silence. She went rigid and Jonny involuntarily stepped backward as if he expected her to launch an attack. I watched her mouth "It's not time" repeatedly until she relaxed her shoulders and unclenched her hands. With effort, she smiled at Jonny. "That should be fun."

He hesitated as though weighing a decision before blurting his question. "Would you like to come to the Grand March at the gym to see us?" When she didn't answer, he added, "Mo wanted me to ask you."

"I would like to come," she whispered. "I would like to come very much."

***

Surprisingly, Dad was the most reluctant to acknowledge her progress. Perhaps he acted out of self-preservation, daring not to hope for more than he was willing to lose. Still, he accompanied her to every appointment with her therapist. Sometimes, at Mother's request, he sat in on the sessions. As soon as they returned home and Mother had gone to her room to rest, Dad would update us.

"We can't expect a cure. We can only expect that she'll be able to manage her condition." He drummed his fingers on the kitchen table. "The therapist warned that this is our honeymoon period. Your mother doesn't want to go back to the hospital, but there will be good days and bad days."

"She seems so much better," Jonny argued.

"Yes, but a lot of that is the medication. More than likely, she'll need to adjust it as time goes by."

"Then we'll just watch her. We won't let things escalate like they did before. We'll do what we have to do."

"Yeah," Dad nodded, but there was no conviction in his voice. "We'll do what we have to do. What we should have done all along."

FIFTY

Student **Senate members had outdone** themselves. Their theme for prom was *Marking Time,* and they had transformed the gym with yards of black metallic fabric, white luminescent columns and tiered chandeliers. Three huge pearly clock faces, softly back-lit and framed in black, glowed beneath towering arches through which the couples would walk. Those of us packed into the bleachers quieted in anticipation when student techies dimmed the lights.

Over the loud speakers, Cyndi Lauper's "Time After Time" blared. When the last notes of the song faded, the senior class advisors took their places at podiums on either side of the gym. As emcees, Mrs. Ayers and Mr. Felson traded corny banter before announcing the names of seniors and their escorts in the Grand March.

When introduced, each couple appeared from behind the shimmering curtains at the rear of the gym, waved to the audience and then made the long walk through the arches toward the bleachers. A single spotlight traced their progress, the pace often determined by the beat of the music and the reaction from the spectators.

Miss Marta Anselm and her escort Mr. Paul Hackbarth. Polite applause.

Mr. Vincent Gruber and his date Miss Kim Brislawn. Hoots and wolf-whistles from the upper tiers of the bleachers.

Some boogied to upbeat rhythms while others glided along to wistful ballads. Even if we didn't know anything about the couples, we could make solid guesses about their personalities . . . everything from painfully shy to cocky and self-assured.

Stacy Ingram wobbled on her spiked heels. Celeste Krueger tugged self-consciously at the panty line beneath her stretchy cobalt-blue gown. Bruce Leurkin's date strutted like a runway model, spinning just as he struck a pose suitable for the cover of *GQ.* Todd Svendsen, statue-like, offered his date the crook of his right arm, and she, in turn, grasped it as though both her hands had been welded there.

Trey was restless. The evening had been over-long, and it was way past his bedtime before the emcees reached the end of the alphabet.

Mr. Le Tharwani and his date Miss Rachel Lyman
Mr. Gary Vogel and his date Miss Bonnie Trachta
Miss Maureen Webster and her escort Mr. Jonny Garrison.

They were stunning. I had never seen Jonny in a tux before, but he looked as though he'd been born to wear it. He had opted for a three-button jacket, perfectly tailored, with a pearl-gray vest and black silk tie. Mo, unlike most of the other girls who preferred too-tight strapless dresses in jewel tones, was simply elegant. She wore a softly-draped Grecian-inspired dress the color of pussy willows and strappy, low-heeled silver sandals. Somehow she had tamed her long hair into a loose chignon at the nape of her neck, secured with a spray of tiny red rosebuds.

The Stones were just finishing a funky promise that time was on their side, yes it was. Inspired, Jonny crooked his finger in mock demand and lip-synched his certainty that Mo would come running back. To the delight of the audience, she gestured an emphatic No! and then pretended to reel him in to her like a hooked fish.

Because of their showmanship, they had navigated only a third of the distance across the gym floor when the next track began, a Jim Croce tune I knew by heart. Throughout the intro, a haunting melody played on acoustic guitar, Mo and Jonny stood beneath one of the arches, frozen in the white heat of the spotlight. Only when Croce's soulful plea filled the gym did they resume the Grand March.

No more lip-synching or play-acting. They held hands and slowly walked in step, hoping, perhaps, that they *could* save time in a bottle.

FIFTY-ONE

When Uncle Kurt helped coach the Ralston track team, he wore an analog stopwatch around his neck on a lanyard of red and white cord woven together. Whether at the meets or during practice, Uncle Kurt constantly palmed the stopwatch, his thumb poised over the timing button. The starter's gun would fire. Click. He pulled a pencil from behind his ear and jotted notes on the clipboard he had tucked under his arm. Then, intent upon capturing the exact moment his runners crossed the finish line, he would raise the stopwatch to eye level and click the timing pin with such force he looked as though he were pounding a nail with his fist.

Odd, isn't it, that we place such importance on beginnings and endings, always waiting for something to start, to be done? We anticipate or we dread. We rejoice or we endure. And then we begin the cycle again.

Jonny and Mo were naive. We can no more save time than we can suspend it. But if it were possible, I would have hand-picked moments of that summer—fresh and ripe with possibilities—bathed them in a sustaining syrup, and packed them into unbreakable sterile jars. In the cold of winter that followed, I could take those memories from the shelf, unscrew the lids, and savor them again as if they were new.

Diving, dancing kites at the Waukesha Kite Fest Tour. Cutler Park and the Memorial Day parade. Jonny hoisting Trey on his shoulders to see the honor guard. A long Fourth of July weekend in Ralston to visit Heather and Kurt before they left for a river cruise on the Volga. Trey clapping chubby hands as fiery peonies and crossettes and palms exploded above us in the Omaha sky. Season passes to the Milwaukee Zoo, and hours spent at the polar bear enclosure. Trips to the farmers' market for squash and ripe tomatoes and sugar-sweet muskmelons. Trey's Seussian-inspired second birthday party in August, complete with pink ink, green eggs and ham, and Mo and Jonny dressed as Thing One and Thing Two.

And then those last bittersweet days before Mo's departure for Atlanta, moments which ticked by on a watch Jonny was powerless to stop.

He rode with Mo's parents to deliver her on Emory's doorstep and texted her before Mr. Webster's Chevy Trailblazer hit the I-75 ramp north toward Chattanooga and home. Back in Waukesha, he lived in front of the computer, emailing, logging on to Skype, or instant messaging her.

Atlanta was culturally rich, she said, an exciting, cosmopolitan city. She loved the Druid Hills area, the craftsman-style bungalows and the Colonial Revival homes, elegant two-story structures with elevated porches over the doorways and sloping, manicured lawns. Her favorite spots on campus were the Bell Tower of Cox Hall and McDonough Field, a huge green space where, even as she was typing on her laptop, a group had gathered to play laser tag. Helen, her roommate, was a pre-med student from Temple whose father owned a chain of restaurants in central Texas. They liked each other instantly and enjoyed Orientation Week activities together. She described Song Fest, where first-year residence hall students wrote and performed songs praising their respective houses, and the appearance of Emory's iconic Dooley, "The Lord of Misrule." She planned to go "all in," she vowed, writing for the *Emory Wheel,* taking in a performance at Fox Theater or an Atlanta Falcons game with friends from her residence hall, attending the Last Lecture series and Wonderful Wednesdays, themed activities at Asbury Circle. She had never felt so busy, so *engaged.*

The more animated she was about college life, the more despondent Jonny became. He was still enrolled at Carroll, but he had mentally checked out before the semester was a month old. When he told Dad he planned to drop out, work extra hours to save money and move to the Atlanta area, Dad was disappointed but not surprised. He could not convince Jonny to change his mind, nor could he soften the news for Mother.

She had been almost docile through the summer, complying with court-ordered counseling, taking her medication, exercising uncommon self-control when in Mo's company, even prudently choosing to leave the room to avoid a scene. Where she had once been reactive, she was now working to be proactive. Even so, she had been curt and abrasive when Jonny left to take Mo to Emory, visibly relaxing only when he returned home. Dad knew what Jonny's decision would mean to her, how she would react. He was right.

"What do you mean you're going to quit?" she demanded.

"Mom, I told you. I hate going to school here. Don't get me wrong, Carroll's a great place. Just not for me. I'm wasting my time and I'm wasting money."

"No, you're wasting your life. You're throwing it away for some . . . some girl." Her tone was shrill, harsh.

"I thought we were done with that. She's not 'some girl,' Mom. And I'm not throwing my life away." Jonny tried to take it down a notch. "Look, I'm not quitting school completely. I'm just quitting it *here*. Maybe I'll enroll in a tech school down there. I don't know. But I can't keep going through the motions. This was never my plan, Mom."

She was unmoved. "Are you blaming me for wanting something good for you? Something good for your future?"

"Jesus, Mom. This isn't about blame. This is about me making my own decisions. For once, just give me some room."

"If you quit school, you'll get no help from us. I'll be damned if we pay your way to move to Atlanta just to be near her."

"Bets," Dad tried to intervene. Jonny stopped him.

"Nobody's asking you for a single dime, Mom. I don't expect you to do anything for me. You never have, really. Why start now?"

"What is that supposed to mean?" She was coiled tighter than a spring. "I've done *everything* for you."

Jonny stopped, considering. "You're right, Mom. You have done everything for me. And that's exactly what's wrong."

FIFTY-TWO

Jonny quit school. He took a night job working for a janitorial company and Dad grudgingly gave him extra hours at the mill after one of the loaders had surgery on his rotator cuff. I barely saw him through the fall, and even Trey complained that Uncle Jonny didn't play with him anymore.

Mother was a mess. Dad said she was still taking her meds, but if so, they weren't working as they had before. Pharmaceuticals might ease Mother's condition, but they could not erase it.

Although it was out of character for Jonny to be secretive about anything, I don't know if he told Mo he was leaving Carroll. Looking back, I doubt it. Jonny's staying in school was probably the only thing Mother and Mo had ever agreed upon, and his quitting would have been hard to confess. He might have intended to surprise her, to just show up one day at Emory, unannounced, and resume where they had left off.

If he were honest with himself, I think once he made his decision he worried if it had been the right one. As October wore on, he had far less news to share from Mo than he did in those first weeks after she left. She was busier than ever, he said, but there was something in the way he hesitated whenever I asked about Mo that sounded forced and false.

"She's got a full load, Luce. I don't expect her to drop everything just so she can give me a play-by-play of her life," he explained. I sensed he was trying to convince himself, not me. Then, as if to prove a point, he might mention something she'd said about an exhibit she had seen at the Carlos Museum or the campus movie fest at Glenn Auditorium.

"Not many details," I observed, "just headlines." I hadn't meant to be unkind, but Jonny's mouth tightened into a grim line.

"I told you, she's busy."

"Backing off," I assured him. "I didn't mean anything by that. I'm sorry."

"Forget it," he said. "She is busy. Sometimes too busy, I guess."

"Do you want to talk about it?" I asked.

"Nope. But thanks."

FIFTY-THREE

I wish we would have talked. I wish he would have told me how worried he was, how the distance between them was measured in more than miles. Mo was immersed in the university culture, meeting people from all over the world, following her passions for writing and volunteering. She was exploring possibilities for international studies and celebrating opportunities Waukesha could not possibly provide.

He did not expect to see her until Christmas break, so when she called on the Friday after Thanksgiving to say she was in town, he was elated. At first. And then he knew. He knew she had not booked a flight home at the last minute. He knew she had deliberately kept her homecoming from him, and he knew the reason why.

He left his half-finished plate of leftovers on the dining room table. Almost as an afterthought, he leaned over Trey in his highchair and kissed his forehead. He nodded to me and then to Mother.

"Where are you going, Jonny? We're having dinner."

"To Mo's. I'm going to Mo's."

"She can wait until you finish your dinner. Jonny. Did you hear me? She can wait."

"I can't," he said. His mouth seemed to have dried up, sealing his lips together.

Dad offered him the keys to the Jeep. He declined. Wooden and colorless, he put a heavy sheepskin-lined denim jacket over his gray thermal sweatshirt and grabbed a pair of leather gloves from the shelf by the kitchen door. His blue eyes looked nearly as gray as his sweatshirt.

When he left, trace amounts of snow lingered on the lawn. A weak afternoon sun had melted the dusting from the driveway into a glistening film, and the temperature hovered around the freezing mark. Jonny's Superhawk roared to life and he was gone.

PART TWO:
AFTER

FIFTY-FOUR

Thursday, December 4.

In the predawn hours, the Waukesha county sheriff pulled his cruiser into the driveway, killing the lights as if to delay announcing his arrival. He did not wake us. We were waiting for him. His boots were heavy on the porch, his steps a halting cadence of death.

Mother tried to keep him from entering, willed him not to speak of Jonny, but his duty was stronger than her denial. He knew my parents, knew me and Jonny, and so he accepted the burden he could so easily have assigned to one of his deputies. He shared the news we could not bear to hear, shared the details we had to know.

The underwater search team had recovered my brother's body from Lake Five. The Superhawk was also in the water, mangled and almost completely submerged. Someone navigating the sharp curve south of the lake on County Road Q had seen a glare where no glare should have been. Otherwise, the news might have come to us in weeks, not days.

He was found in the icy water, tangled in dead grasses a few yards from the water's edge.

My mother whimpered and sank to the floor. She drove the heels of her palms into her eyes and drew her shoulders to her ears, curling into herself. An unbearable ache, hollow and bloated, filled my chest with emptiness, but I could not cry. Not until I looked at Dad. He stared unblinking, eyes bloodshot and vacant. His fingers were laced together on top of his head as if to lift his chest so he could take one more breath . . . and then one more.

"And how did he . . . what caused . . . ?" Each word labored, the question impossible to ask.

The sheriff could only guess at the cause of death. Most likely trauma when he crashed his bike against trees ringing the lake, but he couldn't say if Jonny was conscious when he went into the water. Until an autopsy was complete, he could not rule out drowning.

"He missed a tight curve alongside the lake, Nolan. Probably going too fast. Posted limit is only twenty through that stretch, but I figure he was going nearly sixty . . . sixty-five. Slick roads didn't help. He just couldn't hold the turn. I hate to ask you, Nolan, but what was he doing near Lake Five? It's so remote there. Did Jonny have any reason to . . . ?"

My mother unfolded. Launched herself at the sheriff, screaming the desperate wail of a dying animal.

He backed away, his words fading with each step. "I'm so sorry. Now's not the time. So, so sorry." From the door, he turned one last time. "Nolan, I'll need you to come in later this morning to . . . just whenever you can . . . If there is anyone I can call . . . anything I can do . . ."

But, of course, there was no one to call. There was nothing to do.

FIFTY-FIVE

The organist scanned the lines of mourners who waited to be seated, replaying the prelude until Reverend Wolfgarth could wait no longer to begin his call to worship. He signaled for the congregation to rise.

"We are gathered to celebrate the life of Jonathan Ian Garrison. Let us rejoice and be glad for God's steadfast love. Let us glorify the God whose ever-living Christ is among us."

I tried to do my part. I spoke the printed words of response. I opened the hymnal to "Lead Us Heavenly Father," obediently moved my lips in soundless unison with the voices behind me:

> *Saviour, breathe forgiveness o'er us;*
> *All our weakness Thou dost know;*
> *Thou didst tread this earth before us,*
> *Thou didst feel its keenest woe. . .*

I did not question Reverend Wolfgarth's selection of scripture although I heard no prayer in the passage, only a cruel reminder of my loss: *Save me, O God; for the waters are come in unto my soul. I sink in deep mire, where there is no standing: I am come into deep waters, where the floods overflow me. I am weary of my crying: my throat is dried.* And when Uncle Kurt read from Ecclesiastes, assuring us there was a time unto every purpose, I tried to believe that there was a purpose in Jonny's death. I tried, but I could not.

Many stood to share memories of my brother. Acts of kindness. Funny, childish pranks. Uncommon courage when he backed down a bully. Foolish dares.

As I listened to each speaker, I convinced myself this was not my brother's funeral. The polished marble cremation urn placed before the offering table was too small to contain everything that was Jonny. Surely, he would be hiding among the mourners, a modern-day Tom Sawyer reveling in the tearful tributes as he waited for the perfect time to reveal his joke. I smiled through my tears, spoke his name out loud, and turned to search the pews for his dimpled grin and unmistakable eyes. In a sea of black, pity stared at me. Sorrow met my gaze.

"If everyone who wishes to speak has done so . . ." Reverend Wolfgarth looked at me with patient expectation. I shook my head. "Then let us accept that there is grief in our loss. We will miss Jonny, but this is a day to look forward, a day to trust that God's love never ends, a day to find beauty in the promise of eternal life."

Reverend Wolfgarth paused, smiled, and pressed his fingertips together as he began his message of hope.

"Every life is a work of art drawn by the hand of the Master. Jonny Garrison's life was no exception. We cannot deny that his time with us was painfully short. It ended too soon. It ended tragically, yes. But where we might see the life of a son, a brother, a friend as an unfinished sketch, the Artist in Heaven knows Jonny Garrison was a masterpiece. With His brush, He painted Jonny rich with color. He shaded Jonny's life with depth. And then He invited us to be witnesses to the perfection of His creation.

"We who are gathered here have an obligation. Ask yourselves today what you must bring to the viewing of a masterpiece. What do you see in the portrait of Jonny's life?

"Is your first reaction to protest? *No, this can't be finished.* I confess, mine was. We fancy ourselves to be art critics. We believe we can find fault when the lines of Jonny's life fade, when the perspective narrows to a single point and then vanishes from our sight. But remember this: where the lines of Jonny's life recede to a vanishing point on this earthly canvas, they blossom beyond the easel into a gallery of eternal light and peace and joy."

I saw Grammy Elnora pull Mother close to her, listened to Aunt Heather's shushing as Trey fidgeted, but I heard nothing more. I was not aware when Reverend Wolfgarth concluded his remarks nor when he gave his prayer of thanksgiving. Only when Grandfather Aldrich gently placed his hand on my shoulder did I rise for the closing hymn. I remained standing for the blessing and dismissal and passively followed others to the fellowship hall where I withstood endless whispers of "So sorry for your loss" and endured mindless pats on the back that felt like hammer blows.

The hall cleared slowly. When only a few remained, people I did not recognize, I escaped to the restroom in the church basement. Silence echoed in the tiny space, but I wanted the quiet. I wanted walls to block out words of sympathy and I wanted walls to shield me from faces of pity and sorrow. I wanted to stay there forever, to lean against the tile until I became part of it, hard and cold. I flattened my forehead, pressed it into the wall until my neck knotted with the effort. I ground my knuckles against the ridges where tile met grout, twisting them, scraping them, welcoming the pain.

Someone rapped on the door, tentatively, almost an apology.

"It's occupied."

"Luce? Luce, it's me. It's Mo. Can I come in?"

I had seen her briefly with her parents among the mourners. Knowing she could not approach my mother, she had stood apart from the others who waited in line to pay their respects, hoping, perhaps, to steal a moment with me.

Dad had been the one to tell her when Jonny's body was recovered. She felt guilty, he said. Responsible. She wasn't, of course. But I had not spoken to her then, and I could not now. I could not lighten the weight of her pain when mine was so heavy. I did not want to try.

"Luce? Can I talk to you?"

I answered with my silence.

"Luce, I don't blame you for not wanting to talk to me. But you have to know how sorry I am about . . .," her voice trailed to a whisper. ". . . about Jonny. About everything." She waited. "He meant a lot to me, Luce. Even though we weren't going to be together, he was special. Please, please, Luce. Just let me in."

Words that should have been automatic, words of forgiveness and absolution, words I felt but could not say died in my throat.

"I never thought he would . . ." She was crying. "If I could go back . . ."

If we could only go back, all of us.

Somehow we managed to find our coats and gloves, murmur our thanks to the church volunteers, make our way across the parking lot and climb into the Jeep. Dad secured Trey in his car seat before sliding behind the wheel, but he didn't start the car right away. It was almost as if he had forgotten what to do. And then he sighed, folded his arms over the steering wheel and leaned in, resting his forehead against his clasped hands. Tired. He looked so tired. He sat like that for several minutes, but we said nothing. We were silent in our suffering. Drained. Empty.

The trip home was a funeral procession of two cars—ours in the lead, my Pennick grandparents following with Heather and Kurt in Grandfather's sedan. Mother, eerily calm, cradled Jonny's urn with both hands. She would not release it even to wipe the tears which dripped from her chin onto its polished surface.

As we drove north toward home, an unexpected ray of late afternoon sun pierced the heavy gray clouds pressing down on us with their dark weight. To my right, the light cast crisp shadows of our Jeep. I saw silhouettes—Mother, Dad, Trey, and me—imprisoned in a black, boxy hearse and watched as our shadowy counterpart hurtled through leafless tress, road markers, scrubby bushes and deserted intersections, heedless of any obstacle through which it passed, unscathed.

I envied the occupants. They could not be injured. They were beyond hurt.

FIFTY-SIX

How often are we told that time heals all wounds? It does not. Time is an incompetent field surgeon, called upon to bind jagged flesh of the foolish or the brave or the unlucky. Held together with clumsy and uneven stitches, we return to the front to fight or—if the injury is too grievous—we are sent home, crippled and useless. Regardless, we never heal completely.

Kurt and Heather stayed for a couple of extra days, helping where they could. They addressed envelopes for thank you notes to acknowledge memorials in Jonny's name. They delivered floral arrangements and green plants from the funeral to nursing homes in Waukesha. They transferred enchiladas and lasagna and chicken casseroles to Tupperware containers, wrapped cookies and breads for freezing, washed pie pans and Pyrex bakeware and labeled them for return to the families who had left their food and their condolences at our kitchen door. They filed away pictures of Jonny which had been on display during the visitation and service, and they cataloged phone messages from the answering machine requiring responses. They dusted furniture, vacuumed carpets, wiped countertops, scoured bathrooms.

Dad stepped in only when they proposed going through Jonny's closet.

"Later. She's not ready."

And so they went home to Ralston, resigned to leave our lives neat, ordered. But not normal.

Dad resumed his routine at the mill, but he stopped in frequently during the day to check on Mother. He could interest her in nothing, and her withdrawal was more frightening than her outbursts had ever been.

A week after the funeral, when she could rouse herself from the stupor of the medication she took to help her sleep, she began her day with a cup of hot tea and a piece of dry toast. She would wander into the living room and stand at the base of the stairs leading to the second floor. Beginning with the picture of Jonny as a baby, she stared at each portrait hanging on the stairwell, slowly ascending the steps to drink in the images of her son. I would watch her reach out, tentatively, but as soon as her fingertips touched the smooth glass, she would moan. Every day, there on the stairwell, her grief was new again. There was a barrier between them—had, in fact—always been a barrier, transparent but still there.

We forced ourselves to celebrate the holidays. Despite Mother's apathy, Dad insisted, for Trey's sake, we cut a tree and decorate it. He and I spent the Tuesday evening before Christmas at a local shop selling handcrafted toys. We bought a wooden circus train carrying a giraffe, tiger, and rhinoceros for Trey and wrapped it in paper with penguins dressed in Santa suits. For his stocking we selected coloring books and chubby crayons, an enormous red apple, and several packets of animal crackers.

At a second-hand boutique, we bought a lovely antique frame for Mother and inserted a picture of Jonny in his tux taken the evening of Mo's senior prom. Mother had often said Jonny never looked more handsome than he did that night. Dad and I both hoped this would be a gift to cherish, but when we placed the package in her hands on Christmas morning she seemed unsure what to do with it. She traced the outline of the wrapped box and fingered the silver bow before placing it on the floor beside her chair.

Dad kneeled before her softly urging, "Bets, it's Christmas. Try. Do your part for Trey."

She nodded like an obedient child and picked at the tape, careful not to tear the paper. When she had finally freed it from the layers of glittery tissue, she held the frame in both hands, staring. To our horror, she hugged it to her chest and began rocking back and forth. Her eyes were closed as if in pain, her lips parted only enough to emit a whining high-pitched wail, almost like a distant siren that grew ever louder and more urgent. Dad tried to calm her, unsuccessfully, before leading her back to her bed and her sedatives.

"I'll call on Monday," he promised when he came back into the living room. "She needs to see someone. God knows we can't do this alone."

I nodded. "It will be okay, Dad." How automatic the assurance I offered . . . and how meaningless because I did not know.

I did not know the depth of her suffering, the cold, lightless hell of her loss. I could only imagine that she must be like an amputee who, long after a limb is severed, still feels the phantom pain for which there is no cure.

FIFTY-SEVEN

Under pressure, Mother resumed the therapy she had suspended since Jonny's death. Most days she refused to get into the Jeep until we threatened to commit her again for psychiatric evaluation. If neither Dad nor I could drive her to her appointments, Grammy Elnora would step in. It wasn't that Mother was unable to drive. She could not be trusted behind the wheel, either because she could not concentrate or—worse—because she might concentrate too much on the debilitating sorrow which enveloped her.

Slowly, after months of work with the doctor and repeated adjustments to her lithium and Risperdal, she seemed less mercurial, less susceptible to crippling depression. Having been morbid watchdogs for so long, we were able to lower our guards, to take comfort in her increasing stability, to celebrate watersheds promising better days ahead.

The night she suggested we go to Jonny's favorite burger joint in Delafield, Dad and I did a little victory dance in the kitchen. Her therapist had suggested she visit places meaningful to Jonny to embrace the parts of his life which held good memories.

We bundled Trey against a sharp spring wind and made the twenty-minute trip to Five Guys where we ordered bacon cheeseburgers and Cajun style fries for the three of us and a grilled cheese for Trey.

With a hesitant glance toward Mother, Dad recalled the first time he and Jonny had stopped at Five Guys. They had been pheasant hunting with Gunther Sorenson, one of the mill's regular customers, a nice guy but a notoriously poor shot. Jonny was acting as bird dog, flushing roosters from the cover of dry, rustling corn stalks, but even though he scared several birds to flight, Dad's hunting partner could not bring a single one down.

"You should have seen Jonny. He was cold and tired, but he didn't quit."

Finally, late in the afternoon after the three of them had walked dozens of fields, a fair-sized bird fell at the sound of simultaneous shots.

Gunther agreed to come home only after Dad convinced him his shot was the one to hit the mark. Happy with his trophy bird, Gunther offered to buy burgers for everyone from a new franchise just off I-94. Jonny was so hungry he ordered three burgers to go. Dad said he shook his head and gave Jonny one of those *You're being greedy* looks, but Gunther said no, Jonny had earned every single one.

"He fell asleep halfway through the first sandwich," Dad laughed.

As we finished our meal, Mother dabbed at her eyes.

"This was a good idea, wasn't it?"

"Yeah, Bets. This *was* a good idea."

She smiled. "I can almost see him here. He loved his cheeseburgers."

I can almost see him here became our mantra. We could picture Jonny playing third at a high school baseball game or imagine him plopped next to Dad on the sofa watching the Cubs. Because he would have shopped half-price music stores for recycled CDs of the Plain White T's, Waylon Jennings, Garth Brooks, so did we. At a flea market or rummage sale we might happen upon a toy similar to one Jonny had as a toddler. Inevitably Mother would buy it "for Trey" she said, but most often she squirreled away her purchases in her closet or in Jonny's room. She said they made her feel closer to him.

Bit by bit, we navigated the minefields of first anniversaries without Jonny: Christmas, New Year's, Easter. Mother's Day had been the hardest. We made an egg strata layered with spinach, feta, and sausage. Trey insisted on crescent rolls wrapped around marshmallows dipped in butter and cinnamon sugar. Dad picked out a box of hand-dipped chocolates and a delicate hot-house orchid in a ceramic planter. Early that morning, I ironed her best ivory tablecloth and set out the red *You Are Special* plate at her place right next to the cards we had made for her. Somehow, the sentiments of drug-store cards did not ring true. Instead, Dad and I wrote our own messages: his of love, mine of support. Even Trey had scribbled something approximating a flower on the front of folded cardstock and had proudly inscribed a skewed but legible capital T beneath it.

When we called her, she did not join us for breakfast. She locked herself in Jonny's room for the entire day, refusing to come out or to eat from the trays we left outside the door. Dad tried the lock a couple of times before placing both palms on the closed door.

"Bets. Are you okay?" Hearing no response, he leaned in, his ear flush to the door. "Bets, can you hear me?"

"Yes."

"Do you need anything? Can I help?"

"You can leave me alone. All of you. Just leave me alone."

We complied. The next morning, without speaking to any of us, she took a few bites of a leftover crescent roll and disappeared back into her room where she slept most of the day. When it looked as if the pattern would continue, Dad scheduled another doctor's appointment. Medication was adjusted, lamotrigine added. Weeks of counseling with molasses-slow progress.

As much as she was capable, she rejoined the world. Occasionally she still spent entire days locked in his room, but her depression seemed to have leveled. We moved on.

We planted a garden like the ones I remembered from my childhood. Rows of beans, corn, lettuce, tomatoes. Hills of potatoes and cukes. She weeded and watered early in the morning before the heat and humidity took its toll. From the harvest she fixed food Jonny had loved, sometimes forgetting to set only three places at dinner instead of four. Those nights, we were vigilant lest the reminder of his absence from the table and from our lives send her into despair.

By the end of the summer, she had regained a little of her lost weight and muscle tone from working in the garden. Her skin had lost the gray pallor of winter and Jonny's death, but her eyes were deeply creased with lines of sadness that even her rare laughter over one of Trey's antics could not erase.

She still refused to sort through Jonny's belongings, insisting his door remain closed to anyone but her. It seemed a small concession to make if the solitude and familiarity of Jonny's room helped to calm her. Surprisingly, after the Mother's Day scare, her stints in Jonny's room seemed to lessen her agitation if not alleviate her depression. We might hear a Tim McGraw ballad coming from the CD player that sat on the bookshelf by his window or dialog from *30 Rock* or *Friday Night Lights*, two of his never-miss shows. Sometimes, even if there were no sound coming from the television, we might see light from the screen flickering in the crack beneath the door. All mindless distractions. Who could deny them to her?

FIFTY-EIGHT

With **forced cheerfulness, Dad double-checked** the load stacked in the rear of the Jeep. Our luggage shared space with the portable crib and collapsible stroller, a small cooler powered by the cigarette lighter, a much larger Coleman, and the bag stocked with Trey's books, games, and snacks. "We're all set. Anybody have to pee again before we get on the road?"

Thanksgiving was to be spent in Ralston with Heather and Kurt. It was our turn to travel, but even if it had not been, Dad would have insisted. We risked too much staying in Waukesha so near the anniversary of Jonny's death.

When Dad first broached the subject with Mother, she flatly refused to go.

"I can't, Nolan. I can't leave. I need to be here."

"Why, Bets?"

"Jonny is here. I need to be here, too." She offered this explanation as though the logic were unassailable.

Gently, sorrowfully, Dad countered. "No, Bets. Jonny is wherever we are. He is always with me. I can't go anywhere, do anything, without thinking about him, without feeling him. Isn't he with you, too? "

She nodded.

"Then he'll be with you in Ralston. You'll see. He'll be with you."

Nothing seemed settled for several days until the morning before we were to leave. I came down with Trey to find her at the kitchen sink, her arms submerged to the elbows in soapy water. Cabinet doors stood ajar, counters were dusted with flour and littered with mixing bowls and measuring cups. Sweet potatoes were peeled and quartered, broccoli had been rinsed and waited in the colander, a saucepan of rice simmered on the stove, and a block of cheddar had been shredded into an untidy mound. A pecan pie cooled on the table and two unbaked shells stood ready for pumpkin filling.

She must have been up most of the night, cooking as though she were possessed. Her manic episodes had been controlled fairly well with medication, but it took so little to upset her. We could never be certain whether she would withdraw or explode into relentless motion. Both could be dangerous.

"Oh, good. Luce, you're finally up. We have so much to do if we're going to have everything ready by the time we leave tomorrow. I was thinking I should make that carrot cake Heather likes so much."

"I'm not sure we need it, Mother, not with all this. You've been busy."

"It's no trouble at all. Besides, Heather and Kurt are always inviting some poor soul from the base to have Thanksgiving dinner. Who knows how many of us will be there?"

I paused, sensing a meltdown when she realized who would *not* be there, but she jabbered on in a frenzied monologue.

"I'll send your father to the store for cream cheese and crushed pineapple. There's not much going on at the mill today, so it shouldn't be hard for him to get away. Why don't you help by grating the carrots? Does Trey want pancakes this morning? Let me see, I thought I had a box of raisins out . . ."

She did not let up throughout the day. When she could find nothing more to prepare in the kitchen, she went into her room to pack. I heard her footsteps as she moved repeatedly from bed to closet to bathroom and then to the hallway adjacent to the kitchen where she called to me repeatedly.

"Luce, do you think I should take the brown wool slacks or the dark green ones to go with this sweater?"

"Luce, did you remember to pack the baby shampoo?"

"Luce, are you taking your flat iron?"

"Luce, is there an extra dental floss in the linen closet in the bathroom upstairs?"

Even before Dad came home with pizza, she had her luggage ready by the kitchen door. She had also packed the Coleman, rearranging the contents until she was satisfied the desserts and vegetable casseroles would fit securely among the freezer packs. Then, obsessively, she drew a diagram so she could duplicate the order before emptying the cooler and returning the food to the refrigerator.

I did not look forward to the trip. Trey was an active little boy who protested long confinement in his car seat. We would need to stop frequently, thereby extending the travel time. But Mother, in her mania, could prove to be even more difficult. Carrot sticks and coloring books would not calm her.

I needn't have worried.

Whether simply exhausted or captive to the pendulum swings of her disease, she spent much of the trip through Wisconsin and across Iowa in silence, sometimes sleeping, more often staring out the window. The narcotic monotony of Interstate 80 soothed us in its tedium, leaving each of us to our thoughts.

FIFTY-NINE

I had never been more grateful for Heather and Kurt than I was that weekend. Knowing instinctively leftover turkey and cranberries would conjure memories of the last meal Jonny shared with us, my aunt refrigerated Mother's sweet potatoes and the broccoli casserole and instead served succulent barbecued ribs, crunchy slaw, and cheesy corn soufflé.

To share our Thanksgiving picnic, Kurt and Heather invited three guests—friends, yes, but likely selected for their unique, collective abilities to inject variety into the conversation.

Benjamin was a young airman from Offut and had just returned from a hop to Japan. As we ate, he described an old *papasan* he met in Okinawa who made highly lacquered chopsticks inlaid with mother-of-pearl to sell to the tourists. He produced a pair as a gift for Heather before passing the rest of us wooden ones in paper sleeves. Trey giggled as he watched Dad try unsuccessfully to pick the meat from the ribs or stab the peppers and carrots in the slaw.

"This is impossible," he complained good-naturedly. "My ribs are getting cold."

"If Asian kids learn to use chopsticks when they are about a year old, I think you can manage," Benjamin laughed. "Let me show you a trick." He pulled a rubber band from his pocket and wrapped it around the thick ends of his own chopsticks until the band was as tight as it could go. Then he folded the paper sleeve over and over into a thick wedge which he slipped between the two sticks until it touched the rubber band.

"Okay, now just use the sticks like tweezers," he said. He demonstrated with a couple of bites. "Easy, right?"

He made another set for Trey who grabbed them and spent the rest of the meal intent upon cleaning his plate with his new toy.

Our second guest was Hannah, a senior at Iowa State who was student teaching in a kindergarten classroom at Seymour Elementary in Ralston. Her cooperating teacher, a good friend of Heather's, had arranged for

Hannah to spend Thanksgiving with us because she didn't have the funds to fly home to Kingsport, Tennessee, for the long weekend.

I found myself thinking how much Jonny would have liked Hannah. She was terrific with Trey, singing funny little counting songs with him and offering to read *Red is a Dragon,* a book she used with her students to teach colors. She entertained us with stories of a challenging student, Kevin, who defied her at every turn.

"The first few days at Seymour when I was in charge of a lesson, I nearly drove a screwdriver into my ear," she laughed. "Every time I would give a direction, Kevin would do this." She stood from the table, straightened her right arm and raised it above her head like an angry activist. She closed her eyes, put her chin to her chest, and in her best Kevin impression, yelled, "Never."

Heather clapped her approval and then the rest of us laughed as Trey mimicked Heather's performance.

"Nevah," he repeated.

"Oops," she apologized. "Maybe this wasn't such a good idea." She turned to Trey. "Try this, big guy." She raised her arm as before, but this time she smiled broadly and said, "Right on."

"Ride on!" he chortled.

I looked over at Mother. Although she hadn't said much during dinner, she was smiling. She looked almost relaxed.

Thank you—thank you—thank you—thank you. The words were carousel ponies circling on a ride I didn't ever want to end.

Then there was Vern, an elderly widower and former electronics engineer who had helped design communications equipment for the final lunar mission. After the meal, he retrieved a photo album from the sofa table. With astonishing recall, he provided details surrounding Apollo 17 and shared glossy, vivid pictures from the mission.

The most striking one was taken by Harrison Schmitt of fellow astronaut Eugene Cernan against the stark backdrop of the moon's Sculptured Hills. In the picture, Cernan is flanked by an American flag and the lunar rover's umbrella-shaped antenna. The tread of Cernan's boots leave perfect, crisp impressions in the dust of the moon's surface.

"Hard to believe that was nearly forty years ago. Those two were the last to ever walk on the moon," Vern said. "The end of an era. And believe it or not, Commander Cernan's footprints are still there today. Intact. No wind. No water. Nothing to destroy them."

He thumbed through several other shots—Cernan on the lunar rover at the Taurus-Littrow landing site, a replica of the official NASA Apollo 17 patch, Cernan, Schmitt, and Evans in publicity photos prior to the launch.

Trey was especially fascinated by the "Blue Marble" image. The Earth appears to float above the moon's cratered surface, South Africa and Antarctica brilliant as the swirls in a prized aggie. "Show me more," he demanded. And Vern did, patiently.

Our guests had so stimulated Trey that he was nearly impossible to put down for the night. He protested all through his bath and though he was overly tired, he stretched the evening by giving hugs and kisses all around and then insisted on repeating the cycle. I excused the two of us and took him, his ratty teddy bear, and the little blanket square he always rubbed against his cheek to the upstairs bedroom we shared. I read two of the books we had brought with us and rocked him until he went limp against me.

He was so vulnerable, so innocent. I prayed, as I did every night, that somehow he would retain his innocence for as long as possible. Reluctantly, I brushed a final kiss goodnight across his forehead and eased him into the portable crib next to my bed.

"Night, Trey. Mommy loves you," I whispered.

This was a sacred ritual, the night incomplete if we deviated from our routine. I wondered if every mother, watching her sleeping child, felt the same odd combination of limitless joy and dreadful sorrow. Joy for what lay ahead. Sorrow for the day just ended, for the impermanence of the footprints we left behind.

SIXTY

The evening had been pleasant. No hysterics, no crying from Mother. But in the silent hours of the night I could hear her moving like a rat on a wheel from the guest bedroom on the main floor into the kitchen, the bathroom, the living room, and once, even outside. Her insomnia was as familiar to me as the soft little sucking sounds Trey made in his sleep, so I didn't go down to search for her. Instead, I stared at nothing in the blackness of my room until I heard her enter the house and once again begin the downstairs circuit.

In the morning, she was pale but composed.

"You doing okay, Bets?" my father asked softly as we sat around the kitchen table. "I know this is . . ."

"We all know it, Nolan. I'm fine. Just tired."

"Bets," Heather said, "I thought maybe, with the weather being so unseasonably warm, that we might get out of the house today. Temps are supposed to climb into the fifties, so we could scout around Omaha, maybe visit the Creighton campus. Luce can show you all her old stomping grounds, can't you, Luce?"

Mother hesitated. "I don't know. I don't think I'd be very good company today."

"Or, if you like, the zoo is open on winter hours. Wouldn't Trey love that?"

She glanced at Trey and nodded. "Yes, he would."

"No pressure," Kurt said. "But if you're up to it, we could all use the fresh air and some exercise. We can come back anytime you say."

"I suppose," Mother conceded.

"Well, then," I said, "let's start with the zoo. That way if Trey gets tired, he can nap this afternoon in his stroller."

"It's settled then." Dad turned to Kurt. "You and Heather are in charge."

We arrived at the zoo just minutes after it opened at 10:00. Although the day would grow far warmer, temperatures still hovered in the mid-forties. We opted for the indoor exhibits first, starting in the Lied Jungle just inside the main entrance where we wandered the dirt path through recreated rain forests of Asia and the southern hemisphere. Trey climbed into rock niches and stuck his hand into the spray from one of the towering waterfalls. He squealed as sleek otters glided through pools on the rain forest floor and I had to scramble to keep him from the stepping out onto the suspension bridge.

From there we wandered through the Desert Dome and, beneath it, the Kingdoms of the Night exhibits where Heather involuntarily drew back from the flitting shadows of bats in their caves. No less cowardly, I stood a respectful distance from the emerald tree boas and watchful tarantulas.

At the Scott Aquarium we spent all of our time at the penguin enclosure. A regal king penguin held court in the center of the sixty-foot-long exhibit. He stood nearly motionless, allowing visitors to admire his dress tuxedo of black and white, smartly accented by the triangle of yellow beneath his throat. A fat cousin with the silhouette of a party balloon swam directly in front of us. Trey pressed his nose to the glass and called to the penguin as if summoning a dog. "Here, bird, here."

We stopped for lunch at the Sea Turtle café before catching the zoo tram and a quick visit to the children's area. I think Mother would have gone back to Ralston at that point, but Heather and Kurt were like tour guides on steroids.

"What do you say to a quick tour of Creighton?" Heather proposed. "The campus is so beautiful and if Trey falls asleep, he won't miss anything."

"Yeah, that's a selling point," Kurt laughed. Maybe you should quit teaching and start doing ad campaigns for the university."

"You know what I mean. It's just the one thing he's probably least interested in."

To be truthful, it was the thing Mother was least interested in, as well. In my four years as a student there, Mother had never once visited, had never asked about my time on campus. Even on that day she seemed reluctant, and I wondered if she were thinking of Jonny's decision to quit Carroll. To quit everything.

Strolling the tree-lined brick walks through the center of campus we paused before the flame-shaped sculpture in the fountain right outside St. John's Catholic Church. Symbolizing the Holy Spirit, the gracefully curved helix tapered to a point which rose toward the sky. I had spent many afternoons sitting on the adjacent bench staring as its coils caught the sun and threw the reflection like a white laser back at me. Although Mother did not seem to be listening, I pointed out the two places I spent most of my time outside of class, Reinert Alumni Memorial Library and the Skutt Student Center, the heart of Creighton. By the time we had stopped to read the plaque beside the statue of Ignatius of Loyola, she was ready to go.

We decided to finish the day at Old Market near the riverfront. Dad suggested Trey could select a treat from Fairmont Mercantile with its endless aisles of retro candies if he'd just hang on until after dinner. The promise of a PEZ dispenser turned the tide.

"Does he even know what a PEZ dispenser is?" Kurt asked.

"Nope, but it doesn't matter," I said. "He just likes saying the name."

On cue, Trey chimed in until the words ran together. "PEZ SPEZ PEZ SPEZ."

And so late that afternoon we took our seats in a tall booth at Upstream Brewing Company on Eleventh and Jackson. Heather and I split a Mediterranean pizza, Dad ordered braised pot roast and Kurt opted for the blackened burger with pepper jack and guacamole. Trey polished off a side of creamy mac and cheese, but even though her Thai chicken salad looked spectacular topped with clouds of crispy rice noodles, Mother only picked at her meal.

Despite Kurt's protests, Dad picked up the check.

"You treated us to the zoo. This is the least I can do. For all you've done." Kurt nodded his understanding, left the tip, and steered us toward the Fairmont for Trey's PEZ.

"Hey, before we go home, why don't we walk a little of the bridge? It's right along the riverfront," Heather suggested. "It's great during the day but amazing at night. What do you say? Anybody game?"

She was referring to the Bob Kerrey Pedestrian Bridge connecting Omaha to Council Bluffs, an artful span of pylons and cables stretching nearly three thousand feet.

"Sure," Dad agreed. "Bets?"

"No. I'll sit in the car." There was an uncomfortable silence as we waited for her to say more, but she simply turned north toward the parking ramp on Harney Street.

"I'll drop the rest of you at the bridge and wait with her in the car," Dad offered.

"No, Dad," I said. "Let me stay with Mother."

"You share the time with Trey, Luce. We'll be fine."

Dad hurried to catch up with Mother. When he reached her side, he adjusted his stride to match hers. The rest of us gave them their distance.

As we started up the ramp on the west side, hundreds of spotlights along the footbridge suddenly illuminated the structure. The cables running from the bridge to the two support towers looked like string art on a grand scale, filaments of steel as delicate as a spider's web.

Kurt pushed Trey in the stroller. Heather and I followed, zipping our jackets against the night air. We did not walk the entire length, stopping instead at the line on the bridge marking the division between Iowa and Nebraska. My uncle positioned the wheels of Trey's stroller to straddle the line and then snapped a picture with his camera phone.

"Well, big guy, you're in two states at the same time. That's a lot for anybody to do in just one day. What do you say we head for home?"

"Head for home," Trey echoed. "What do you say we head for home."

Kurt turned to me and gestured toward the Omaha skyline. "Look at that. It's too bad your folks missed this."

The sun had set and there was no wind to ripple the water beneath us. The river became a mirror reflecting the violet sky, a canvas for the city lights, blurred and elongated, stretching away from their source.

Sixty-One

We said good-bye to Heather and Kurt early Saturday morning. Although forecasters promised another warm November day, the sun had not yet burned the chill from the air. Dad said ending a trip was never as much fun as anticipating one, but it would be good to be home. Mother didn't respond, nor did I. Only Trey chattered as we drove east on I-80 toward Des Moines.

"Mommy, see the big plellers. Look. Lots of big plellers!!"

"What are you talking about, Trey? What are plellers?" I leaned over nearer to him in his car seat to peek at the book he was holding. Are they in your story?"

"No Mommy. Not big plellers in my story. Look. Out there." He pointed at the wind farms stretching across miles of countryside, the blades of the turbines spinning air into energy.

"Oh, you mean 'big pro*pell*ers,' don't you?" I asked.

He nodded vigorously. "Big proplellers. Big proplellers for big airplanes. Where are the airplanes, Mommy?"

When I couldn't convince him there were no planes missing their "pro*plell*ers," he lost interest and returned to his book. I turned to look out the window again.

How many times had I driven this stretch of highway, indifferent to the landscape until I saw it through Trey's eyes? Could I harness his imagination?

Just as I used to do with the old Magic Eye books, I stared at the massive towers, smudging the gray skies and barren horizon behind them into a drab background.

No, I decided, Trey was wrong. The turbines were not propellers. They were clocks without numbers, marking time in a land of giants. For all their size, they were useless as timepieces. The blades remained equidistant from each other, ever in motion but ever separated, the seconds never adding to minutes, the minutes never advancing the hours.

Sometimes our lives felt like those silent turbines, moving in place at the mercy of forces we felt but could not see.

Sixty-Two

Unlike the year before when we were paralyzed in our grief, we readied ourselves for Christmas by cooking, shopping, decorating. Our actions were often forced, artificial, but necessary just the same.

Dad clipped strings of big multi-colored bulbs over the junipers near the porch and stacked bales of hay by the driveway to serve as a staging spot for a hand-carved crèche that had belonged to Grandmother Lucinda. Inside the house we wrapped garland around the handrail of the steps and set out Mother's collection of Santa figurines. Trey's favorites were the ones we hooked to the ceiling and suspended from stretchy springs the width of a pencil. When touched, they bungeed up and down. He called them "flying Santas," and one of them, posed like an airborne Superman, actually had wings that flapped as the figure bobbed.

One afternoon, admittedly after much cajoling from me and some emotional blackmail from Trey *(Nana, please?),* we baked all the favorites I remembered from my childhood. Caramel bars, pecan tassies, Santa's whiskers rich with coconut and candied cherries, rolled butter cookies cut into snowmen and angels and bells. Dad would want Cajun-spiced party mix; I requested dark fudge with sea salt. For the span of a few hours, we devoted ourselves to measuring and mixing, shaping, baking. In the end, we gave most of it away, beautifully arranged sampler plates wrapped tightly in plastic and finished with strands of raffia. The mill workers were profuse in their thanks, to which Mother responded with a dismissive, "It was nothing." But it *was* something. It was a whisper of promise.

Gifts for Mother were always the most difficult. The framed picture of Jonny in his prom tux had been disastrous, so I decided to forgo surprise in favor of safety. I suggested we cut square blocks from old T-shirts Jonny had worn so that Mother might make a quilt from them. My gift would be helping to prepare the T-shirts, purchasing all the materials, and buying a book with definitive step-by-step instructions from an expert quilter, according to rave reviews on Amazon.

Mother was enthusiastic. "Luce, that sounds wonderful. Thank you. But I wouldn't know where to start. Jonny always wore T-shirts. I have them upstairs. There must be dozens of them." She paused, considering. "I guess before we go shopping for quilting material we ought to figure out which shirts we'll use." She insisted we begin sorting through them immediately, but when I followed her upstairs toward Jonny's room, she blocked my way. "Don't bother. I'll get them."

"Why don't we just go through them in his room?" I asked. "It would be so much easier than carrying all of them downstairs."

The lightness of her mood just moments before disappeared. "I said I'll get them."

"Okay. Okay. No problem. I just thought I'd help." I backed down a couple of steps before turning around and heading downstairs.

Her arms piled high with rainbow stacks of shirts, it took her seven trips to and from Jonny's room before we could begin. We spent nearly ten minutes debating whether we should first sort them into piles according to their worthiness and, if so, what the criteria might be—shirts associated with particular memories or ones representing times throughout his life. Then it was another half hour deciding if we should group them by color or size or theme. Mother was as animated as I had seen her in a long time, and I mentally patted myself on the back for suggesting the project.

During the next two weeks, we worked at least part of every day when Trey went down for his afternoon nap and in the evenings after his bedtime. The quilting guide suggested a simple grid suitable for beginners: four rows of four T-shirt blocks. Because she was having the devil of a time trying to choose which shirts to use, Mother wondered why we couldn't just double the number of blocks and rows.

"We're making a quilt, Mother," I laughed, "not a tarp to cover the infield at Miller Park." She conceded only when I suggested we could make other quilts from those shirts not selected for this first effort.

We washed the final sixteen tees, turned them inside out, laid them flat, and ironed on a non-woven fusible interfacing to help them hold their shape. Then we traced around the designs with a square template to keep the sizes uniform. The sashing she used to frame each block was made from faded denim because, as Mother reminded me, Jonny always wore jeans. Methodically she stitched the blocks together, added a denim border darker than the sashing, attached puffy batting, and finished with a pale blue flannel for the backing.

When the last thread had been clipped, she asked me to stand and hold the quilt for her. "Luce. Luce. It's so amazing. Every square . . . every square reminds me . . ." Tears brightened her eyes. "It's the story of my Jonny." She read the words from each block as though they were Scripture.

> *Mommy's Man. YMCA Little League. Ellie's Deli All Stars. Apple Harvest Festival. Waukesha JanBoree. Camp U-Nah-Li-Ya, Chute Pond. Earth Week Extravaganza. Northstar Baseball. Kiwanis River Run. WNHS Homecoming.*

"It's a great quilt, Mother. Lots of memories." Do you want to put it in your room?" I asked. "Or maybe you'd like to leave it in the living room as a throw. It's so cozy and warm."

"No," she insisted. "I want to wrap it and put it under the tree so I can open it on Christmas morning."

"Sure," I agreed. "I'll go get the paper and ribbon from the closet."

"Get the gold foil paper. And I think there is a big bow, too. Oh, and we'll need a big box. I don't want to wrinkle it."

I retrieved the foil, a metallic gold bow with curly silver streamers, a sleeve of tissue paper, Scotch tape, and scissors. In the meantime, Mother had gone to the mill to find a wide cardboard box, a tape gun and a box cutter. With the precision of an engineer, she fashioned a large but shallow container and lined it with layers of tissue. She folded the quilt in fourths and nestled it inside the box, placed several more sheets of tissue on top, and secured the lid with tape in multiple places on each side.

When she asked me to find a wooden yardstick in the broom closet, I couldn't help myself.

"Are you measuring it for a suit of armor?"

"Don't be ridiculous. I just want to make sure I make straight cuts. I don't have any more of this paper, so I don't want to mess up."

Every step was meticulous. Centering the box on the paper. Taping the edges so there were no ripples. Creasing the paper at each end and folding it into crisp envelopes. Because she didn't have enough ribbon to circle the package, she played with the placement of the bow until she was satisfied with the effect.

"There. Finished. It's the most beautiful package ever, don't you think, Luce?"

"It should be," I agreed.

"I'll just need a tag for it," she said.

"Yep. Otherwise, I'm not sure we'll know whose it is." Even as the words left my mouth, I felt ashamed of my sarcasm. She was so happy, so excited, and I had no right to dampen that rare joy. "I'll see what tags we have in the drawer. It needs to be just as special as the package."

I brought back the assortment of tags from Christmases past and present for her, but she was already cutting the front from an oversized card we had received from one of Grammy Elnora's friends to use instead. An expensive reproduction of a style popular in the early 1900s, it was a vintage Ellen Clapsaddle print on heavy cardstock. The artwork featured two children facing one another in a flurry of lacy snowflakes— he in tan knickers, brown coat trimmed with fur, red hat and red mittens; she in white leggings under a blue dress, the hem just peeking beneath her white coat, and black hat fringed with white. Each was shielded by an umbrella and they both carried quaint baskets full of silvery-green holly leaves with clusters of red berries. The caption inscribed at the bottom read, "The good old Greeting take from me, Happy and glad may your Christmas be." The artist's name appeared in faded gray script near the lower right corner.

Mother rolled four small strips of tape into circles, sticky side out, and fastened the card to the box. "This will do," she remarked, as though she had been forced to settle for a dimestore lick-it and stick-it tag. When I left the room, she was looking for a fine-tip Sharpie so she could address the package to herself.

SIXTY-THREE

For the remaining few days prior to Christmas, Mother stopped
several times to pick up the shimmery package, shake it gently and
laugh. "I wonder what this could be." She would press her lips against the
card, hug the box to her chest, and then almost reluctantly tuck the present back under the tree, making sure as she did so that it was visible but
protected.

Privately, Dad told me how much he appreciated the thought I had
put into my gift, how surprised he was at Mother's anticipation, how delighted that I had given her reason to smile again, to laugh.

Heather and Kurt arrived from Ralston late in the afternoon on
Christmas Eve. We served a buffet of appetizers: little sausages in a spicy
chili sauce, hot artichoke and spinach dip, pot stickers, meatballs on
skewers, raw vegetables with dill spread. In deference to Mother's medication regimen, we debated whether or not to mix the champagne and
brandy punch.

"That's ridiculous," she said. "It's not Christmas without tradition,"
and she seemed perfectly happy to sip on club soda and cranberry juice.
She could barely stay in her seat, hopping up and down to refill drinks or
replenish trays of food.

Trey was allowed to open one gift. He unwrapped plastic Mega Bloks
and worked the rest of the evening building wonky-shaped garages for
his collection of toy cars. Despite his protests to play "just two more minutes, Mommy," I bathed him, gave him one last drink of water, read *B
is for Bethlehem* and tucked him in. "Remember, buddy, Santa comes
tomorrow, but we'll have to wait to open presents until Grammy and
Grandfather come."

In the morning, I heard my Pennick grandparents arrive just as I was
changing Trey. Before going downstairs, he banged on the door of the
guest room. "Unca Kurt. Aunt Heather. It's Santa time."

"They'll be along in a minute. Let's go say hello to Grammy and
Grandfather."

He clutched his teddy bear with one hand and held onto the spindles of the railing with the other as he descended one step at a time. "It's Santa time. It's Santa time."

Santa had left a play kitchen complete with charcoal grill and burners that clicked when turned. I had found it at a rummage sale in a ritzy development in Whitefish Bay at the end of the summer and Dad let me store it at the mill. The woman who sold it to me said her daughter never really used it much, which explained its near-new condition, but I knew Trey would love pretending to flip burgers with the big plastic spatula.

His stocking bulged with plastic food for the grill—burger patties, hot dogs, corn-on-the-cob, squares of yellow cheese and white onion slices, puffy sandwich buns dotted with fake sesame seeds, and bottles of picnic-fare condiments—all of which he insisted on carrying to his place at the breakfast table. He began to take orders for dinner on the grill before I had taken my first sip of juice, and throughout the meal he kept seasoning his eggs with fake ketchup, encouraging the rest of us to do the same. As we cleared the table and loaded the dishwasher, Kurt kept yelling "order up" and listing outrageous burger combinations, much to Trey's delight.

In the living room, we gathered around the tree. Mother enlisted Trey's help to hand out some of the smaller presents but she delivered the larger ones herself. We all watched Trey unwrap his gifts—a make-your-own monster puppet kit from Heather and Kurt, zoo-themed foam floor tiles from Grammy and Grandfather, and stackable, weighted spheres from Dad and Mother. He squealed when he opened the mini-trampoline from me. Dad and Kurt had spent nearly an hour the night before threading the nylon cording through the grommets on the trampoline bed, pulling it tight and tying it off. They assembled the soft safety cushion to cover the frame and attached the handle Trey would hold to stabilize himself as he jumped.

Mother's disapproval at my choice of toys was palpable. She had watched the assembly in silence, but as I covered the trampoline with an old green blanket and wedged it behind Dad's recliner, she scolded, "Little boys can get hurt all on their own. Trey doesn't need any help from you."

"Reviews on this model are really good, Mother. Besides, it beats him jumping from the couch and the bed. Think of it as controlled chaos."

She said nothing more on the subject, but her dismissive *I'm going to bed* took on the tone of, "I can't stand to be in the same room with such a negligent mother."

Her surliness was gone Christmas morning, however, and she even managed to join in the family chorus of "Go, Trey, go," shouted in sync with his bouncing.

With Trey engrossed in play, the rest of us opened our gifts in turn. Heather and Kurt each received leather travel kits and a year's subscription to a travel magazine. Mother and Dad gave my Pennick grandparents gift certificates for a swanky restaurant downtown, and I gave them a calendar featuring pictures of Trey I had created online. I gave duplicates of the calendar to Dad and Mother—one for the mill and another for the kitchen wall.

Mother cooed over her gift set of luxury fragrance and rich, scented body cream from Heather and Kurt and the crystal fruit bowl from my Pennick grandparents. Dad was equally pleased with the tackle box from my aunt and uncle and a cordless drill from Grammy and Grandfather. For one another, Dad and Mother did what they always had done, electing not to exchange gifts in lieu of some promised future purchase they would never make.

Finally, there were only the gifts from Trey and me to Dad and Mother. Dad opened his first. I had splurged on a wireless remote for his television and media components. His reaction was almost comical as he balanced his weak protestations of "Luce, this is too much," with the far more exuberant, "What a great gift. I mean a really great gift."

Mother had saved the quilt for the grand finale.

She slipped a finger under each corner of the vintage card and lifted it slowly lest she tear either the tag or the gold foil. And then, as carefully as she had wrapped the package, she removed the paper with bow intact, sliced through the tape on the box, and peeled the layers of tissue one at a time. I found myself holding my breath. Silly, I suppose, since I knew what was in the box, but Mother's reverence created an aura of anticipation I could feel.

When the quilt was finally revealed, Mother spread it over the back of the couch. Dad walked over to her and held her from behind. I saw him whisper something in her ear, and she smiled in response. Grandfather said he had never seen anything quite like it.

Heather knelt on the floor to examine each square more closely. Grammy Elnora leaned over her shoulder and stretched to touch the lettering. "I remember him wearing this one. And this . . ." There was just the slightest catch in her voice.

"Bets," Heather turned to Mother, "the workmanship is incredible. And what an inspired idea."

"Yes, yes it was," Mother answered. I waited for the acknowledgment I knew must be coming, but instead she joined Grammy and Heather to recall events memorialized on the quilt.

Dad slipped beside me and wrapped his forearm around my neck in a loose embrace. He kissed my temple. "Luce, you've given her an amazing gift today. Thank you. She hasn't been this happy in long time."

It should have been enough to see her happy. It should have been enough to know I had been the source of that happiness. I convinced myself it was enough, for a time.

But later, when I was setting aside reusable bows and crumpling scraps of torn wrapping paper for the garbage, I picked up the neatly folded foil and the Clapsaddle card Mother had used for a tag. Beneath the picture of the little boy, I read *To: Mom*. And under the picture of the girl, *From: Jonny*.

With deliberate malice, I tore the card in half and stuffed the pieces in the bag with the rest of the trash.

SIXTY-FOUR

If I had a place to go and the money to do so, I would have left home that afternoon. I was finished with Mother. Done.

Logic told me I was being childish. Gifts are just that. Gifts. Something offered to another person for the sole pleasure of the recipient. No conditions. No strings attached. No reciprocity needed.

I would have made a lousy philanthropist, I guess, because I wanted payback. I wanted her appreciation. I *needed* her acknowledgment. At the very least, I needed her to know I was hurt. And I wanted her to suffer because she had been the one to hurt me.

That would have been Mother's gift to me.

SIXTY-FIVE

During the weeks before Christmas, when Mother's cheery focus fooled me into thinking she was truly, finally, ready to move on, I had applied for the graduate program in community counseling at UW Milwaukee. Classes were to meet Mondays, Wednesdays, and Fridays in the afternoon with the occasional seminar on Tuesday mornings. On most days Trey would be down for his nap and I thought I could count on Mother to babysit. Earning a degree a few credit hours at a time would take longer, but I was willing to start slowly.

After the Christmas quilt incident, I withdrew my application, ate the loss of my registration fee, and made other plans. By the third week in January, I had taken a job at La Petite Academy on Woodburn. Free tuition for Trey was the biggest benefit at La Petite, and I planned to squirrel away every last penny so I could rent an efficiency apartment and move out within a few months. Dad was still paying me for part-time clerical work at the mill on weekends, but that wasn't enough to live on.

I passed the required physical, completed the mandatory training in CPR and first aid and signed up for one of the in-house professional development classes. The pay wasn't great, but it was a start.

Because Trey had always been an early riser, I accepted a job as the opener, starting my eight-hour shift at six in the morning. I was stationed in the lobby to assist parents who, armed with the PIN number for our electronic lock, signed in and shunted their children to the various toddler and pre-K classrooms or to the infants' rooms. On those dark, frigid mornings before the academy opened, many parents with weeks-old babies were there before I arrived. They waited in cars with heaters blasting, anxious to be on the freeway before morning rush hour made the commutes impossibly long. Most clients, however, had toddlers who dictated a later arrival time. I loved seeing the children every morning, their eyes often puffy with sleep, hair unruly beneath stocking caps. Some carried their favorite stuffed animals, either protectively wedged between forearm and chest or dragged nonchalantly over icy, salt-sprinkled sidewalks.

I prided myself on remembering the names of these "auxiliary" enrollees which thrilled Cathy, our director.

"Good morning, Sophia. How is Lady Roxy today?"

"Max! Is that Bodhi with you? He looks hungry."

"Gus. Did you remember to give Wrigley Bear a hug for me at bedtime last night?"

I enjoyed my status as greeter far more my afternoon counterpart, Julie, liked hers. She had the sometimes unpleasant job of verifying identities of people claiming their little ones at the end of the day. Less than two weeks from my start date, Julie and I were sharing lunch when she described an ugly encounter with a divorced dad who had been called upon by his ex-wife to do pick-up duty. The mother, a corporate VP, had missed a connection in Chicago and had been unable to reach her sister, the usual back-up. Her ex must have entered the PIN wrong, perhaps transposing numbers. When he couldn't gain access, he started pounding on the glass and yelling obscenities. Julie asked him to produce his driver's license. He refused. She tried, unsuccessfully, to calm him and simultaneously alert other staff that children should be cleared from the lobby area. Ultimately she had to call the police because the man threatened to get a sledgehammer and "break the goddamned windows" if he didn't get his daughter "right this fucking minute." In the meantime, the little girl's aunt showed up and bundled her into her SUV just as the police hauled her father away in handcuffs.

I had not been a witness, but I had no trouble imagining the scene. I only needed to substitute Mother's face for that of the irate father. How many times had I watched her lose it, watched her frenzy reach out with claws of brass to rake her victims? And when those on the fringe of her fury realized she was a mother, a wife, how many times had I curled and withered from their stares of disbelief or—worse—their pity?

"Whose father was it?" I asked Julie. I had to know.

"Lily. In pre-K. You know, that little red headed girl with the freckles? The one who wears . . ."

"Lily." I knew her immediately. No matter how early she arrived at La Petite, she was always put together, always dressed in coordinated leggings, patterned overskirt, matching sweater, expensive coat. She could have been a child model in a fashion magazine, but her designer wardrobe would not protect her. She would remain a pawn in the chess game her parents played until the ultimate checkmate. And while the academy staff would try to minimize the risk with math games and writing centers and craft time and character education, Lily would always be vulnerable. Vulnerable as Jonny had been to Mother's obsession. Vulnerable as I was, still.

Sixty-Six

At the end of my shift, rich from dependable days full of children bright and capable, children who struggled, children who laughed easily and who threw tantrums over the disputed ownership of a Lego block, I could manage the emptiness at home.

The euphoria which sustained Mother over Christmas had vanished, as I knew it would. On the morning of Valentine's Day, she rose early and baked a four-layer German chocolate cake, Jonny's favorite. She had attacked the caramel frosting, chunky with pecans and grated coconut, beating it until it was satiny smooth. She placed the cake on Grandmother Lucinda's heirloom crystal pedestal, covered it with the glass dome, and propped a framed picture of Jonny beside it.

After dinner, Dad told Mother her cake was a great way to honor Jonny's birthday. She smiled, nodding. But when he lifted the dome to cut the first slice, she placed her hand gently over his.

"It's for Jonny." Her matter-of-fact tone, more frightening than the absurdity of her words, paralyzed Dad. He looked at Mother as if, by staring into her eyes, he might find something to remind him of the woman she used to be. He replaced the lid, slid the knife and cake server back into the utensils drawer, and walked out of the house. He did not come home until the following morning, but I don't know if his absence even registered with Mother. She spent the night locked in Jonny's room.

After that, each day replicated the day before. Like copies of copies, they faded and blurred and bled into one another until they were indistinguishable.

Mother was never out of bed when I left for La Petite in the morning, and when Trey and I came in late in the afternoon, she was in Jonny's room, the door locked against intrusion.

She still joined us for dinner, but she had no more substance than a watery hologram. Most nights she sat with her head down, looking at none of us. She did not eat. She did not speak. The weight fell away until she was knobby, all cheekbones and shoulder blades and ribcage. Blue smudges circled her eyes. Her complexion dried, grayed, flaked, aging her until she was a caricature of herself.

Only Trey's chatter and my anecdotes chased silence from the kitchen table. One evening I shared stories of Marie, a precocious two-year-old who assembled floor puzzles as though it were her job, and Rocke, who memorized George Strait songs as easily as nursery rhymes, belting out the lyrics as he ate his morning snack.

Another night I described little Ryan, a Down's Syndrome child who incessantly tugged at my pant leg several times a day chanting "Miss Luce, Miss Luce, Miss Luce, Miss Luce" until I looked down to acknowledge him. Each time I asked, "What, Ryan? What do you want?" he would smile and point out something in the room. I would dutifully smile back and murmur, "Yes, Ryan, I see the picture of the lion. Yes, Ryan, I see the yellow block. Yes, Ryan, I see your shoes are tied."

We had replayed the scenario at least six times within a half hour when he began his refrain again. "Miss Luce, Miss Luce, Miss Luce, Miss Luce."

I turned to him with more exasperation than I was willing to admit. "What *is* it, Ryan? What do you have to tell me?" Happy to have my attention, he said, "Miss Luce, I *luuuuv* you."

Dad snickered. "Guess you felt pretty small, hey, Luce?"

"You have no idea."

"So what did you do?" Dad asked.

"What else could I do? I knelt down and said 'Ryan, Ryan, Ryan, Ryan, I *luuuv* you, too."

His mouth full of peas, Trey mimicked me. "I *luuuv* you, too."

Dad laughed, turned to Mother and said, "Bets, isn't that a hoot? Can't you just picture that little guy?" She simply rose from the table, scraped her meal into the garbage disposal, climbed the stairs to Jonny's room, and locked the door.

One night in June, Trey was fitful. He had a wicked summer cold and was clammy from a high fever. I was refilling the cold mist humidifier in his room when I heard a whispered conversation in the hall. I half expected to find Mother speaking to Jonny as if he were standing in front of her. Instead, she had planted herself at the threshold of Jonny's room, barring Dad's access.

"Bets, come to bed. Just for tonight. Why don't we talk for awhile?"

"About what, Nolan? What do you want to talk about?"

"God, I don't know. Do you need an agenda? Note cards? Let's start with this—Jonny's gone, but we're still here. We're still here, Bets. Do you hear me? Jesus. I lost him, too. He was my son, too, and I miss him. I'd do anything, Bets, anything to make it better. Let me help you. Let me help us."

"Can you give Jonny back to me?" She waited, punishing him. "No? Then at least give me this." She gestured to the room behind her. "It's the only place I can breathe, Nolan. This is the only place where I can still feel him. Please, Nolan. Please don't do this."

"Do you even want me here, Bets? Am I in your way?"

"No. I just need you to understand," she pleaded.

"How can I understand when you don't talk to me? You spend more time with Jonny's ghost than you do with the living, breathing members of this family. For Chrissakes, Bets. Tell me what there is to understand. Tell me what to do. I'm going crazy here. You're killing me."

I stepped back into Trey's room and eased the door shut. I sat in the rocker by his bed, but I did not sleep, haunted by my son's labored breathing and by the hollow desperation in my father's plea.

In the morning, Trey was still spiking a fever so I called Cathy at La Petite to ask for another family illness day. I gave him some children's Tylenol and went downstairs to start a pot of coffee. Dad was already gone. I didn't expect to see him until lunch, so I was surprised when he came through the kitchen door a few minutes later carrying a couple of cardboard boxes. They had apparently been stored for a long time because they had gone soft with age. The sides bulged with the weight of their contents, and I sneezed at the unpleasant odor—part mill, part mold.

Dad hefted the boxes to the counter and dropped them with relief.

"Coffee ready?" he asked.

"Soon. What's this?"

"They're for your mother."

"What's in them?"

"Jonny's stuff. From when he was growing up." He took a mug from the cabinet and stood impatiently by the coffee maker. "There are several more like this in the back room at the mill. I'll haul the rest over today when I can." He pushed the power button to stop the brew process, poured himself a cup and rested his hand on the top box. "She wants to go through them. I don't what good it will do. Everything just seems to make her sad."

"I heard you talking last night, Dad. I didn't mean to eavesdrop, but when I heard voices . . ."

"Don't worry, Luce," Dad said. "And don't apologize. I just don't know how to help her. She said she can't go forward unless she is at peace with the past. I don't know how she thinks she's going to find peace dredging up memories, but she wants to go through the boxes, save important things, donate the stuff she can stand to let go, throw away anything too far gone to save."

"Actually, that sounds pretty reasonable, Dad. Maybe this is a good thing," I offered.

"I'd feel better if she'd let me be a part of it." He shrugged. "But she won't. She thinks Jonny's death happened to *her*. She thinks she's the only one who suffers." He shook his head. "You know what she said to me? She said I just go on about my business like Jonny never existed, like it doesn't matter. She said I didn't love Jonny as much as she does." His voice cracked. "She even said I didn't love Christopher the way she did."

"Dad. Dad, I'm so sorry. You shouldn't listen to that. You can't."

"I told her it was like cutting out my heart when they died. But I can't stop living. I told her *we* can't stop living." He rubbed his eyes. "I think the only time she listened to me is when I asked her if this is what Jonny would want her to do. I said, 'Bets, would he want you to give up? Would he want you to be sad all the time?' She got real quiet, like she was really thinking about it."

"So this is her solution?" I asked. "She wants to sort through all these boxes?"

"Yeah, but she's hell-bent on doing it alone."

"Then let her, Dad. Let her."

By the end of the day, boxes had been stacked outside Jonny's door, two deep, three or four high. Freckled with fuzzy mildew, they were musty and, I feared, an attractive nuisance to Trey. If the bacteria from the mold didn't aggravate his allergies, then certainly the urge to climb the boxes was an accident in the making.

Surprisingly, Mother agreed. She offered to empty each box onto the floor in Jonny's room where she could take her time with the sorting process. Then she would dispose of the moldy cardboard and haul out everything she wasn't saving in plastic garbage bags.

She was so thin, so frail, but she wrestled each box into Jonny's room. Crouched as though she were the anchor player in a tug-of-war, she backed them across the floor, dragging one corner toward her, then the other, until she had cleared the hall. Jonny's room wasn't very big, and I imagined her as a demented hoarder, happily surrounded by all the precious trash she couldn't bear to toss.

SIXTY-SEVEN

Several days passed before I saw evidence of progress. When Trey and I stepped off the bus after work and made our way down the drive, Mother was standing a few feet away from the burn barrel in the field adjacent to the house, iron poker in hand. Judging by the ribbons of heat rising from the barrel, whatever she had fed to the flames was still smoldering.

She reached into a brown paper grocery bag and grabbed what appeared to scraps of paper and glossy photographs. These she dropped into the barrel, jabbing at them with the poker until delicate fragments like blackened butterflies rose on the heat.

"Do you need any help, Mother? I can get a snack for Trey and give you some relief," I offered.

"No. I'm nearly done anyway."

I had trouble imagining her destroying snapshots of Jonny, but when I moved closer to see, she hurriedly upended the bag over the barrel. Two pictures fluttered errantly to the ground. One was of Jonny standing beside the Superhawk. In the other, a torn remnant, Mo's face in three-quarter profile grinned toward the absent half of the picture.

"I have duplicates," she said defensively as she scooped them up.

"Okay," I said. "I'll see you inside."

Her criteria would be simple, then. Anything perceived to be a threat to Jonny would be purged. Who else, I wondered, had been ripped from her son and cast aside?

SIXTY-EIGHT

White plastic garbage bags with red draw strings lined the porch. There were a couple of boxes piled with wooden puzzles, picture books, a lap-sized chalk board, and children's board games like Candy Land and Mousetrap and Operation. Another box held a kid-sized easel and a Fisher-Price farm, silo attached, complete with plastic cow, horse, sheep, and pig.

"Are you sure you don't want to have a rummage sale before fall sets in?" I asked Mother. "Baby gear is always in demand. We could just wash these removable covers and sanitize the rest with disinfectant. Really, high chairs and baby swings are big-ticket items."

"No. I want everything gone."

I tried to salvage a few toys Trey might use, but when I pulled an Etch-a-Sketch free from one of the boxes, Mother insisted I put it back.

"I'll buy a new one for him," she said.

"Mother, that's crazy . . ."

Dad cut me off with a murderous look. He was loading the Cherokee under Mother's direction, mindful to keep the items destined for Goodwill separate from those headed to the landfill.

"Leave it, Luce," he said. "I promised your mother she could decide what we'd do with all this. But then it's over." He turned to Mother for confirmation. "Right, Bets? We're going to move on? Just like we talked about?"

If she acknowledged her agreement to such an arrangement, I missed it, but Dad seemed satisfied.

"Anything left in the house for this trip?" he asked. "Okay, let's go."

Mother settled herself on the passenger side and looked straight ahead as Dad turned around in the drive. I expected her to cry as they carted Jonny's things away, but she was stoic.

There would be many other similar weekend trips, different from the first only because they hauled away smaller, fewer loads of clothes and boxes of toys meant for increasingly older children.

A kind of pathetic determination seemed to drive her. She was methodical and thorough, detailing each item on a spreadsheet for tax purposes. Often, at the end of the day, I could hear the printer in Jonny's room cranking out the paperwork documenting every donation. Given Mother's obsessions, she would describe each item, note the manufacturer, the condition, the fair market price and then print multiple copies *just in case*. The process stretched on until I could not believe there was anything left in Jonny's room, but she kept boxes and bags coming as regularly as shipments on a factory conveyor belt.

She had promised Dad she would finish before Thanksgiving, before Heather and Kurt joined us for the holiday. It looked as though she intended to keep that promise.

SIXTY-NINE

I **woke to Sevendust's "The Past."** From the iPod in the kitchen, Daughtry's throaty vocals played against smooth harmonies and soulful guitar. It was as though he had written an anthem of rebirth just for me.

I felt alive. The week before, I had signed a year's lease for a one-bedroom apartment in the Hillside Village complex on Swartz Drive. The check for my deposit and first month's rent had cleared, and I needed only to set up electrical service in my name. Trey and I would be in our own place the first of December. I had landed the cheapest unit in the building by virtue of its sub-level location. The rooms were boxy and unimaginative, the walls starkly white. They would be a blank canvas, a clean start.

I could not anticipate Mother's response, so I would delay telling her until just before we moved. She could explode or be indifferent, but I was beyond caring. I just didn't want to hurt Dad. My resolve had been strong until I actually broke the news to him.

He reacted with ambivalence. Selfishly, he wanted me to stay. Realistically, he knew I needed to go. "I can't lie, Luce. It'll be tough not seeing you and Trey every day," he said, "but it's time you took this step. Past time, really."

Fortified by his blessing, I nearly crumbled. "If you need me to stick around for a couple of months, I could probably . . ."

He drew me in to him in a fierce hug. "Where did you come from, Luce? Who taught you to worry about everybody else? It sure as hell wasn't your mother or me." He held me at arm's length, searching my face. "No, I need you to be your own person, not run interference for me. I've made so many stinking mistakes for such a long time. But I'm not going to mess this up."

"I love you, Dad. I don't want this to be hard on you."

He shook his head. "Sometimes I wonder if you can ever forgive me. I did things . . . stood by when . . ."

"Stop it, Dad."

"No, Luce. I've never told you, not once, how sorry I am. Jesus, I sent you away . . ."

"It wasn't exactly Siberia, Dad. And you had to do something. If you remember, I wasn't winning any congeniality awards with Mother."

"If I ran the mill the way I ran this house," he managed a rueful smile, "Mr. Matthews would have fired me years ago. I'm supposed to be good at managing people. It's what I do, Luce. I'm the fix-it guy there. But for the life of me, I don't know where the tipping point came with your mother. Was she gone before Jonny died? Was she, Luce? You'd know better than me. I lived with her every day and I can't tell you when she crossed the line, when there was no more going back, no way to repair the damage. I should have been able to tell, Luce. And I should have stopped her. God, things would have been different if I'd stopped her."

I was crying, then. He pulled his handkerchief from his back pocket and held it to my nose as though I were four. "Blow," he commanded. He pulled me to him again, whispering against my forehead.

"And then Jonny died. I tried to understand. I knew what he meant to her, what she was going through. I couldn't deny her anything. My God, Luce, I helped him buy that goddamned cycle. I just felt so guilty. I just didn't want her to hurt anymore."

He was silent for so long, I leaned back to look at him, but he pressed my face into the hollow beneath his chin. I could feel the tiny, steady drum of his pulse against my cheek. "I lost Christopher. I lost Jonny. I'm losing your mother. I don't want to lose you, too. If you stay here, she'll swallow you up. You and Trey. You need to go, Luce. You need to go."

I hugged him to me. If it had been possible, I would have pulled him into me and through me.

SEVENTY

Thanksgiving.

Following Heather's last class on Wednesday afternoon, my aunt and uncle drove straight through from Ralston, arriving in Waukesha sometime after one in the morning. When I heard them come in, I slipped on a sweatshirt and went to the top of the stairs to say hello and offer help with luggage, but they waved me away. "We're fine. We'll unload in the morning," Kurt said. He grinned. "I mean we'll unload later *this* morning. Go back to bed."

Despite their late arrival, they were in the kitchen with Dad when Trey and I came down for breakfast. Danish pastries from Kurt's favorite bakery in La Vista were arranged on a platter and thick bacon strips sizzled in the iron skillet. Heather was whipping eggs with half-and-half while Kurt sliced apples, oranges and bananas for fruit compote. Dad was at the sink, seeding a pomegranate.

"Lady Luce and Little Man Trey!" Kurt grinned. He wiped his hands before swinging Trey around in dizzying circles.

Heather gathered me into her arms. "Sweetheart. It's so good to see you. Happy Thanksgiving."

"How was the drive?" I asked. "I bet you're exhausted."

"I never understood the school board's thinking when they set the calendar," Heather complained. "Even though a fourth of my students are absent on Wednesday because they're traveling for the holiday, we still hold classes. Why couldn't they eliminate one of our professional development days and extend the Thanksgiving break?" She shrugged in apology. "Listen to me. I'm sorry. It's just been a bad week."

"What's going on?" I asked.

"Just one of my students . . .," Heather began.

"Do we really have to talk shop today?" Kurt interrupted.

"She didn't offer. I asked." I turned back to Heather. "Spill it. You'll feel better."

"I don't know if anything will make me feel better about this. I've got an incredibly gifted young man, a senior, intent on throwing his life away. I had him in AP Lang and Comp last year. Brilliant student. He asked me to write a letter of recommendation for him because he wanted to apply to Northwestern. Early decision candidate. I made him sound like the Messiah—and, from what I had seen in class, he deserved every glowing word. He was accepted, declared the first of this month, and you know how he celebrated? He smoked weed, evidently a perk from a little enterprise he had going on the side. He'd been selling it as well, or—at least had the intent to sell. All this came to a head on Monday. I guess his parents found bags and a scale in his room along with a wad of cash. They called the cops. In the meantime, the kid ran. He hasn't been back to school since, and I don't know if he's hiding out with friends or has skipped altogether."

"That's rough. I'm sorry. I know how much you invest in your kids at school, Aunt Heather."

"Sometimes more than they invest in themselves, apparently. Anyway, thanks for listening. I appreciate it, but my disappointment is nothing compared to what he's doing to himself. Foolish, impulsive kid. Half of me wants to take him home and straighten him out. The other half wants to knock him in the head with a two-by-four."

"And on that cheery note, my darling wife, drop it. Take a vacation from worrying, okay?" Kurt said.

"Right. You're always right," she laughed.

"Anybody catch that on tape?" Kurt asked. "I'd like video documentation for future reference." Aunt Heather punched him playfully in the shoulder.

"Not to change the subject . . .," he paused, considering. "Strike that. I very much want to change the subject. Luce, my brother says he's finally getting you out of the house. He told me this morning that he couldn't stand your mooching off him anymore, so he's throwing you out on your ear."

Dad chuckled. "Yep, that's exactly what I said. She and Trey can't vacate fast enough for my liking. I've already packed her bags for her."

"It's no wonder you want out," Heather shot a look of mock sympathy. "Living with a Neanderthal can be so trying."

"Seriously, Luce, congratulations. You have to be excited."

"Yes," I said. "And a little sad, too." Unexpectedly, tears welled up. "How embarrassing is this? I'm pushing thirty and I'm blubbering like a homesick baby. I haven't even moved out yet. Geesh." I grabbed a paper towel and dabbed at my eyes. "Okay, enough. I'll pretend to be a big girl."

"Who's hungry?" Heather said. "You'll be able to bounce these eggs like rubber balls if they cook any longer."

"If you want to put Trey in his booster seat, Kurt, I'll help Heather fill the plates," I offered.

"Okay. I'll just go upstairs and get Bets," Dad said.

"Upstairs?" Kurt asked. "I thought she was still asleep."

"She is probably sleeping," Dad answered, "but she sleeps upstairs, not down here in our room."

"Upstairs?" Kurt repeated. "In Jonny's room? How long has that been going on?"

"That's none of your business," Heather said.

"Hey, man, sorry. I didn't mean to overstep."

"Forget it," Dad assured him. "It's not like we can hide it. Bets has been . . . working through some stuff. I think she's trying. For the past few months she's been going through all those boxes I kept over at the mill. You know, all those things of Jonny's she's saved over the years? Believe it or not, she's been really good about sorting through it all, hasn't she, Luce?" He looked to me for confirmation.

"Yeah," I agreed. "She's thrown some stuff away, but most of it she gave to Goodwill. Mother and Dad have made enough trips to the donation center that they're on a first-name basis with the staff there. Who knows, we're probably on their Christmas mailing list."

"I think it's the healthiest thing she's done in a long time. Maybe she's finally letting go," Dad said.

"Okay, but why is she sleeping there?" Kurt insisted. "Is *that* healthy?"

"Again," Heather said, more insistently, "need-to-know basis. You don't need to know."

"Like we have any secrets here," Dad countered. "Through the worst of it, Bets seemed to be better when she could be in his room. Calmer, you know? Not happy, but she could function. I never thought she'd part with anything of his, but she has. Now, maybe since the physical stuff is gone . . ." He looked at each of us and shrugged. "This is a tough time for her, especially today and tomorrow. If being in Jonny's room helps her, well, . . . it's hard for me to say no."

"Got it," Kurt said. "Okay, enough meddling. Why don't you go up and tell her artery-clogging bacon, primo pastries, and Heather's *eggs extraordinaire* are on the menu?"

"Thanks. We'll be down in a minute."

Dad took the stairs two at a time and rapped gently on Jonny's door. "Bets? Babe, breakfast is ready."

When she did not answer, he knocked more forcefully. "Bets. Heather and Kurt have breakfast on the table and Trey is starving. Bets?"

Out of habit, he tried the door, expecting to find it locked as usual. Was he surprised when it opened at his touch? Was there no longer a barrier separating them?

He found Mother, her eyes bright with accomplishment, sitting on the edge of a bed that had not been slept in.

We followed his anguish, the siren of his wordless whine, to stand beside him in Jonny's room.

SEVENTY-ONE

Had her grief turned to madness, or did it simply forget to latch the door, a lazy gatekeeper who beckoned demons to crowd the chambers of her mind until only darkness, confusion, and surrender remained?

Dad surrendered, too, but I could not call him cowardly. He gathered the meager remnants of his resolve and waved a flag of retreat, a flag gray with exhaustion and unbearable sorrow. He could not muster strength enough to fight her illness anymore. I could not blame him. He held the line longer than I had.

But now there would be no going back, no way to repair the damage, no sanity left to salvage.

SEVENTY-TWO

Jonny's **room whispered. It spoke** with a thousand tongues, beguiling in its awful beauty. Mother had become the master builder for the tomb of her boy-king, and in it she had assembled the artifacts of his life.

Walls. Ceiling. Windows. Closet. Shelves. Nightstand. Dresser. She had cloaked them all beneath a shroud of loss. The media of her transformation? A lifetime of memories—photos and papers and drawings, diary pages and long, rambling letters written to Jonny after his death—cataloged with no chronology, no pattern discernible to anyone but her.

She had begun at the baseboard, fixing each piece of paper, each picture, to the wall with a dab of hot glue. When she had completed a full circle of the room, she started over, the second layer barely overlapping the first. Tier after tier, a living mosaic emerged, dreadful and fantastic, each piece individually prized because Jonny had made it or used it or owned it or earned it.

I could not turn my eyes away. I could not move. But I could see Jonny when I read and remembered. And I could see Jonny in the years I never knew him.

The certificate he earned in the high jump on Track and Field Day in fifth grade.

A line from a school assignment when he was eight: *If I had one wish, I'd play baseball with the Cubs and live an easy life.*

Jonny's name in hand-lettered calligraphy on a "Mr. Hustle" Sportsmanship Award for middle school wrestling,

Impossibly small fingerprints on heavy cardstock from Police Safety Week: *Jonathan Ian Garrison, age 6.*

Participation ribbons stapled to a North Side Elementary Gymnastics Meet award certificate.

Pages from an eighth-grade Spanish assignment: *Vivo con mi familia en Waukesha, Wisconsin. Tengo me madre y padre. Mi familia es muy importante a mi.*

Labored printing on wide-lined penmanship paper: *"LiDDl Antz Frist Piknik" by Jonny.*

Elementary Pupil Progress Report for Jonny Garrison: *Jonny understands basic ideas in science.* And on another: *Acceptable progress in spelling.*

Illustrated first-grade alligator poetry: *Alligator cheese/alligator cheese/if I don't get some/I'm going to freeze.*

The driving test score sheet from the Wisconsin Department of Transportation, imprinted with "pass for class" by the examiner.

Jonny's entry in the end-of-year fourth-grade memory booklet, addressed to the custodians Mr. Ranes and Mr. Harris: *You always cleaned up our messes. Thank you.*

The Presidential Academic Fitness award, complete with a gold lapel pin rimmed in blue and embossed with the official seal—an eagle holding an olive branch in one talon and arrows in the other.

A handwritten note from his social studies teacher: *Jonny did a fine job on his Colonial Days report today.*

A worksheet from Dinosaur Crazy Day. *Directions: Circle five things that don't belong in this picture.* Jonny had earned a smiley face sticker for correctly identifying a balloon, a soccer ball, a rocket ship, an elephant, and a caveman.

Perfect attendance certificates.

A hand-made card for Mother: three construction paper triangles pasted into the outline of a pine tree and decorated with Christmas lights cut from scraps of wallpaper.

A self-reflective essay presented at conference time: *I am most proud of getting better grades last quarter. When I get bad grades Mom doesn't get mad unless I don't try my hardest.*

Annotated notecard for a speech on why music and sports don't mix: *Could you picture Elvis in a baseball uniform? (Pause for laffs).*

Mother did not discriminate. Nothing of Jonny's was too insignificant, too inconsequential to post. For every piece of paper, there were thousands more. And scattered among them, hundreds and hundreds of pictures.

Jonny, age 4, dressed in denim jacket and black cowboy hat, clutching a fistful of leaves.

Jonny in a puffy orange life vest holding his first catch, a fish no bigger than his palm.

Jonny sound asleep in his high chair, his face smeared with spaghetti sauce.

Jonny pretending pain as Dad faked a wrestling hold.

Jonny busy with shovel in plastic turtle sandbox.

Jonny, #34, crouching as he balanced a Wilson Varsity basketball on his right knee in the seventh-grade team photo.

Jonny hoisted high above Grandfather Pennick's head.

Jonny peddling a Power Trac toy tractor.

Jonny posed as a Halloween pirate with black eyepatch, penciled-in moustache and red bandanna.

Jonny wearing a white Oshkosh shirt with red piping and blue stripes in an undated school photo.

Jonny peering over the edge of a Little Tykes football toy chest.

Jonny in new braces, captioned in his own hand: *Metal Mouth. Railroad tracks.*

Jonny washing his tricycle.

Jonny, slender but athletic, in maroon *Metro YMCA* T-shirt.

Jonny belly surfing on a water slide.

Jonny holding a plaque, shaking hands with the distinguished presenter; behind him, bleachers full of students on their feet, applauding.

Jonny straddling a low-hanging branch of a massive oak.

Jonny with three friends, all in Badger football helmets and red jerseys.

Jonny in footed sleeper, old Gunner at his side, staring out the window at snow.

Jonny was everywhere we looked, and we looked everywhere. Mother had even lined his closet walls with pictures, but my brother appeared in none of them. Instead, each toy and game she had willingly given away were photographed and displayed, a shrine to his every childhood passion.

In a tragic room, Mother was the greatest tragedy.

"Nolan, Nolan. It's finally finished. Everything's ready for him."

SEVENTY-THREE

Mother told the hospitalist on staff in the psych ward that Jonny spoke to her through the car radio. He whispered in her ear the location of misplaced house keys. Like the good son she had raised him to be, he always remembered her birthday and Mother's Day, and last year he gave her the very best Christmas gift ever. She couldn't wait to see what he had planned this year. Her Jonny didn't need a special occasion, though, to show his consideration for her. Even as busy as he was, he took time to respond to the letters she wrote almost daily. She kept them, she said, in a safe place at home where she could see them whenever she wanted. Wouldn't the doctors and nurses like to read them?

She had been committed less than twenty-four hours before Grandfather Aldrich began the search for a long-term community residential facility. Determined his only child would not wither in a mental hospital, he researched alternatives which might provide rehabilitation for Mother. The best places were out east, he concluded. Most did not accept insurance or third-party payers, but cost didn't matter. He and Grammy Elnora would insist upon a place specializing in treatment of severe, persistent mental illness, but it must, *must,* feel like home. No lock-ups. No bars on the windows. No physical restraints.

His search led him to the Greystone Program associated with the Friends Hospital in Philadelphia. Their credentials were impeccable. Family members of present and past Greystone residents wrote glowing testimonials citing the individual, personal attention their loved ones received from the treatment team.

Most importantly, Mother fit the admission criteria, headlined by her prolonged mental illness. She was over twenty-one, she didn't suffer from a major physical disability, nor was she typically destructive. Mother's psychiatrist provided documentation of her illness, previous failed treatment protocols, and his recommendation for placement in the program as soon as an opening became available. Her spot on the waiting list was expedited, no doubt, by the financial statements my Pennick grandparents tendered with the application and by the letter for special consideration Grandfather Aldrich submitted on stationary bearing the name of the law firm he founded.

The Greystone director screened Mother, found her to be one who could benefit from the program, and initiated the necessary paperwork.

"Patients stay at Friends for a minimum of three months with the hope of moving to a more independent setting over time," the director advised. "Still, her placement might very well last years, perhaps even a lifetime. Much will depend upon Elizabeth herself."

"Bets," my grandfather corrected. "You'll need to call her Bets."

SEVENTY-FOUR

Dad had instructed the auctioneer to hold nothing in reserve on the day of the sale. Except for clothes and personal items, everything would be put on the block, even the farmhouse. The buyer could take possession at closing. Proceeds from the sale would go toward rent on a furnished one-bedroom apartment not far from Friends Hospital.

Mr. Matthews had been generous. Immediately after Mother's breakdown, Dad took an unpaid, personal hardship leave of absence from the mill, but at his boss's insistence, he had continued to collect a paycheck for "unused vacation." It was a bruising act of charity for Dad.

Once Mother's admission into the Greystone Program had been secured, he gave notice of his retirement, with one caveat. He would appreciate a letter of recommendation when he sought employment in Philadelphia. Mr. Matthews offered to personally contact potential employers and, should my father ever return to the Midwest, he would need to make only one phone call to secure a job.

On the morning before the auction, staff from Estate Liquidators prepared the sale site. They loaded tools and equipment from the machine shed onto huge flatbed trailers. These items were offered first when crowds were large and the bidding aggressive. As the day wore on, buyers thinned and enthusiasm waned. Most of the household items were sold in lots at pitifully low prices. Dad didn't seem to notice.

Despite a young entrepreneur's curiosity about the unusual, extensive damage to the plaster walls in an upstairs bedroom, he bought the farmhouse and land for just under a hundred-thirty thousand. It was a steal worthy of jail time, according to the auctioneer. The new owner planned to reconfigure the main floor, update kitchen and bathrooms, and make cosmetic changes upstairs. He intended to market the property as a rare, rural acreage close to urban amenities. He would make a killing.

Seventy-Five

Dad's flight to Philadelphia had been delayed because of fog. Worried about missing his connection in Chicago, he checked the board near the concourse tunnel for departure updates. We sat side by side, his arm circling my shoulders as Trey played with his magnetic sketch pad.

"Have you made up your mind, then?" he asked. "You're sure?"

"I'm not sure of anything, Dad, but yes, I've made up my mind."

The letter to Hal was ready. I had debated with myself for days whether to call him or to write. If I called, I could hear his voice when I told him he had a son. His disbelief. His hesitation. Hal was a good man, a compassionate man. If he felt hurt and anger over the betrayal of lost years, he would try to mask his pain. If he felt pressured—or, worse, indifferent—I would know. He would not be able to hide the truth from me.

He deserved better. He deserved to dismiss me or to forgive me on his terms, not mine. And if he could not forgive me, I deserved his blame.

I would offer him the gift of his son and I would wait. I would pray for his forgiveness. I would pray for my redemption.

Could there be redemption for any of us? Jonny's death had tested the fragile threads that bound our family. It had cemented Mother's madness and it had forever tied Dad in cords of obligation, imprisoning him in an ill-fitting cocoon.

"You're doing the right thing, Luce. Trey's a great kid. He deserves the chance to have both his parents." Dad squeezed my shoulder and twisted his body to face me. "He should have what you never did."

Gate change notification. US Airways flight 3777 to Chicago will be boarding at gate C19.

A smooth, modulated voice reminded passengers to report any unattended packages or belongings.

"That's me, Luce. I need to clear security." He stood reluctantly.

I glanced at my watch. "Looks like you'll make your connection." I turned to Trey. "Come on, buddy. It's time to give Gramps a big hug and kiss. We won't see him for a while." Dad knelt down to gather my son in his arms.

"I want a big hug. A great big-boy muscle hug." Trey tightened his grip around Dad's neck until his little arms quivered. "You be a good boy. And take care of your mama, okay? Promise me you will."

"I will, Gramps. I can do it."

"I know you can. I'm counting on you."

Attention, gate change notification. US Airways flight 3777 to Chicago will be boarding at gate C19.

"Let me know when you get in. It doesn't matter what time you call, even if you're delayed. I won't sleep 'til I hear from you. And let me know about Mother. Tell her . . . tell her I'm thinking of her."

"I will. I'll call. Luce, I wish I didn't . . .," his voice cracked.

"I know, Dad. I wish it more." He grabbed me, his arms a vice. I could feel his hands at the small of my back, the fabric of my jacket clutched in his fists. "I miss you, Dad. You're not even gone and I miss you already."

"You'll be good, Luce. You'll be okay."

Attention, passengers. US Airways flight 3777 to Chicago will board at gate C19.

He picked up his carry-on bag and gripped my hand one final time before turning to go. Through my tears, I followed his broad shoulders until he disappeared into the crowd.

PART THREE:
NOW

SEVENTY-SIX

In my dream, I am late and in a hurry to go—where, I don't know. I pull a cumbersome piece of hard-sided luggage from Mother's closet and open it. Like the covers of a favorite old book, the suitcase lies flat, inviting. In haste, I throw clothes from my dresser drawers into the suitcase. They pile in a jumbled mess—the pajamas and socks, shirts, skirts, blouses, underwear and pantyhose. From the closet I take handbags, belts, shoes. The more I stuff into the compartments, the more room there seems to be.

I cannot find enough in my closets to fill the valise, so I wander from room to room, hefting Mother's candles and jewelry, Dad's shaving gear and ledgers from the mill. Pans from the kitchen, cookie sheets and mixing bowls. Trey's toys and stuffed animals, old sleepers and onesies, blankets and bibs. Draperies and throw rugs. All goes into the suitcase.

I lift one side of the luggage to test the weight, but it is lighter than air. And then, as if the contents have taken on a life of their own, my bras and panties, the colored T-shirts and denim jeans, the print skirts and Capri pants swirl together and reassemble themselves into a portrait. Boots and leather shoes dissolve into a molasses-like liquid and snake around the edge of the portrait, framing the picture formed there.

The lines clarify, solidify, and Jonny's face smiles at me.

I lift the picture, intending to hang it on the wall of the stairwell, but as I try to suspend it from the nail, it softens and sags. The image of my brother dissolves, melting onto the stairs. It dribbles slowly down to the landing where it puddles, finally gelling into a tangled heap of wadded fabric.

I close my empty suitcase and step out onto the porch.

SEVENTY-SEVEN

In the light of morning, I buckle Trey into his car seat. I drive to County Road Q, navigate the turn Jonny missed, and pull the car onto the hard-pack shoulder. From the trunk, I retrieve a canvas sack. Trey helps me carry it as we walk together to the curve.

For a time, we sit on the grassy slope, saying nothing. The summer day is quiet save for the reassuring drone of bees and the cries of plovers angry at our intrusion. In the gentle breeze, leafy coins of silver-green flutter against a cloudless sky. A glare on the water shimmers from the reflected sun, not the handlebars of a partially submerged motorcycle. For a moment, I close my eyes, preparing myself.

The small cross Mother stuck in the ground the spring after Jonny died is still there, near the water's edge. The wood is weathered, splintered and gray from the elements. From the canvas bag, I pull two identical crosses for the parents who are lost to me in ways Jonny never was and struggle to push them into the grassy turf. The wood is new, raw. In time, it will age too, but I will not revisit this spot. I will not be witness to the decay.

Taking Trey's hand, I walk with him back to the car. When we are ready, I glance only once in the rearview mirror before pulling onto the road.

ACKNOWLEDGMENTS

Little is ever accomplished in isolation. In this venture, I was rarely alone.

Thanks, first, to Brick Mantel Books and Jennifer Geist who took a chance on an unknown to launch her literary imprint. I'll forever be grateful for her enthusiasm and professionalism, and for her belief in the work.

J.A., you were the impetus. You are one of nearly six million who suffer from bipolar disorder. To my son, Bryan Netolicky, MD, I could not be more proud of the compassion and commitment you show your patients every single day. Thank you for sharing your expertise in diagnosing and treating those who struggle with the unthinkable challenges of bipolar disorder. Thanks, as well, to other experts in their respective fields: Herb Chafin for the guided tour of your feed mill (yes, I'm still stinging from the buck deer joke); Jake Daubs, for your crucial knowledge about underwater search and recovery (and Lt. Greg McGivern for helping me find you); Karen and Curt Jamieson–can you say *Road Trip*?; Vernon A. Jones for your Apollo artifacts; Dionne Kraklio of Unity Point Home Health Care for access to a wealth of information; Jess Netolicky, barista extraordinaire in a former life; Kelly Netolicky for the Lake Five expedition; and David Rhodes, my literary hero and my friend, for your invaluable suggestions regarding the opening passages. Lin Settle, your discerning eye and thoughtful questions helped immeasurably, as did early feedback from Erin Becker, Karen Jamieson, and Rod Turner. Family members Bryan, Jess, Greg, Emily, Chad, and Kelly, thank you for indulging an obsession. Jorita Jones, Jae and Ty Menzel, Birdman, G.A., Bud, J.P., Emsy, and Keels I owe you for the anecdotes. To the littlest Netos, Gus, Sophia, Max, Hank, Lincoln, and Cooper, I hope you see the best pieces of yourself in Jonny. And of course, Rick, you are my rock star.

Discussion Questions for We Dare Not Whisper

1. Luce believes Midwesterners, when shaped by hardship, typically give thanks at the "altar of resiliency." Does resiliency prove to be a noble or crippling characteristic for members of the Garrison family?

2. Each major character is flawed in some way. In your opinion, whose flaws cause the greatest suffering to him/herself? To others?

3. Pictures, portraits, and photos are a recurring motif throughout the work. Discuss their importance in the depiction of each character:
   - photos of Bets as a child
   - wedding photos of Bets and Nolan
   - portraits of Jonny on the farmhouse stairwell
   - portrait imagery used by Reverend Wolfgarth at Jonny's funeral
   - photos in Jonny's room, found on the second anniversary of his death
   - the portrait in Luce's dream

4. Are snapshots, captured for an instant in time, reliable evidence of an event or personality? If you were to design the cover for the book using a snapshot of a person or scene from the story, what would you choose?

5. After Jonny's accident with the snow shovel, Luce notes her scars were "entirely hidden" but no less disfiguring. Discuss the effects of hiding one's emotional scars.

6. Do you think, on some level, the accident at the photo shoot was subconsciously planned? Was there an intent to harm Jonny?

7. Headlines are rife with examples of horrific events brought about by those who suffer from untreated mental illness—events in which they and/or others are harmed. Discuss societal trends in dealing with mental health. Are we making progress? How far have we come? What still needs to be addressed?

8. Consider Luce's "exile" to Ralston to live with Heather and Kurt. What positive outcomes, if any, did the experience provide? Negative? Should Nolan have allowed Luce to be gone for such a long time? Was it fair for Heather and Kurt to offer such lengthy sanctuary?

9. In Ralston, Luce is drawn to Bella, the Down's syndrome child, Sadie-Lady, and the "misfits" at Java, the Hut. What is compelling about these associations?

10. Compare and contrast Luce's grandparents: Grammy Elnora and Grandfather Aldrich Pennick to Grandmother Lucinda Garrison.

11. Discuss Luce's decision not to tell Hal about her pregnancy and, later, her choice to tell him about Trey via a letter.

12. Some readers speculate that Jonny's death was purely accidental; others argue there might be evidence Jonny wanted to take his own life. Where do you stand?

13. Mo Webster feels guilty after Jonny's death, but Luce is unwilling to offer comfort when her burden is so heavy. What would you say to Mo if given the opportunity?

14. When did you first suspect the depth of Bets's illness?

15. The first impression we have of Bets is the anger and pain Luce describes as she silently screams at her mother. Detail your feelings about Bets as the book progresses. Does knowing about her mental illness and the stunning breakdown she suffers absolve for you the hurtful things Bets says and does?

16. Do you support Nolan's decision to sell the farmhouse and move to Philadelphia? Why or why not?

17. When Luce visits the site of the motorcycle crash at Lake Five for the last time, she places crosses for the parents who are lost to her "in ways Jonny never was." In your view, is this an act of resignation or one of resolution? Will Luce be okay?

ALSO BY TESSA McWATT

Out of My Skin
Dragons Cry
There's No Place Like . . .
This Body
Step Closer
Vital Signs

TESSA McWATT

Higher Ed

RANDOM HOUSE CANADA

PUBLISHED BY RANDOM HOUSE CANADA

www.penguinrandomhouse.ca

Random House Canada and colophon are registered trademarks.

A portion of this novel, titled "A Taste of Marmalade," was published as a Kindle Single in September 2013.

Excerpt of six lines from "Howl" from *Collected Poems 1947-1980* by Allen Ginsberg. Copyright © 1955 by Allen Ginsberg. Reprinted by permission of HarperCollins Publishers.

Library and Archives Canada Cataloguing in Publication

McWatt, Tessa,
Higher Ed / Tessa McWatt.

Issued in print and electronic formats.

ISBN 978-0-345-81476-0
eBook ISBN 978-0-345-81478-4

I. Title.

PS8575.W37H53 2015   C813'.54   C2014-906353-9

Book design by Jennifer Lum

Cover images: (hand) © Wolfgang Kraus, (letters) © Kmitu, both Dreamstime.com
Interior images: (hands) © Sergey Siz`kov / Dreamstime.com

Printed and bound in the United States of America

2 4 6 8 9 7 5 3 1

Penguin
Random House
RANDOM HOUSE CANADA

For the students

CAST

(in order of appearance)

The Administrator—Francine

The Film Professor—Robin

The Law Student—Olivia

The Civil Servant—Ed

The Waitress—Katrin

SUPPORTING PLAYERS

The Anthropology Professor—Patricia

The Film Student—Bayo

The Motorcyclist—Dario

The Driver—Rajit

The Driver's Wife—Mrs. Mahadeo

The Medical Student—Ryan

The Admirer—Nasar

The Civil Servant's Colleague—Sammy

The Civil Servant's Brother—Geoffrey

The Student Union President—Moe

The Waiter—Alejandro

The Café Manager—Claire

The BFF—Jasmine

The BFF's Mum—Jasmine's mum

The Law Student's Mum—Catherine

The Head of Quality Assurance—Lawrence

The Administrator's Brother—Scott

The Film Professor's Ex-girlfriend—Emma

The Administrator's Ex-boyfriend—John Clarke

The Law Student's Granddad—Granddad

The Law Student's Uncle—Eric

The Waitress's Mum—Beata

The Med Student's Mum—Mrs. Broughton

The Film Department Head—Richard

The Philosopher—Gilles Deleuze (as himself)

The Deceased—Anna-Maria Hunter, Keith Meyers, Jonathan Henley, Diyanat Bayar

. . . who passed through universities with radiant cool eyes hallucinating Arkansas and Blake-light tragedy among the scholars of war,
who were expelled from the academies for crazy & publishing obscene odes on the windows of the skull,
who cowered in unshaven rooms in underwear, burning their money in wastebaskets and listening to the Terror through the wall . . .

—Allen Ginsberg, "Howl"

THE OPPOSITE

OF THIRTEEN

FRANCINE

Sayonara, sucker! Francine swipes the back of her hand across her mouth, pushes the handle, straightens up, and watches the water swirl in the bowl. Air alone will do; she can live on air. Sometimes breath puffs her up so much that she feels like she will explode.

She pushes the handle once more so that there is not a shred of pizza left in the bowl, leaves the staff washroom and returns to her office, the door clicking open but needing a hip shove before it budges. Everything in this building is swelling. She smells barf. She picks up the cup of cold tea from her desk and sips, washing it over her teeth. There are fifteen course specifications and twenty external examiners' reports on her desk, which need to be checked by her and passed back to programme leaders before she leaves today. She sits. Buck up, get yer ass in gear; pull yer finger out, as they say in this country. It's unlikely that the whole department will go, isn't it? Surely Quality Assurance and Enhancement is key to any university. She has to admit, though, that her department, like her, is a little fat. There are times when, if she wanted to, she could spend the rest of the afternoon sitting blankly in front of her screen and still get her job done.

She sees her reflection in the screen saver's swirling shapes, which dice up her features and blend them back again in hexagonals of eye, nose, mouth.

A raisin Danish and some Mentos before lunch are also now gone. It's only two in the afternoon, 1400 hours, and she's thrown up everything she's eaten so far. Excellent. She sits up straighter, pleased with herself for her conversion to the twenty-four-hour clock. Time stretches out with the higher numbers. Calories, they say, should be consumed in the early hours.

She is beautiful today.

Running her hand over her belly (okay, but . . .), her hips (a bit, sure), and along her thighs (yes, still!) doesn't change her mind. All her friends back in Philly regularly told her she had a pretty face, after all. And it's not that she doesn't want to hold on to this confidence that normally scurries off like a startled mouse; it's just that at fifty-three this big ass and slackening skin are not about to disappear.

"Men like big butts," Cindy from Philly always says, but Cindy has a black girl's perfect ramp of a rump, which men like to rest their heads on after fucking. Stop. Francine Johnson (good, honest name) will feel beautiful today, all day, she promises, or she will expire in the trying.

She does one last Google search for John Clarke. Stupid name. John-ordinary-everybody Clarke. There's the one who is the minister, there's the poet, the trader, the actor, the leader of the Church of Latter Day Saints. There's even a marathon runner named John Clarke. But there's no IT director who by now has surely procreated with the young IT star at his office, who was oh so smart and jaunty and you-would-really-like-her too—she's kind of like a guy; we talk about sports—while Francine went to England for a once-in-a-lifetime opportunity to work for her accounting firm in its new British office. There's no John-the-prick Clarke who led her on for eleven years, past the last days of her fertility, into the promise of a peaceful, childless life where adventures like the English one were just the beginning. And since the accounting firm's European demise, there has been no John Clarke, supreme asshole, cuntface, cocksucking bastard, with the guts to upload an internet page that would explain himself or just say a simple, fucking sorry.

"Sayonara, sucker," she says as she clicks onto the Guardian Soulmates icon on the desktop, entering her log-in name, ReallyYouandMe, and her password: Isoam.

No one has viewed her since her last log-in.

She has no fans.

She has five favourites.

She has no new messages.

She clicks through the favourites.

"Hear, hear!" she says, raising her mug to the screen at the fifty-five-year-old widower who describes himself as "wanting to feel beloved again." The rest are all too young for her, and they will never contact her. But their presence there, beside her profile, is better even than feeling hunger. Hunky single guys with lots of hair and good teeth—she primps her hair with her fingers, feeling the soft straightness, her most reliable feature.

She shuts down the site and turns towards the reports.

Give a damn, she urges herself, trying to waken her family's work ethic, to keep her duties from slipping. She feels suddenly sick—barfed perhaps too soon—at the idea of losing her job. Returning to the States would be one failure too many. But the announcements have made it clear: there will be a round of redundancies. They will affect every sector of the university, and every department will be scrutinized. She tries to focus on the programme report for the BA in Multimedia Studies, which her colleagues call the Mickey Mouse degree. Appreciating the historical impact of Mickey Mouse is right up her alley and she would like to see the programme stay open, but with low retention rates it seems unlikely. And the data on employability is even more damning.

How did she end up on this side of the divide? Back in the States she marched in campus demonstrations at Penn State against the local nuclear power plant. Okay, she was never arrested, but she'd been willing to be. Now she's the lock-'em-up voice of right and wrong in this university where senior managers look to her to tell them whether people a whole lot smarter than she is are teaching to regulation. She should have finished her master's and applied to the PhD programme in Landscape Ecology at Duke as she'd planned, but cranky John Clarke told her that studying more would be a waste of time and money. And she let his crankiness get to her and took a financial management diploma to be practical. But she knows what good learning is. She could teach her own programme, one that fits with national quality guidelines to boot. And her students would get jobs; they'd be relevant in tough times. She'd call her programme Environmental Containment, or a BA (Honours) in Curb Your Enthusiasm.

She needs another cup of tea. Brushing her hips to smooth down her skirt, she leaves the office.

She's beautiful today, all day, even if the atrium smells like cheese, even if the students irritate the shit out of her with the way they clump together. She waits behind a boy clump in the line-up for food.

"Alright then, Francine?" says Patricia over Francine's shoulder. She turns. Oh Patricia. Pat to friends and colleagues, Patty on the dancefloor, no doubt. Patty in front of the mirror going "Oooh, I feel love, I feel love . . ." Always asking Francine to go out with her to salsa at Ronnie Scott's on a Saturday night when they give you lessons. Patricia is late fifties, slim but buxom, with unplucked eyebrows and big hands, all of which she pulls off with enviable moxie. And she has a big smile and nice, straight teeth, which is something for an English woman her age, so Francine doesn't mind her, really.

"What do you think that smell is?" Francine asks Dancefloor Patty, who lectures in anthropology (because this gal never hid her brains so that some half-pint would love her). Francine nudges Patricia, who sparks at the touch and leans in, so that Francine has to step back.

"There's a hint of vanilla, I think," says Patricia, and, oh shit, Patricia has just sniffed her.

"I mean . . ." she waves her hand in the direction of the atrium, "out here," Francine says, and she retreats to the tight corner of her I-am-beautiful day.

"What, you mean the Starbucks smell? It's a disgrace," and Patricia shifts side to side, as though the topic has revved her engine. "The choice of this or Costa—brilliant—at twice the price of last term, to a company that pays no tax in Britain, to a company—"

"That's not what I meant . . ." Francine says. She takes another step back. Patricia comes across stern and composed, but on the right topic she's a struck match of opinion. "What are you up to these days?" Francine asks her. Wood, metal, plastic, cloth: each distinct smell comes wafting in, one after the other.

Patricia looks down at her feet and this seems to stop her hips from swaying, delivering her back to perfect composure. "It's always hectic at the beginning of a term," she says, raises a shoulder, and tilts her chin to it like a cat cleaning whiskers. The hair on Francine's arm rises: Colgate toothpaste, Dove deodorant, Aussie shampoo. There's more of this every day: the "change"—she's still goddamn changing.

"Seen anything good recently?" she asks, forcing her eyes away from Patricia's shoulder, wondering if she should ask Patricia if she thinks there will even be an anthropology department next year.

"No time," Patricia says. "Anything in mind?"

Damn it. Francine always falls into this trap, this feeling of being the one who has to follow through. "I'll see what's out there, and, yeah, we could"—she doesn't have the guts to stop there—"get together."

"Excellent," Patricia says. "Friday?"

"Yeah."

Shit.

Francine finds herself doing the thing with her silky hair that John Shitface Clarke used to tell her made his heart melt— that pulling down of her fringe in an attempt to cover her eyes. She doesn't mean to do it; it just happens. She smiles nervously as Patricia takes her in, and Patricia responds with a smile so full and ripe that the little part of Francine that keeps being the sucker is warmed.

ROBIN

He doesn't want to go mad. If this is madness he can't have it.
The wind whips off the river in front of him and slaps his cheek.
Robin counts the ways madness might bear down on a man: 1) he
could be born mad; 2) he could slowly, over the course of years,
lose the capacity to see that actions and thoughts are separate; or
3) the self might become only a threshold, a door to multiplicities.
This final point is from Deleuze, whose critical theory Robin has
mined for the article he must write on motion capture and animation. Deleuze has hypnotized him with *A Thousand Plateaus*,
but in truth Robin is most worried about number 2.

He downs his double espresso in the Styrofoam cup, his
regular mug left behind in his office this morning. This forgetfulness is surely a sign. He picks up his briefcase and makes
ready to face the lecture room. He has to remember to keep his
glasses high up on his nose, because Emma told him that he
looks like an old man when they slide down towards the tip.
Thirty-eight is the edge of old. He stands and braces himself for
this second-year class in Cinema Poetics. Where is the poetry?
Where are the stressed syllables and open vowels? The wind
stings his chin. Father does not rhyme with much.

The river whips up again and only facts remain. Fact is, in 1963 this river froze, the Beatles sang "Please Please Me," and Fellini released *8 ½*. These are thoughts that don't require action, and this is what he's more used to, what he's certain, almost certain, he would still prefer.

In the atrium he nudges the glasses up further before he enters the lecture room. One, two, three . . . only four students are there ahead of him. Not a promising sign so early in the term. Bayo is in her seat in the front row, ready to take him on. Formaldehyde, he wants to say to her. *Formaldehyde* is not an easy word to spell—it was she who challenged his typo on the PowerPoint last week. In that need to act on her thought, Bayo revealed her madness. A mature student from Nigeria, her bosom broad, her hair long and straight from extensions—a swath of it wrapping over her forehead and across one eye like a pirate's patch—Bayo's madness is a slow-burning constant. Last term Robin caught her behind the Samuel Johnson Building setting fire to the essay he had handed back to her minutes before. Jake, Dan, and Miles also set fire to theirs, but it wasn't lunacy; they did it together in full view in the university square. Jake is from a small northern town where a bloke is not allowed to like film and art; Miles is a thin Afro-Caribbean DJ wanna-be, and so shy that he talks into his hand as though the hand were clutching a microphone; Dan used to sell drugs to celebrities: these young men aren't mad. Their actions were pure performance.

He walks to the lectern and places his briefcase on the table beside it. He takes out the pen—*I'm the pen your lover writes with*—stolen from the Epicure Café. More students stream in, and they are loud. He looks down at his Doc Martens and starts to hum.

He's fucking going to be a father.

A sheet of paper slips from his notes and floats down like a leaf. At this portent of chaos, he rushes out of the room, gripping the stolen pen, and crosses the atrium to the student union shop.

The chocolate is along the back row with bags of Haribo, Basset's Mint Imperials, Fruit Gums, Starbursts, Minstrels, and Jelly Aliens. Kit Kat is the one sane choice. He reaches for one and catches sight of familiar curly hair and wide cheekbones. Olivia is a third-year law student who took Cinema Poetics last year as an option and was the best student in the class. Her face is like Cleopatra's, her hair like Shirley Temple's, her confidence as thin but as certain as cellophane. In the second week of classes she towered over him as she asked if poets wrote only about things that are impermanent. He considered the question so thoroughly that he lost track of time, right there in front of her. Love, and water over stones, she said and brought him back. Yes. Yes, they do, he said.

Olivia catches his eye from across the aisle, but on remembering their final meeting last year, he bows his head and ducks behind the rack of greeting cards, pretending to look for a suitable card for the now confirmed autumn event. *Happy Birthday: Son, Daughter?* Oh God. He doesn't want to be a man. He wants to be a lightning bolt.

He returns to the lecture room with the Kit Kat in his breast pocket. Bayo is sitting straight, like an actor ready for a cue. She stares at him, but he bends down to pick up his notes from the floor. Image: the hands of the woman from the Epicure Café on Upper Street, the way she holds his cup as she walks towards him, the way her thumb releases the saucer as she places it before him. He arranges his notes, turns on the computer and projector, and opens the PowerPoint presentation.

"I celebrate myself and sing myself," he says, and the room goes quiet. This worked on him as an undergraduate at Warwick, and he knows it will work now. He looks over at Bayo, who appears agitated. "And what I assume, you shall assume . . . " he continues, and when the students realize he's quoting they will relax, but for now he is content to unsettle them, to confound them with the possibility that he might be saying something real. Except that Bayo has begun to wring her hands so he breaks out of his performance sooner than planned.

"Whitman refers to his book *Leaves of Grass* and the American Civil War as though they are one, making a link between them to the democratic soul, and the struggle for unification." He sees Bayo look down into her lap. "Not dissimilarly, Elsaesser and Hagener explore the reflective and reflexive potential of cinema, using the mirror and the face as a motif for understanding the self and the other . . . "

Bayo looks up again. Robin cannot push away the face of the woman in the Epicure Café, which beams like his grandmother's in a photo of her at the foot of the Eiffel Tower. A tiny stranger who smiles at him in a way that makes all things seem possible.

FRANCINE

Living on air is harder in the drizzled dullness of February, chilling at six, when Francine leaves the university. Hungry. Trying to stay that way. But sleepy as she drives west across London and the radio repeats the news of Gaza violence she heard at lunchtime. Her flat is too far away at this hour of the day. She presses the dashboard button for Kiss FM and sings along behind the wheel, because it's true, everybody wants to rule the world.

It's an hour before she nears home, turning towards Kilburn Park, then up Salusbury Road towards Willesden Lane. John Clarke would have hated Kilburn, hated its pound shops, cheap garments and kebabs. The dark brick, the crowded-front-teeth of a road that leads onto hers. John fucking Clarke would–

There's a sliding, screeching, wet bang. A body flies above the car in front of hers and glass hits her windshield. Her car smacks the back bumper of the small red sedan. Now only one sound: a low pumping vibration all around. She puts the car in park. Fuck, fuck, fuck. And opens the car door. Near the oak tree at the side of the road is a small, contorted body, face down. She has trouble breathing. She trains her eyes on the jeans, twisted

around impossibly bent legs, the black leather jacket, the motorcycle helmet, tilted up just enough to have broken the neck. The
clothes are emptied, breath having wrinkled them in its leaving.
The pumping vibe deepens: a bass line that moves up the back of
her own neck.

"I think it's a girl . . . " a voice says, and cinnamon wafts
through the fugue of voices. "Ooh, look at the legs." Francine
looks at the legs again to try to see this girl, but she is sure
this pile of clothing belongs to a man (beer, cigarettes, stale
cologne). She walks towards it: or just a boy. His bent leg shimmers like it's going to dissolve, like particles are separating to
show her the skin, twisted tendons, broken bones within.
Thank God his mother isn't here to see. Thank God it's she
who witnesses this, not his mother, who will next see him when
a sheet is pulled down to reveal a face, scrubbed and bloodless,
in the morgue.

The driver of the red sedan, over which the boy flew, is
slumped at his steering wheel, window open, his body unin-
jured and his face a stiff mask. Francine stands among the
strewn motorcycle parts. Someone is asking for an ambulance
on 999. Someone else whimpers, "He wasn't going fast." And
the driver slowly gets out of the red car. Mum, she thinks, but
doesn't know why all this mummy, mummy for the shattered
boy by the oak tree.

Sitting down on the curb, dizzy, as the others keep talking—
"It's not a girl, look"—she spots a young man running towards
them.

"Don't touch him; leave him, let me do it," the young man
yells. He tells them he's a medical student and will try to help.
His accent is Scottish. She watches his curly head as he turns the

body over and lifts the helmet's visor, then tilts and blows, one, two, three, again, one, two, three, through the broken, bloody face. Once more, harder.

The driver of the red sedan leans down to say something to the Scottish doctor. One car later and it would have been she who hit the boy. One car later and it would have been Francine who had to see his mum's face in court. Her knee begins to tremor. Fuck, fuck. She takes a deep breath. (Rubber, asphalt, and a burst of aftershave.)

"I'm sorry, I'm sorry," the med student says as he stands up. His eye is in a wink, sealed partially shut by the blood from the motorcyclist's face. Francine stands up, retches, then throws up and, from habit, stares down at it on the pavement.

She looks again at the med student's face as he wipes blood from his mouth. He catches her eye. *Cry. Cry*, she thinks. But he doesn't. It's the driver of the red sedan who begins weeping.

"I only saw him fly through the air," she's able to say to the police when they finally arrive. "I have to go," she says, adamantly, and her tongue touches a fleck of vomit on her lip. But one officer keeps asking her questions, while another questions a Filipino nanny who is worried about being deported. The med student whose name—Ryan Broughton—she listens carefully for, speaks to the third officer on the scene. The driver of the red sedan is led to the back seat of the second police vehicle. "I have to go," she says again and heads to her car before the paramedics have lifted the body into the ambulance.

Ryan Broughton catches her eye just before she climbs behind the wheel. At which stage of medical school do doctors become impassive to dead bodies? How is Ryan Broughton digesting the taste of the crushed face he sucked on? How respectfully he had turned over the ruined body. Takes just a little to be decent.

At home she dreams that every wall in her flat is painted yellow. In the middle of the night she wakes to a gush between her legs and throws back the duvet to reveal a blood-soaked mattress.

ROBIN

It's safe to leave. The atrium is in darkness; the drizzle outside will set the tone for his evening. Robin walks out of the building. The usual few students, the security guard. He looks around for the curvaceous American woman who works in QA—the body of the mature Mae West, the face of Vivien Leigh's Scarlett O'Hara. She is always staring at him, always on the verge of chatting him up, but she must have left already. Fact is that rain can fall as fast as twenty-two miles an hour, so this drizzle isn't the worst it could be, but home would be a better place just now. He takes the path towards the bus stop and waits.

Emma left two messages on his voicemail while he was teaching. She doesn't trust his reaction to the news about their baby. So she shouldn't. It's a beautiful thing, she says; it is for me, is it for you?

Deleuze: Bring something incomprehensible into the world!

In his kitchen he wipes down the white subway tiles behind the gas hob, dotted with bolognese sauce from last night. Emma's news came just after dinner; he would never normally have missed these spots. He scours the stainless steel hob itself, the wood counter, scrubs the corners, presses hard against the rings from cups, enjoying this cleaning more than anything else today. Fact is that tomatoes are not as benign as we consider them. Their Latin name means "wolf peach." Cleaning takes over from reading some days, and then he allows himself to go to bed. But he has to make two phone calls this evening, before he falls asleep with the BBC World Service at his ear. Today, the third of February, is his mother's birthday and she will have been wondering all day what might be taking him so long to call. His father will have taken her to lunch in Falmouth, possibly to Rick Stein's Fish, and now they will be reading in front of the fire, toasting each other for another day of a long, relatively happy relationship in a predominantly happy life. His brothers will have already called, from New York, from Manchester, and Robin will be the only missing element of his mother's measured happiness.

The other call will also be to Cornwall. Emma's move was right for her, and when he tells his parents the news his father will secretly wish for a granddaughter and will offer to build them a summer house in their garden that extends towards a cliff over the sea.

He turns the volume down on Emil Gilels who is playing the Beethoven piano sonata that his mother tried to learn throughout his entire childhood, her failure to do so remaining one of her only regrets. He dials Emma's number first.

"Hi, hi," he says, and listens for the right thing to say next. "Not bad, tired," he says, which is obviously wrong. "Long day, you?"

Emma describes her mother's reaction to the pregnancy in such detail that he cannot keep his eyes open. Then her sister's, then the fact of driving to the sea and walking the cliff path, the path he himself showed her. At this he perks up. He has a twinge of panic for her safety, but then the thought of his child growing up in Cornwall brings pleasure. Gorse, heather, pyramid orchids in the rolling dunes, golden samphire in the cliffs, salt marshes, slanted rain, flavoured air.

The day he and Emma broke up he said, I wish you love in the sea cliffs; I wish you everything you want. She had wanted a baby, but neither of them had really wanted each other.

"And the news from your end? How has that gone over?" she asks him. He hasn't told a soul. Emma hears this in his hesitation. Her silence shames him further.

The phone tucked under his chin, he starts to buff the stainless steel kettle, heightening the double-arched reflection of the kitchen window within it. They had come together out of inertia. Friends for years, they had turned to one another after the breakup of far more necessary and romantic connections, she to him for comfort, both of them for sex, and even that wasn't necessary. His relief at her decision to quit her job in dentistry and move from London to the southwest to teach yoga was manifest in his saying, blithely, I love you, before having sex one last time in an effort to marry theory and practice.

"How are you feeling?" he asks, wanting to take the morning sickness away for her, to make everything good for her, wanting at the same time to bury his face in the straight blond hair of the Polish waitress at Epicure and to tell her how her lack of awareness of her own beauty has loosened the tiles of his sanity.

"Still woozy in the mornings, but a bit better. Skin looks great." Her voice invites him to intimacy.

"Oh, good," is all he can say.

FRANCINE

Francine is bent over the toilet basin for the third time today, fingers deep in her throat and the omelette and toast high up in her belly, and for the third time unable to coax anything out.

This has happened before, through the years, when it stops working, when she has to find another way. Damn. She straightens up. The phone rings and makes her jump. She has already made her excuses for her third day of absence from work. There is no one else who would call.

"Patricia," she says to the woman's voice. And because Patricia has a gift for extraction, she finds herself telling her everything, from the wet bang to the crinkled jeans and finally the young doctor's face. What she doesn't tell Patricia about is the flood in the middle of the night and the disappearance of her craving for sugar. She doesn't say, that's it, last friggin' hurrah, a final shove towards change. But this change feels like a reversing, back to age thirteen, when things swirled like this, were scary like this.

"Ronnie Scott's," Patricia commands, "tonight, come on." Francine looks out her window. The plane tree's branches have recently been pruned and the knotty limbs are clothed only in translucent bark, like gauze over veins. She can see into her neighbour's front room. He has no shirt on. Nothing is opaque anymore.

"Sorry, no, can't . . . really not feeling up to it," she says, standing firm against Patricia's persistence. And to her surprise Patricia lets her off the hook with a warm wish to see her at work soon and an offer to bring around food and magazines. Francine promises she'll be back at work tomorrow and will check in with Patricia around lunchtime.

"Sure, sure," Patricia says. Yeah, like there is anything that is.

—

The next morning the atrium smells different—like Dr. Pepper in the summer. When they were teens her brother told her that Dr. Pepper was for losers. Scott knew who the losers and winners were, being so popular with other kids that he spent weekends at their homes or cottages. She'd take those opportunities to order Dr. Pepper at the A&W, her father's treat to make up for his desperate widower cooking and her loneliness without her brother at home. It was around this time that she learned the trick—the two-fingered flick on that flap at the back of the throat and whoosh—gone was the strawberry ice-cream sundae, the hot dog and French fries, the Dr. Pepper. Scott, whose annual Christmas conversation on the telephone consists of lecturing her on how she needs to think about her long-term security, will never know just how right he had been about Dr. Pepper. Maybe she should try the Atkins diet again. All that meat. She checks her butt with her hand, making a show of brushing something off her skirt— another little trick. *Plop, plop, fizz, fizz, oh what a relief it is.*

She asks for a skinny hazelnut latte, rhyming off the order comfortably now that Starbucks is on campus. She feels students behind her, their pushiness, like she's taking too much time. One of the two dark brunettes behind her glares at her and Francine finds the face hard, blunt, the first opaque thing she's seen in days. She touches her throat, sore from the failed barfing.

"Order me a cappuccino," the other woman says to her friend who says something back in a private language, then they giggle and Francine feels a lurch in her gut like she's going to release air. Nothing is solid; now even the hard mask of the woman's spite seems porous.

As she leaves with her latte, she spots that guy, the young lecturer. Robin joins the queue and Francine reaches for a napkin, a small delaying tactic. Ten years younger and she'd be following him around like a stray pet; Robin is the kind of guy she should have gone for instead of John Cuntface Clarke. Robin has eyes that squint when he's thinking, and he's always thinking when she sees him. It's not his looks—fine, but nothing special—it's something else, maybe in the way he walks. Can kindness show in a walk? Teacher of film studies and befriender of students, Robin would know the real her. He walks like he'd be a good kisser. *Annie Hall,* she wants to ask? Does he teach it? She follows him out of the atrium, leaves him behind in the square and heads back to her office.

Three days = 198 unopened e-mails.

Google is the only tolerable option.

There are three news articles for "motorcycle accident Queen's Park," and now she knows his name: Dario Martinelli, 24, of Barking. A boy. She also reads the name of the driver of the red sedan, but she can't hold it in her sights, skips over it to find that he has been charged with dangerous driving causing death.

She searches Facebook, where Dario Martinelli's timeline has photos, postings in Italian, and recent posts in English about how much he loves riding his motorcycle and how the horrendous London winter has kept him off it and wouldn't it be great to be back in Bologna and going fast, with you, friend. Her throat tightens. The most recent post is from Roberto Martinelli—brother? cousin?—in Italian, but she can make out enough to know that la famiglia grieves the loss and that the (airless, shrunken) body will be brought home for interment. She clicks off quickly. His wrinkled clothes. He is Dario. He has a family. Dario will have an interment, and Dario's Facebook page will remain forever, his beloved motorbike preserved there in mint condition.

Dario is dead. People die every minute of every day. What's going on with her?

She seeks the young doctor, Ryan Broughton. Finding Ryan will help. Ryan knows what death tastes like. But she can't find him, so she returns to Google and asks it a question. There are countless answers: "Death tastes like blackened carbon"; "death tastes like almonds and spoiled fruit"; "death tastes like McGriddles", and her favourite: "it tastes like feet."

Sayonara.

OLIVIA

"Robin?" Olivia mumbles. Oi. But he won't hear; he's got those wanna-hide shoulders hunched over the row of chocolate in the far aisle. Robin. If she could steal Robin, right, she'd give him to her mum, she would, because he would make her lighten up; his words would open her. Instead there's Ed, and what is she to do with him? Right. Six days now, six days it's been since finding him. Edward of the lonely dead. Edward like a rabbit in a high-beam when he first saw her; Edward whose life's work has been to bury the unknown, unloved, unmoneyed people of Barking and Dagenham. Ed. Her dad.

Olivia makes a sound with her tongue. It's cicada-like, not the sucking of teeth that her mate Jasmine has perfected in wishing she'd been born a Jamaican. This sound is not hip, not hop. It's a sigh in reverse.

"May I have some aspirin?" she asks the cashier. One foot, then the next, back and forth, gotta slow everything down. Right. The spindly woman, who looks like she is already a mum of many even though maybe only twenty-five years old, turns to the shelves behind her and reaches for the yellow Anadin pack, turns back, slides it on the counter and waits—like a mother would—for Olivia to sort through her change for £1.20.

"Spindly," Olivia says, under her breath. The woman looks up at her with don't-mess-with-me eyes like rectangles. Olivia holds on to other words—*tattoo, milk, nicotine*—takes the box of aspirin and leaves the shop. She sees Robin retreat down the atrium. Robin's walk is like a bird's, even though she's never seen a robin walking, but he bops like something that is used to flying instead. Robin is a bebop bird. And Robin is the only bloke on the planet who has seen her cry.

Right. She weaves through the people in the atrium—the fat, the small, the smelly, the limping, the arrogant—every one of them in last-minute coffee-and-sweets-buying mode to keep them awake through class. Their choice is limited; Thames Gateway U has been branded. The dinner ladies from last year look sad in their new brown uniforms and baseball caps. The new cafeteria food is sadder than they are. *Sad and Sadder*: a Netflix blockbuster. Olivia is on the student union committee that has been lobbying the governors against outsourcing to corporations for months now, but times such as they are is all she hears. Does no one see what's happening here? Right. She lowers her eyes to avoid the faces, the sadder than sad, dumber than dumb, bleaker than bleak. Don't take it all on yourself, Robin had said. How not to? She weaves through the bodies, weaves like that girl's hair, like that man's jacket, like this boy's lies he's telling his girlfriend, and like that boy's flying Paralympic-style wheelchair. She heads towards the finance office. Maybe today the panting, pink-faced man will tell her when the last loan instalment will appear in her account. Her debt is already five times what she planned when all of this started. You can always ask for help, Robin said. If and when she becomes a solicitor will she really have chosen correctly over becoming Lara Croft instead? Right, but the law, really? The wheelchair boy is stuck—another thing she has to get sorted, so that being at this uni in a wheelchair gets easier than being a tuna in a can.

Sorry. Right. She speeds up.

Who will bury these people?

Two and a half years of law school but there are questions they have not taught her to answer. All these questions she's now in the habit of asking. She adjusts the satchel on her shoulder—books, court decisions—and pushes through. Who will bury them?

"Lonely," she says, slipped out like all the other words these days, like fish from a hand. She is going to be a rubbish lawyer.

One foot in front of the other heading out of the atrium. There's fog. Something clangs against metal, like a stay against a mast. She dips her chin into her scarf. In the square she searches for Robin. There's a man with wild hair like his, but that one walks like a zombie. Students stand in clusters in front of the Watson Building where she's headed. Smokers, listeners, worriers, huddlers. One of them could be Nasar.

Nasar's last message said: *hop u r fine. When I meet u first time it was like a dream. I like to have a friend like u trust me if u agree to start good friendship pleas text me. I really like you . . . !!! Nasar.*

The first text had been short, sharp, friendly—*hi how r u?*—but when she asked who it was and got only his name, well, what's up with that? The next two were check-ins, how are you today? This latest one is swag. Who is he and how did he get her number? The bloke she met in the student bar? The one in the kebab shop with Jasmine last week? The skinny, floppy emo from Robin's class? Skinny, floppy emo boys are not called Nasar. Jasmine thinks Olivia should have taken the Italian boy up on his offer—the short, funny man who chirpsed them up at Nico's bar. He wanted her to get on the back of his motorcycle in order to Moto and Guzzi to Bologna. Jasmine egged him on. Jasmine placed his hand on Olivia's lap. Jasmine knows shite about anything except shagging. But for Olivia shagging has been put on hold for so long, while there was shite to sort out, that even if she is secretly chuffed by being Nasar's dream to meet, oh crikey. She will ask Robin—and plan not to blubber like the last time—why, oh why love feels like a threat.

She could probably take out an injunction against Nasar, charge him with harassment under the 1998 Malicious Communications Act, because she's entitled to protection from indecent, offensive or threatening electronic communication. But, only the lonely: Nasar might just need a friend.

It's her father's fault. Six days of having to hold her tongue at home in front of Catherine, six days of thinking so much her head will burst, the image of Ed standing behind that desk, all strawless scarecrow-like and them talking all casual-like until she could see from his face that both of them were putting two and two together to make the twenty-two years of age that his daughter would be. If it hadn't been for her father she wouldn't be needing to enlist Robin, give Nasar a second thought, or do anything other than study because she needs to get a first.

Her final-year project was meant to be a simple route to a first-class degree, on account of it being straightforward while the rest of life wasn't. The law is the law, after all, and not a *Tomb Raider* game. But now even that has come unravelled, and it's like she's dubstepping to Unkle's "Only the Lonely." It started simply enough: getting more details on paupers' graves—like depth, how many, how much, how weird—and on how the council was dealing with the foxes, because this whole idea came about when she heard that foxes were ravaging paupers' graves. She got hooked and started to research the rights of untraceable, unknown deceased residents to a funeral. When Olivia called the council, the clerk corrected her use of "paupers' graves" and transferred her call to the Safeguarding Adults Team. The next day, out of nowhere, no-how, no-possible-way, she was standing in front of the funeral officer who looked too weak to do a job that might entail a bit of digging and lifting coffins. And then he started to look at her all funny, like the fall-down-on-his-knees scarecrow of Oz. When she asked Edward Reynolds if he knew a certain Catherine Mason, one time of Romford Road, the look on his face made the whole entire room a Rubik's cube, the colours lining up, like for the first time ever.

Her friend Jasmine says "Ah, Jeezus" when things like this happen. Jasmine's mother is a born-again, on account of her husband moving out seven years ago, but when Jasmine says *Jeezus* it sounds more like something from the devil, because Jasmine is bent on showing her mother that her dad was justified. Jasmine's not her real name. Eleanor is only Jasmine because in secondary school, when her dad left and the ground dropped out of her life, she had to find something different to hold on to. So Jasmine loves this kind of thing that bonds blud and happens regular-like in their ends. "That's extra . . . " Jasmine said, first thing, when Olivia told her about the Rubik's cube moment, and she touched the side of Olivia's head. "Why did your dad leave again?" she added, now coiling the end of her own long hair around her index finger, as though the leaving of dads could be measured like curls.

"Jaz," Olivia said, "my father is a caring man," and that shut her up, but truth is that's what Olivia's mother said, over and over, "Your father is a caring man," when Olivia's questions at the age of thirteen turned to why Catherine was letting different blokes kiss her in the sitting room of the house they share with Granddad and Nan, and why there was never a bloke who stayed, and where, after all, was the one who was responsible for Olivia? Wouldn't you save kissing for someone who wouldn't be leaving? And maybe he left because you were giving it away so easily? And wouldn't it make sense to avoid that ever happening, ever?

Catherine keeps the secret of Edward the way a girl in Olivia's primary school kept a snake in a terrarium. The girl loved that snake, tended it like she could do anything the boys did, but one morning when they went into the classroom the snake was gone from the glass tank: only a circle of moulted skin was left; snake-shaped lace draped over the large rock at the far right of the terrarium. From that day on the girl was terrified of all snakes, but mostly scared that the one that got away would show up at any moment, larger, slimier, wild. When Catherine talks about Edward at a distance, she says things like this—"he cared"—but when the question of why he left crops up there's the girl-with-the-snake sound in her voice. And for Olivia there's a once–upon–a–time of a father who sang a song to himself, over and over. A simple, spiralling song that Olivia hears sometimes out of nowhere. When Catherine says these things about him and then returns to her fashion magazines and makes deadpan comments like *Innit a nightmare that some women of her age wear short shorts*, the song comes back. Tra-la-la-la-la.

Olivia walks faster.

"Robin," she says again.

Robin let her sit there and cry, not asking her to stop, not asking her to do anything, just telling her that you don't have to fix everything all by yourself.

Right.

When she arrives at the finance department, she is hot and opens her jacket. She leans over the counter trying to catch the attention of the pink-faced man she usually talks to. Her jumper rides up, her waist rubs the melamine rind of the countertop, and ahh, she catches the eye of the black-haired woman with glasses, who, oh please, this time, will not say that these things take time.

ED

It sounds like the earth's turning too fast, the planet louder than last week, and the traffic on Ripple Road hungry-hungry for getting to work, when work is the last place anybody really wants to be. Ed waits, waits, waits for the traffic that does not cease. He should go farther up to the zebra crossing near Sleepwell Bedroom Furniture, but man he'd be tempted to stop in for a lie-down rather than head to work. His toe is throbbing, stubbed last night on the damn ledge that juts up outta the floor towards his bathroom, because he was too fired up, too buzzy to stand still: there is so much to tell her.

He is going to be late, and even when he gets there he won't be able to concentrate, with only two hours' sleep last night thanks to—all night—practising there in his kitchen how to say it. A car comes close up to his foot and he has to pay attention now or he'll be mash-up to slop and never get to tell her a thing.

He hurries towards the crossing, his shoes pinching his toes, and he takes it at a pace. If she's willing to meet him again, if her mother hasn't poison-up her mind, then he will tell her that in Guyana there is fair and there is unfair, and some people does resist their coexistence and they will resist and resist until something changes or explodes, yes man. Yes, this is one of the tiny amount of the things he will tell her. Even a child who is a grown-up now needs to know things about where she is from. And who she is from, never mind the jumbies of the past. He cannot lose her again.

Miracles happen, man, miracles happen. In she walked to his offices six days ago, and there in her face was something he knew like his hand. Funny, funny feeling, that: when you know a face as a baby then all of a sudden it's there, same face, but a woman face. He has to tread softly-softly in this new world, to expect nothing, and to mention Catherine only when it feels safe to do so. How he loved that name, loved it so much he has barely said it for eighteen years. To anyone he met later called Catherine he would say, hey Cathy, or all right Kate, but never Catherine. He rubs the bald part of his head first, then runs his hand over the short dog-like pelt at the back. Man, there are miracles.

Inside Sydney House the hall is smelling better than yesterday, when that limping, overcoat-and-sandals man who sleeps on George Street in cardboard came in especially to piss and shit, as if to say, here, look after that, Safeguarding Adults Team, and he left a trail of he foulness, piss running all along the floor for so. The cleaners have done good.

What is the price of miracles?

If he loses his job just as he regains his daughter, he will consider himself one giant step ahead of the Barking and Dagenham Council, so never mind. Out of the three Protection, Funeral and Conference Officers, he is the least educated but the oldest. Sammy has the most experience and seniority, and Ralph is a specialized social work graduate, so he knows he's the one most likely for the chop, if it comes. But never mind, because even though he's losing bulk except in the belly, he's still a man with arms that could wrestle a cow like daddy did when the cow in Berbice had her foot caught up in wire and thought daddy was trying to kill she. That cow fought hard-hard, and his daddy took the cow head by the horns and bent it so, and the beast twist up and fall down to let the men hold she there and unwrap the wire slowly, slowly, for her to be released.

"Alright, Wood," says Sammy when Ed enters the Safe and Sorrow room as the two of them like to call their office. Ralph is too serious to make fun of their work and the kind of people they have to watch out for, but Sammy's all for lightening things up a little. Sammy is the real thing, though, and takes on his job like these people are family, goes into their homes and bears the smells and the sights always with a smile. Sammy is a damn good fella. Sometimes when there's not much happening in the way of advice-giving to the public or securing council flats that have been abandoned or making sure pets get sent to the shelter if the resi-dent has died or is in hospital, or when there are no care homes needing recalibrating or help with the basics, Sammy likes to lime and watch football on his brand new iPad. Sammy might be younger than Ed is, but Sammy is the main man. The two of them alone held things together for the longest time, but with the previ-ous government their budget was increased and they were allowed to hire Ralph. The three of them get along fine, never mind Ralph's damn seriousness. But now it looks like one of them is going to get shafted. And it won't be Sammy, because he's too good.

"Good, good, Sammy, You?"

"Fuck yeah, Hammers winning at last."

Sammy breathes football night and day and loves it more than his wife, who doesn't particularly seem to mind. Days are easier with him around because Sammy is always full of hope—even when there's nothing better to hope for than a draw.

"Whatever it takes, Sammy, whatever it takes, right? I'm glad you're happy."

"Better than the dogs, Wood, that's all I'm saying." And it's true, Ed does succumb to good odds at the track now and then. Ed isn't big on sport. Besides the dogs, he can get fired up about horse racing, but he has trouble seeing that as a sport, except for what the horse does. If he hadn't come to London as a young man in 1974 because President Burnham had dreams of being Fidel Castro, he might still be at the betting shop below sea level in Georgetown or at the track a metre above sea level in Berbice, and he might still be just watching them run instead of meeting Catherine, nearly tripping over his own feet for those green eyes, putting up with vexation from her dad, and getting to help Olivia grow to the point when full sentences were coming out of her mouth.

When you tell people you used to live below sea level they think you mad or joking, but true-true, that is where Ed moved to as a young man from Berbice, and where houses are built on stilts, where the whole of the town is pouring out into the sea with the Demerara River, in the effluence of loam, gold and sanity of an entire country. Is that the kind of thing you tell a daughter? And if you start, do you stop? Are there ever things a father should leave out? Olivia will need to know these facts about her father and the kiskadee-kaieteur-foo-foo-garlic-pork trimmings of what makes him.

"You okay, Wood?"

"Yes, Sammy, fine, fine. Just miles away."

Sammy is forty and fat with lots of hair. But he's a good man. And that's another thing Ed has to tell Olivia: that in Guyana black and Indian men used to have to work together in public but didn't like each other in private, but that is changing and things are better since the time he had to go back there in '85 to help his ailing daddy and ended up staying too long, when, man, it was bad and the Guyanese dollar was worthless. Blacks and Indians, like him and Sammy, they are fine-fine now.

Ed sits at his desk and turns on his computer. The requisition order for an Italian family to secure the belongings of a now deceased lodger was drawn up yesterday but the landlord was contacted only late in the evening, so this needs immediate processing. Martinelli: a good name; has its own steel band behind it. Aged twenty-four. Lord. This is the vex-he part of the job, the bad news arrows that get launched across the internet to land in who-knows-whose heart on an otherwise good day. Ed prefers the practical tasks. Before he checks the Safe and Sorrow office e-mails he fights sleep by uploading the photo he sent to himself from his home machine last night, one he found in the box beneath his bed, the one with photos of Catherine and Olivia before life bruk them up. In the scanned photo of the three-year-old Olivia, she wears a white party dress with lace and frills at the shoulders, white ankle socks and black patent leather shoes. Her face is dough-like round and slice-my-heart happy, and she holds up a T-shirt that says *I want my mummy*. Yes, girl, true-true.

"Edward," Catherine would say, her voice coming from the kitchen. "Edward," drawing out the last syllable. "Edwaard!" Then she'd tell him all the things that needed doing and fixing. "Wood," Olivia would say, trying to copy her mummy. "Wooood . . . open," as she toddled up to him with her lime-green plastic box that was a toy enough just to open, fill with stones, grass, buttons, pennies, and close again. And Wood he became.

Man, those miracles.

"You have a funeral," Sammy says, and raises his hand in the air above his keyboard before hitting send to sling the e-mail over. Ed's heart does a little hiccup; these funerals seem to be coming more regularly, and Sammy has given over most of them to him.

He checks the e-mail. The woman who needs the funeral is from Malvern Estate in Castle Green. She was forty-two, died alone, of an overdose, and the police say there is no one to bury her. So he will do it. This he is better at than knowing what to say to a grown-up daughter he last saw when she was four.

Now that he thinks of it, returning to Georgetown to attend to his family gave him good training for this very job. In Georgetown he met a man who was real bruk up at the side of the stall where his friend Sanil sold cassava and eddoe and plantain in Bourda Market. The man had been there every day he walked through the market for the five months of money-hunting that Ed had been doing to help his brother, to keep his mother in her house in Berbice because she refused to move, and this man was worse off than Ed. There were a whole lotta them worse off, but this very-very man he felt for: his hair was natty, his feet were torn up, his arms scabby, but in his face was something you could see that was quick-quick. Ed took the man home and gave him a shower and cleaned up his feet and let him sleep in his bed for twelve hours before sending him on his way. And, boy, this was the best Ed had felt since leaving London, missing his woman and his daughter. He wanted to keep the feeling, so he did this time and again with this man and others in Georgetown.

So, Carol at Rippleside Cemetery will be contacted on behalf of Anna-Marie Hunter, dead at forty-two, and there is the vicar to book, and he has to see about a place in the community plot, or whether she must be cremated. Of all the London jobs he's done—insurance, accounting, his stint in Housing—this job is the proper place for him.

And that is another thing he must tell Olivia: that after Catherine moved and told him not ever to try to find them, he learned to feel lucky for the things he didn't lose. In Guyana plenty people have nothing.

Olivia is training to be a lawyer, imagine. She already knows these things about life. Could be she got that from him? It's a notion he keeps in his cheek like a squirrel keeps winter food. When he thinks of the man in the Mazaruni River, Ed knows that the proper teaching like Olivia is getting would have helped him to know how to act, what to do in the face of a crime, no matter who committed it. She will not be like her father who was expelled for truancy and bad grades from Corentyne High School. Even so, there are things she can learn from him: he can tell her about Marabunta Creek where he played as a boy, and about orange hibiscus with red veins, about frangipani, about Gafoors Shopping Complex in Rose Hall, the town where he was born, about Bartica and the wide Essequibo River like a thick vein in his own neck. Okay, yes, he has to stop thinking or tonight he will not sleep either.

Anna-Marie Hunter is his priority now. But the most important thing about this woman's death? Man, he is ashamed to admit it, but the abiding boon to this sad event is that it will bring him Olivia again. She wants help with her research, needs it to complete her studies this year, and this, this is what a father must do.

ROBIN

These departmental meetings are more frequent, the days for his research less so. His head is filled with jargon: *research income*; *collaborative partners*; *knowledge transfer*; *impact*. These are the terms that govern all of them these days, and those who rarely showed up for meetings when he first started at this university now attend regularly. "Concepts are centres of vibrations," says Deleuze, and his more politically astute colleagues are tightly wound to the academy's tradition of knowledge for its own sake. Until a few days ago and the announcement of his fatherhood, Robin was ready to stand alongside them, to take strike action in support of the principle of excellence. But now, in this meeting called for the film department, he sits at a desk near the back of the room like a third-class student and doodles with the Polish waitress's pen on the last page of the agenda. Richard, department head, tells them that the dean is implementing the first measure of restructuring ordered by the vice-chancellor's group. Film Studies and Film and Video Practice will merge, beginning in September.

"There's an initiative towards practice-based programmes as the key to our students being better prepared for employment," Richard says, and Robin doesn't disagree or make much of this. The other theorists hum with indignation: the closing of courses will mean a streamlining of outlooks, a lack of choice and the return to the values of a polytechnic, further marginalizing the students of this underprivileged borough, when once widening participation—a university graduate in every home—was the key goal. Knowledge for its own sake.

"And this is what management think students want?" Mark, reader in cultural theory, says. "From their 'client satisfaction' surveys?" he adds, his fingers doing air quotes.

"'Key performance indicators,'" says Albert, a professor in visual theories, mirroring Mark's air quotes. They have been here before—the hardcore old guard bemoaning the MBA management-speak that has permeated the academy. Edu-business stocks, Robin has been told by Mark, have tripled on the global exchange markets over the last five years. The Epicure waitress is called Katrin. Her lips are like Emmanuelle Béart's in *Un Coeur en hiver.*

"As a result, there will be new job roles and titles, and a department structure that reflects the redefinition of how film is studied in the school," Richard says. This brings grumbling about who will decide what, how will they define "new," about the lack of consultation. "New job specifications will be posted in the coming weeks, with interviews and decisions before Easter."

Interviews? Now the room erupts. Robin resists sitting forward in his chair, the panic too obvious. "Are these new roles advertised externally?" he asks.

"No," Richard says, "but they won't replicate the posts as they currently exist. New job specifications."

"But what will distinguish the candidates—among us?" Robin asks, aware that he is the most junior in the room. Richard looks flummoxed, and the others stay silent, underscoring the challenge.

"You will take the views of the students into account, I assume?" Robin says, and sits back again.

He pictures what is growing inside Emma. Will his long nose take shape there? Or her blue eyes? He hopes for her hands, not his, but it would be a disaster if the baby were so often as sad and angry as Emma.

He can't lose his job.

"There are key performance measures," Richard finally says. "Research, teaching, community engagement—you know the deal."

"Not everything is measurable," Robin says without leaning forward, but it's loud enough to be heard at the front of the room, and Mark slaps the desktop in a right-you-are gesture of agreement, and others offer up "Exactly," rallying against Richard who was once one of them. Robin wishes he were able to talk like a poet. In school he wanted to write poems, to acknowledge his contradictions, to challenge his own reason. And his own foolishness.

———

He hides out in his office at the end of the day again. Image: a child's booster seat for his piano bench. His groin moves with the wrong kind of excitement. Everything is confused.

A polite, faint knock on his door. He can't hide the fact of the light on, so he says, "Come in." He turns towards the door to find Olivia.

"Robin, hello, sorry to bother you," she says.

It's her hair and face that make her striking: curls like tangled seaweed, open gaze, features awkwardly set. "No problem," he tells her and although he hopes desperately that he won't make her cry this time, he feels grateful for the relief a student always offers. Their needs come first from the moment they sit in the chair beside his desk and, oh, what respite not to be engaged with his own petty thoughts, indecision trying to become action. He pushes his glasses up on his nose.

"I wanted to ask your advice, or maybe your help," she says as she sits.

That was his word. You can always ask for help, he said at the end of last year, and she erupted in sobs. She had come to his office about a missed deadline, apologizing, detailing the facts of her life: the unmanageable workload in her law courses, the fact that her mother supported the whole extended family, the fact that her mother kept secrets, and, with each disclosure more intimate than the last, with him leaning forward, on the verge of comforting her, finally she said that the young men her age merely wanted her to do more than she was already doing for everyone else, and this she could not stomach. He sat back, shunting his chair a little away to the left. But when she continued about all the things that needed fixing—the university, the gender divide, immigration laws—he began to admire her for the clarity of her sense of obligation, her easy recourse to action.

"Go ahead. Ask away," he says. He notices that Olivia is carrying a hardcover book whose spine reads *Death in the Nineteenth Century*. She surveys his office, up and down the shelves and over towards the window.

"You have even more books than last year," she says. He looks up with pride at the shelf piled with film theory, cinema history, books on their sides, books standing, rows and rows of them. Poetry chapbooks and pamphlets line the window sill. He must ask the school office for another shelf.

"My one bad habit," he says.

She looks down to the book in her lap. "I was wondering if you would help me with something . . . part of my final year law project. I wanted to investigate paupers' graves," she says and looks up at him. Her brown eyes are slanted and he sees now that there might be Chinese as well as African and Caucasian blood in her. These eyes go into a squint as though she's now embarrassed about what she's just said.

"Oh yes," he says and sits forward, wanting to show enthusiasm but not yet knowing where this is going. Parenting will be like teaching—he can do this.

"Not just about the people who can't afford a burial, you know, but also about those who have no one," she says. Her enthusiasm is undercut with anxiety.

"Yes, okay."

"Well, whose responsibility is it?" Her eyes go wide with the question.

"I suppose the state's—"

"I don't mean for the burial, I mean to honour them," she says.

"I don't know. No one's, I guess," he says. His sadness meets hers and waltzes through the room. She shifts and begins to tap her foot. He finds himself wanting to tell her about his baby, about Katrin and his heart.

"My research isn't about this, exactly," she says.

"Oh?" He holds her gaze, not wanting to press her.

"But I was just wondering if in films, like, in film history, there is anything that deals with that, with how you can remember the dead, how they can be honoured."

He leans back. He is trying to grasp her vision. As a father he will have to entertain ideas more oblique than this. In the Mexican Western, *The Three Burials of Melquiades Estrada*, the quest is to honour Melquiades, to find his home, to do right by him. But that is a stretch. Then there is that romantic comedy that rebranded British cinema, but that's just—but still, yes, here is something to say.

"Well, poetry is one way it's been done in film.... " he says, leaning forward. Her face lights up. "'Fear no more the heat of the sun,'" he says, but sits back; in this territory he is merely an interloper, and Shakespeare is surely not what Olivia has in mind. But her question has him churning now. A song: everyone needs their own song. He is tempted to mention "Brokedown Palace," his secret signature tune, the song he'd like played at his own funeral. Instead he says, "But my area is really film—I use philosophy to discuss images: movement and time. Sometimes that intersects with concepts from literature, with poetry, but . . . that's not the same."

She looks disappointed.

"What are you looking for, Olivia?" he says, thinking that this young woman holds truth as a cup holds water. He himself is a sieve.

"A link, I suppose," she says, and her face looks encumbered in a way that has nothing to do with the law project. "I don't know.... "

He allows a silence to fall.

"Yes, well. Maybe it's something to keep thinking about. It sounds like you need more of a legal angle, for the dissertation," he says, annoyed at himself for not showing her that he sees where she's going with this. He is off his game. She looks disappointed again, but nods. She thanks him, and the curls at the back of her head jump as she walks to the door and leaves.

Deleuze: The shame of being a man—is there any better reason to write?

FRANCINE

Lawrence's tie has bold red stripes. Francine watches him walk through the cafeteria with their colleague, Simon, both of them holding lunch trays loaded with lasagne and bread pudding. But she smells oranges. And lavender. (*Oranges and lemons, say the bells of St. Clemens, for you and for me, from Chef Boyardee . . .*) Across the table from her, Patricia is watching her watch them, waiting for the answer to her question. How the hell can you know why you obsess on one thing and not another? The mother of the motorcyclist keeps coming up, simple, but this has not been enough of an answer for Patricia, who is tracing the path of Francine's eyes as they jump from Lawrence to the students in the queue who are doing the hokey-pokey on the spot, earphones in, all of them jangling inside themselves. Francine can almost hear the music, can almost feel the tremors in their legs. The orange smell is heightened, peeled—all of it, everything excoriated.

She looks again at Lawrence, who is not dancing inside or anywhere else. One day last week he wore a bright purple tie. Lawrence thinks he's outrageous, but Francine can see through his tie to his shirt, through his shirt to his skin, through his skin to his heart to see that it's big but broken. She knows that last year his wife told him she was having trouble seeing how they could live together in the same house for the rest of their lives. Lawrence, who heads up Quality Assurance and Enhancement, used to talk to Francine on their lunch hours, on away days, when they'd break from the group and walk and he would smoke and she'd pretend she did too. At one point in the past few years Francine thought Lawrence was starting to see her as more than a sympathy buddy, and she even started to find his fat fingers sexy. The gossip is that Lawrence had an affair with a woman at his gym, his wife moved out, and even though he's single he no longer misses her. But Francine sees through the red stripes, through all of it. Oh Larry. Lawrence is maybe like Mary Tyler Moore's Mr. Grant (*Oh Mr. Graaaaaant*). She holds back her smile and turns her attention back to Patricia.

She answers finally: "Well, what would it be like to get that call from the cops—the English cops, while you're in Italy and maybe planning to visit your son who moved to London for work?" The cafeteria hums. On his way past, Lawrence beams her a smile, which Francine returns.

"You're romanticizing it," Patricia says, and Francine sits back, wary that Patricia, who doesn't seem at all like Dancefloor Patty here in the throbbing presence of all these young people, is turning her into one of her anthropological subjects, doing psychoanalysis on the fact that Francine has been constantly sick and disoriented since the sight of Dario's bent, emptied legs.

"Explain," she says, pushing the chicken thigh on her plate through the sauce.

"You like to think you had a connection to him, because you saw him die, but this is about you, not him," Patricia says, and maybe this is a step too close to the truth or maybe it isn't.

"Maybe it was yourself you saw lying face down on the road," she says, and after a pause, "or maybe your son—a son."

"What are you talking about?" Francine puts her fork down. The Atkins diet isn't working for her and Patty should stick to the dance floor. She looks up again as Lawrence laughs with Simon. His gappy teeth look like a ten-year-old's.

"I mean," Patricia catches Francine's eye. "I mean, you seem traumatized."

Francine looks back down at her chicken. Maybe she should try the raw food diet. She could sprout her own sprouts. She won't tell Patricia that she knows the name of the driver of the red sedan—Rajit Mahadeo—and that he is charged with dangerous driving causing death. Rajit Mahadeo is a name far removed from Francine Johnson. "And how have you been, Pat?" she says, trying out familiarity.

"Fine. Busy, but this term is lighter than last, so, fine."

"Your book?"

"Mmmm. I might have lost the lust for it," Patricia says softly, and Francine wonders how one has lust for a topic like the anthropology of water ("not water itself," Patricia said when first explaining it, "the necessity of water") in the first place. At least Patricia has the lust for something.

"Shame, sounded cool," Francine says. Patricia would never say cool. Francine is merely trying to keep the kindness floating.

"I'd rather be in the garden, all year round if it weren't for winter. I'm trying orchids this year. I'm not very good," says Patricia.

This shared interest in plants is not something Francine is willing to acknowledge just yet; besides, lots of middle-aged women like to grow things. She used to grow vegetables when she lived with Auntie T, but hasn't touched a garden in decades.

Dancefloor Patty lives her passions. But there's also something delicate about her—in a horsey-woman blond-bun kind of way. Those white shirts. And blue . . . slacks . . . you'd have to call them. And Oxfords. She comes from academic stock, from a long line of philosophers and mathematicians, but she prefers people science. She writes about people as they walk towards water, as they tilt towards the sun, as they bend in fields. Francine looks at her hands now and sees that despite the desiccated skin, Patricia has girly fingers that played with dolls. Probably made them perform passion plays and tragedies. Patricia would have been a girl who put on shows, who could skip faster than all the other girls, who built ant farms.

"We'd make a good singing duo," Francine tells her.

Patricia's brow twitches, and a wrinkle at her mouth deepens.

"I mean the names—Patty and Francine—a bit fifties, don't you think? Or an ice-cream franchise . . . " Francine laughs, and this makes Patricia's face go Times Square bright. Francine looks away, looks around. Lawrence is talking with his mouth full (*Well, it's you girl and you should know it . . .*), the students across from them have plates loaded solely with chips, which she wishes she had instead of this chicken. (*Love is all around no need to fake it . . .*).

"It could have been me," Francine blurts out, turning back to Patricia.

"What?" Patricia asks in a way that sounds like she already knows.

"Not me, on the road, but me in the car. I could have been the one who hit him," Francine says, but feels stupid so she also laughs and a small bit of snot runs from her nostril to her top lip. She wipes it off and holds Patricia's gaze long enough to blush.

"I see," Patricia says softly.

"People get hit, all the time, all the time, you know, by buses, scaffolding, by lightning. It's all over the place, you know?" And Francine is surprising herself now (*You can have the town why don't you take it...*). The hair on Patricia's arm is like the peach-fuzzy down on Virginia Cooper's top lip when they were ten years old. Virginia Cooper, veterinarian's daughter, saver of fallen baby birds, who lived on her street in Philly.

"Have you spoken to your brother?" Patricia asks. Scott is the opposite of a motorcyclist—a rich, high-flying financial manager with his own driver, in NYC.

"Why would I?" Francine says, her lip starting to tremble.

Patricia doesn't shake her head at her in that way that Aunt T would when met with the same tone of voice, time after time through Francine's orphan adolescence. What was it her mother would say to her? What was it? That thing her mother said to the eleven-year-old Francine about love? That final speech she always tries to grasp the tiny thread of—to hold on to what her mother left her with. About how "love comes with . . . "? What was it that love came with? Patricia looks at her.

"My brother isn't a phone guy," Francine says.

"Do you ever wish he was?" Patricia says. Francine can't stand the compassion, the wise tone of concern, and she puts her knife and fork together on her plate, scrunches up her napkin and places it on top.

"I've got tons of work," she says before standing. "I really should get going."

—

Her office smells of banana. She clears her desk and awakens her computer.

There's a message about the restructuring plans: "Have your say" forums are to be held throughout the rest of the term. Please, God. The wide streets of Philly will feel too big, the Julys too dry and hot. Please, God. She really needs to keep this job.

She checks other mail, but can't concentrate. She clicks on to Soulmates. There's a message from bringmesunshine:

I like your profile and pic. Would love to know more about life stateside. If you're interested, please e-mail me at matthughes794@ hotmail.com.

She clicks on to bringmesunshine's profile. Oh man. She tries to be gracious. Matt is fifty-nine, describes himself as a genuine kind of guy with a childish sense of humour. He would like to find an attractive, intelligent, and sophisticated woman "because underneath the quiet, unassuming exterior lies a wheelbarrow of surprises. (OK, I've nicked that line from AA Milne, but there is some substance to it.)"

Help.

She goes back to Dario Martinelli's Facebook page. Someone has posted a YouTube video called "My friend Dario." She plays it. A jumpsuited woman, backed by bikini-ed girls in American football helmets and silver high-heeled boots dance to "my friend Dario, drives, too fast, drives, too flash . . . . doesn't care about to crash." The video has been posted by Roberto Martinelli. Such ease that a brother has with crashing and dying?

She clicks off.

Good God.

OLIVIA

Fog gone; air rusty; time tight.

Right.

She's cold. The sheepskin bits of her jacket are tattered now, the hide ripped for shite. How to afford new clothes is anybody's guess. Olivia pulls her collar up, grips her leather bag, lets her curls fall over her right eye in the very second that she spots a dark male across the square watching her walk towards the Templeton Building. Clenching her legs, she holds herself in at the place no one has entered yet—sure, yeah, the fingers of Mark from year 10, but nothing like what that bloke might have in mind. Can't be Nasar. Nasar's texts don't make her feel like she has to fend off invaders. If Jasmine knew this is what happened to her when some peng bloke took a look at her, she'd send out the fam and make some kinda virgin intervention. Olivia speeds up and heads to the doors of the atrium but stops short of going inside, waits. For what?

"Fire," she whispers.

She will try hard to get through the me-me-me of the Student Union meeting, try to remember that the May '68 geezers were really something, that some things did really change, even though a bunch of them became Tories, and then she will go home to her room, to her sites and her books. She'll never have the guts to join Anonymous, but saved on her desktop, the shortcuts to Hactivisimo, Ninja Strike Force, and Cult of the Dead Cow remind her that there are people who are not asleep at the wheel.

"Olivia, y'all right?"

She jumps; shit.

"You coming to the meeting?" It's Moe, like molasses, Moe the slowest talker in the SU or maybe the world. His face is pale, his eyes circled by shadows that might have come from once being a kid who had a lot of pressure on him to be something other than just a kid. Moe for president, Moe for a bit of caffeine, more like. Moe's American and changed his name from Moses to Moe-nearly-like-Joe when he was thirteen.

"Moe, we gotta do something with the Heston Bridge people," she says, because Moe is good with things outside of uni life, Moe is fired up internationally even if it is a slow burn, and the illegals sleeping under the bridge are bound to be rounded up soon. Slow-Moe looks at her like he's making a political calculation.

"Sure, sure, let's bring it up at the meeting," he says.

Moe is sleep-inducing, but she needs to be more like him. She should've chosen refugee law for her dissertation instead of dead people. "See you there," she says and starts to open her satchel so that he thinks she's got something important to attend to. Moe turns and plods inside. She rummages for chewing gum and waits for him to reach the automatic doors and disappear into the atrium.

She moves off; the pebble inside her Ugg boot rubs her big toe. The strumming of a guitar comes from across the square. The busker sings. She wants to stay and listen, but what if the hoodie over there is Nasar? She walks slowly. The singer hits a note that makes the hair on her arms stand up. She knows now how Robin might help.

THE TASTE

OF MARMALADE

KATRIN

This morning she has no paper for the toilet. Forgotten yesterday, no time, too tired, passed the shop, to bed. To sleep. She washes herself in the basin, on tiptoes, thigh on the sink, water splashing on the floor. Washes her hands a second, third time. Glances out of the window at the flower box, the frost that didn't come, and feels again the waiting inside. The tick-tocking of morning, watching. But she must go to work. Work takes her away from the window boxes, the waiting on the shoots in the soil, but in the café there is the man who comes every day now, to smile at her. He will never love her if she cannot even have paper for the toilet.

Outside: the crocuses, purple, white, maybe, the ones she saw last year and named Beata one, two and three, for her *mamunia*, but cannot remember which is which, along with the toilet paper. The tips, there, just beneath the dirt around the tree. This makes the hair on her arm stand up. This England sight, this not-Poland sight, this evidence that she is making her life on her own and for her *matka* when she will come in May. February in Gdansk is snow. February in London is the poking heads of purple and white.

Katrin swallows. The taste of marmalade.

In the coffee shop there is angry Claire from Tottenham and

Alejandro from Madrid and she is Katrin not from anywhere now, not from Gdansk, not from her father who left, not even from her mother who sleeps at the edge of the big bed where the pillow beside her is still dirty with her husband's hair oil.

"You take your time," Alejandro says, as she walks in, and she looks up at the clock to see that she is not yet late.

"You take the piss," she says, and they smile, because this is a sentence he himself has taught her. "Second person singular, showing improvement," he says, and her day will go well, now, here on Upper Street where the man might come back and Alejandro will make her laugh.

But Alejandro is not fun today, having a fight with his girl-friend by text, and there is a sourness from Claire: "This country is fucked. They are ripping us off." And when police sirens sound in the street: "It's all kicking off." These words make Katrin go curly inside. Claire throws slitted eyes at her and complains that Katrin is not doing enough refilling of the coffee machine. And when the man comes to the Epicure Café at the end of her shift she tries not to look unhappy.

"You need a pastry, too, sir," she tells him, holding the smile in her mouth and his coffee in her hand.

"You must call me Robin," he says, and she looks away, not because she is shy but because she loves this name. This man is one of the birds, the early morning bird, she has learned in English.

"Robin," she says and waits to see if he will take up her sug-gestion, but she thinks he is not really a pastry man. He has long eyelashes under his glasses. He is a man who lives through his eyes not his mouth.

"Nothing else, thanks. This is fine," he says and his long fingers, the fingers of someone who plays the piano, take hold of his coffee cup. "Did you see that film?" She does not remember the name of the German-Turkish director of this film, but its title in English, *Head-on*, is a way of speaking in this language that she must practise.

"Not yet, I will, I will," she tells him, and wishes she was not so tired at night. And there is Claire with a look like there is a snake in her throat, watching her, so Katrin moves to clean the table beside him, even though there is not dirt there, but there is the ribbon of the sun. When London first loved her it was always night time, Soho, films to help her English, and quiet bars on nights off from the loud one where she worked with Ania who went back to Poland, Ania who could not love these English men. Ania said, you are educated, they think you are cheap because you work in this bar, and they will never treat you as you deserve. Katrin would loosen the pony tail of her straight blonde hair, letting it fall towards her face to make it look less angular, more oval and English, but Ania said she would never fit in. Ania went back to Gdansk, where she is working in an office for less than one quarter of what Katrin makes in the café. Okay, so it is not anymore a bar; things are better: she works in the day.

A tall woman with a pink scarf wrapped high around her neck, covering her chin, enters Epicure. She walks like a soldier towards another woman at the back table, who stands in time for the pink woman to fall towards her and into her arms crying, like she is remembering what children do. The friend holds her tight, while the pink-scarfed woman cries and says not a word. They stand like that for a long time. Katrin watches until both of them sit down. When she looks back over at Robin he is staring at the women, before he looks at her. He nods at Katrin with a face that says, yes, sometimes things are exactly so.

Ania told Katrin's mother a lie. A lie that Ania knew was the only thing to say to her best friend's mother, because mothers are all the same. She told Beata that by the time May came and she was ready to move to her daughter in Islington, England, that the twenty-six-year-old Katrin would be married to an Englishman who would help her to find a job suited to the economics degree her daughter achieved at the University of Gdansk.

No matter. This is Robin, who teaches at a university and said her English is perfect, and this is a job in the day, and the crocuses are coming up.

FRANCINE

Almost nothing. After a whole pizza and some Doritos—a proper Saturday night feast—all that comes is a sore throat. Francine pushes at the tiny window in her bathroom, the paint chipping on the frame as she shoves it open to the cold air. She should move. This flat has done its time with her: six years, beginning with the early wailing—the wasted tears over Fuckhead on the rented bed—through the more hopeful middle period of repainting the bedroom walls, of forcing the landlord to replace the boiler, to this last stage of plumping the comfy cushions, lighting scented candles, dimming the lights: the patient waiting for someone who would change everything.

She breathes in the bronze-smelling air from outside. Traffic noises scratch the night.

Mom—what was it she'd said? *Love is . . . blah blah, Francine. Love comes with . . . blah blah.* She must remember. She walks to her living room and the couch is barely solid. Everything in the room is in *Star Trek*'s transporter room. She can't sit down.

She picks up the phone and dials.

When Scott answers his cell phone he's got his I'm-an-important-and-busy-man voice on. It's Saturday, for Christ's sake.

"Just checking in," she says.

"Hey, surprise, surprise. Whassup?" he says and oh Christ—whassup? Maybe he's just shocked that she has called again so soon after Christmas.

"Do you remember," she says, "something that Mom used to say—"

"God, Fran, really?"

Scott hasn't had a moment for their mom since she died when he was nine. Scott claims basically not to remember her, not to miss her, not to need to talk about her. But Francine knows there was something their beautiful, cancer-ridden mother said on her bed as she wheezed away her last few days in their bungalow on Minerva Street, a bed brought home by their kindhearted dad, who is the one Francine must have got the tending plants thing from, because what she remembers most about him is the dirt on his knees from kneeling in the garden. He tended to her mother like she was the last orchid on the planet. The thing her mother said about love was said in that bungalow, and it felt like a chiming in Francine's ears, but the chiming gradually stopped, because the pulp of a teenage brain is porous. It was something that should have stayed forever. But now she can't find it, can't get back to it somehow.

"How's the winter treating you guys over there?" he says.

"Relentless, totally relentless. You?"

"Same, but at least it's sunny here—and not so goddam damp. You should come back." This is Scott's thing: to find a way to make Francine feel there's always something she's missing out on or not got quite right. And so she must stay in London if it kills her, even if, as Scott has told her time and again, the US will always be the future and England will always be the past. And damp.

She searches for something else they have in common, given that their dad, who raised them on his own for eight years, seeing her through high school and Scott through to his driver's licence, had a heart attack and left them to join his wife.

"Melissa okay?" she asks.

"Been laid off," Scott chirps, as though he's somehow pleased. Poor Melissa: no job and no kids, because her dickhead of a husband didn't want them. Ten years ago Melissa replaced a longing for children with a love for Jesus and has perpetually tried to get Francine to join her in the promise of rapture.

"Oh, I'm sorry to hear it. Any prospects?"

"Sure, sure, though the job market's tough. But, you know, she doesn't really need to work anyway. I do just fine."

Okay, that's enough. (Death tastes like Dr. Pepper.)

"She might get into charity work," he continues.

As Scott chirps on about charity being more and more important in times like these, Francine wonders whether he would be a beam-me-up Scotty if he were in this room. Would she be able to see through her little brother, or would he be an odourless, opaque mass of Scottness?

They sign off formally—Well, brother . . . Well, sister— and Francine doesn't put the phone back in its cradle properly. A few minutes later she picks it up again and books an evening out with Patricia.

ROBIN

On his route home from the tube station Epicure is a short diversion. Katrin is coming towards him as he enters, but she has her coat on, her knapsack slung over one shoulder.

"You're leaving. I was just stopping in for tea."

"It's the end of my shift—Alejandro is closing," she says and looks towards the dark-haired man at the counter who gives her a sly smile. Jealousy sketches a shape in Robin's chest.

"Are you going home?"

"Yes."

"Do you have time for tea then? We could go somewhere else."

She smiles. "Tea is not my drink, but I am learning to be English."

Her proficient English humbles his pathetic French, his effete attempts at German and Spanish. He wants to take her hand. They walk down Upper Street, something he tells himself he's doing every time he's doing it, but today he doesn't bother with the joke. Today he has the sensation of going down a tunnel. The lane behind Camden Square snakes off to a cobblestone alleyway where Moment Café is squeezed between a dress shop and an antiques dealer. The owner, Martin, has been selling records for twenty years; he added the coffee, tea, hot chocolate and pastries five years ago in order to address the rising rent, and he sells more of them now than he does records.

"This is something," Katrin says as she pulls out the bar-stool to sit at the high table next to the Decca wind-up gramo-phone. Her voice comes straight from her belly; he's never heard anything so clear. He orders tea from Martin, who brings it over to them and chats about the recording of Bach partitas that he suggested for Robin the last time he was in. Robin tries hard not to look too much at Katrin as she pours tea from the pot.

"He's gentle," Katrin says, when Martin leaves them to each other. She tells him about her Polish friend, Andrzej, who has a zipper tattoo on his arm, which gives the impression that his flesh could be unlocked if you tugged at it. Like Martin, she tells him, Andrzej is a gentle man. As she describes the rooming house where Andrzej lives with five other men, flashes in Robin's cere-bral cortex convince him he knows this already, that he and Katrin have not only had this conversation before, but that they have fea-tured together in numerous scenes accompanied by their own original soundtrack, in another time-space continuum. In *Matter and Memory*, Bergson pushes further the Cartesian split of mind and body to assert that the body is the abode of the present, while the spirit is anchored in the past, continually arriving, here, now.

"Here," he says as he offers her more tea. He lifts the petit fleurs porcelain teapot and pours. He tips it too far over, the lid tumbles off, clangs rudely off the tabletop and smashes onto the floor in two embarrassed halves. "Oh hell." He looks over at Martin who gives him a shrug. He would like to be more like Martin. He picks the two dainty pieces up, holding them together along the fracture line and making it look like nothing at all has been broken. He returns to the stool, puts the lid on the table, and as it opens again along its fissure, he turns back to her face. She has a look that says he is not a bumbling fool, that she doesn't mind if he's nervous. What if hers could be the features of his baby? He's insane, this is all insane. It's hot in here. And he is a cliché: Rath consumed by Lola in *The Blue Angel*. He is every poor bloke who ever wrote a sonnet.

"You're very funny," she says, smiling, her eyebrow hitched up.

"Funny?"

"Not funny, like the way you laugh. Funny the other way. You know: weird. Weird-funny."

"I wouldn't use weird if you're not trying to insult me . . . "

"Oh no!" She laughs. "No. I like weird." She touches his hand and he takes a breath, and is now very glad that it is hot in this café, so she won't know that the temperature of his skin has everything to do with her.

"You said you studied economics," he says, because economics has facts; facts are hard lines, real.

"Yes, but I don't like this so much now," she says.

"Why not?" he asks. She looks at her hands to consider the question, as though she must build him the answer. He knows little about Poland, and mostly through film images and phrases—shipyards; Solidarity.

"We have two kinds of university. In public universities in Poland you have only one way to look at economics. In private you have all ways open to discussion, but in state universities at first cycle—this is what we call BA—they cannot afford to teach you to challenge. Economics is not prescription, I think," she says and looks to him to see if she's right, but there could be nothing more perfect than what she has said.

"My grandfather owned a small company that made aluminium panels for prefab houses after the war," he says. Does she understand the meaning of prefab? "My father was an engineer . . . so maybe I should have made things instead of watching them."

"But it is your passion!" she says, and he feels off balance. He's embarrassed to say the things he wants to about film, but he finds his courage.

"There is a wonderful scene in three of my favourite films— an image of old people trying to recycle bottles. In one film the scene is shot in hues of blue, the other in white, and the last one in red light, for liberté, egalité, fraternité."

"But he is mocking them," she says, and of course she knows the work of Kieslowski probably as well as he does, so he nods, can't stop nodding, because there are images they share, and he is giddy with them.

Robin begins to talk on as though he is continuing the single thought they have shared for years. By the time his phone rings, he has told her everything about the year he was ten and how he built a whole village out of balsa wood, the church being the centre, the church—even though, no, no, he doesn't believe . . . it's not like they were believers—as big as the television in his parents' front room as they watched *Dad's Army* and he took strips of balsa wood and fashioned a utopia for . . . for her—he doesn't say this, of course; he doesn't say it was for her, but now that he thinks of it, it must have been for her, for who else but her has he been piecing cusps and zeniths together for all these years?

"Hi, Emma," he says softly into his mobile, but he should not have said her name, not in front of Katrin, who perhaps has not heard but who nevertheless looks away, unwittingly getting out of the way of his conversation with the mother of his child. When Emma tells him that she's done a lot of thinking and she has decided that it would be better if he moved to Cornwall with her, he turns his back on Katrin, not meaning to snub her, not wanting to do anything other than protect her from all the action-images of his life.

"Can I call you back in an hour?" he says to Emma. He hears her struggle to be gracious—of course, of course—and he rings off, looks back at Katrin, and wishes again to be a lightning bolt.

OLIVIA

"Tell me about him," Olivia says, plonking down on the bed. How can a mother lie in so long even on a Sunday? Ginger. The smell of the bed is like the herbal tea that Jasmine's mother serves over at hers while they study. The sheet has the uneven feel of her mother. She touches Catherine's pale cheek, the fold at her eyelid. Catherine doesn't like it when Olivia calls her by her name, but Catherine has never been Mummy, more like Kat Slater in *EastEnders*, less nasty, less of a slapper, but same-ish looks, same-ish secret ways about her.

"Where is he, Catherine?" Olivia says softly in her mother's ear. She will tell her she's met Edward only when she has had an answer. Catherine turns over under the sheets, blinking, looking at her daughter, through her, all the way to somewhere without secrets.

"Baby, I'm not awake."

The sleepy Catherine is the best. Olivia nuzzles into her mother's neck; powdery, plump, permanent. "Tell me about Wood."

"Oh, for God's sake," Catherine says. As she pulls the sheet up over her shoulder, Olivia smells her mother's ginger breath, all girly, while deep down Olivia has snakes and snails and puppy-dog tails.

"He didn't fight for me," Olivia says, stretching out her legs along her mother's body; silken. The melty feeling takes over her legs and then her arms. "He left. Or did you kick him out?" Nearly whispered, that last bit, on account of the eggshells in Catherine's heart.

Catherine turns over on her back and wrests her eyes open to the ceiling. "Why are you asking me this now? What's up?" she says, and turns her head to Olivia's face so that their cheeks touch.

"Nothing's up." This is whispered too.

"I don't know where he is," her mum whispers back, and they lie still; everything is soft.

Until the song Ed used to sing chimes in and there are all the things she needs to put right and, when she does, she and Catherine can move away from Granddad and Eric and take Nan with them. She'll get a first in her degree, get a job, get a flat—

"Stop shaking your foot," Catherine says, "it's shaking the whole bed."

And one thing that Olivia can't compute in all of this is how Catherine went and had a baby with a black man when her whole life she must have heard Granddad hollering Enoch Powell's rivers of blood at the telly. Her whole life she would have been made fearful of the very thing that's lying pressed up against her right now.

"You need a hubz," Olivia says.

Catherine turns her head closer and looks directly at her daughter. She brushes the curls away from Olivia's face and stares in her eyes as an optician would, looking for changes. "Do you have one?" Catherine asks, and oi, of course this is what she's wondering because this is the topic her mother loves to raise, softness or not.

"I don't need one, but you do," Olivia says sharply, turning her cheek towards her mother's mouth.

"I've got a 'hubz,' thanks," Catherine says, and argh, Catherine is talking about the swag gas man who calls himself an engineer. Even Granddad has seen through him.

"What, once-a-week William?" She feels her mum's lips swell and hears a little giggle. "He bought you dinner yet?"

"I'm getting up now," Catherine says and leaves Olivia clutching the imprint of her curves in the bed. "You get back to your studies."

Olivia pulls the sheet and blanket over her. Ginger, grape-fruit and the scratchy cheap sheets her mother can't afford to toss out. She feels her idea taking shape, and Robin's role becoming clear.

KATRIN

Epicure is a place to feel proud. It serves French macarons, has specialty in panettone and Brie-wrapped phyllo, and they order from their special chefs the best wedding cake in London. Epicure mixes tart and sweet and bitter: apple and frangipane; lemon and custard; cheese and carrot; coffee and mascarpone. These new words she loves because they are nothing like the ingredients in other jobs, nothing like paper or plastic or metal.

Katrin counts the day's earnings and rolls the elastic band over the bills, twists it, doubles it over again, and puts the cash in the bag with a lock that Claire leaves for them in the evening. Epicure makes money, Katrin makes tips, and she does not have to scan bar codes like her friend Andrzej, or check that the sports food supplements are packed in each box, eighty hours a week, twelve hours a day, for £5.93 an hour. She is not in a factory. She is on Upper Street and she takes one bus to work. Her father made £400 a month for all of them. She makes this for herself in one week because Epicure gives the service charge to the server. She is proud, even though this England freedom comes with tiredness.

But tonight she is going to meet Robin for dinner. And she is clean. She is not tired.

—

To arrive. To sit. To smile. These are verbs in the intransitive form. But transitive verbs give her the trouble, because in Polish they do not only have a direct object. He sees her. She is seen by him. In Polish these are both possible. It is this form that she must stop confusing in English. Robin is sipping. He is sipping his wine, but his wine is not being sipped. Before this wine he raised a shot glass and swallowed vodka, her suggestion, because Bison was her father's drink, and they winced at the same time with the heat in their throats. But now talking in Robin's language—not only English, but the language of art and film—she is not so confident. This is the space that is opening inside her for words and pictures, and she does not want to be stupid in this. But he is kind. He looks at her as though anything she says will be a poem. She tries not to disappoint him.

"In Poland film is so poor they light it with candles, and this is what made Kieslowski so famous." She waits. He smiles, and now she can too. She sips her Spanish wine. Plum and vanilla.

"And where will you live when your mother comes?" he asks her, this fact about her remembered from weeks ago as she stood at his table, drawing her out, drawing her in.

"She will live with me, where I am." The waiter puts paella in front of her.

"It's a bedsit, right?" he says, with neither judgment nor pity.

"We have been in much smaller, it's fine." She doesn't want to talk about herself any more. "And you," she says, "you live alone?"

Behind glasses his eyes dart left towards a poster of the Alhambra. She adjusts her hair, runs her finger over her ear, before he looks at her again; something is not the same.

"I might be moving soon," he says. Her stomach bends.

"I'm coming back," she says as she stands up, not too fast, so that he will not be worried.

In the toilet she tells her face in the mirror that this is nothing, nothing. That her *matka* is coming, that she has a job in the day, that England is not Poland, that there are many fish in the lake, that this is Robin, named for something that flies, and that she must ignore this *czekam* feeling like she is the pet at the door when he is turning a key to come in.

She washes her hands.

"Are you okay?" he asks when she is back in front of his kind face.

"Yes, fine, thank you," she says and smiles.

"I'm not avoiding your question. I live alone right now," he says. The *czekam* swells and she takes a sip of wine. She must not drink too much because she will be stupid with wine.

FRANCINE

Galumphing—is that what she's doing? When she first met John he would tease her, telling her that her walk was a waddle, but then when she gained weight he started to call it a galumph. She feels her hips and tenses her thigh muscles so that she doesn't galumph along the pavement from the underground, where she has just emerged from Covent Garden tube station. Driving only on completely confident days seems to be working out for her nerves, and all this walking will work for her thighs. But right this moment she is naked in the middle of London's west end. Naked to the smells. What does soot smell like? Like damp potatoes. Naked to that woman in the hijab who has looked at Francine's legs in these stretchy trousers that expose every single bulge. Naked to the voice of the man with his head down, mumbling (*Dog Chow makes me very happy* . . .). Covent Garden station is a joke of pressing bodies, and she is exposed to them all.

It begins to rain.

She pulls her scarf tight around her, dips her chin, raises her shoulders, and looks out for the restaurant as she heads towards the Royal Opera House.

Patricia loves opera. Patricia can *Così-fan-tutte* with the best of them, and tonight they are seeing *Rigoletto*, and, when Francine asked to be briefed on the basic story and if there'd be tunes she'd recognize, Patricia corrected, "Not tunes, arias."

Of course Patricia is already at the restaurant when she arrives and this, Francine knows, is what women her age do now, what it means to be past the pause, with no time for pausing, no time to be late. You've gone all meno, Cindy used to say to her mother when she and Francine were teenagers. She never got to pause, Francine would say of her own mother. Meno-pause: the lying in wait . . . for what?

The restaurant Patricia has chosen is French, and Francine feels uneasy about the tablecloths and soft lighting because flickering up through the romantic chroma is Dario's bent leg. She pulls her chair out to take her seat across from Patricia. The knife, spoon, fork are a quivering silver (one of Dario's arms was tucked under him, the other bent back, almost curled). The plates on the table are matte white, which makes them appear almost solid, but she's not fooled, she knows that none of this really exists, and that molecules and breath and sympathy are an illusion.

"I used to come here with my ex," Patricia says, lifting up the wine list. Francine wants to block Patricia's radar, so she lifts her menu too, in front of her face. This is the first time Patricia has ever mentioned a partner, and Francine waits for a pronoun.

"We'd argue about whether it was right to eat foie gras and veal; of course, it was not what we were really arguing about. It was my way of telling him he was thoughtless, his way of telling me I thought too much."

Francine lowers her menu, feeling safer now, and looks at Patricia. "How long were you together?"

"Five years, not that long, in the scheme of things, but he was the first person I'd ever lived with. I was a late bloomer." Patricia puts the wine list down. "I'd never pinned myself down before that."

Francine would not in a million years eat foie gras, but she briefly considers it now.

"I travelled a lot—on field research trips, and he was just there, happy when I got home."

Francine might order escargots—she used to love them in her twenties when eating French food was exotic and showed you knew a thing or two about love and garlic. Love comes with . . . blah blah.

"So did you only argue when you came home?" she asks.

Patricia doesn't answer. She looks for the waiter, signals to him, and orders a bottle of Chablis. Then she looks at Francine so sternly that Francine feels she is in school again, in trouble for forgetting her gym shorts. Patricia's mouth twitches like it doesn't know what to do next. And then her face softens. The tears that might have flowed aren't coming after all. The English: they know how to do that.

"I think I just needed him to resist me, somehow, resist just being there and happy. I don't know. I'm not easy."

And in Patricia's voice is that little girl who tortured dolls, collected butterflies, made life difficult for others because it was hell to be Patricia. Francine looks down at her menu, but she has begun to perspire and has to wipe her brow.

"How about you and John. Did you fight?" Patricia asks.

I'm speaking for myself and you're perfectly welcome to speak for yourself. I take full responsibility for my own feelings and am not blaming you, but I feel angry when you don't respect my space, said John, in his gobbledy-gook, self-help jargon, so that whatever anger she might have had about him not calling her for two days was redirected back at herself and her so-called responsibility for her own feelings, which she knows now was just the Fuckface's way of shutting her out, shutting her down. So that when the day came— when she finally was able to raise her voice and yell: "Why is it always about you?"—well, he slammed a door and she ended up foetal on the floor. Only when he declared that he would never have children, even though he claimed regularly how great he'd be at it, did she finally twig that John Clarke was not the man she had imagined him to be; twig that she had known this all along; twig that John Clarke was a fuckwit. But he was her fuckwit, and she believed in sticking with things.

"No, John didn't like to fight."

"Like to fight? That's not what I asked," Patricia says with a smirk. And suddenly Francine can see through Patricia's skin, through to the blood in her veins, through to her bones. It makes her tummy rumble with hunger and makes the Chablis smell like vinegar. She sits forward in her chair, her elbows on the table, and clears her throat.

"Patricia. What is it, exactly, that you would like to hear from me?" She holds this forward tilt for two, three, four seconds, then sits back and picks up her menu, but she can feel her lip starting to tremble. Peeking over the menu she sees that Patricia is smiling, that Patricia has enjoyed Francine's defiance, and now, oh shit, she's really done it now.

—

The cup lights that line the balconies—their shimmering make the Royal Opera House appear to be on the verge of being beamed up. And it smells of . . . what? Nina Ricci, that's it. She has to hold her nose, but a little cough comes, just beneath the soft music, an aria not a tune, into the second half of *Rigoletto*. She has been struggling to stick with it and has been lulled along by the arias she recognized from Bugs Bunny cartoons, and by her memories of working on the high school production of *Oklahoma*, doing costume and makeup, sewing petticoats and bonnets, and going home singing about how the cowboys and the farmers should be friends and the elephant-eye height of the corn.

But she's sleepy. Her eyes are sliding shut. Okla, Okla, homa, homa . . . O.K.L.A.H.O.M.A. She rubs her eyes, keeps her eyebrows raised.

When she jolts awake it's the hand she feels first—Patricia's on her arm—but then she realizes that her head has dropped in Patricia's general direction, looking to be patted. Straightening up, she flushes, sweat welling like tears, and the baritone is singing like he is crying too. Patricia's face is fixed in concentration. On what? The words? Does she know Italian? The notes are sad. Patricia glances over, gives a little smile and rubs Francine's forearm just before Francine moves it away.

The next day at work, and all that week, Francine makes tea in her office and brings parcels of protein—tuna, ham, even roast beef—for lunch so that she doesn't have to appear at the Starbucks in the atrium or the Costa's in the Watson building. She doesn't answer her phone when she sees Patricia's number come up on the screen, and when Patricia leaves a voicemail message wondering how she is, Francine writes a polite text back telling her that she's incredibly busy and that all the work is keeping her mind off troubling things. She doesn't tell Patricia that it actually felt good to be tilted towards her at the opera or that she has found out that the man who killed Dario—Rajit Mahadeo—is a fifty-five-year-old night shift Quality manager at Kandhu Ltd., supplier of branded and own-labelled snack food to major UK retail centres. Rajit Mahadeo lives in Harlesden with his wife, mother-in-law, and four children aged between ten and nineteen. He was released on bail the night of the accident, having been charged with dangerous driving causing death.

The charge continues to be the disconcerting fact in the case. She saw no dangerous driving from the red sedan on that night. The others must have seen something more terrible. She should have stayed longer. Slumped over his steering wheel in tears, Rajit had not been dangerous in any way.

It could have been her.

OLIVIA

Olivia, you make heart singing. Nasar

He's probably in the queue. That's well-dred. Has he seen her? She looks behind her but sees the wheelie bloke in his Paralympic vehicle, whose name she knows for sure is Christopher. Who the fuck is Nasar? She throws the phone into her satchel. She wouldn't get in that queue in any case; she can get water from the tap in the caff and pick up a regular coffee there too. It's hard to keep her eyes open on account of how much reading she did last night so that when her tutor, Stan, looks at her and asks which EU statutes apply to jurisdiction and immunity in international law, she'll have something to say. But she's done with answering people's questions, really. All those answers have exposed her, and Nasar might be a phony name for Clive or Richard or Amir, trying to humiliate her. She's answered enough questions for a whole degree, and all it's given her is—what? No, what she needs now is continue her boycott of Costa and Starbucks, get a first on her dissertation project, and find a way to persuade Robin about her idea.

She heads down the atrium, passing another queue. How can they afford this shite, anyway? The cost of coffee in this uni has doubled since last year. Brand me with your beans. If Nasar is among these sheep, she'll never find him. And she wouldn't want to.

Head down, hands in pockets, Olivia is a panther up the stairs—oh oh oh oh, talk to me some more, Robin. But at his office on the first floor the lights are off, computer shut down.

—

Jasmine is smug-arsed and floaty. Olivia wants to pull Jasmine's hair until it comes loose at the roots. "It's fine," she says, instead of tugging. It's fine: the fact that it's been weeks since Jasmine shagged the Italian dude they met together and is only now telling Olivia about it, on account of thinking that Olivia would have been merked to know earlier.

"I know you had your eye on him," Jasmine says as she gathers up her long brown curls and makes a pile on her head, pouts like a model. Eleanor-turned-Jasmine works hard at her curls, wears Rihanna tops, and too much lipstick to make her lips look thick, all the while them being thin as shite, because Jasmine was cheated at birth, should have been born something more sexy than an Eleanor. Olivia has known her since primary school, when Eleanor was the quiet, slim but dim girl that Olivia made friends with because no one else would. Eleanor was generous, always doing things for other people, always bringing treats for Olivia, who grew to depend on her kindness, depend on her house as an escape on the days when Granddad would beer-up and go off on one. Then something happened to Eleanor in year 10, when her father started staying out all night and her mother became a Christian. Eleanor started having sex like it was her own Jesus. Her generosity turned to giving head, and giving up the inside of her, night after night, like it would change her into someone else. And so Jasmine emerged.

Jasmine sucks her teeth.

"You're always playing so hard to get, so I figured he was fair game," she says, but what does Jasmine know about fair and what does Olivia know about any game. The Italian biker would have made everything shut up for her like the seaside in winter, because she's not going to end up like Catherine with some guy riding off into the horizon, so he's better off having done Jasmine if that's what he wanted.

"He's bang tidy," Jasmine says, "and he lips like a prince." Jasmine would know. Jasmine has kissed a prince from Benin, even though both of them know that the Nigerian dude said he was from the Royal Edo people as a way to get Jasmine to open her legs. "I'm sorry," she adds, "he would have been a good one to add to your list."

Olivia nods and looks disappointed as she plays the girl with a list who might want to add yet another hubz. Jasmine admires Olivia for her brains, but also because Olivia is nearly black and surely has had it—like, lots—surely. A misconception Olivia has never tried to correct.

"We texted after, for, like, days. He called me, and once we even did it over the phone," Jasmine says. But her face goes mincy all of a sudden.

Olivia can tell there will be no studying tonight. And she is not going to get a word in about how she's going to her first funeral ever tomorrow to meet Edward Reynolds, or about how paupers' graves were a thing that people thought had disappeared with plagues and horse-drawn carriages, but that her thesis will show . . . dang, what will her thesis show? That she has a father, that her father buries these people, that maybe her father left on account of her or the shite he had to put up with in the very household she is dying to leave. And she will try to make it all better again. And then?

Olivia plants her face in the pillow on Jasmine's mother's sofa. She's always thought of this as the Born Again pillow; it's silky, packed with eiderdown. It takes the weight of her chin so tenderly—like it loves her—that she bolts up.

Right.

"I have to do some revising," she says and takes up her notebook. Jasmine gives her that look saying don't be jealous of me, it's not my fault blokes like me, but Olivia starts to make pretend notes and ignores her.

Back in the day, workhouse poor had paupers' burials, even if they had family. Coffins made of cheap wood would crack with the weight or be too small, but it's all they had. Families wanting to make coffins special put ribbon or hair or cloth over the box, and there was no affording a cart or horse; only lifting and walking would get the coffin to the plot. Olivia has sifted through letter after letter from family members asking for bodies to be exhumed from paupers' graves after the family had saved enough for a private burial. People care about these things. But do we still have rights in death? And what about a lonely death with no relatives to come claim you?

"I think I'm going now," she says to Jasmine as she closes her book.

"Look, Liv, I'm sorry, okay?" The pity in Jasmine's face is confusing because, without her knowing what for, there's lots of pity that could be heaped on a girl who hasn't got time to be touched.

"Jaz, I'm gettin' it plenty other places," Olivia says and makes a black-girl zigzag with her neck that she knows gets Jasmine's blood racing. "See you soon."

ED

Cannon-ball tree, kufa, yellow allamanda, soldier's cap, parrot beak, stinky toe: they are the flowers a child should know, would know if she was to visit she grandmother in Rose Hall. These flowers Ed's mother taught him to say when he was a child, she thinking that learning was about reciting things one after the other. But here in the chapel entrance, Olivia has her eyes on the lilies in the vase he himself bought this morning to make an impression on her, and he hopes she's thinking it is proppa good. Ed cannot take his eyes off Olivia's face because if he does it will be like losing her again, and Catherine too because Catherine is there in the girl's cat-eyes, in her straight-straight but gappy teeth. Olivia is the most beautiful thing he has ever seen.

"Please take your seats," the vicar says.

Ed is standing at the front of the chapel next to the coffin of Anna-Marie Hunter, known for her quiet and polite demeanour. Her neighbours say they didn't see much of her outside her flat for the two years she lived there: no trouble at all, just quiet and polite. Anna-Marie has no known next of kin. Anna-Marie will be cremated at 13:30. Ed will make sure this happens smoothly and quickly because he is meeting up with Olivia after. When

Neil—the vicar he regularly calls on for these funerals—is finished his few words about how life brief fa so, Ed will swing into action. It is action he was missing, back home on the river, standing doing nothing while blood spread out in the water like octopus ink. He could have said a word or two, then and there. He could have.

"'I am the resurrection and the life. He who believes in me will live, even though he dies,' says the Lord (John 11:25)," Neil says and he continues quickly, because he knows this will be the short version. Even God is going along with Anna-Marie being quiet and polite.

There are only three people, other than Ed, Neil and Olivia, to bid goodbye to this woman, and they are neighbours who have not prepared anything to say about her. The ceremony is over in no time and the neighbours leave quickly, not even talking to one another, and this is another thing that Ed must tell Olivia: that West Indian people talk to one another, even if they are strangers. *Wha gwan, gal? When last we see ya?* He wishes Olivia would talk to one of Anna-Marie's neighbours, but the girl puts her head down and looks sad when they leave the chapel.

"Wait for me in the A13—it's a caff down Ripple Road," he tells her outside when the wind blows, cold-cold, burning up he cheeks and making him hold tight to his flimsy jacket, which is the only good one he has that fits him, now that he has a paunch. He must attend to the business of Anna-Marie's remains but he desperately wants to speak to this beautiful daughter standing right here. The first time he talked to her in the staff room at the Safe and Sorrow office he was so schupity that she had to do all the talking. This time he wants to talk—to talk to her like a father.

"Will you be long?" Olivia asks, her voice like the one he has heard in his sleep.

He tells her to meet him at two o'clock, and that he hopes that is not too long for her. And it is relief like cooling rain when she agrees.

—

The A13 caff is a pitiful sight and, blast, not right for Olivia. He should have known better: this outdated box with six tables covered in plastic cloth, salt and pepper in cheap old-fashioned shakers, brown sauce for egg and chips, the signs old, the waitress old, the chairs old-old. Man, he mess up with this one. He sits down in front of her. Olivia looks up from her book.

"Hi, hi," she says and smiles, uncomfortable, but a smile in any case, so his chest fills up. "This place is nang," she says.

"Nang?"

Her face says, oh God, dotish old man.

"It's good!" she says and her fingers start tapping the table as though current is going through them at high voltage. Is *nang* a cuss word? When he was young he could cuss for Guyana. He was rass this, mudda skunthole that. If he tells her these perhaps she will be impressed, but this is wrong, not what he really wants to tell her at all.

"So, the law," he says, feeble, man, feeble, but this is where they left off first time.

"Yes, yes." Her eyes go on a tour, starting at his balding head and moving from exhibit A to B to C like she is cross-examining her origins. He lets her do her tour because it lets him do his. "How did you end up doing this job?" she says.

Nothing has been deliberate since the love that produced her. Nothing at all, so what is there to say? It's all been chaos since that day with Geoffrey at the river's edge, leading to losing Catherine and ending up just trying to keep up, a broken but decent man. One small moment in all the moments of a man's life should not stand in the way of some kind of hard-won decency.

"You know, Olivia." Okay, so that's better, saying her name is good, the name he himself chose for her. "I wasn't good at my studies, not like you. I got expelled from school . . . " He pauses to give her a moment to feel ashamed of him, but in her face there is nothing like judgment. "And, you know, when you told me you were studying law, man, that was something, and I said to myself"—he is about to say, I bring my pigs to fine market, but it's not he who has brought her up, not brought her to any market at all. "I said to myself, man, Catherine is a wonderful mum."

There, he has said it, said the name.

She nods.

His insides are twisting.

"And you know, as to how I've ended up in this job, well, it's because of lots of disruption in my past. You know I went back to Guyana, right?"

"No, I didn't. She doesn't talk about it. She just said that you had to leave us but that I was not to hate you."

Oh Jesus. She has been taught not to hate him; so she doesn't know. He takes a big breath.

"When I was about your age I came to London because I felt I was clever—more clever than I really was, mind you." The look on her face humours him, and the truth is that he doesn't know what more to say to her. Should he tell her about the politics? About how Burnham was telling people that all labour was now part of the state, along with the Berbice Bauxite Company where he got his first job when he left school? About how suddenly after independence the government couldn't afford its own labour? And the same austerity slogans the politicians shout now are what Burnham shouted then? Should he tell her that when he lost his job he was raging vex and thought he was more clever than Burnham so he and his brother left bauxite and went to the Mazaruni river where, man, there was gold, and he worked on a dredge like a real porkknocker? Would she have sympathy for him if he told her he got malaria, was too lonely, and quit gold, and while the country was starting to topple he arranged to stay with his cousin in London? And that he never had any intention of going back?

He has to simplify it. "Guyana was a place that faced a lot of hardship, after independence; a lot of hope, but a lot of trouble too." And maybe that is enough to say at this point. How much of a Guyana-lesson does the girl really need, after all? About fast money, gold, and the benefits of having a jungle to hide it? About how Geoffrey ran, and he just stood and watched? About how a whole place can go mad?

"I came to London and I had no training; it was hard then, hard for black people," he says.

Olivia nods her head; she is an educated girl.

"Then why did you stay?"

"Well . . . " Good question, good question. "I had hope for good work, Olivia." And saying her name again is another thrill. She fidgets; her hand taps the table and beneath it her leg is shaking. This girl is wound right round, and certain things set her spinning. She is like Geoffrey. Oh Jesus, she is like Geoffrey.

"I worked in different places—in the docks, but also in some shops. And I took some classes—City and Guilds," and looks at her to see if she knows about this. She nods. "And I learned accounting, then office management . . . so you see, it's still a bit of that."

"Accounting?"

"Well . . . " He laughs, and man that feels good.

"But then you went back," she says.

That's the problem, he never should have left, never should have listened to Geoffrey's nonsense. "I was cold all the time!" he says, but he knows that the girl doesn't want foolishness. "My brother had a scheme—in Bartica with a gold mine, and he was making money for so." This is enough about Geoffrey. "So I went back home. And shortly after that, my daddy died, and I had things to look after, and my mummy . . . and Guyana was harder than London, because the government bankrupt us." And he doesn't say that it's because of Burnham and Geoffrey that his daddy died, that the man's heart gave out because Burnham was steal-ing the country's money and Geoffrey was scheming-scheming and making bad deals and stealing money from the gold dredge on the Mazaruni River, and telling lies, making and spending so much money that one day he was driving a Jag and the next day he was taking a bus—all of that just a hint of what would happen years later, that April he left when Olivia was four.

"I stayed for three years," he says, "then I came back to London, but it was even harder to find a good job." He was older—and still black. "I did a night-time diploma in health and social care at the Barking and Dagenham College, a different kind of accounting . . . "

Olivia smiles and picks up the pen beside her notebook as if she's going to write something, but she just holds the pen and rubs the top of it. "When did you meet Mum?"

"Catherine," just to say it, because he is allowed, "came into the council office—I worked in housing then. She was so beautiful." He takes a breath. "Like you," and oh Jesus. He waits.

She smiles again. The girl is good at smiling. "Love at first sight?"

"You can be sure of that . . . for sure . . . " He nods, but even he is not convinced by the gesture. "Maybe not for her . . . Her folks didn't like black people so much."

"Still don't," Olivia says, and he wants to catch the hurt that falls from her voice. "Granddad is an angry geezer," she says, and she goes on to tell him about his former in-laws, how Catherine's brother is much the same. "Nan is ace. Mum . . . keeps to herself."

Christ. How can life come to this? Catherine had wanted to be a dancer before he went and made her pregnant and caused her to lose her shape. Now Olivia tells him how Catherine works in the box office of the Theatre Royale so she can still be close to people on the stage.

By the time they have to leave—because he has to get back to work and she has to get back to classes—he hasn't told her anything near enough. "Guyana's money is still in some Swiss bank account in the ex-president's grandchildren's name," he says. But he's left out so many of the good things—like Christmas in Rose Hall when all of the neighbours make the rounds, visit every single house of every single person they know and drink punch de crème and dance like Mother Sally, just dance, dance, dance.

"Will you ask your mother if she will see me?" he says. Olivia's cat face goes broad to bursting and maybe she thinks this is a fine idea. But then he sees different.

"Sorry, sorry. Never mind." Is that pity in his daughter's eyes? "You have so much studying to do, and your project—did this help, today?"

She studies him further, like there is an exhibit she overlooked on the first tour. Like she knows that every rope got two ends.

"I want to come to another one, to find out more—like what happens for refugees. Do you know about the men at Heston Bridge?"

He does not, and shakes his head.

"In any case, I have more research to do before I write, so will you tell me when there's another one?"

But that could be months from now, you can't predict these things, and he can't just wish for someone to die alone so that he can see his daughter. "My job is uncertain; they don't need three of us. I don't know when that will happen," he says because he would prefer to set an earlier date, like tomorrow, or eighteen years ago. But Olivia's face looks panicked.

"What?" She is bobbing again, at the knee, in her fingers. "You're going to lose your job?"

"I don't know for certain, but, you know, this is what is going on across the country," he says. Rass, man, rass.

"Oh." She looks at her notebook, picks up the pen and clicks the top over and over. She scribbles something on the page. He has let her down. "Okay, well, I'll ring you. I'll ring you," she says. She stands up and he has to let her go. He follows her to the door. Waits there to see if she will hug him or offer her hand. Is it wrong to kiss her cheek? She nods at him as if to say, yes, man, yes, it's very wrong. She turns and heads out the door of the café.

Callaloo, pepperpot, Rupununi, arapaima, Karanambu, Essequibo: words he still must say to her.

FRANCINE

Ryan Broughton is a slight, bony, young man, slouched on the velvet couch in his living room while his mother hovers just outside the door, listening, sniffing, like a wary sow. When Francine laid eyes on him again for the first time since the accident, as he floated down the stairs of his house to greet her at the door (burnt toast, bacon, toothpaste), he seemed much more slight and bony than on the evening of the accident. How in hell's name had he turned the dead weight of a body over to try to breathe life back into it? Ryan's face is pointy and pocked near his temples.

"What about tea?" his mother calls from where she is hovering.

"Mum, nothing," Ryan says. She had answered the door when Francine arrived without notice and was reluctant to let her in. Francine had paid for their phone number and address on a web directory, and the woman's Scottish brogue was burdened with suspicion. At the door she described in clipped sentences just how Ryan hadn't been able to return to his medical studies at King's College because he thought he was a failure. "He's not well," she said. "That accident has changed him." Oh God, oh God, Francine thought as she clutched the flowers she'd brought in a plastic bag: death tastes like failure.

Now Ryan shifts and pulls the zip of his hoodie up and down beside her on the couch. Francine wants to tell him that what he tried to do was the bravest thing she's ever seen. She wants to say, *I love your lips, and your breath, and the guts you must have,* but as they sit on the understuffed couch in the overstuffed living room of his mother's house, a few blocks away from Francine's flat, she is speechless. She tries though:

"You did all those things, pounding his chest . . . it was something . . . "

Ryan looks at her like she's a dumbass, but she sees the memory of the clotted blood on his lips. They stay silent and his mother pokes her head around from the kitchen again. And then Francine begins to cry. For the first time since the accident.

Ryan sits up straight with a look that says, oh hell. He waits and watches her wipe her eyes.

"He begged me to save him," he says.

"What?" She sits up as straight as he is.

"The driver, he came over to me and held on to me and begged me to save the guy." Ryan gives the couch a gentle punch.

"I'm so sorry," she says as Ryan's mother comes in and stands, hands on hips like a warning. "I wanted to give you this," Francine finally manages as Ryan's mother picks up random objects around the room—a framed photograph of a graduating Ryan, the TV remote—and she's embarrassed by what she's brought, but it's too late now. Ryan deserves a medal, a badge, whatever it is they give to heroes these days.

"Here," she says and takes the red champion anthurium out of the bag by her feet. She sees in Ryan's face that this is okay, that a living thing is an antidote to kissing death.

"That's nice," he says as he picks up the small pot and examines the waxy, almost fake-looking red petals.

"You're kind," he says.

Francine holds on to her composure. "Not anything like you," she says, and looks over to his mother. What does it take to make a good kid? When John Clarke said he didn't want children, Francine looked into his face to consider her options. They would move in together, he said, of course they would, not now, but of course they would, and they would travel for their holidays. His face said to her, I'm the best thing that has ever happened to you, kiddo, so don't push your luck. All the while John-the-liar-from-Lakawanna Clarke was considering his own options for depositing his oh-so-precious genetic coding into a more compelling vessel.

"I feel I should have stayed with you," she says. "I should have helped you. I'm so sorry."

Ryan looks up from the anthurium. He is so young, but seems so calm. "They'll need more witnesses if he doesn't plead guilty. They'll need you to testify."

She hears the trauma now, like steel-wool in his voice. "But he's not . . . " She doesn't know how to define danger. "It was an accident," she says.

"What are you talking about? Did you see how far he was flung?"

Ryan's mother sits down on the arm of the couch. She looks at Francine like she dares her to say another word that will upset her son or KAPOW!—she'll land her one.

Francine clears her throat. "Sometimes they reduce the charge," she says to Ryan's mother, but the woman is looking over at the bay window as though someone is climbing through it. The doorbell rings, and it's a relief when the woman gets up to answer it.

"If they do, they're wrong," Ryan says.

God, oh God. She folds up the bag she brought the plant in and pushes it into her coat pocket.

"Maybe if you'd stayed, you'd know that," he says.

"But he was dead," she says, and Ryan wrings his hands slowly. "But you still tried," she adds quickly.

He looks at his hands. "Of course."

"And that must be awful for you. Very painful."

His face loses its tension. He tells her that he has Rajit's phone number and that he's often thought of ringing to shout at him. And Francine wants to tell Ryan about how as a teenager she planned to become a conservationist, to save all the species and creatures she feared were becoming extinct—tigers, or even the frogs that had started to disappear from the lake that her geography teacher took the class to year after year. But her thoughts get knotted up and instead she says, "Frogs go first if the lake is polluted, so you have to watch for the frogs."

Ryan looks startled, confused. She picks up her handbag, buttons up her coat. "I'm beginning to think it's all about watching out for the frogs," she says, but Ryan's face stays the same, so she concludes, "We have to be careful."

Idiot.

"Thanks so much for seeing me," she says. "You did an amazing thing." She reaches the front door and squeezes between Ryan's mother and the *Awake* pamphlet that is being offered up by the black woman wearing a Sunday bonnet who is standing serenely at the door.

—

At work the next day she deletes the e-mail from Human Resources that contains a checklist of the elements required in the annotated job specification she is supposed to prepare in a few weeks' time so that the vice-chancellor's group can make decisions on restructuring and rationalization. She does a quick search in the *Guardian* job section and decides to branch out: environmental jobs, marketing jobs. Nothing.

She opens her deleted items box and retrieves the checklist from HR. She starts a new Word doc:

> Quality Assurance Officer:
> 1. Servicing officer to Validation Review Panels.
> 2. Advice and guidance to academic schools on QAE processes delegated to schools.
> 3. Working below my capacity, to hide my light under a bushel, to be forever sidelined and invisible, because I forgot to do all the things most other women have done by now, and have just been trying to get by on my own.

She exits without saving and reaches for her phone in her bag, to retrieve the number Ryan gave her. Deciding to work at capacity rather than below it today, she picks up the phone and calls the Mahadeo household.

—

Like Ryan, Rajit won't come to the door when Francine shows up at his house on Saturday morning three days later. Rajit, his wife tells her, is not talking to anyone, not even his favourite son.

Francine peers in from the threshold and sees someone cross the hallway, a young man, perhaps the favourite son. When the figure returns, it's back-first, as he drags a wheelchair, and a sari-ed old woman sitting in it, her legs wrapped in a blanket. There is a muscular smell of ghee and garlic. And the sad sound of daytime television.

"He is in the same clothes he was released in," his wife says.

"But he's home; he's released, right?" Francine says, watching the blanketed legs disappear across the hallway.

"Bail, madam. We have family, you know," and Francine can't tell if she means that family gave them the money or if, of course he's out on bail, his family needs him.

"And the charges?" she asks.

"My husband is not dangerous, madam. He is not good at paperwork, that is sure," Mrs. Mahadeo says, and again Francine is confused but she doesn't want to push it. She remembers what she's brought. She holds out the rubber plant. Mrs. Mahadeo stares at it then her head goes into spring-necked shaking mode, back and forth.

"Thank you, but we don't want this."

Francine draws the plant closer to her chest in gracious acceptance of the rejection.

"I'm sorry to have bothered you," she says.

"Don't be sorry, madam. You were doing what you thought was a good thing. Too much sorry sorry in this country."

Francine nods at Mrs. Mahadeo, then turns and leaves.

Sayonara.

But she wants more from this visit, wants to do something for Rajit, who might merely have been looking down to check the time or change the radio station. She walks down the Harrow

Road back towards Kilburn without any idea of what doing something for him would look like.

She's hungry.

Her flat smells green. She walks to the kitchen and opens the fridge door.

Juice, cheese, salad dressing, anchovies, mustard. She pinches an anchovy from its jar and lobs it onto her tongue. She opens the Dijon mustard jar, scoops a dollop with her fingers and smears it on top of the anchovy.

She wants her mom.

"Never spit, baby, never spit—it's vile," Mom said. They had been walking down Race Street near Franklin Square in Philly, the trees yellow, red, the leaves kickable at her feet, the fountain making a dome of itself, and a great big horking gob had come out of a fat man standing on the corner of Sixth and Race. Her mother had grabbed her hand, pulled her closer as she declaimed loudly enough for the fat man to overhear her, and they'd quickly moved across the street towards the store where she would buy her daughter a new dress for going back to school. For fifth grade and all its pressures, like knowing the thing that love comes with: the other thing her mother had said to her on that day. They'd bought the dress and her mom had said it, that thing about love, for the first time, and it was less than a year later that she had repeated it, for the last time, in her hospital bed.

Now Francine needs a kind of back-to-school dress again, to wear Monday, to be seen in, because invisible is not the right choice now. She has to keep her job. "Love comes with . . . not panicking," she says to the jar of creamy French vinaigrette in her right hand.

OLIVIA

He's not Slow-Moe now. Moe is not molasses today. Too right. Student union leader Moe has his hoodie up, a fag between his fingers, and is walking like for once he hasn't been blazing all night and is clear-headed in motion towards the M4 bridge where the Bridge Men of Heston will still be sleeping. Olivia feels the swoosh of the traffic on the M4 up above, even this early in the morning darkness. Her knapsack is heavy, filled with water and tins—tuna, beans, soup. Her fingers are falling-off-cold and she shoves her hands into the coat that she's sick of wearing, sick of patching, sick of pulling on every morning when the end of February is supposed to be the end of winter not the beginning. Everything is arse backwards and, shit, if Ed loses his job like he said he might—shit. She has to think. But her heart is racing beside the mostly racing Moe as they hurry along Heston Road to make it to the bridge and the men of Little Punjab below the M4 flyover before daybreak. Moe has agreed to help her out, even though he really wants her to help him organize #Demo, as it was her emphasis on an ENTIRE GENERATION that was being affected, saying, "E-E-E- entire, Moe," which he went on to adapt into the movement's manifesto: to educate, employ, empower the young people of Britain. But Olivia has too much going on for all that. This visit is different; this is specific, contained, urgent; and she has to get right back to the library. She has to do her project, and all she thought she had to do with Ed was to help him make things pretty, the way Catherine likes them. Catherine and her lacy bras, her underpants that look like they're supposed to be on a cake. She thought that if Ed just made things a bit more frilly then Catherine would be sure to go for him again. But Catherine will not go in for a jobless bloke. Sod it. Catherine is not going to like all that death shite in any case. Catherine thinks death is for dead people. But the funeral wasn't so bad—even a few flowers in a glass vase at the front of the chapel, the priest said good stuff, and it's not like she saw a dead body or anything; it was just a box, not bad for cardboard, not something that someone could fall out of. Death isn't so scary. Catherine's got to respect that. Oh, Wood. It was his chin mostly, as he talked about gold and towns that sound like ships—his chin that she stared at because this was the bit of him that she thought she remembered: the feeling of it, the stubble along it when he pressed his face to hers or tickled her belly with it, making her squeal with his raspberries. And then she remembered his song more clearly, and the tra-la of the girl in the ring, over and over in her mind. This is fucked up.

Moe walks even faster and she spots the row of sleeping bags under the bridge. And there's an acid stench, all piss and shit and burnt wood. The traffic vibrates the ground beneath her Uggs and she stops, feeling it in her toes and all the way up her legs. There's a flutter along her shoulders with the swooshing tires overhead, and for an instant she has wings.

"We have provisions," Moe says to a groggy man at the entrance to the encampment as a few of them emerge from their sleeping bags. Olivia knows they leave the camp early and head to the carpark at the Southall Sikh temple, where sometimes they get selected for casual work. Olivia slips her heavy knapsack off her shoulders and brings it to her feet. She unzips the large compartment and takes out some of the tins, the bread, squished now, but hell, better than anything she sees around her: plastic bags of rubbish, rotting food, socks. What's with the socks? She takes out the bottles of water. They don't have long. Once the sun comes up the neighbours will be poking their heads out and adding her and Moe to their list of complaints, until that list is long enough that the Home Office and the police do something and get rid of these damn homeless, jobless illegals—even though that's not even the case for all of them. Some had visas, but they can't find work and now they can't go home or stay here either. Some were sold false papers back in India, Pakistan or Bangladesh; some stay here all day and drink and piss and shit.

A siren chirps into the underpass and now there's all kinds of stirring and moving and mumbling from beneath the blankets. A police car parks beside the camp and two officers get out and slam their doors, all TV-like, and Moe walks towards them. Moe is well-sick when it comes to talking to police, on account of his Americanness and the fact that nothing scares him. Moe would take someone like Granddad and say, *Sir, with all due respect, anti-miscegenation laws in the US were repealed on the 12th of June 1967 by Loving v. Virginia. The British created what your daughter tells me you call half-castes in every port that a cargo ship docked in across the colonized world.* And to extend the point of this long continuum of inter-everything, Moe would say, *Sir, gay marriage is becoming legal in one territory after the other. What in Abraham Lincoln's name is your problem?* Moe would point out to Granddad that his very own flesh and blood was *really, I mean, really, sir, as you can obviously see, a very simple emblem of the future.*

"You need to be moving along now, please," the officer who is barely older than Moe says to him, shooing his arms towards Moe who has gone into slow motion now, nodding and pausing with something on his mind, and taking up all the officer's patience before he says, "We're British citizens, sir, and we're helping out some people here." Moe turns to Olivia and nods, which she takes as her cue to make sure the tins and the water are handed out. She digs deeper into her sack and takes some beans, peas, and sweet-corn tins and begins to walk towards the sleeping bags.

"Miss," the other officer says. This officer is older, with one dark fucker of a unibrow. She turns towards him. "That's enough. You have to leave," and his voice is not as polite as the young dude's. She looks at Moe, but Moe is nearly smiling. She realizes that maybe Moe doesn't blaze as much as she imagined; maybe Moe appears stoned when he's in his highest power. She turns towards the men at the sleeping bags who have all been watching this as the sun comes up behind them under the lip of the bridge. She sees only heads in silhouette, at different standing, sitting, squatting heights, like a city's skyline. She looks back at the unibrow officer and starts to move towards the sleeping bags.

"Miss!" he says, his voice closer now.

That was the truth of it right there: no one had ever picked her up but Ed, his stubble against her face as he carried her. "Pumice," she whispers and delivers the cans to the first man she reaches.

KATRIN

The snake in Claire's throat is bulging this morning. All the sunshine that Katrin collected on her shoulders from walking and not taking the 38 bus is useless now in the chill of Epicure, where Claire is filling the coffee machine and *fuck-fuck*ing at every knob or lid that resists her.

"Today is beautiful," Katrin says, to charm the snake.

"Don't get used to it—March is brutal," Claire says.

The twist in Katrin's stomach has been getting worse over the last two months. At first Claire was her friend, was her guardian against the men who came into Epicure and were not like Robin, and she was fair between Katrin and Alejandro. But now there is nothing Katrin can do right and Alejandro can do wrong.

"You didn't put the chairs up at closing. How do you expect the cleaner to do her job, for fuck's sake?" Claire says.

"I put them up," Katrin lies. The simple past tense means that the lie is not so big. She once did; she was not always doing. She walks to the back office and ties on her apron and changes her shoes to be ready for when the café opens. The exact moment that Claire started to hate her: when was it? It has something to do with Robin, so she has told Robin not to meet her in the café;

they meet at Angel tube station, or in the Green, where for one day or two this week the sun was pointed and white.

They walk; they do not sit much these days. Along the canal, through the streets around Upper Street and under trees that make her gulp at the sight of sweet white flowers over delicate green branches, and pink petals on the high bows of others. On these walks she is rewarded for *czekam*.

"I love how you smell," Robin said one day, and so she is trying every day to smell the same.

Claire wins against the machine and the coffee becomes ground. Alejandro is the one who is late today, but Claire only stands in front of him with her hands on her hips like a cowboy. He walks around her.

"Does she give breakfast at least?" Katrin says to Alejandro with eyebrows up.

"Breakfast of champions," he says, eyebrows also high. She is relieved he is here now.

"She hates me," she whispers to him and nods towards Claire now at the front table doing the accounts.

"She does," Alejandro says as he takes off his jacket and puts on the apron she holds up for him.

"Why?"

He shrugs. "I met her sister one time; she is very beautiful."

Claire laughs and they both look over to the window where she is sitting. Outside there is a man with chains looped along the bottom of his leather jacket. The man is holding a beer bottle towards his German shepherd, who is licking the opening while the man tips the beer into the dog's mouth. The dog is thirsty; it drinks and drinks. The man then lifts the bottle to his own lips and drains the remaining beer from the bottle.

"HA!" Claire says and laughs more.

Katrin runs to the door and is suddenly outside. When the man sees her, he smiles, which takes away all the words—words she might have had to express her thought that to make a dog drunk is to kill it. The man holds his beer bottle up to her like he is saying *Na zdrowie*, a cheers to the things that Katrin is not entitled to say. She goes back inside, not catching Claire's eye, but returning to the counter beside Alejandro, where she wipes the top again, going over the same spot to make it shine.

"For her sister, things probably come easy," Alejandro says.

This makes no sense. Claire goes outside to talk to the man with the German shepherd and their laughter seeps through the glass. Katrin looks at Alejandro who shrugs again, and in his shoulders he is saying, look, see, she is competing with you. Katrin carefully sets up the sugar and the stirring sticks on the small table beside the counter. In English to talk *about* something is very different from to talk *on* or *at* or *in* something. She must remember that English freedom is like the prepositions that she has difficulty to always put in the right place.

NED TIME

ROBIN

Anita Ekberg in Fellini's *La Dolce Vita*: splashing about in the Trevi Fountain, casting her spell over Marcello Mastroianni. Ekberg and Mastroianni engage in sexual foreplay to the point of eruption, the fountain showering them and then suddenly shutting off, as though spent. Deleuze cites this film as exemplary of the crystal image: the power of art through mirroring to create a moment both virtual and actual, the here and now of life. Deleuze doesn't discuss hormones, but Robin has been reading up on them and contemplating the limitations of academic discussions of art. How can poetry and science, for example, help him to understand the hormones reigning over him right now? He has snuck into his office again, third time this week, so early that no one has seen him arrive. He has read about the chemical components of the hormones possessed by a clownfish. Fact is, clownfish schools contain a hierarchy, at the top of which is the female, and when she dies the most dominant male changes sex and takes her place.

Emma arrived at his flat last night, having apologized for her unreasonable phone calls, for forcing him to think about moving to Cornwall, saying she will stay only as long as it takes for them to figure out what they will do, insisting that he is under no obligation but that they will discuss this like adults, like the friends they really are. But her mood is more fierce than before she left London—the effect of the wilds of Cornwall, the feral muliebrity of pregnancy, or merely the fact of her knowing the contents of his heart better than he does.

The knock startles him. He turns to the door. Rarely is anyone else here by 8 a.m., but when Bayo enters, her ebony face shining from perspiration as though she has run here, he is reminded that early mornings are for people whose thoughts need to be let out first thing and walked like a dog.

"Robin, this is not a bad time, is it?" she says.

"Come in."

She sits and immediately takes out papers from her large cloth bag in which she seems to carry the contents of her entire day. "I was wondering if you could look at my essay and tell me whether I'm on the right track." She hands him a sheaf of papers.

"Of course, later today, maybe. We can have a word after class." He glances at the first page: "The aim of this essay is discussing theories and films like french new wave and criticisms like textuality and spectatorship, I personally will go through the films to have the groundwork's of the theories and how the films are made in these groundwork's."

"It needs editing," she says, noting the look on his face. "I've been having a bit of trouble. Lost my disability benefit."

He looks at her with concern.

"If I go off the medication they don't give my money to me, but I have trouble to focus when I'm on it. I'm taking it again, but it takes time for the money to be put back in place, so my landlord is not happy. I have no one in this country. I've had to move twice since August. I'm not sleeping. I am sorry."

His chest goes heavy. Bayo has thoughts, actions, regrets that require medication. And this heavy feeling in his chest confirms, every time, why he teaches here, still, after three years of frustration that he has no A students—this feeling of being nothing if he's not at the centre of a real and honest struggle. Cornwall, toffs, jobs, correct grammar. And then there is this place.

"Don't worry. We'll work it out. I'll have a look, and you go and get some rest, or at least some coffee before class," he says.

When he's finished preparing for the Cinema Poetics lecture, deciding to show a clip from *The Blue Angel*, he checks his e-mail.

The job specifications have been posted on the HR website and have been e-mailed to the film lecturers. He scans the positions. There are five of them for the seven lecturers currently in the department. His shin starts to feel sore—a hiking accident in his twenties, a hairline fracture. He skims the titles: practitioner, practitioner, practitioner, technician, theorist. He reaches down and rubs his shin. They have allowed for one theorist from the three currently in his programme. The other two are more senior than he is.

Robin's father lost his first engineering job, he told all his boys when they were young, because he wasn't fierce enough to fight. But he learned from it, got a better job, and was promoted time and again, landing him at the head of the company. If Robin doesn't move to Cornwall, if Emma doesn't stay in London, if he has nothing more to do with her than send a cheque every month he is still fucked. And Katrin will not want to be with an unemployed theorist who if he had to do anything else would be writing useless poetry for her eyes only.

Their next date will be their third, so he is hesitant to ask her out. Do the Poles acknowledge the third date as pivotal? Does every Polish woman expect sex on the third date like English women do? He will tell her about the baby. She will hate him and refuse to see him again, but he will be nothing if he doesn't tell her.

Until then he will not go mad, will keep his thoughts from being actions except for those thoughts that will result in a successful application for the job he already performs.

—

The sunlight in the atrium makes spring feel like a real possibility, even though outside it is five degrees. These rare, crisp days need to be marked. He walks to the student union shop and in the queue for coffee sees the American woman from QA, who stares at him. He wants to tell her it's rude, that people don't stare like that in England, and if she wants to talk to him she should do so. Last year he received an e-mail from her informing him that he had not responded adequately to the external examiner's comments on his course evaluation. The examiner had made a wholly positive statement about his treatment of theory but noted that some of the students hadn't incorporated it as effectively as others. QA read each of these reports to monitor course improvement, and he was required to create a course improvement plan based on the fact that some students don't do as well as others. Some students don't do as well as others, he wants to say to the middle-aged Mae West. They have had one meeting together and she seemed like a pleasant enough woman—shy and yet so constituted of that shyness for it to seem almost arrogant. But that's cruel and stereotyping of her Americanness. Sorry, he would say to her if he could bear to say anything to anyone. He pays for his coffee and Kit Kat, and leaves.

—

Olivia is at his office door when he arrives back upstairs.

"Robin, me again, sorry, sorry . . . " she says, and throws the long ringlet that covers her right eye back behind her ear and tucks it in there. He opens his office door and lets them both in. As he puts his coffee and chocolate on the desk he notices after she sits down that Olivia's knee is bobbing up and down like a needle on a sewing machine and that her finger is worrying the top of her pen, back and forth, rubbing it as though for magic.

"You okay?" he says and holds up the Kit Kat, offering her some.

"Yes, yes, really," she says, declining the offer, straining to smile.

The wideness of Olivia's face obscures a clear reading of her beauty. She can be hard to look at: there is so much to take in.

"The project," Robin says, to get her started. "It might be better to approach it in terms of basic social tenets," and before he knows it, he is saying, "Does everyone have the right to be remembered somehow, and would it be meaningful, after death, to be identified with something specific? I'm not speaking in terms of legalities—that's your area—but I thought—"

"There's this man, works for Barking and Dagenham council . . . " Olivia's interruption feels like a rejection. "He looks after paupers' funerals. You know what people call them, in the papers?"

"No, I don't."

"The lonely dead," she says, her shoulders hunching. "They are mostly people without family, or if they're foreigners we don't even know who they are, they have no papers, or they are old people whose family have fucked off—they don't get funerals, not proper ones. But in my research . . . " Her knee is bobbing up and down still, her fingers wishing the pen into action. Robin sits back in his chair to try to make her feel more comfortable. "And well, you know how in Amsterdam there's a lot of drugs 'n' all?"

He nods.

"They get a lot of lonely deaths—like drug mules, like from Colombia—girls who carry drugs in their stomachs or up inside them and the drugs leak or someone kills them and they don't have real names on their passports, and nobody can find out who they are . . . or . . . " She looks at him with her wide face like an urgent, flashing sign. "And then the city has to bury them. There's this man there, a civil servant, and he looks after them. He has made it his thing to visit their homes if they had one, and he chooses music to play at their funeral. He puts flowers on the coffin and makes sure each one gets buried. With dignity."

He sits forward, "I was going to say something about music . . . in fact, about music at the funeral—" he stops himself, because he shouldn't be encouraging this tangential thinking when Olivia should be working on her dissertation, "but that's not something you can legislate; the idea of rights seems to me—"

"That kind of politics doesn't work," she says, as though that is all she needs to say to him and he will understand. And he does, but there's so much understanding developing between them that he has to draw that line, the one he must draw as a tutor—the line that says I can't go there, no matter how much I see you and agree with you: this is just my job. So he simply nods.

"This Dutch man," she says, "decided that they needed praise, like, real eulogies, even if there was no one in their lives."

Yes, this is the kind of thing he was trying to say at the beginning. "That sounds like a beautiful idea."

"And that's what I was thinking . . . " Both knees start to bob now, and she is a jackhammer to his office floor.

"Okay," he says calmly. "And coming back to the law project?"

"He got a poet to write poems for them, as their eulogies—a poem for each of the lonely dead. Somebody knows them, even if it's just in their imaginations." She sits back in the chair and her bobbing subsides.

"That is a lovely notion, Olivia. But without meaning to undercut it, have you thought about how it will inform your dissertation?"

She sits forward again. "In England's community graves, it's the same. So many people. The man at the council, he's an old man, well, not old, really, but not like you, older—and I think we need to do something." She hesitates.

"What do you mean?"

"The council is to cut its budget, and he might just be one of the people to go. But . . . " Her face becomes even wider as she looks him directly in the eyes. "If we started this new project, brought attention to it like they did in Amsterdam. If there was a poem for each of the people who dies alone, who the council has to bury, who this man has to look after, and if the council has to find the money to pay him because it's the right thing to do . . . and . . . if you could write the poems . . ."

"What?"

She sits back.

He takes her in. His grandparents died quietly, unceremoniously, his father's mother going to an early grave when his father was twelve. They were not a family for big events. He doesn't know the words to hymns; his father was adamant when he was growing up that church was nowhere for boys who needed their minds stimulated not shrunken.

"I am not a poet," he says, and she straightens up.

"You wrote that poem last year," she says, and it's true. He did use a poem of his own last term, in a moment of shameful vanity.

"That was different, that was just to make a point," he says.

"Exactly," she says. And he does not know how to respond. "You're the right person," she says firmly. "You care."

He thinks about the impact and knowledge transfer indicators he has been told he has to address in his research, and how projects should extend into the community at large, should demonstrate that there is no longer such a thing as an ivory tower. For a cynical, self-serving moment he considers a practice-based research project that combines cinema poetics and visual eulogies. He stops himself.

"I don't write poetry, really, Olivia," he says, and watches her shoulders drop. He would embarrass himself in the eyes of the avant-garde poets he loves—the Language Poets; the New Sentence poets. "Really, really, Olivia. What you're saying is great, interesting, but not for me. I can't do that." She begins to gather her things.

He searches his bookshelf and reaches up to pull out the slim volume. "You might like this," he says, as he hands it to her.

Olivia takes it and nods. "You used Ginsberg last year," she says, and nods. He winces and she smiles, thanks him, then leaps up from the chair and leaves his office.

Deleuze: What is an unconscious that no longer does anything but believe, rather than produce?

ED

Zihan restaurant—not as in Lawd bring me to the land of Zion—
is Somali and not the one he's looking for. There's a restaurant
called Pepperpot on Longbridge Road because he is sure he
passed it a year back, when he thought, man, he should be going
in. But those days he wasn't too fired up about things Guyanese.
He wasn't looking back at anything that would smell like home,
because if home hurts you have to mash it out. But don't mind
how bird vex, it can't vex with tree. So now he has to find it
because Sammy is counting on getting some pepperpot, cassava
bread, mauby or guava drink to wash it down with, after all the
bragging Ed did in the office.

"You walk fast, mate," Sammy says, catching up with Ed on
the pavement outside the Pepperpot, which is more brukadown
than Ed remembers it. "You must be hungry to walk like that,"
and Sammy takes a fat bloke's inhalation on Longbridge Road.
Ed breathes in with him. The air is a blend of petrol and . . .
what? What is that smell? Bleakness, if that can be a smell.
Petrol and bleakness. "And why is it that you West Indians feel
like if you don't have grog—and that is your word and not
mine—with your food it ain't a meal?"

Sammy has agreed to come along to Pepperpot on the condition that he is not expected to drink rum, which he detests. Ed has brought beer—Cobra, a big bottle that he holds up like a trophy—because Sammy is a one-drink man.

"You people can drink, innit," Sammy says.

"Let's go," Ed says, and he pushes open the door to the restaurant. With a ting and a pang and a parrang braddups and a whole band playing in his head, he is back home inside this bad-lighting plastic-flowers room. Guyana maps and flags, bird of paradise, and pan playing in the tinny speakers hung up in the corners above the counter, below which take-way patties, peas and rice, and rotis are growing crusty behind the display glass. Music happens somewhere in the heart and not in the ears, true-true.

After they have ordered their food and opened the Cobra, split between them, it's time for him to ask Sammy: "Do you think a daughter should know that her uncle is in jail?" Coming right out with it is the easiest, after batting it around in his head for weeks now since Olivia found him. Straight ahead, at least with Sammy. Sammy looks at him as if to say, man, why on earth you bring this surprise 'pon me when my team is failing, like it's the worst thing he might have done the day after the Hammers have lost to Spurs.

"What you on about then?" Sammy says.

So Ed starts slowly, because this is the way the details must come while Sammy does the inevitable re-examining of the exhibits A, B, C of his face to find where there is a likeness to criminals. "I told you about Geoffrey, but I never told you he was—is—in jail."

The food arrives at the table and Sammy looks into his pepperpot like it's the dark stew of Africans who boil up white people, and maybe Indians too. He picks up his fork with purpose though, because Sammy is a good bloke.

"What happened?" Sammy asks and it takes a second before Ed realizes he's asking about Geoffrey.

"He killed a man. On a gold mine. He tried to steal, got caught, killed him: simple. So simple it's nearly ridiculous, like in a Wild West movie," Ed says.

Sammy nods and tastes his pepperpot, nods again, pleasantly surprised.

There's a long silence as Ed watches Sammy slurp up the slimy oxtail and wipe his lips with the back of his hand. Sammy is the best bloke there is, but in the silence Ed sees the man in the river, Geoffrey in the distance, running, running, and the inky blood following the path of the river like it needed a new home. He is not able to describe this to Sammy, or to explain what happened next.

"It's why Olivia's mother didn't want anything to do with me." Sammy looks up at him like this is nonsense.

"I went back to Guyana when Geoffrey asked me to help him . . . begged me like he was dying, and when I saw him he looked so bad, but he was still boasting like a big man, and he asked me for money. How was I to get that money? He said I should borrow it from people I knew in London, from Catherine." Ed shakes his head and looks to Sammy for confirmation that he was right not to ask Catherine, but Sammy is looking at his food, moving it around on the plate. "Catherine had no money," Ed says. Nobody he knew had any. "Geoffrey and I had a big row, man, and I told him he was mad as shite. And then he stole the money he needed and he was caught in the act. He killed the man who was chasing after him, just so.

I have never understood that. Never." He should have found the money for his brother. His brother was in trouble; that's what family is for. "When I told Catherine, she said she didn't want me around, thought I had something to do with it."

"And did you?" Sammy asks him, his face as open as a net. And of course that's the question. The only reason you don't let a man see his daughter is because you think he did something wrong and because you believe all the seh-seh from other people like your knack-about father and brother.

"I followed Geoffrey that day, it's true, but I had no part in it, no part." Even to Sammy he can't tell the whole truth, because what Ed did that day—or rather didn't do—was witnessed only in his own heart, and that was the place where Catherine lived, so she might have felt it too.

"I had to pay for lawyers, help move my mum, pay her bills because it was Geoffrey who had been doing that all along —and I had no way of getting back to London. Catherine said, you stay there then."

Sammy is shaking his head now, and Ed can't tell if it's at the food or at what he's saying.

"She was wrong, too hard . . . " Sammy says. And Sammy starts with his fork and is eating at a pace, man, and Ed wants to tell him to slow down, but he watches, waiting for what is to come next, as it seems Sammy has something more to say; he just needs to fill his belly first. And then the rice and pepperpot are all gone, a swig of Cobra to wash it down, and Sammy wipes his mouth.

"When I was a teenager, my cousin burned down the community centre because they took away the sports club on Saturday afternoons. Right nutter, he was, and brought shame to

the family, but you know, he was pissed, and I didn't blame him."
Sammy releases a whoosh of air in a silent burp, covers his mouth
too late.

"But Catherine has never told Olivia about my side of the
family," Ed says.

"The past is the past, Wood."

"You think she shouldn't know?"

"Of course she should know, of course . . . but she doesn't
need to know now, not yet. You're just getting reacquainted. You
take your time on that."

Sammy has a point, but the hell in Ed's belly rumbles. And
Ed knows that while a young man wants freedom, an old man
wants only peace.

OLIVIA

Maybe it's not going to work out fine after all. She stares out of the window of the number 364 bus. Parsloes Avenue is chocka with people who must do decent jobs, what? Offices, restaurants, shops. Everyone needs an electrician, for example, like Catherine's Once-a-Week William. Everyone needs a plumber; everyone needs a barber or a salon for the weave. All of it there, necessary. And stale as shite. It's not real poetry she's looking for; it's something that will make a man seem special, the way Robin was special when he gave those lectures, the way even a small dude like him can make a whole room of barely awake wankers go oh wooo he's talking good shite here that's meaning something, like the time he did that Holy, Holy, Holy riff last year. Poetry for Ed to make a point with, even if it's just for nobody but the dead. If Ed can do that, that hushed voice thing that Robin does at the beginning of the class when no one knows he's starting the lecture, when people just think he's talking about himself, well.

What if Nasar has some of that? What if Nasar appears in front of her and has that riffing thing that makes her feel like all the world is joined up by the wind on her skin?

The 364 stops just near Jasmine's on Osborne Road. Jasmine will be a good diversion. Her house on the square is bang opposite the Dagenham Evangelical Congregational Church, which is dench for Jasmine's mum and a horror for Jaz herself.

At the door, though, she's never seen her gal so cranked. Jasmine lets her in and turns around, expecting Olivia to follow. Jaz's arms are long, her head big for the rest of her, and she walks back and forth in her living room holding that head between her flattened palms, her elbows stuck up and out like bat ears. Olivia sits on the sofa and wraps up in Jasmine's mother's pink-and-brown knitted blanket that gives her that baby-love feeling.

"He had a crash," Jaz says and it takes one, two, three long WTF moments to figure out that Jaz is talking about Dario from Bologna. Jasmine starts to explain, but Olivia can't follow, because, hell, this is something. This is one thing too much in a month that is way over much. And Jasmine is talking too fast.

"Jaz, you gotta chill."

Jasmine's pacing picks up speed. "Chill? Do you get this? He's dead, Liv, he's dead."

Olivia nods.

"He coulda been the one," Jasmine adds. And this is where Olivia has to get her head out of Jaz's wonderland, because this is the line Jaz has for every dude who rides her once and never shows up again. "It was real, this one, and now he's gone," Jasmine says with her elbows still up in the air beside her head. Olivia takes out her phone and while Jasmine paces the room she searches, finds it, and types a short but simple reply that is at least ten days late, but maybe not too late.

It's "heart sing," not "singing." Thanks.

And with that she feels lighter, what with making sure that Nasar is still alive and all. By the time she leaves Jasmine to herself to pace and be administered to by her mother with the Bible, Olivia is wondering how many more things can get in the way.

—

Eric has the TV turned up to garage-house decibels because if he fills the entire sitting room with the sound of Man United in their home stadium on a Wednesday night, then he can pretend that he's alive, and that his life is not worthless. Uncle Eric is a waster who has been living off his sister and their parents' pension for the last five years. Eric is a no-show in the game of life, let alone football. Olivia closes the door to the sitting room and heads to the kitchen with her heavy satchel. Two essays due and one exam in three weeks and nowhere to study now that staying late at uni feels like she's being caught on hidden camera footage that Nasar gets to see. She should never have texted him back. First rule of harassment cases: don't engage. Something tells her that Nasar is legit and different, but she shouldn't have. She has to be careful not to turn soft.

"Honey, it's late, have you eaten?" Catherine says, looking up from her magazine.

"Not bothered," Olivia says, but tries to control sounding cheesed off. It hasn't worked on Catherine. Her mum closes the magazine, puts her elbows on the table and her chin between her hands.

"What?" Catherine says.

When Catherine has nothing to do, no worries about bringing food home for everyone and keeping Eric full up in beer and cigarettes, nothing to dream about in her magazines, and no Once-a-Week William to be giggling for, she is a mother. Olivia has tried to resist it before, but it's tough when Catherine puts on that soft voice.

"Nothing. Got shitloads of pressure, is all," Olivia says, not looking at the big green eyes of her mother that make her look like an old version of Adele and that also make Olivia want to be picked up, even though she's taller than Catherine now. She sits down at the table. "If you ran into Wood, would you just ignore him?" She looks up at Catherine, whose eyes go squinty.

"What are you getting at?" Catherine asks.

"Nothing, just, would you?"

Olivia can tell that her mother wants to open the magazine now, her fingers itching to turn those pages so that she won't have to talk. But this time she's not going to run, maybe this time.

Olivia hears shuffling—the sound that makes the hair on her neck stand up, and if Granddad would just buy proper slippers instead of wearing the paper ones Nan got in hospital when she was ill, the shuffling would not grate on her nerves so much, but he is a stubborn old git and here he comes just as Catherine is struggling with her instinct to run, just as there might be a moment when something becomes clear.

"Olivia love, our bin was stolen again. You call the council—I'm sure it's over the road behind. They paint them over, sell them, must be." Right. Granddad hasn't combed his hair, and what's left of it is sticking up like a troll's.

"Who would they sell the bins to?" Olivia says. Catherine is back at her magazine and Granddad has won. Again. She can feel her pulse. There's thunder at her neck.

"Tendril," she says. It comes out a lot louder here at home. Because at home everyone is their own Jack-in-the-box, springing up, nattering, when the pressure is too much. Granddad's the worst, the things he has to say getting front and centre most of the time, whether they're trivial, ignorant, bigoted, or plain obnoxious. She knows that her very presence makes him the Grand Jack-in-the-box, and that her being his so-called half-caste winds him up and spins him out. Granddad also loves her, and it is this confusion in his very own cells that makes him so unpredictable, makes him blame everything and everyone else in the world instead. It's not that Granddad is such a bad man; it's just that he is the most scared of them all. He's the kind of geezer who fools you, who is clever and doesn't raise his voice except at the telly, talks like he has schooling, talks like he reads books, but deep down Granddad's ignorance is as deep as his unknowing of his own soul. Nan meanwhile has stopped hearing. Nan has taken to being sick all the time, needing to stay in bed, needing, even, to be in hospital for big bouts of delirious time when she's coughing so bad and yelling a lot and she can't hear how loud she has become. She can't hear how much she just wants Granddad to shut the fuck up and leave everybody alone and give her some peace so that she can pay attention to something other than him. Ed is not in any way like Granddad, and maybe Catherine just wasn't used to having air time of her own, so she couldn't handle it. Maybe Catherine's magazines are like Nan's deafness.

"What's everyone on about here, then?" Eric says as he enters, his belt and top button undone like he's just come out of the loo but forgot, like the stupid baby git he is. Granddad launches in about the bins, and he and Eric go on about who's stealing what, until the topics switches to Man United, because

Uncle Eric is nearly as bad as Granddad when it comes to need-ing to say what's on his mind.

This is where she's from; it is not who she is. She does not have to stay here. Nan is small, doesn't take up too much room when she's well, and Ed and Catherine will give each other space so that no one has to fold up inside and disappear.

Who will bury these people? God bloody help her.

Her phone pings. Catherine looks up at her like she should be told who that is. Olivia gets up from the table with her satchel and heads upstairs.

Thnk you for writing me. My heart sing to read you. Maybe you meet me?

Now she's gone and done it. But a little part of her is relieved, and maybe even more chuffed than before, to hear from him.

KATRIN

A promenade: the English have stolen this word, but it is right. "At my university," Katrin says to Robin as they take this slow walk along the canal leaving Camden Market, "each day we met at the main fountain in the square, some classmates and I, and we would stand or sit, winter or summer, and discuss our reading. We had big, waving-arm debates, loud arguments about Malthus and market politics." She does not dare to try to translate the concepts because she will be stupid in these. And Robin knows them better than she does, but she is happy that when she talks he nods like she is not boring.

"My students meet to get high and to talk about how they can pass without doing any work," Robin says. He shakes his head. "That's not true, no, I am being harsh. Some of them are among the most inspiring people I have ever met," he says and looks at her, smiles. "But it's not like you describe. They don't have the luxury of so much debate." He takes her hand. His is warm in this not warm air and she looks at the faces of others on the canal path to see if they notice how her breathing is shallow.

It is the second time he has touched her. The first time was her chin. And that touch said *I'm so surprised by you.* And for real he said, "I had given up." They had been sitting on a bench on the canal like the one they are passing now where another couple are sitting, not talking, not touching. When she asked him what he was meaning about giving up he said there were things he'd like to tell her, but she became worried about time because she was on a break and Claire was more and more angry, and she said, no, don't tell me, not today. She has not yet found out what he had given up.

Now, more than a week after waiting for him to come into Epicure – his absence like rejection – she is content on this walk. He has asked to meet during the daytime, not evening, and this is not how she understands English men. By now they are expecting much more that Robin has asked for.

In Camden they ate lamb and spinach stew from the African stall, also sweet chocolate banana crepes, and she is a snail on this promenade, while Robin is alert with talk about his university and his wish to be more useful. "Film studies," he says, "is not what students want. They want to make movies, not interrogate how they work or what they mean; I don't make films, I'm from the old school, in which you need to know things deeply, first, before doing anything that is decent." In this sentence there is a darkness like stepping inside a cupboard. Katrin does not hold tighter to his hand, but she is more aware of its strength.

He keeps talking. Where does he want to take her with this talk?

"There's this woman," he says, and her hand loosens. Her mother will arrive in two months. She has things she must prepare. She has to get back. He holds her hand tighter and looks at her now. "I was with her, yes," he says.

"Oh, good, that's good," she says, releasing her hand, looking down at the holes on the front of her Converse trainers.

"But this is what I need to tell you."

Katrin holds the hem of his jacket and tugs him towards a bench. She has had enough walking now.

"You loved her," she says before he is even sat beside her. His face looks surprised.

"I didn't," he says, sits, pauses, then, "but I wanted to believe I could."

He is perfect in his words, always precise, and this makes her weak in front of him.

"And now?" she asks and watches as his eyes in his glasses go towards the canal, to find the right words there, in water.

"And now," he says like in a show where they are going to announce a winner and they repeat the question and make you wait, "now she is expecting a child."

She is surprised how alert she feels; her shoulders straighten; she pictures her grandmother's house by the river in Gdansk. His forehead creases with worry that she will run, so she doesn't; she doesn't want to hurt him. She wants to whisper something to him, but doesn't know what she would say.

"I want to explain it to you," he says.

She nods.

"We were friends first, and then we got together for about a year. We were never right for one another, but we stayed on, as friends, mostly. She's a year older than me, thirty-nine, and she asked me to get her pregnant. I said no, but then, when she was moving away, we had sex. I'm an idiot. I felt like nothing would ever happen for me again, so I didn't care. I'm an idiot."

The white blossoms of the tree behind Robin's head remind her how far time has come since the first days of him coming into Epicure, when shoots of daffodils had a promise. How long has he known about this baby? She is all of a sudden tired. She has worked two times her normal hours this week; she has bought a duvet for her mother. She wants to lie down with Robin, whisper to him, and fall asleep.

"Well," she says. There is nothing to say. He will be a father and fathers will live with their children, no matter what. Fathers will not leave the mothers of their children to sleep on one side of the bed forever more.

"I don't want to be with her. I want to be with you," Robin says.

She looks at his face and knows he is saying the truth. "We are very different in age." It's all she can think of—that and the fact that her *matka* will bring trinkets and books in her suitcase—unnecessary things for which there will be no space in the bedsit. She must remember to send Beata a list of things she should bring and things that should stay in Gdansk.

"No, it's nothing, the difference between us. We are exactly the same," Robin says, but stops and merely looks at her. "You're far away," he says, and this is true.

"I should go," she says. "We will talk tomorrow." She stands and puts her hand on his face. His eyes fall shut, then open wide again. "I will see you tomorrow," she assures him.

—

But the next day she is not sure of anything. And even though Alejandro has been kind as always, his joke today is about a Mexican, and it has made her uncomfortable because she is learning how racist she was in Poland. She needs London even more for all the things she has learned, for all the fingers it has pointed to her stupid ways of thinking. What will her mother do when she sees this place?

Claire is busy in the back room with accounts and supply orders, but all morning she has had her eyes on her as though someone has told her how Katrin as a child used to make monkey sounds with her friends when they saw black people on television. Katrin has a headache and her throat has become sore. Claire knows all the things she has thought and all the things she has said.

"So, it's simple: he tells her she cannot have it," Alejandro says of Robin's story with the baby, because that's what Alejandro does: finds solutions to the problems of all the people in the world. Alejandro should be a counsellor, or a judge. He has so many answers for everything. He wipes the top of the counter and straightens the napkins, moves straws to the edge of the glass top, and turns the basket of almond biscuits towards the front. Alejandro is the tidiest man Katrin has ever met. Robin, too, she has noticed, is tidy. His clothes are neat and ironed and in place; his taste is for clean lines and white spaces. The furniture shop she passes every day on Upper Street has things for Robin's kind of home. She loves this so much about him that she has to stop thinking about it. She slides the basket of almond biscuits back from the edge where Alejandro placed it.

"What?" he says.

"I don't know," she says. A customer who has finished an espresso and croissant holds her finger up for Katrin's attention. Katrin moves towards her just as Claire comes out of the back room and catches her eye. "Can we have a word?" Claire says. Katrin hunches and becomes small like a bad dog. Claire turns and walks back into the office, expecting her to follow, but Katrin must bring the customer's bill and ask Alejandro to cover while she's in the back room. When she goes into the room, Claire is already red-faced.

"I had a customer," Katrin says, and this stops Claire from saying what she had wanted to, even though she has stood up to talk.

"I thought you had more hours on your timetable than what appears to be there," Claire says.

"What do you mean?"

"If you look at the number of hours you worked in the last three weeks, it doesn't add up to what we really needed coverage for, does it?" Claire says, trying but failing in her intonation to sound kind. "We're really busy, more busy as the weather gets better, so we actually need more not less from people. You need to be able to work when we need you."

"What do you mean? I worked double hours last week."

"You covered for Alejandro's hours, but we need coverage on Sundays," Claire says, "and then at the end of the day, the early evening shift," and Claire's face is very close to Katrin's. Not angry or threatening, just close. "The business is doing well; we are opening a branch in Soho."

"I asked you for the maximum hours. You told me that was all you could give me," Katrin says. She does not know about laws in this country, how much is too much, but when Andrzej scans bar codes for too many hours the laser machine makes a stinging take place around his eyes.

"The owner might be interested in hiring another person to help."

"What does that mean?" Andrzej sends all his money back to Gdansk; he is not lucky like Katrin who can live in her own bedsit. When he visits her on Sundays his face is cold and pale.

"What do you mean what does that mean?"

"Why are you telling me that?" Heat walks up Katrin's neck.

"I just noticed, that's all. You're working fewer hours and you told me you needed hours. Times are hard but this place is doing well . . . go figure."

"I need hours." Next Sunday she has invited Andrzej to eat lunch with her, but she could work at Epicure instead.

"Then you should be working them," Claire says, one step back on her right foot.

"Is that what you wanted to say?"

Claire plays with the gold chain on her wrist, twists it, and looks back at Katrin, which brings the curling in her stomach, and the failed-exam feeling across her chest. She turns quickly and walks out of the room.

Claire will hold this too against her.

Behind the counter Alejandro is busy, with many customers before him in a queue and maybe Claire is right, she is not working enough, she is letting him down and making customers angry, but they do not look angry. He nods his head to the left, telling her to serve the customer in the front.

She makes all the coffees and rings in all the pastries and bread and salad for the next two hours and barely says a word to anyone except for very kind and helpful phrases to each of the customers. Espresso, macchiato, latte, chocolate marquis, Chantilly cream, tiramisu: English is not in so many things at Epicure. She smiles at Alejandro and he shows her with his own smile that all is fine between them.

At 8 p.m., Claire has been gone for three hours—her early day when she drives her teenager to football practice—and for three hours it is safe to believe again that Epicure is a place to feel proud. If Katrin can hold on for one year, her mother will get used to London, her savings will grow, and she can look for a job that is not with coffee.

"I have never had this kind of relation with anyone in my life," she says to Alejandro as he sweeps beneath the chairs that she lifts onto the tables. "What is wrong with me?" She wants him to tell her the truth.

"There is nothing wrong with you," he says. "She needs a good shag, that's all." Katrin doesn't like it when people say this kind of thing, but a small part of her is grateful for it.

"Maybe you could help out," she says, smiling. He gives a face like he has swallowed vinegar. "My mother will not come if I do not have a job," she adds.

When they have closed the café she feels heavy, and her tongue feels coated in butter. Her feet drag along Upper Street. Her shoulder has a pain where it meets her neck. It is not good to think too much. She takes her phone from her bag and taps a message.

Two, three, five, ten minutes and nothing from him, and the failed-exam feeling in her chest is there again. Stupid. Of course he is with the mother of his baby. You stupid. She rereads what she has said to him.

I am sorry to take so long to reply to you. I can cook you dinner so maybe we have more time to speak, and I will listen better. I will work on that for Ned time. x

Ned time? The phone she uses is not smart like it is called. It pretends to know what she wants to say, but it is as stupid as she is. She thumbs it to obey.

I mean next time.x

Before she gets to her bus stop a simple ping makes everything good again.

I like the idea of Ned time very much. Maybe that's a place where everything is as we want it to be. What about Saturday for dinner? xxx

She thumbs the screen impatiently.

Saturday is good. xxx

OLIVIA

"Darling, you used to be a child who never cried. And I used to worry that there was something wrong with you, that I had done something bad . . . " Wood says and Olivia feels all tremor-like sat here at the melamine table at the A13, on account of the fact that this man knows she's a baby who never cried and the fact that when he says *bad* Wood is like a sheep crying in the dark. This man – who is kind-hearted but a little feeble, if she is allowed to think these things about her father – held her when she fell and didn't cry, and wondered if he had done something wrong.

The A13 is familiar now, but it's like a caff out of time, all bacon grease and sticky-topped.

"Do you cry?" Right. This is a lot to ask a geezer you barely know any more. "I mean, at the funerals, ever?" What she really wants to say is please let my oddness come from somewhere legit, directly from a particular chromosome on a particular bit of sperm that created me; otherwise, I'm just a weirdo living among white people who don't get me one little bit.

Wood looks over his shoulder, Olivia turns round to follow, and there is Mary the waitress who sits and does sudoku while her punters eat their toast and drink their builders' tea. "Condensed,"

Olivia says softly. Ed doesn't hear her or doesn't let on he does, and maybe he does this kind of slippery thing too, and maybe for Ed this is normal. After a few seconds of staring at Mary, Ed looks back at Olivia.

"I used to cry a lot," he says and then smiles, "used to . . . when I couldn't get to see you. Funerals are not the same. They remind me I'm a lucky man."

Right. Right. Alice Sampson. Ed has been telling Olivia about Alice Sampson, eighty-three years old, who has just gone into a care home. Ed has been put in charge of her property, to make sure it is cleared out, to secure it and dispose of things that need disposing of. Alice. Ed says it's important to hold their names, to keep naming them, like you know them. Olivia pictures all the stuff at home—Granddad's fantasy junk that makes him believe he is better than everyone else. Right.

"What do you believe then, Wood?"

Ed's shoulder twitches like she has tickled him.

"What do you mean?"

"I mean . . . " when she was ten she found a secret shoebox in Catherine's cupboard with small scraps of paper with a few words on each, in Catherine's handwriting, as though she'd jotted down wishes and allowed them to pile up in the box instead of making them come true, " . . . what it's all about," and she waves out at the wide world.

If she tells him her idea now, makes it seem all about her project, impresses him, Barking and Dagenham Council will think he's a saint, he'll secure his job, get a promotion, Catherine will see what a man he really is.

"You all right, Olivia?" Ed asks her and touches her hand. A quick, father's touch. "You're shaking," he says.

"No, no, I'm fine, I'm thinking is all." She breathes in deeply. "Maybe we could work together. You could help me," she says, appealing to his instincts, "we could help each other," she adds, looking around and, yep, right, all melty here in the what-you-want-will-never-come café.

"Okay," Ed says, simply. "Okay," again.

Holy the solitudes of hospitals and malls! Holy the casinos filled with the millions! Holy the mysterious whispers of doubt beneath the sheets! She needs to chill. She can't tell him her plan just yet.

KATRIN

He kisses her like it's the last thing he will do in his life. Maybe she has not known kissing before. This is how they kiss in English. This is why everyone is here. He tastes of fried onions and sauerkraut from perogies she cooked for him, but there is also vodka, and one small thought comes that maybe he has drunk too much. But this kissing like the end of the world is too good to stop. His body moves if she moves. One leg for one leg, one hand for one hand, on top of her and then still if she is still. She cannot find where she ends and he begins.

And so she cries.

He pauses, caresses her cheek. "Are you all right?"

She has no words.

He slides to her side and holds her tight. She turns and he gathers her into a spoon and this feels like something that God has done.

"I'm sorry," he says, but she does not want to ask what he is sorry for in case it is something that will end this. So she makes believe and pushes everything out of the room that God did not mean to happen.

"You sing," she says, not asking but telling because he has before named Bach and Beethoven, then Bartok and Berlioz, and all the music he could think of when she played the game at dinner. Name all the music you love, she said, and only after Bartok did they notice the Bs. She slides from his arm—"Wait for me"—gets up and on her toes, crosses the cold floor, and is happy for once that the room is small. She brings the guitar.

"I sing one; you sing one." And she sits; her fingers clutch for C, then D, G—as she has learned from the book. Pick and strum. It is this song that Beata taught her on the dulcimer, but in London a guitar was £40 in Brick Lane. And she can give this kind of music to him because her mother was a girl in Warsaw and learned Czerwone Gitary's "Biały krzyż" to sing to her baby. "The translation is 'White Cross,'" she says and closes her eyes to sing to him. When she is finished she opens them and his face is like grace.

She passes him the guitar and smells their bodies in her sheets. "Do you sing?"

His fingers curl over the guitar neck and make her wet again.

He picks the strings like he knows how. And she knows this song because her mother was a girl in Warsaw when Czerwone Gitary was merely a copy of this band, and so when he sings "Blackbird singing in the dead of night, take these broken wings . . . " she does not understand how he can know her like this, or how this other B music will not make her die, right here in her own bed.

There are two more songs, more elaborate, more foreign, before he stops and looks at his wrist, but the watch was taken off in Ned time, so he picks it up from the floor and makes a face that has pain.

"I should go," he says, and the pain is now in her chest.

"Why?"

He draws her to him, pulling her down and spooning again as God decreed.

"I promised. I promised I would be there for her," he says. She does not ask then why are you here for me; she slides out from the spoon and sits up, pretends that everything is okay.

"Of course, of course," and she tells herself that she is doing this for a baby, and so it is fine. "Go quickly."

ROBIN

Her bedsit has been made beautiful. Robin touches the silk cushions on Katrin's only comfortable chair. She has dessert for their return from the Spanish restaurant, their regular now, several nights in a row.

The first night he was here she cooked a Polish dinner for him, and he touched her lips with his finger before he kissed her, and when he kissed her it was a disappearing.

Katrin has not mentioned Emma or the baby, doesn't talk or ask about them, and when he told her the bare facts before their first night together, she didn't flinch, didn't recoil, but said, simply and with force, "It's good to be a father." This is an extraordinary response. He wants to assure her that he doesn't take it lightly, that her equanimity inspires the sort of awe in him that he has previously only experienced in the presence of nature. He worries, however, that it might mean that she is not investing and that the small parts of himself that he leaves behind every time he visits her will be unsafe.

How will he manage all of this? Emma is bigger. Her face is more beautiful than it has ever looked, her cheeks flushed, but her moods more fierce. She stayed at his flat for almost a week before she reacted to his frequent evenings out, and now she has moved to a girlfriend's house, saying there is more room there, but in fact there is less room. He has told her about Katrin, but has under-played it, sparing everyone's feelings, grappling with Deleuze's principle of courage, which consists in agreeing to flee rather than live tranquilly and hypocritically in false refuges. He hugs Katrin's green silk pillow to his chest. His guilt is adamantine.

"You are very serious, Mr. Robin," Katrin says as she approaches him on the chair. She kneels down and sits back on her heels, watching him. "You could play some guitar for me."

He shakes his head, "I'm better on the piano."

"But that I do not have!" She taps his knee. "You are a real musician," she says. He shakes his head, knowing he would per-form only for her. He loosens his grip on the green cushion.

"If you could be any animal in the world, what would you be?" She smiles, encouraging him. This is a game, and his heart lifts like a child's.

"Goshawk," he says, and sees her eyebrows go up.

"What is this?"

He drops the pillow, sits forward and draws her in closer, moved by her attempt to reach him. "A bird, like an eagle, but not quite . . . "

She resists him and stays firmly planted on her heels.

"And why, why this animal? I want three words to describe it." She is still in the game. He thinks about this question, but he can't concentrate; she is so beautiful and he can't take his eyes off the small imperfection at the left side of her lip.

"It's a predator, it's free, it's beautiful." When his baby is born will Katrin agree to be part of his life; will she play games like this with his child?

She nods, taking mental notes, taking this all very seriously.

"If you couldn't be a . . . what is it?"

"Goshawk . . . a northern goshawk, to be precise."

She resists a smile. "If you couldn't be this, what would you be?"

He doesn't want to play, wants only to kiss her. She looks at him as though she already knows his every thought.

"Clownfish."

"And this is a fish that lives where?"

"Warm waters: reefs, the Red Sea," he says. He does not have to go home; he can stay with her tonight.

She nods, serious again, learning something more about him.

"And three reasons why you would be this fish?"

He is not going to be drawn into talking about their hermaphroditism, but she is the sea anemone to his clownfish. "Colourful, loyal, free," he says.

She nods again, taking more mental notes. "And if you could not be this bird or this fish, what would you be?"

This is hard now; he can't concentrate. He doesn't see what she's getting at. She already knows him.

"Green mamba," he says.

"What is that?"

"Snake."

"Oh dear," she says, and looks alarmed. He laughs.

"Snakes are beautiful," he says.

"I hate them," she says, and what an idiot he is to want to be a snake. But it's true. Snakes are a form of magic incarnate.

"But no, really, they are amazing, so smart. They are perfect form and content," but she doesn't look convinced. "And when are we going to have that dessert? I'm still hungry," he says, trying to divert her disappointment in him. She holds firm, puts her hands on his knees, and rubs them.

"Three words to describe snakes, then," she says.

There is nothing to consider: "Beautiful, clever, free."

She nods and adds this information to the list she is clearly making in her mind. "You are very strange," she says. And if it weren't for the look on her face he would be worried, but it's clear that she likes whatever she means by strange. "You want others to see you as a predator, free, and beautiful; you see yourself as colourful, loyal and free; but you really are beautiful, clever, and free."

His eyes fill. He grabs her shoulders and pulls her up to him. He touches the left side of her lip and then kisses her with all the life in him.

She starts to laugh, pulls away.

"What?"

She can't control her laughter and he climbs inside it, wants never to leave it. She takes a big breath in order to speak. "You want to be seen as a predator . . . " but she loses it again, and he goes with it, until they settle down with her in his arms.

"Dessert," she says, and starts to get up. He pulls her back, but finally lets her go.

"I didn't make it," Katrin says as she puts down on her small dining table a plate and two forks. "It's from Epicure—simple, but pretty, no?"

"Why is the world suddenly possessed by cupcakes and over-decorated biscuits?" he says.

"You don't like them?" she says, timidly.

"Oh, no . . . I do," he says. Idiot. He takes her by the shoulders and turns her to him. "I do." There's nothing he wants more than never to disagree with her. He kisses her and they stand in an embrace almost like dancing. Her hair smells of flowers. And it comes to him. She reminds him of Mona, that's it—Mona was a girl he knew at school in Falmouth whom he slow-danced with but never got to kiss. A girl who told him he was an anorak and that the silly things that went on in his brain should be kept in his brain. And yet he wanted to kiss her more than any girl he'd ever known. Unlike Mona, Katrin does not seem to mind hearing the things that go on in his brain. Yesterday he spoke to her for nearly an hour about afterimage—the optical illusion that takes place in the eye—and how it is easily replicated in cinema. "In a medical condition called palinopsia," he said, "you develop the capacity to perceive afterimage." Katrin looked at him and for a moment he thought that she was finally seeing his flaws. But instead she said, "When a baby is first born, it sees the world upside down."

She releases him and reaches for the plate of cupcakes. She holds one up towards him.

"Maybe for breakfast," he says. At this she puts down the cake and touches her fringe. The smell of her hair, the taste of her.

"And Emma?" she says softly.

"She's living with a friend."

Katrin pulls out a chair and sits at the table. Oh God. He sits down across from her.

"And how will it be with you and your baby?"

"I don't know yet." But this is not what he means. Deleuze: Desire stretches that far: desiring one's own annihilation or desiring the power to annihilate. "I have to get through this thing with my job." It's the job that will dictate everything, the thing that will tell him how he is to live. This is what he can count on: that he has this simple task to complete, this deliberate act of determining his future. Everything else will fall into place.

"A lot of questions for this uni to answer," she says, knowingly.

"I don't know what else to do," he admits to her.

She looks at the cupcakes on the table. "Maybe in Ned time it is not as difficult as this." She looks back at him, and he's relieved she's smiling. "During the war, when a Polish scientist asked Einstein if he thought it was possible for human beings to change, Einstein said, 'In historical time, no; in geological time, possibly; in mathematical time, absolutely.' Perhaps anything is possible in Ned time."

How is she possible? And how would life be possible without her?

FRANCINE

Lawrence is seated at the head of the boardroom table. Today his tie is orange. Orange alert: high-level threat. Francine shifts in her chocolate-coloured pencil skirt, too tight, too short, damn it. She fingers what is becoming a wide run in her pantyhose. She coughs, nervously. The four others at the table chat and tease, waiting for Lawrence, who is reading something on his Blackberry, to get on with the last item on this meeting's agenda. Sarah, Paul, Simon and Mohammad do not appear to have done any special dressing for the occasion.

"It's a good thing she went back; she was worried it would be the last time she'd see him," Sarah says.

"And it was," Paul adds. Ya, duh, you idiot. Francine notices that Paul has a stain on his collar. They are talking about Samita, who took sudden compassionate leave to go to India to see her brother. Samita is the key QA administrator, who liaises with field QA reps in each department. Francine has not until today noticed her absence.

"How old was he?" Mohammed asks.

"Young," Simon says.

"In his forties," Sarah says.

"Young," Simon says, nodding.

"Doctors can't tell you . . . they think they can tell you . . . but they can't tell you," Sarah says.

"Like the weather," Paul says, and Francine snorts, then holds back her laughter, pretending that she's coughing again (*Who can turn the world on with her smile . . .*).

"The VC group," Lawrence resumes, "has announced that the second round of redundancies won't be voluntary, like we'd thought at the beginning of the year. To be blunt with you, they're expected to be brutal." He looks at each one of them in the eye like some tribal judge, and Francine holds his gaze the longest, swallowing back what could have been another snort in less serious circumstances. She smirks but doesn't mean it and then tries to smile, but Lawrence has looked back down at his documents, then his Blackberry, checking the time.

"Any questions?" He's still looking at his phone.

That's it? Francine looks at the faces of her colleagues: Paul has started to fiddle with his nose, the fingers dangerously close to entry. His fingers go transparent and she can see cartilage and the hands of a four-year-old boy picking his nose and eating the boogers. Sarah is smiling and Francine can see through her teeth, to the feathery canary secrets hidden behind them. The other two are blank-faced.

"It's not going to be easy going forward, but we have to assume that we're all in the firing line, so to speak," Lawrence says, and he sounds like a complete jerk. She finds herself suddenly hot for him.

"Larry," she says as she adjusts her thighs in her chair. She has no idea why she has collapsed into cute familiarity with him. "How much warning do we get?" She's perspiring, more than a hot flash—this is like dripping sweat after running a long race.

"There's a protocol in the HR guidelines, but I'm told there'll be more time than usual. It's now March; the end of our fiscal year is July. Expect some kind of announcement in the next month or so, to take into account due notice."

Francine wipes some droplets before they slide from her eyebrows and she looks at Lawrence's tie until its orange colour separates into component yellow and red and everything about him is only the sum of its component parts laid bare.

"Any other business?" he asks. The others mumble a no, and Francine bolts out of her chair, the creases behind her knees soaking wet.

—

It's dark, everyone gone home but her. She has finally been productive. After the meeting she patted herself down with paper towel in the ladies', took off her pantyhose, retreated to her office in bare legs and boots, and stopped asking herself what her mother had said about love. Instead she thought about one of her father's favourite lines that he had tried on her as a teenager, when she didn't want a part-time job: "Take Cinderella, for example; she had a good work ethic, and she had a thing for fancy shoes . . . " She hunkered down and cleared the backlog of reports and specifications that had piled up since the beginning of February and the last breaths of Dario Martinelli.

Now she is starving; her bare legs are splotchy with cold. As she closes her office door she catches sight of Lawrence ahead of her in the corridor.

"Larry!" she calls out. He turns and smiles. His orange tie is loosened, drawn down, rousing. She swallows and thinks of her splotchy legs.

"Working late—that's not like you, Larry!"

"You don't know me then," he says and she's aware of all the things she doesn't know, one for sure being how to talk to a man who once told her that his wife never appreciated him in bed; another being how to hide her legs; and the last being why she feels that Lawrence is necessary right now.

"You have plans for dinner?" she asks.

"No, not really. Starving. Shall we?"

And suddenly she is in Philly again, in the hospital room, and her mother's mouth is dry and her lips are like snakeskin. She's not at all sure, but she thinks the thing that her mother might have said, the thing that love comes with, might have included shame.

She follows Lawrence towards the parking lot.

—

His hand is on her waist and she sucks in her gut, not moving a muscle as she gauges what her skin must feel like. The hand moves down, towards her ass, and she grabs it suddenly and does that thing she learned long ago, in another place: she kisses his hand and puts his finger in her mouth slowly, deeply.

Oh shit.

The evening started out obviously enough: the Crown Tavern on the docks, haddock and chips, from which she'd peeled away the batter and ate only the fish, a few chips, but it was the four glasses of wine and her drinking them all like water and then not feeling safe to get in her car—not knowing if Rajit pleaded not guilty of danger, not guilty of negligence, maybe pleading plain old dumb—that has brought her to this moment. This ever-so-stupid Francine who has Lawrence's finger in her mouth like a popsicle.

"Oh God," Lawrence says, and, shit, now she has to live up to the promise of this gesture.

"It's just head-count, nothing more, nothing less. You can't take it personally," Lawrence said at the Crown, well into their second bottle. "It's better to be seen to be cooperating," and he held her eyes, staring into them, but looking more like he was trying to see his own reflection.

And now with his finger in her mouth, she is desperate to be seen to be cooperating.

Dario's nose flashes into her mind. It had been driven flat to his cheeks from the impact on the road and then Ryan leaned his face over bone and blood and pried open his broken teeth and blew himself into a stranger.

"Oh God," Lawrence says again.

After glass of wine number two, he'd asked her if she would go back to the States if she lost her job. Shit no, she'd said. She didn't know what she'd do; she had options, she said, with her breath getting caught on the "p" and her mind getting stuck on an image of Scott and Melissa's spare room: the single bed with the cream-coloured satin comforter and tubular satin throw-cushions like giant butterscotch mints. The crucifix over the bed, the night table with its doily and glass of water. And now she sees that room again, the light from the window that slashes the single bed early in the morning and exposes the fingerprints and lipstick stains on the rim of the water glass.

She takes Lawrence's finger out of her mouth and licks it, rolling her tongue around it, sliding it back into her mouth.

"God," he says again.

When everything is off but her bra and underwear, his shirt unbuttoned, only his underwear and socks remaining, she looks at his belly. Then lower, to the tent-like pouch of his briefs.

Shit. She tries to back out by shuffling herself away on the bed towards the pillows, hoping he won't notice, but she sees her own thighs jiggle, and when she rests them on the duvet, the orange-peel complexion is spotlit in the track lighting overhead.

"The lights?" she says softly as she raises her knees and hugs them.

Lawrence complies then quickly takes off his shirt and whips off his socks, leaving only his briefs that look like they will rip with the force of what's inside them. Larry is packing.

When he arrives at the bed it's with a ferocious grunt as though he's already come, but she lowers her knees and allows him on top of her, and shit, yeah, there it is.

His kiss is wet; she flinches. But a kiss—it's been a long time coming, so she examines it with every inch of her tongue, tastes its haddocky tang and remembers not to probe too forcefully, to let him do some pushing forth, to allow him access to the depths of her throat, to make him think of other depths. And this seems fair enough. He has been kind to her; he has offered to protect her as best he can from the ravages of the upcoming culling; he has offered to read her job description for her; he has, bless the fat little functionary, said that she'll be the first he will give a heads-up to if he hears anything significant. And as he takes his somewhat oddly shaped—more impressive in its width than length—cock out and aims it at her, she remembers all this and starts to help him by taking down her underpants, sorry that she hasn't shaved or waxed or trimmed, but right now Larry could care less.

While he's in her she can't stop worrying if he has something that she might catch and why on earth she hasn't insisted on a condom. Then it's there: an image she hadn't realized had imprinted. The image she had not even known she'd experienced until just this second: Dario's face as his body flew across her windscreen—his visor open, the only discernible feature his white teeth bared in a silent howl.

"Ow, ow, ow," she says and pushes Lawrence up to get him to stop.

"What? You okay?" he asks, terrified he has hurt her, but she hugs him to reassure him he has not, no, not really . . . it's just . . .

"Sorry, just a second, let's . . . just . . . Stay there. Don't move," she says, "I like that," and she remembers how to be helpful and how to make it seem like everything is just right and the guy just never has to do anything but the perfect fucking he believes he's been born to do. She remembers that this is a crucial part of all of this. So she whispers: "Oh God, that feels great," and in a moment so graceful and swift that it feels like it is enacted by a petite, confident woman half her size and age, she turns over on her stomach and raises her red ass in the air like a baboon and offers it to Larry as the last thing on earth that might save her.

ROBIN

The gods are back. This day confirms it. And they are toying with him again. Since the last warm days of October, through the misery of November and his last hurrah of sex with Emma in December, and all through the dark winter, the gods said, you deserve this, you are lost in a grim forest, you are not Kurosawa's samurai, you are merely a common, irrelevant man. And now today's sun—the evil light like the cinematography in Rashomon—is their joke on him. Things were easier in the irritating shadows, the itching cold. This light, this warmth on his neck; daffodils, crocuses, a million shades of green: these will hurt without her. And those birds. God. The birds are torture. There is one tree, one supernatural tree that he must pass on his way to the tube, and this tree persecuted him this morning; this tree with branches dressed in white lace petti-coat blossom, circled by sparrows calling like fools. And the afterimage of Katrin seared into his brain: her hair, skin, the way she takes him to her. These, along with the ultrasound image of his baby, Emma's tears, and the fact that he has agreed to her request to move into his flat for the baby's birth, are torture here in the sunshine.

Today the river smells nearly like a river should. The sun makes this space behind the library feel nearly like a real shore. Robin looks around him, aware of noises near the derelict spot at the back of the Samuel Johnson building. He sees the broad back of Bayo, her weave of black hair, long down her back, her shoulders hunched over something, and then the flame opens and she drops the thing in her hand and stands back. The essay. He didn't want to, he tried hard not to, but he had no choice but to fail her. It would never have got by the external examiner, would in no one's eyes but his own have been worthy of a pass just because she has tried so hard and needs a break so badly. Is he doing them justice—these students who don't need theory but who, like Bayo, just need a job?

The inevitability of bad news awaits him in his office. The last round of e-mails from the dean reveal that there will be no hourly paid lecturers for next year, and class sizes will increase accordingly. Even if he keeps his job, he'll never have time to write another article. Students will consume him, making a film would be out of the question even if he could, and, fact is, without being submitted to the REF he'll never get further than the lecturer grade. He needs to make a mark in a different way, but his application for his job has been sent to Human Resources; his article on motion capture and animation has been submitted to *The Velvet Light Trap*, and he now must ensure that he doesn't botch the interview. The one for his current job is the only interview he hasn't botched in his life, except maybe the one for a stock boy position at Sainsbury's when he was sixteen, when he jabbered on about the importance of fresh milk.

Bayo spots him as she walks away, the blackened leaves of her burnt essay fluttering on the ground beside the cement wall. He nods, but she doesn't acknowledge his gesture.

Olivia paces in the corridor; a scowl, eyebrows close together. Robin slows down in his march back to his office. Bayo, Olivia: too much today. But as soon as she is in front of him at his desk, the born teacher in him, the part of him he wishes he could bottle so that he could sip it during other less resourceful moments of his day, arrives to shore them both up.

"That man who works for the council," Olivia says. She is ticking inside, something about to give. He puts his hand on the desk.

"What is it?"

She rubs her face. "I didn't tell you this before."

He waits, expecting that her bobbing will spin out meaning like cloth.

"He's my father." She looks at him with something akin to a dare.

"Oh," he says, and waits for her to explain.

"So, yes, that's why, that might be why."

He waits, giving her space, not wanting to force her to that place she was last year when she revealed more than he could rightfully handle.

"I haven't seen him for . . . like forever . . . and he . . . " She shifts in the chair. He waits for her to finish, but she shakes her head and doesn't look as though she will.

"Is there something else?" He lifts his baby finger to the bridge of his glasses and nudges them slightly.

"He just seemed so pathetic, is all." The tension in her face slackens.

"I don't understand," Robin says, but really he does, and there is something pathetic about a man who is responsible for heaps of lonely dead people who might lose his job because of budget cuts and shrinking economies and the careless, idiotic way we live.

"I just had to tell you that, is all. I just thought, oh, I didn't tell the whole story, and it wasn't fair, so I had to tell you that." Olivia picks her satchel up off the floor.

Now it all makes sense, her tortured, confusing designs disguised as research.

"Are you worried about him?"

"He's just this man; he sounds a bit foreign. I didn't use to think so, when he was my dad," she says.

The boundary that Robin is perched on is a dangerous one, he knows.

"What do you want to happen?" he says.

Her eyes are very clear as she looks up. "To do this project with him," she says, "so he can keep his job, and he can become—" she stops, her confidence spent.

If there are no rules, there is no game. But what kind of parent will he be if he doesn't respond with his truest impulse?

Afterimage: Katrin laughing uncontrollably: you want to be seen as a predator.

"I could talk to him," he says, and she is calmed. He is not promising anything; he doesn't have to commit to action just because that is her way of handling strife. Talking to Olivia's father would be like breaking the fourth wall in theatre. There might be no worse or better moment in his career to do so. Though coming up with a better way to eulogize over a communal grave will not save Olivia's father's job.

She rests the satchel on the floor again. "Will you? Oh, that's ace; you will? I'll set it up."

"Yes," he says with a firm nod. Formaldehyde is a difficult word to spell; Bayo knows this. Yes, he will do this small thing.

When Olivia has gone he looks at the sky through his office window. The beryl through the atrium's aperture confirms that the day has not yielded in its outpouring of painful sunlight. Skin, tongue, hips. God. It's palinopsia.

OLIVIA

Jasmine is wearing a cross the size of a door key. She looks like a jailer with it hanging around her neck, and Olivia can't hold back her smile. Even if Jasmine looked up now from her praying to see Olivia's face, she wouldn't get the smirk. Nah, Jaz is gone. Jaz has a dead-man-has-been-inside-me miracle of Christ's love to distract her from feeling duped, on account of finding out how many girlfriends Dario had at the time of being splattered on the road. Jasmine is straining towards Christ as a way of eliminating the competition.

"Jaz—we should go out, to the park or something, get some air, innit. It's stuffy in here. The sun is out—the birds are singing—feels nearly spring," Olivia says.

Jasmine looks up and glances out the window. "It won't last," she says, "and there's nowhere to go except to Jesus, Liv."

"You know you don't believe that. You didn't even know the guy, Jaz." Olivia stands and gets her coat on. "I'm off—got a ton of work to do. I'm danged, Jaz, but you just keep praying." And out she goes into the sunshine that says, cool it, cool it, right.

But it's week five of the term already, and she has to get down to it. All she has is an outline on the history of paupers' graves, a bit of research on poetry, ceremony, and commemorations, and some jacked-up ridiculousness from Jasmine on how souls who don't get praised don't go to heaven. She's bound to fail her degree now. This sunshine is not helping, not one bit. She wants to sprint like mad the way she used to in Parsloes Park on the March days when Miss Temple from Five Elms Primary school took her year-four class to the park and said, "Run wild," because she knew they'd tire themselves out and be better behaved for the rest of the day. Olivia could outrun Jasmine-who-was-then-Eleanor, Athina, Sally, and even Rufaro, Olu, and Beverly, who were the sporty ones with a lot of speed but too much attitude. There was nothing keeping Olivia back because she knew where to focus. She knew you didn't look at the finish line; you looked at your own two feet running. Right.

And now she has to do the same and not look up again until this dissertation is finished. Robin told her that he would meet Ed at his office; Robin is a man who will not let you down. Something will come, and the next time Ed has a funeral and reads a poem for the lonely dead, well, she'll take Catherine. That will be the moment, and all will be unveiled and all will be right. Suddenly she feels tired.

Her satchel buzzes.

She flips up the flap and reaches in for her phone.

You disappearing from me, but I still try, and hope. Nasar.

It's not anger she feels, no. If he's so determined, he will wait. What's in her fingers is more like the need to brush the curls away from her eyes.

Very busy now. How do you know me anyway? You're amping this don't you think?

She keeps walking. The bus will be quiet this time of day. She can read her printouts on participatory rights in international law on the way. Uni food is too expensive and too shite since they dumped all the real dinner ladies, so she'll get off early and get a sandwich from the shop, and—

You meet me on the cuts march at SU bus.

Nasar. That was him. Of course, on the student union march. Of course he isn't a random stalker. That dude was something different. A tall bloke, a small tingle, and just enough of a wish that this Egyptian will be around when she's finished her course work and that there will be an Arab Spring in London.

The 173 stops directly in front of her and the driver takes his sweet time opening the door. She was right, it's nearly empty, but even though she could without harm take a disabled and elderly seat at the front, she moves to the back, sits, and takes out her notes. As they make their way around corners and through intersections, she feels something in her knickers—a bit of wetness, which makes her uneasy. She looks around to make sure neither of the two women in the seats around her take any notice that there might be something going on inside her.

ROBIN

Sydney House, the offices of the Safeguarding Adults Team of the Barking and Dagenham Council, is drab and boxy, with the kitchen-sink realism of *Kes*, and overhead lighting to match, as though revealed through the lens filter of a cinematographer invoking the 1970s. Robin walks the corridor to the Protection, Funeral and Conference Officers. The door is open and a black man behind one of the three desks in the office stands up when he sees him. "You are Robin," the man says. "I'm Ed," and he smiles. His head is balding at the front, closer to a number-two trim elsewhere. "Or Wood," he adds, zipper teeth towards a laugh. The Caribbean accent is as mild, but present, as Olivia said.

Robin shakes his hand. "Wood?"

Ed comes out from behind the desk. He leads Robin to a small room along the corridor, where there is a table, chairs, a coffee machine, cups, and a kettle. A tiny *To Sir with Love* staff room.

"Wood is what people call me when they know me," Ed says. The man pulls out a chair at the table and sits, inviting Robin to do the same.

"Why Wood?"

"When my daughter—when Olivia," he raises his hand in a yes-of-course-you-know-her gesture. "A nickname she gave me. You go ahead, call me Wood. Olivia says you are very good to her." Ed's voice is higher when he talks about his daughter. His accent is less controlled. Robin feels both familiarity and fresh-ness on the other side of the boundary he has crossed, and he sits up straight to resist getting too comfortable here. He will find out what Ed thinks of Olivia's eulogy project and see if he can offer any suggestions. That will be all.

"So, this must be a demanding job," he says, and shifts a little in his chair.

"No, no, not demanding—not in an ordinary way." Ed turns over a napkin on the table, folds it, opens it again and straightens out the edges.

"What sort of training do you need?"

Ed begins to talk quickly, as though he's being interviewed, and this uneasy dynamic is not what Robin intended.

"I have a lot of experience," and Ed rhymes off a range of courses and diplomas. "I wanted to be a teacher myself, once. Teachers are as important as parents," he says, but he laughs uncomfortably at this. Although he's fifty-nine, he says, he still thinks he can be a good parent. "Olivia is lovely, isn't she?" he says.

Robin nods, wanting to tell him how Olivia seems worried for him, but he will not breach her trust. And mostly what he is not saying is that you are a lucky man and if I get a child who cares about me like this I will be undeserving. He closes his eyes then opens them again quickly.

"And what about her idea?" Robin asks.

Ed shakes his head and smiles, big, wide. "Her dissertation, you mean? Oh, yes well, you know, I helped her a bit, but not too much, really, just told her a little about community graves and what goes on through the council . . . I'm not the best source; she needs to be doing the history, I think, and I—" He pauses and looks serious, nearly unhappy. "But it's all right, isn't it? My helping her a bit?"

Robin takes a deep breath; he has been set up. Olivia has obviously not told Ed about the poetry, and now Ed thinks he's here to check up on him. "No, no, it's great; it's fine." He shifts in his chair again. "Have you worked with academic researchers before?" Maybe he can salvage this without embarrassing either of them. If there's a real project here what's the harm?

Ed nods his head and begins to answer, his voice dedicated and professional. Directed by the Social Care Institute for Excellence, their work is pan-London, partnered by the police, the NHS, local authorities, and the fire brigade. His job is a small part of a bigger strategy, because, according to Ed, the whole world is going wrong. The things he does, day to day, don't change much, but there are always strategies for finding more partners, more money. He looks after the elderly, the mentally incapable, people who don't have family or friends to represent them and can't make their own decisions. Ed gets them the right help.

Robin sees the feathery blackened remains of Bayo's burned essay at the back of the library.

"Does it get you down?" he asks, looking around the room. The only books in sight are the paperback manuals piled on the table beside the kettle: phone books, regulations, government reports.

"Ah, no-no," Ed says, shaking his head. "Just the opposite."

That's the thing, yes; he knows this from teaching: it keeps you in the world. Afterimage: Emma's tiny mogul of a bump beneath her white T-shirt. "Hope you don't mind me asking . . . your accent, where are you from exactly?"

Ed is reluctant at first when he tells Robin about Guyana, but he slowly opens up and talks about the variety of landscape— sea, rivers, bush. He describes the swell of forest in the middle of the country making it sound like lungs for a hemisphere. Robin breathes in and holds his breath, thinking, yes, yes, there are things I could do to help. As they talk more, across random subjects, Robin finds himself at one point saying, "I fix nearly everything in my flat with duct tape," at which Ed nods, knowing exactly how important duct tape is.

"Did you learn to read from young?" Ed asks him.

"Sure, sure," Robin says, and they smile at one another, mirroring language as well as smiles. Ed fidgets, and Robin knows he must either take the conversation somewhere new or tell Ed about the poetry. Although the idea seems less absurd in this precise moment than it has all along, he doesn't have the words right now.

"Catherine is Olivia's mum," Ed says, saving Robin from raising his own random subject. He thinks of his own, Polish Catherine. There's nothing left to say.

"I'll think about possible research projects, a film, perhaps," and he makes moves to leave, but he doesn't want to return to the university; he wants to return only to the moment of standing with Katrin in the curve of the eaves in her bedsit, holding tight, only a slight, rocking movement, a dance, a silence.

"Olivia's project is good," Ed says, proud, maybe a bit defensive. They stand.

"I'm sure it is," Robin says.

He shakes Ed's hand. He doesn't mind that he has been stitched up by Olivia; he wants to be necessary, like this man.

FRANCINE

It might appear like a normal day if you didn't look too hard—students sitting in lecture halls taking notes, lecturers bitching in the staff room, coffee being drunk, cigarettes smoked out in the square—but London in March is not supposed to have snow crushing the daffodils poking up through the brittle ground, so Francine is shit sure that something is going down today. A few days ago the skies were like oh-hallelujah-it's-here! But now the skies are pewter, flecked with dandruff. This might be the day she hears that her job is kaput. She decides to call the States. "Scottttttt . . . " she says, playing with him, in a way they never did as children. But when he doesn't rise to the invitation and instead responds matter-of-factly, asking her why she's phoning him so early on a Monday morning, she speaks plainly.

"I might need a job," she says.

Scott tries, in his way, but he is not comfortable with comforting, and when he says, "Things are tough there, I know, I've heard . . . " she understands that is the best he can do.

"I'll be fine . . . it's not really any of that . . . " And she finds herself telling Scott about the accident and how lousy she has felt—minus the menopause, minus the sex with Larry—and he is more at ease now, back in familiar territory with his sister who was always a bit of a case, and so he reverts to his favourite mantra of all:

"You need a good man," he says.

The silence between them feels the same as it did when their mother died: the size of the ocean that divides them.

—

After some progress on her job specification, and completion of the overview of QA for the last six months, which Lawrence has specifically asked her for today, Francine is ready for tea. The snow has melted, but she doesn't feel like trudging across the square, so she settles for the staff room. She struggles with the handle of the door.

"Pull it up a bit, then out."

Almost whispered, the words make the skin goosepimple on Francine's neck. Patricia is smiling when Francine turns around, at the same moment the staff room door becomes unstuck with a click. There's heat not unlike a hot flash, but she feels caught out. She knows this door, for God's sake; she isn't breaking in.

"Subsidence," Patricia says. "The whole building is tilting. It'll be in the river soon."

"What are you doing over this way?" Francine asks. That smell again. She knows now that Patricia brings the smell of France—croissants baked with lavender.

"Meeting with your lot about our MA programme," says Patricia. Her engine seems quiet, nothing Patty about her today.

"Oh?"

"Not enough students."

"Oh, I see," Francine says, and tries to think of something clever that will make them both feel more comfortable, but she can't, and ticking seconds of silence build and build.

Patricia stares at her now. "I'm not desperate, Francine."

"What?" Francine's face burns.

"Enjoy your tea . . . no, it's coffee, isn't it?" Patricia says. She places three fingers on Francine's shoulder (two, three, four seconds) then turns and walks towards the stairwell, disappearing downstairs.

The sudden lump in her throat forces Francine to put her hand there; she scratches her neck.

—

When she's composed after her coffee, she quickly finishes the QA document that she will give to Lawrence before leaving. She prints it out and doesn't bother to proof it again, satisfied that she's accomplished one major thing this week. She takes the document to Lawrence's office and leaves it on his desk. She hovers there, sniffing the air: it brings sandalwood, cheese, musk, and whisky. Larry is like a swamp. Larry is a bit of a jerk. If she tries, she can still feel him crashing against her, way up inside her, she on her hands and knees, smiling painfully at the wall. She leaves his office.

She can try to sneak out early to go home or she can sit at her desk and try to look busy. The announcement is expected in three weeks. She sits at her desk and clicks on to her Soulmates account:

Three people have viewed her profile since her last log-in.

She has one fan.

She has five favourites.

She has one new message.

Chris from Nottingham wants her to get in touch. Chris from Nottingham looks like mashed potatoes. Her throat catches again.

—

When she reaches her neighbourhood later that evening, she drives in the opposite direction of her flat. She turns down Ryan's road and parks outside his house. Lights are on in the living room, and there is movement behind the sheer curtains. She pushes the radio dial and catches the end of the news, not listening. And when a familiar tune of prancing violins begins, she recognizes *The Archers*. She can't stand the voices, the accents, the melodrama. But she finds herself listening.

When the show is over she starts the engine. This is idiotic. So she can barely believe it when the door to Ryan's house opens and out he comes, earphones in, and up goes the hood, down goes the head. He crosses the road towards her and is about to pass the car and she can't help herself. She opens the door and leaps out in front of him.

"Fucking hell!" He's scowling.

"Sorry, sorry," she says as she puts her hands out to touch his shoulders. "I didn't mean to startle you." She didn't mean to even be here, but now that she is she has to buck up, not fail him.

"What are you doing here?" His face has softened and there's room for her now to tell him that everything is going to be okay. Isn't that what her own mother would have done?

"I wanted to give you something—a book," she's not thinking fast enough, "a book that I thought you'd be interested in, but

I realized I'd left it at home. Sorry, I was just turning around to fetch it, and then I saw you." He's not listening.

"I could use a lift," he says quickly.

"Sure," she says, and hops to it, unlocking the passenger door for him.

He's fast, edgy, cagey.

"Where to?"

"Anywhere . . . "

She pulls out and does as he requests, driving slowly, any- where. He smells like beer. There's a silence for a minute or two until he turns to her:

"The driver has pleaded guilty to a lesser sentence of care- less driving causing death. He must have done some sort of deal." She wants to ask him how he knows, but he seems too agitated now. "I don't believe him," he says.

She takes a right at the lights because it gives her a moment to wait for a passing car, and to think. "Don't believe Rajit?" He nods and beer comes at her again. "What's not to believe?"

He turns towards her, his face pained. "That he forgot to renew his licence? Forgot? The car was borrowed. He could have just been taking a chance. But he said he forgot and was about to buy his own car." Ryan sniffs. When she and Scott were teen- agers, living with Aunt T, Scott would do a lot of yelling. *What the hell does that guy think he's doing? Where the hell is the butter?* And when he was most afraid he would blame her and Aunt T for trying to get away with things, for putting one over on him. Ryan's nose is like Scotty's.

"Of course, his family—they need a car—his wife's mother—" She stops, knowing that she can't reveal her visit, can't mention the old woman in her wheelchair. "He would want a car . . . "

"I don't believe him," Ryan repeats. He puts his hand on the dashboard and it shimmers, dissolves, passes through it, into the body of the car.

They are somewhere deep in north London as the sky darkens, but she doesn't know exactly where. Stocky terrace houses, with rubbish bags popping out of bins, everything squashed together in the dinge. "Do you want to go somewhere in particular?"

He shakes his head and puts his hood up again; she keeps driving. (*To boldly go . . .*)

By the time she has figured out where they are, it has started to rain. Shit. Fuck. Shit. The street signs are difficult to see. Her hand shakes as she flicks the signal to turn left. She pulls the car over at the side of the road and puts the hazards on.

"You okay?" Ryan says.

"Yeah, sure."

He takes down his hood. "Let's go back," he says.

"Yep," she says, but she doesn't move a muscle.

"You're a good driver," he says.

"My memory's doing funny things," she says.

He watches her.

She checks her mirrors and blind spots, signals and pulls out, slowly finding her way back towards his neighbourhood.

KATRIN

They say the rain is like spit but it is not. Today the rain is oily. Katrin is inside her hat, hunched like a cat against this rain that wants to bring her low. Claire is right about March, but Claire is wrong about her.

At Epicure when she is dry and ready for the customers, she tries not to catch eyes with Claire. She must make herself brave to ask what is needed, and then be invisible again. Already it has been left too long taking chances with Robin that would give him two babies this year not one. Alejandro has a doctor's surgery that is taking new patients and she will get a prescription. But this appointment is tomorrow. This appointment will mean taking time from work to be doing something that really belongs in Ned Time. This is maybe a bad idea. The good choice would be to stop seeing Robin, to not believe him, to make him choose her or his baby, but she is weak and stupid, and she has never been touched like Robin touches her. Ania held a judgement in her face on Skype when Katrin told her about him. Alejandro says love is rare. Beata would like this English Robin.

"Guy's a fucking twat," Claire hisses in a whisper so that the bald man at the front does not hear. "Wants this heated up," she says and nearly throws the plate with the Danish onto the counter. "Why didn't you heat it up?"

Katrin's heart hammers as she picks up the plate. "He didn't ask me," she says and turns to the oven. How is she doing wrong? If she asks for time off to see the doctor Claire will think she is sick and will fire her. When her father got sick with *półpasiec* and sores broke out on his one side and he could not work, his foreman punished him from then, and from then he started to drink and she started to lose him. She will tell Claire that she needs the day for her mother's papers, to arrange for her to be moving to London in just over seven weeks. Claire at least has a mother. She must understand.

"Claire," she says when she approaches the back office during her break. If you use the name you address the heart, Beata always told her. "May I come in?" Her heart starts hammering again.

"Ha! There we go. Have you seen this?" Claire points to the newspaper and Katrin does not know if this means yes to come in. "A new study using sophisticated brain scans shows that women have more intense responses to pain than men. Bloody hell. These people have obviously never seen man flu in action."

Katrin waits at the door. Claire looks up from her *Daily Mail*.

"You know my mother is coming to live, I told you, yes?" Katrin says.

Claire nods but it looks also like she is shaking her head, so Katrin is more nervous. "She comes in May." Katrin pauses. Claire does not change her face, but of course she is waiting for more. Katrin is slow; she has not practised this. "I need to go to Islington council, to make some applications and some papers, and I need to do this tomorrow in the morning." She waits.

Claire makes a face. There is a big silence. This is a mistake; she should have told the truth about the doctor.

"You know that you have to pay more if your mum is with you, don't you?" Claire says.

Katrin nods, but she didn't know this.

"More council tax."

"My room is very small," she says.

Claire's face goes sour again. "That's not how it works. Tell your landlord too; not all of them go for it." Claire twists the chain on her wrist, like it is something to help her not explode. Katrin regrets every word she has said, and her lip trembles. She tastes pastry like it lives in her throat. "And why do you need the whole day?" Claire says.

"I don't. I will come as soon as I'm finished."

"But how long?"

She waited for two hours the last time at an English doctor and was in his room for five minutes. "Two and a half hours," she says in a firm way. Claire looks to be thinking.

"It's not easy dealing with the council," she says, and Katrin has heard a softness in Claire's voice for the first time since she remembers. "I'll cover for you, but not any longer than that, or I'll have to get Rose for the whole day."

Claire has forgotten to hate her, so Katrin nods and nods before Claire can remember again. "Thank you, very much," she says in a formal tone.

—

It is like *wata cukrowa* at the fair in Gdansk during harvest time: the pink spun sugar, like cotton on a stick that she ate as a child.

This tree on the pavement outside of the doctor's surgery is like a *wata cukrowa* tree, pink with blossoms that looks like she could eat them if she bent this branch to her mouth. A cherry tree also blossoms in her grandmother's garden beside the river and a flour mill, where her father was raised. But these blossoms are different from Gdansk blossoms. Big, as though the tree has been fed too much. Swollen. Like she feels also. An extra hour to stand and look because the doctor was a fast Indian doctor and gave her a prescription without trouble. The sun is on her shoulder. Robin loves her and she will see him tonight. March is not brutal as Claire said. And soon it will be April. Her *matka* will love the promise in this month; she will find work cleaning or making clothes, because Beata has talent and is only fifty-eight and when she is not in the bed where her husband will never return she will not sleep so much.

When Robin is with her everything is in the right place. Before in England she did not always know where to put herself. He is where to put herself. Today everything is in the right place, like this *wata cukrowa* tree.

Ania says that Beata is in panic. That Gdansk is her home, but that Gdansk is impossible without her daughter. These two things are not lying well together inside Beata's heart. Katrin will make sure that London is home for Beata and that they will not need impossible Gdansk. When they are together more things will be in their right place.

—

He has her hand in both of his and rubs it in a gentle way. This rubbing makes her head feel light and maybe she is sick, or maybe she is pregnant already after taking chances before taking the pill, or maybe Beata forgot to tell her that love can feel like illness.

"If I don't get it, I'll have to move out of London," Robin says, and this stops the lightness and brings a heavy feeling. She rests her elbow on the small table that is her dining table, desk, and ironing board. Robin must reapply for his own job. At the university they are restructuring and deciding who they will keep and who they will remove, and Robin for the first time in his life is worried about money, because no matter what will happen with Katrin, Robin will be a father.

"But why?" She returns the rubbing and plays with his fingers.

"There are no academic jobs in London," he says. He stares at her. "I feel calm with you."

She can only smile, because he is being so serious and looks like a sad cartoon of himself. "You are teasing me. I am the least calm person, but I fool people because my face doesn't move much." Now he is smiling and they laugh.

"It's true, except when you sleep: your face dances around when you sleep, as though you're watching a circus," he says.

She breathes in. He watches her in her sleep, he sees her; he, more than anyone else, knows her.

"There's this student," he says, and Katrin gets nervous again. She hates this about herself. She does not want everything to feel like a threat. "She wants me to help her father." But Katrin can barely hear the rest because she wants him to help her, maybe too many people want Robin's help, maybe Robin is like an angel and she must remember that angels do not belong to one person alone. She wants to ask him about the council tax and how things work in the council and whether her mother will be allowed to live with her without telling her landlord. She will not ask him because maybe he will think she is trying to take advantage of his country. But it is not that. It is not.

She takes a sip from her vodka that he poured for her before he took her hand. His hands fall away and he leans back in his chair. Katrin wonders if it is this chair where her mother will sit when they eat dinner, or if her mother will prefer the one she is in, which faces the street and from where she can see the window boxes that now have tulips and *cyklameny*. The bedsit has room for only this table and a small dresser. She will need to buy a television for her mother to watch in the evenings. Where will she put that?

"He buries the unknown dead," Robin says. He is still talking about the student's father.

There is a feeling in her chest from his words, but it is not pain. It is like pain, though. "They do this in the councils?"

"All the people who have no families—the foreigners, or the people without friends who die in Dagenham, and who need funerals."

"And how will you help him?" She will try not to feel jealous. Try very hard. And she will not ask him about the council tax. She will not be in need like this student.

"I don't know," Robin says, and he looks down at his feet— his leather shoes have scuffs on the toes and the laces are frayed. Maybe he is thinking he needs to shine them, maybe he is not thinking about his shoes at all, but when Robin concentrates he is very beautiful. "Let's go to bed," he says.

And everything is in its right place.

BUT NOW I'M FOUND

ED

Long hair; smart-Beatle glasses: is this in truth how a professor looks these days? Robin's open face is not unlike Sammy's. Ed sits in front of Olivia and Robin in the staff room of the Safe and Sorrow office and feels proud. The first time the man was here Ed was worried he'd said something wrong, but the professor is back. And Olivia too. And his Olivia is something else. She's full of the things he was as a youth—Resistance! Revolution!—but she doesn't need to holler in the streets like he and his friends did when the ballot boxes got stuffed and boys in Tiger Bay got shot. She is a tread-softly warrior.

"Wood, maybe you could explain what you have to do, exactly," Olivia says to him. And, man, she's calling him Wood.

"Well, I was explaining last time—"

"But you didn't talk about funerals, not exactly," Olivia says, interrupting him like there is something urgent to organize. He looks at Robin to see if this is what the man really wants to hear. He stands up and clicks on the kettle, searches the rack for cups that aren't too stained, rinses them out, takes two tea bags from the box of Clipper beside the kettle, and drops them into the yellow teapot. "Busy here today," he says, and wipes his forehead, hot as rass with trying not to make a mess of this meeting. For her.

"You know, we see a lot of elderly," he says over his shoulder, then turns towards them. "Family left them long ago and they didn't know they were unwell, you see. And . . ." he looks at Olivia whose eyes prompt him to continue. "And some illegals . . . we don't know where they've come from—sometimes women, mostly men. A young woman—as young as you—" he says to Olivia, "nobody found her for a long time. She had nobody. That's bad, man." He shakes his head and places their cups in front of them. He goes to the small fridge for the milk. The open fridge is cool, and he stands there longer than he needs to. He picks up the packet of Hobnobs and places them on the table before he sits down again.

"And worst is the babies. Yeah, we've had some babies."

"Where from, though? Their mothers, surely . . . " Robin says, looking bruk-up inside.

"You don't know it, but some mothers walk away and leave them. You don't think so, but that's a fact." Olivia is looking at him like he's saying the wrong things. "Stillbirths have to be registered if they take place after twenty-four weeks . . . " What does she want him to say? The poor man's glasses are slid down towards the tip of his nose. "We had one a few weeks ago, was found in the rubbish . . . " He looks in their faces again. "The police had custody of the body and they needed to organize a cremation. Normally there's no funeral under these circumstances, but Olivia has me," and the thing that's been there in the room all along catches him and he can't shake it, "thinking different," he says and pours the tea.

He tells them about the mandatory autopsy. The police have to treat it as a crime and the morgue has arrangements with the crematorium for this kind of thing. He knows the coroner who signs the death certificate in this case, a good bloke who talks to him a lot about his cases, and maybe they should work together, because, as Olivia says, a life is a life after all. He burns out on this last sentence and looks to her, but she is looking at Robin who pushes his hair behind his ear, making him look like a girl.

"But what's there to say at a funeral like this? How could there be anything to say?" Robin's voice is tortured, like bacoo stuck in a bottle.

"True-true," Ed says, and he won't tell them about Keith Meyers. Five years ago it was the fact of Keith that made Ed go out more often, made him keep up with his friends better, call his mum more regularly, because he wanted to leave a trace of himself, didn't want to end up like Keith Meyers, early sixties, whose corpse was discovered only after his rent had gone unpaid for more than a year and his landlords at the Housing Society began proceedings to have him evicted. No one was going to evict Keith because he had already done so himself, thirteen months previously, dead on the sofa in front of the TV which, when the body was found, had one remaining beam of light coming from the centre, like a cataract eye.

"What do you think would make it better?" Olivia asks him, and he knows what she has in mind—this feeling she has that every human being deserves something good. He can tell this in the throng-bang-parrap of her body. She is a girl who feels so much she will bust open. Things don't always work out, he will have to tell her—part of his duty as father. Nah every crab hole get crab.

"Just something honourable," Ed says. "To give a bit of dignity."

Robin is nodding and fidgeting, like he's caught it from Olivia.

"Okay, okay, I see," Robin says. "Look . . . I don't know, I really don't. It's beyond me, really . . . "

Ed is confused by this modern education system—with the lecturer sitting beside the student while she's doing the research. Robin takes his leave—formal-like and polite—like a man whose own folks have just passed, and Ed is sorry for bringing this pain on him.

"He is the most caring teaching I ever met, Olivia." He will say her name until he dies of it.

"I haven't told you the whole thing yet," Olivia says.

"Oh?"

—

She tells him her plan, her crazy, beautiful plan, in the A13 café. He is more comfortable with her in the dull thud of the place that says, man, this is real, this is not a dream you once had. Now he needs to follow this through like a father.

"And what has poetry got to do with the law?"

"Nothing," she says. He waits, because she is a girl who has more, the way a river does after rain. "I don't always know if I'm in the right field."

"It's a good thing to know the law," he says. She nods then shakes her head. He has much to do in the shoring up of this daughter of his.

"Yeah, but the law gets changed, and I have this friend— president of the SU—and he says you don't wait, you don't sit it out; by the time there's a law it's way too late."

This he cannot argue with. What a father can do is encourage her every step of the way. He lets silence fall for a beat before he speaks again. "When you said everyone needs a poem, what about you? Someone writing you poems?"

"Noooo," Olivia says, like what a ridiculous question, but there is a puncture of relief in his chest.

"Why not?" He is pushing it now.

"Too busy, too busy," she says and that's that.

"What about your mum—she have a boyfriend?" Jeez and rice, now he's done it.

Olivia's eyes duck behind her curls. She shakes her head as if to say, man, he has no idea. He's a stupid rass. Of course Catherine's got a million boyfriends. Catherine was a beauty. Curvy, blonde, a Marilyn Monroe even though her face was not what everybody would call attractive. But she was sexy, with skin like cream. Jesus. Why she went for a man like him he can only put down to the fact that he tried so hard, while the blokes she knew treated her with no respect.

"Have you told her about us meeting?" he asks.

Olivia exhales. "No, no, she wouldn't be happy."

"But, darling"—yeah, he's allowed to say that, and Olivia doesn't flinch—"she should know. Lying is bad." He hears the hypocrite-rasshole-worthless nothing of a man he is by saying that, picturing the man in the Mazaruni river, face down in the halo of blood. But Olivia looks at him like it is right. Like, just maybe, he has said the right thing for a father to say.

KATRIN

There is a blond child hitting a plate with a spoon, and his mother does nothing. The noise is getting louder and other people in Epicure look at Katrin like she must do something instead, but she cannot and she must finish talking to Alejandro who is not teasing when he says, "You should have told me that was what you said to her." And he's right, he could not have known, and she is stupid not to have warned him. "You should have told me," he says. But it is too late and Claire knows about Katrin having gone to the doctor and not the council, and now Katrin is trying not to feel sick and not to need the Indian doctor more than before, because of the clanging spoon along with what Claire will now hold over her. Alejandro talked to Claire and by mistake said doctor and not council. And now Claire is being so friendly to her, talking in a little voice, that Katrin is more frightened than ever. Claire's tone of voice has made Katrin feel the same size as this blond boy.

"She will get me," she says to Alejandro.

"How? She cannot fire you. You don't have to tell her where you go. You asked for the time. It's not her business. You did nothing wrong."

"She will tell my landlord that my mother is coming."

"She doesn't know how to find him. And why would she do that?"

"I don't know." The clanging of the spoon on the plate finishes but the child has begun to cry. The mother is asking the child if it is okay with him if they go home now. The child is crying stronger and louder. Is it okay with him that they go home now? Why is the mother asking him? Katrin feels dizzy. "She'll find a way to get me," she says and now she must do it first; she must tell her landlord that her mother is coming to live with her before Claire tells him, and she will have to find more hours to pay the extra tax.

It's fine. It will be fine; if she can stop Claire from making it worse it will be fine.

—

She is walking too fast along the canal in the rain as the day is ending, but she can feel Robin dragging, wanting to slow down, wanting to walk like it is an hour for fun, even in this weather. But Katrin needs to walk fast. She is the opposite of Robin today, and this worries her. There is a time in all the loves she has had when one person becomes faster or slower than the other person in the way love is working in their heart. Robin has not been talking this last week about the coming of his baby. He has not talked about the mother of his baby. He has talked only about this student, Olivia, and her father Ed, whom he wants to help, but she still is not sure why this must be so.

"I can't join you for the movie," she says, and then spots drooping white blossoms that make her mouth water. The rain has made tiny rivers in between paving stones. She breathes in. "I have to look after some things."

He tugs on the hem of her jacket and this slows her so that now she is at his side. "What kind of things?" he says. And he pulls her to him and puts his arm around her shoulder. "What?" he asks.

When Katrin accepted her place at Gdansk university and told her *matka* that she would study economics, Beata was very angry. Beata wanted her to study music, to be a beautiful and free artist, but Katrin wanted to be part of the world, not separate. She wanted to be inside the things that make it go around. But she also knew one important thing that her classmates whose mothers were not sad did not know yet: that you do not rely on others.

"Things for my mother, when she will come," she says. Because it was not fine when she called her landlord Gary, who told her that she must move if her mother will be with her. She must not have two people in this bedsit; he will not allow this in his property and let it become like the Third World. Gary will come and make sure her mother isn't there. He will come every week if he has to. She will find a new flat that she and her mother can share, not too far from work or Robin. She will not make a new pressure for Robin who will have a baby and who has students asking him to help dead people.

"But that's weeks away," he says and holds her tighter, knowing that there is more than she is saying.

"And how will you help this Ed?" she asks, stepping back, making his arms fall.

They both know that the things they talk about now are not the things they need to talk about. "It's a crazy idea, but his daughter believes it will help him to keep his job. I don't know if that's true," Robin says. "Probably not. Probably it won't make any difference. But there is something that—I don't know. I feel moved by it."

"And how will you write for people that no one knows?" she says, trying again not to feel jealous of this student.

"Well . . . how do you know anyone? Maybe it doesn't matter," he says. But this does not sit right in the place of simple love and she lowers her eyes. She is so stupid to be touchy and moody and swinging from feeling to feeling.

"Come to the movie with me," he says, taking her face and holding it, like he has read her mind. "Come. You'll like it; I promise."

When will she visit the flats she has written down from Loot, which are too far out, or from the Islington *Gazette*, which she cannot afford. She cannot put this off, but standing with him like this reminds her that whatever is not possible now is possible in Ned Time.

"Okay," she says and kisses him on his lips.

FRANCINE

In the annual audit of the QAE processes in the Health and Biosciences School, Francine can't keep her eyes off Lawrence's tie: bright yellow. Like a TV news presenter sending a secret message. She wonders what Lawrence is trying to say and checks out his socks: black. Lawrence is not inventive or subversive. Larry might just be a knob.

In the corridor after the meeting, when the rest have dispersed, he catches her eye and jerks his head in the direction of his office, as if she should know this little secret signal of his; as if she should feel privileged to have secret signals with him. She follows him into his office.

"You caused me great embarrassment," he says as he sits down at his desk.

"What?" Her cheek tingles.

"Your QA document for the restructuring." Larry's eyebrows are like dirt smudged across his forehead.

"I put it on your desk."

"I know, but it was wrong."

"How?" Her cheek twitches. He sighs, annoyed at her for being so thick and stupid and not knowing what he's talking about. Larry is acting like a jerk.

"Look . . . " He walks towards his desk and takes the document from a pile near the corner. Hands it to her.

She knows at first glance what happened, what this is, and where her head was when she printed off this track-changes version with the red editing in the margins. She might even remember seeing the red ink as she put the document on his desk, thinking that red was the swamp smell in Larry's office. It's as stupid as someone could possibly be (*oh Mr. Graaaant*).

"Some of those comments would have got us both some bad attention," he says.

"Oh God." She flips through the document and sees his marginal comment at "difficult decisions" where he has added, "glad you didn't use the word hard, I'm very prone to suggestion," and she winces with more disgust than the first time she read it. There are no mistakes: isn't that what people say? Somewhere deep down, didn't she want to expose flabby Larry? She rubs her own waist, her hand coming across her tummy. Bloated and tender.

"I'd already forwarded the electronic version to printing before really having a good look. Then I called Sally and cancelled the print job. We were out of time, so I fixed it myself."

"Shit." The window behind Larry frames him and, if she squints, he is a portrait in an abstract painting.

"Luckily they didn't have it for long, and they're far too busy to read these things," he says, holding this fact of his doing her job over her like a banana over a baboon. The VC group decides who goes and who stays and there is talk everywhere. You can bet that Larry has mentioned her error to Sally and covered his own ass.

"I'm sorry. I have no idea how that happened."

"I do. You're distracted."

"I am?" The abstract portrait of Fat Larry goes into the transporter and starts to lose its solid lines.

"Do you want to talk about it?"

"No, no, I'm fine. Really. Everyone's stressed. Simon has shingles—"

Larry moves closer to her and she nearly coughs. "You shouldn't be stressed . . . " he says and reaches for her hand. She doesn't realize what he's doing in time to pull away. They stand there near his desk, his tiny purple lips like a skinny worm, his hand now on her hip. "A drink at the end of the day?" he asks, his hand not quite moving, but not quite still either. "We should have dinner, yes?"

"Oh, I . . . " she says, stalling. "I have to check . . . there's a friend, a young guy, I think I might have told you . . . we witnessed the same accident. He's been having a rough time and I told him we would meet up." She steps to the side just enough so that his hand falls from her waist.

"There's a new chef at the Crown, could be good," he says. He looks at her like he wants to eat her, and Francine remembers that she is supposed to want this, that there's this man who wants to eat her and she's somehow supposed to be grateful. And besides, he has just saved her butt. Shouldn't she be showing her gratitude?

"Thanks, Lawrence," she says formally, "thanks, that sounds really good. Dinner sounds good."

He licks his skinny lips and her tummy rumbles.

"I'll stop by at the end of the day, then. We can drive over convoy style," he says.

"Convoy style," she says and nods. Shipshape, yep, shipshape. "But I'm really sorry," it comes out more shipshape and peppy and snide than she means it to. "I mean, sorry," she says again, more gently and genuinely, "but I shouldn't let him down, I really shouldn't; we made a plan. Sorry."

Lawrence doesn't look hurt, exactly, but she notices that his face has tightened.

"Another time," he says and walks back to his office.

—

She marches out of the building in search of chocolate. She crosses the square and touches her tummy (smaller), her thighs (wow), her butt, just for a second (hey) and will buy both a Kit Kat and a Dairy Milk bar. She enters the atrium, and there is that film lecturer. She follows him to the student union shop (*When the red, red Robin comes bob, bob bobbin' along* . . .) where she watches him hover over the chocolate bars. She knows his choice will be a Kit Kat. It's destiny. Hello! Hello! She wants to yell across the aisle to him. Hello, she wants to say, really loudly, because they just look at each other this way, regularly, and neither says a word. In a village they'd be pals by now. She watches him leave as she pays for the chocolate.

In the atrium she joins the line at Starbucks, and she arrives at the same moment as a powerful waft of lavender-croissant. Patricia.

"How's it going? How are you?" she says more eagerly than sounds right for an atrium reunion, but since she's been avoiding Patricia the days have become longer and the spring light is creeping up on them.

"Not too bad. You?" Patricia has her guard up.

"Here," Francine says, and holds out her Kit Kat. "I got you one of these," and she pushes it into Patricia's hand.

"What? Why?" Patricia's unplucked eyebrows slide towards one another.

"Just did, that's all." Francine wants to tell her things. Instead she looks at the age spots on Patricia's hands. Her mouth goes dry. "I think it's hormones," she sputters.

"What is?" Patricia says. There's a loud crash at the end of the atrium and Patricia turns around, while Francine keeps looking at her hands.

"The fact that everything smells like it looks, like if something is yellow and gooey, that's how it smells, and if something smells rancid that's how it looks. Everything is flat and precisely so. Flat and also translucent. I can see through walls and under tables." She pauses, breathes in deeply, "Like superpowers."

Patricia doesn't laugh at her, and for that she will agree to whatever the woman says next. Patricia stares a little too long.

"We have that plan for Ronnie Scott's, remember—let's do that soon," Patricia says. "Call me." She is next in line at the till and pays for her cappuccino.

"See you later," Francine says. Patricia leaves and looks back at her like she's smelling blotchy skin.

—

Later is not something Francine understands at the moment. Later is the same as now is the same as then, because time is doing a stupid shuffle. She is sitting in her car with Ryan, who for the first time in the weeks since she's met him isn't wearing his hoodie. Hot today, spring nearly here even though she's only just noticed, and she looks up at the sky behind Ryan's house. At seven o'clock, twilight, it's lighter than usual for this drive through Queen's Park, up into Willesden, sometimes as far as Wembley. She opens the car window. One thing going for her these days is that she can make a statement to herself like the day smells longer and be proud of how precise it is.

"Where would you go if I weren't driving you around?" she says, looking back to Ryan's pointy head like an arrow on his neck.

"Dunno. Just need a break from the books."

"Anatomy?" A cherry tree in front of the house across the street has purple blossoms that look like a party dress she once wore.

"Pharmacology, genetics."

"Is it hard?" White blossoms like pompoms, three trees in a row. And there's a flowering yellow shrub she would like to know the name of—these are the kinds of things she once used to track in springtime.

"No. Just big."

She smells gum and looks over at Ryan, who is chewing ravenously. Does he really want to be a doctor or is he trying to replace his dad in the household? "Do you like it?" she says.

He stops chewing. "What? You don't think I'm cut out for it?" he says, and, oh what an idiot she is. Why is it she hasn't learned to speak to someone Ryan's age? She could have a kid his age.

"You'll be fantastic," she says, signals, and makes a right turn, back towards Queen's Park, where she'll drop him off before this turns into the Ryan and Francine sad-ass-losers show.

"Are you trying to be my friend?" he says, as she turns onto his street and slows down towards his house. She stops the car, puts in it park and turns off the engine. She looks at his arrow-like head. They smile at the same time.

"Tell me about the other students. Do you mingle much with them?"

"Sure, of course. Not recently."

"I'm sleepy," she says. He undoes his seatbelt, reaches over and touches her hand. He gets out of the car.

"See you tomorrow," he says before shutting the door.

KATRIN

Her mother cries like a small animal. Katrin has heard this sound all of her life, but tonight the squeal makes Katrin irritated. The sound grates, and her mother's face is frozen in pain on the screen, because Skype is slow tonight.

"Beata," she says, because she uses the name when it is her turn to be the mother. She calms Beata and tells her that in London it is not a problem, there are flats enough to rent, but that it might mean not in the centre as she has been before, and it might mean they will share a bed for a while until they can afford more, but it is nothing to be crying about. Please, *mamunia*, please don't cry. She talks to Beata about weather, about money, about the price of onions and about the Japanese film that Robin took her to see that made her want to eat noodles, so he took her to a Japanese restaurant afterwards. The food of Japan tastes clean and stops at the back of the tongue like a good wine does. In Japan they do not have gas, Katrin has decided. In Japan they have clean systems. Her mother laughs at her and disagrees with her, and the little animal sounds stop.

Her mother will not sleep tonight, Katrin knows, as she clicks on the red end-call icon and Beata's face disappears from the screen. A bedsit is big enough for them both. She could put a futon in the cove by the fireplace that does not hold fire and she could sleep there and give her mother the bed. She will have to lie to a new landlord to let her mother share with her; she does not want to move far from Islington or Epicure. Or Robin.

Katrin gets up from the table and pushes the button for her kettle to boil. But tea is not what she wants. She bends down to her fridge and opens the freezer. She takes the bottle of Wyborowa and pours a small level in a glass. This is her father's drink. She throws it back but promises herself she will not become accustomed to this, like her father. Her father was not reliable, but Robin is reliable, and if she asked him he would help her. Robin is a man whom both she and Beata could trust. This thought makes her scared.

She calls his phone. It rings and rings until his voicemail comes.

"Hello, baby," she says to his voicemail. She feels silly. She has not called anyone baby before, but this is what she hears lovers say to one another. She doesn't want to be confusing, with baby and babies and his future, but it has come out of her like this. "Hello . . . are you free tomorrow in the evening? Can you come here? I will cook a dinner. We can relax here," she says. "Please call me."

She pours another small level into the glass and takes a sip. The warmth in her throat takes away the scary feeling of almost trusting someone.

—

He is facing her, their knees up and touching. Katrin imagines that from above they look like they form a key hole. And into their perfect fit something perfect also fits. Sex with Robin is not only a place where everything is possible, but where nothing is necessary.

"Baby," she says, trying out this new word again.

"Sweetheart," he says and strokes her face.

"I think you should stay here," she says and surprises even herself.

He smiles. But then his eye twitches and she feels a jolt in her stomach.

"Wouldn't you like this every day?" she says. She looks at his chest and touches the few hairs there; she avoids his face in case there is something she doesn't want to see.

"Of course I would. I think of nothing else, I tell you," he says, and she can look up at him now. But his brow is creased like there is pain there.

"But . . . " she says and nods, yes, of course she knows what comes next.

"I dream of it," he says, "I do. But there is so much to sort out."

She lowers her knees and rolls over with her back to him. He pulls her in and his knees now touch the back of hers. Still the perfect fit.

"My mother will not be able to live with me," she says finally and closes her eyes; she could sleep now.

"I don't understand." His body is alert; she has made him worry, but she does not know how to correct it. When she explains about her landlord it is through sleepy lips. She is so tired suddenly that nothing he says will matter to her. "Please could I live with you, just for a little while," she says. If it was brave she wants a drink of vodka as a reward.

It is possible that she feels his foot twitch then. And now she is alert. She turns her head over her shoulder towards him. He strokes her hair.

"I told Emma that she could move in and deliver the baby

there. She wants a home birth. She has a midwife and she doesn't want to be alone when the baby comes."

Oh God. She sits up in the bed but does not face him yet. Oh God, she is so stupid. He has promised another woman to live with him, and Katrin has been taking this man inside her for weeks now. She has been making it easier for him to make promises to someone he does not love.

She gets out of the bed and puts on her dressing gown.

"Please go," she says very softly. So softly he has not heard. "I want you to go," she says louder, and she hears that she has said "I" very strongly, and realizes that this emphasis has been missing between them.

"Katrin," Robin says. "Please, let's talk."

Katrin ties her dressing gown tighter around her waist and does not turn around. She walks to the window and examines the *cyklameny* in the flower boxes, with their petals wide and holding on by one thread, their stamens fat and long now laid bare. All the *czekam* she did for the spring and now this is what is here. She opens the fridge. She pours some vodka in a small glass. She does not pour any for Robin.

ROBIN

Everything she does is deliberate: her washing up from their dinner in the sink, the way she places her hand flat on the plate then caresses its underside with the cloth. Katrin's movements are pointed and fluid at once, and this makes a hole in Robin's chest as black and deep as something yet undiscovered in science. He watches as she pours herself vodka, waiting for her to pour him one, their nightcap that is now routine. Afterimage: her back turned to him in her bed, curved as she hugged her knees. Please could I live with you just for a little while in the soft skin that runs across her back to her thin shoulders that all he wants to do is kiss.

"Katrin," he says.

"I want you to go," she says, her back still turned to him. He should not have succumbed to his guilt, to Emma's desire to share the birth of the baby with him. He is angry with her, and with himself. But now what?

"It will only be for a little while, until she gets on her feet. She is not my love," he says, and starts to dress so that he can stand beside her without shame.

She turns towards him but doesn't move, her certainty

locked in as she watches him put his shoes on. Her cheeks are wet with tears wiped away before he could see.

"You are," he says, composing himself. "You are." And he will find a way—he will pay for a flat for her mother, he will give his flat to Emma and will move here. He will do something.

"Please," she says.

He looks at his watch: 23:11. He gets up, stands in front of her, then turns and leaves her bedsit. His chest is like fraying rope, holding.

—

The next morning he texts her but there is no response. His sitting room is a tip—his clothes, papers, books for an article he must write on capitalism and schizophrenia in the films of Darren Aronofsky. His bedroom is no better. He throws himself on his bed and watches the clouds through his skylight. No trace of spring here, nothing about babies, nothing about future, just him under a puffy cloud that cannot speak his name. He will give Emma this room and will convert the sitting room. He can sleep and work and work and sleep and make sure he has enough money to feed everyone, to provide the baby with clothes, to send it to school, to football practice or dance rehearsal. God help. He picks up the pad from his bedside table and writes words that come, one at a time, each on its own separate page. Margins. Manure. Manufacturing. Munchies. He hadn't meant to be in the Ms. *Bring something incomprehensible into the world!* He tosses the notepad aside. In avant-garde poetry one strategy in the method of "chance operation" is to pick a routine that would inspire one line of poetry each day, over fourteen days, to produce a sonnet.

A time of day, a name, an association that is repeated fourteen times by taking the first line from an existing work of poetry and using it in the new sonnet, whatever way it comes out. He looks over at his shelf of books. A dare. But he has only an hour before he needs to leave for the university.

At his desk he checks e-mail, sees that there is one from Olivia thanking him for meeting with her father, asking him his thoughts on the project. He has no thoughts. Afterimage: Katrin's wet cheeks.

He writes back to Olivia, suggesting she come to talk to him later today. He holds tight to the pen in his imagination; the pen that was Katrin's.

—

The atrium is quiet. Robin takes the stairs slowly, calmly, to Richard's office. Richard's e-mail had a red exclamation tag: urgent. He slows down, one step, the next.

"Your student," Richard says when Robin in seated in the comfy chair beside the desk. Richard stole this chair from the staff lounge, Robin knows. "Bayo Esima . . . " he says. Oh God. "She's lodged a complaint with the Dean."

Fucking hell. "What?" he says, keeping his cool.

"Says your marking is biased, and that you are picking on her."

"Excuse me, but this is outrageous. Her essay was double marked. Miriam agreed with me; it had to fail."

"I know, and there's nothing to be done about it, and you're not in any trouble whatsoever, but I thought I'd let you know, before you see her again. There's definitely some instability there," he says. At least Richard has confirmed that it's not he who is losing it, but Richard is also holding something back, he can tell, as though there's ammunition now which could be used against him at any moment.

—

Robin stands at the lectern waiting for the lecture hall to fill up. No sign of Bayo. Not in the front row, nor in the back. Miles comes to the front of the room. Miles, his DJ demeanour in full force, holds up the phantom microphone in his hand, dips his chin and turns his nearly black eyes up towards Robin. "I missed the last lecture—and I don't understand the slides on the website. Can I book a tutorial?"

"Of course, of course. Let's talk after class."

"Great, Robin, thanks." Miles is all bones and bad skin. A decent bloke who is a relief to talk to when he comes to his office, even with the phantom mic. A decent bloke who wants to know things, to do well, to pull his weight. Robin checks his notes and starts the powerpoint.

"On the day the world ends, a bee circles a clover . . . " He pauses. This hasn't worked; he hasn't got their attention. He looks up and sees Bayo, snuck in by the back door. He has to pull this off, has to rehearse his presence and power so that next week's interview will not be a complete shambles. "The depiction of the process of art within another work of art—a film for our purposes—liberates the event for all time." He needs confidence, deliberateness. Afterimage: the look on Katrin's face when he said snake.

ED

Resistance? For some mad reason the light in this Great Court of the British Museum makes him feel a child again, playing games in the yard: Dog and de bone, One Two Tree Red Light, and Bun Down House. He is running wild and one of the mothers of his playmates is cussing them for pulling the sheets off the clothesline and telling them not to tek they eye and pass she. Crisscross lines from the skylight in the Great Court make a shadow on the wall of the reading room that catches them in all the clotheslines of all the childhoods of all the world. Resistance has no force here.

Ed hasn't been to the British Museum since before there was a Great Court. It is like morning in the Iwokrama Forest—without the screeches from howler monkeys, and except for the fact that it's still rass cold as far as he is concerned, never mind how others are saying it's spring. He will tell Olivia about the forest, about the trees as big as this reading room, about the cock-of-the-rock bird, the macaws and the electric-blue butterflies.

"You want to get a drink?" he asks her. He doesn't want to break the mood of this special outing—he has not thought to ask about Catherine, and Olivia has not talked much about her project, the reason they have come here in the first place. They have floated along beside one another, through China, India, Egypt, like real father and daughter on an adventure. But she has to leave by four o'clock, and there is so much to say. She nods and touches his arm to guide him to the café at the edge of Enlightenment.

"I like this," he says, when they are sitting with their tea. She smiles, the museum her idea after the nearly two weeks since she brought Robin to his office. She is different today, not electric, not treading-threading, not crease-up in her face, just smooth-like. Something has changed.

"I can't believe you never come here," she says.

"Not for a long time, no."

"Mum said you used to like museums and stuff."

"When did she say that?"

"A few days ago."

In her face is something like defiance more than resistance— a little smirk as if she has done something bad. She has talked to her mother about him, and from what he can tell it seems that whatever Catherine said has not fouled the image of Wood in the girl's eyes.

"And does she know you're here?"

She shakes her head, no. He rubs his hand across the top of his head in search of a part of himself. Catherine has said his name, Catherine has told their daughter about the museums that he liked to take her to when they first met. Catherine has probably mentioned how bad his learning was, how he didn't read books. He hopes she also told her how he taught himself and made himself better.

"We aren't telling each other things at the moment." Her thrumming has been given a poke and resumes while she sips her tea.

"Why not?"

She looks up into the canopy of the Great Court. "We had a giant row the other day because I want us to move," and she looks back into his face.

Jesus. "But you mustn't fight with your mum," he says. Feeble.

"It's fine, happens all the time. She thinks the world is against her."

Of course, this is what it feels like to her. Catherine was happy before she met him.

"Listen, darling," but this time it doesn't sound right. "Did she ever tell you about my brother, about Geoffrey?"

Olivia frowns. "Not that I can recall, no."

And so here goes. Olivia is too clever for the slowly-slowly approach. "My brother, Geoffrey, he is in jail for killing a man." It's not so bad. It doesn't sound so echoey in this hall as a man might think, and doesn't make him feel corrupt and small in his own skin; it just is. Olivia nods her head as if she has known all along.

The details come out at a good pace—how everyone suffered, especially his daddy, how his mummy still watches out for Geoffrey along the road every day, how Ed sends his brother letters and packages once in a while.

Olivia is quiet through the details, but suddenly she sits forward, then back, then forward again, her face a balloon. "She's insane!"

"Well, darling," he says, only after realizing she's talking about her mum.

"Did you do something too? Did you help him? Did you kill anyone?" She is angry at them both now.

"Of course not," he says, slumping back into his chair the way he slumped into the sand by the river, frightened now, as he was then, by what to do with death lying before him like that and a brother running, running, running in the distance.

"Well, that's crump . . . " Olivia says, but he doesn't know whether to agree or disagree. "Didn't she love you?"

Now here's a question. This one and what is a brother to do? Both of them buzzing like a marabunta, for the last eighteen years. Ed and Olivia look into the continental exhibits—Africa, China, South America—of each other's faces. The answers lie somewhere there. They stay silent.

"Will you ask her if she'll meet me?" he says, finally, taking strength now from her face, because he has to know once and for all—needs to know why.

"I will," Olivia says, with pepper in her tone.

They throw away the rubbish—tea bags, napkins, a part-eaten brownie, a piece of lemon cake—put their trays in the rack, and walk through the Great Court towards the exit, passing by an exhibition about the horse: in stone reliefs, gold and clay models, horse tack, paintings, trophies. The thoroughbreds that his daddy looked after at the racetrack in Berbice were Arabians, but skinny for so: hungry horses that raced too much, that foamed at the bit out of vexation. By the time they leave he is nearly used to not telling her the things he really wants her to know: how dredging for gold does make you hungry all the time, how the Mazaruni River drops like a waterfall, how black electric eels, piry, haimara, and baiara fish in the Mazaruni don't measure up to anything like the lau-lau, the half-ton fish which is the next thing down the scary scale from the kamundi snake. But even with all of that, the Mazaruni does bear diamonds like a pawpaw does bear seeds.

OLIVIA

At the buzz in her pocket, Olivia puts down her fork to slip the phone out and read the text, even though she knows this is mega rude at the dinner table. Jasmine watches her with a sly smile.

In media lect showed film of chomsky. You see it?

For two weeks he has been texting her and receiving one word answers in response. It's now a little game they have set up. He asks her questions—*what is name of your mother? where is your favorit place for dancing? do you think government will bring EMA back if there is rioting?*—and she writes back simple answers: *Catherine. Nowhere. Never.*

For two weeks she has eaten crisps, Maltesers, with granola bars to keep things balanced, while she stayed late at the library and did everything her studies demanded of her, and more, even taking Ed to the British Museum to check out death in other times, burials and rituals throughout civilizations. She felt more at ease with Ed. Having a brother who killed a man is surely not enough of a reason for Catherine to refuse to see him. She will find the right moment and find out the real story.

She is at Jasmine's for dinner because, turns out, Jasmine is not as religious as she thought she could be, on account of it meaning you can't be letting new boys put their hands in you up so far that you become their ventriloquist dummy.

"How is your granddad, then?" Jasmine's mother asks as she spoons a tiny bit of mash onto Olivia's plate and then a ton on Jasmine's like she wants her daughter to get fat. The sausages in the centre of the plate spin and slide left, making room.

He's the same old bastard he was the last time you asked a month ago, but Olivia doesn't need to say this, because Jasmine's mother is being polite and all Christian-like, all the while knowing that Granddad hates her and her Christian ways as much as he hates the rubbish bin thieves.

So, "Same old, you know," is all she says, and now that everyone's plate is full they can eat.

"Bless," Jasmine's mother says.

"Mum, I'll say grace and then Liv and me are going to take our plates up to my room, 'cos we have so much, like so much reading to do we don't have time to take a break, really, really," Jasmine says.

Her mother looks at her as though Jasmine has told her that the next man she's going to shag is the devil himself.

"Olivia, I'm sure you are very respectful of your mum," she says.

Olivia isn't fast enough with the right words to slip in here between mother and daughter. Jasmine's mother bows her head.

"Peak," Olivia says quietly, but only Jasmine hears, and in any case, Jasmine's mum wouldn't understand their language and how there're some really fucking sad times going on here. Jasmine's mum bows her head, not giving over that bit, at least, to her gnarly daughter. She mumbles a little prayer over the bounty they are about to receive. Amen.

—

"Liv, when a bloke says he wants to get to know you, means he doesn't fancy you," Jasmine says, with her head upside down, dangling off the bed, so that she really does look like a puppet. "Means maybe he wants help with his coursework but not that he wants anything romantic." Jasmine smacks her lips because she still thinks she's got big ones and her new boy is from Grenada and even if she did shag a dead dude she's back into trying to be West Indian. From this angle her mouth does look mega. "And you can get who you like, don't need no Arab who can't spell," she says.

"Shut the fuck up, Jaz. Shut your ugly lips." Olivia picks up her satchel and makes a show of putting books back into it so that she can walk out of this hellhole of a house where mother and daughter are God and the Devil playing draughts. Jasmine's upside-down eyes go wide and she sits up, then stands, furiously, like she has heard what Olivia was thinking, and shit, what's happening? Is Olivia in some freaky place now where absolutely nothing is kept inside?

"Right," she says as she too stands.

"What's the matter with you?" Jasmine says.

When Olivia is silent for too long, Jasmine walks over to her, holds her hand and pulls her down gently to sit with her on the floor. Olivia follows like it's a dance, and they sit face to face at the foot of the bed. Olivia can smell Jasmine's breath and it is sweet like she has been chewing on fruity Mentos. Jasmine touches Olivia's shoulder and the sweetness and the little tickle of fingers cause a lump to form in Olivia's throat. She can see why blokes get all gooey over Jasmine; she understands that now.

"Filigree . . ." she whispers.

"What?"

"Nothing. I'm sorry, Jaz, didn't mean to snap before."

"Your dad is just your dad, you know. It's mums who do all the work and mums who get left, even if she did turf him out—you found out why yet?"

Olivia shakes her head and then takes Jaz's hand off her shoulder and folds her fingers into Jasmine's—doughy, smooth. Jasmine's fingers rub hers, and there is calm.

"I'm a virgin," Olivia says softly.

Jasmine's fingers stop their rubbing and go all alert and stiff.

"Hoooo!" Jasmine's laugh is long and pigeon-like. She can't control herself now. "Ah! Whh . . ." she holds her tummy . . . "What, they making born-again virgins these days?" Jasmine manages to squeeze out in her fake West Indian accent. "You think Nasar wants a virgin, is that it? Some Arab shite you're riffing on?" Olivia's fingers fly-away-home from Jasmine's, who pigeon-laughs again and it must be her new boyfriend who has taught her this. Her new hench hubz who is a garage house DJ in some basement off Romford Road. What would Ed think about Jasmine?

"Flipping," slips out, but Jasmine doesn't react; she's still hooooing.

ED

The boombox speaker is scratchy; embarrassing, man. Borrowed from Ed's neighbour who plays music too loud, the sound is raunch but at least he has tried. Olivia is the only one in the pew of the Rippleside chapel, so for her alone he plays this hymn he found on a CD of greatest hymns in the check-out queue at Tesco. He tried out a few others—"Abide with Me," "There Is a Green Hill Far Away," "The Lord Is My Shepherd, I'll Not Want"—but this one has the best melody, and the words, well . . . *now I'm found.*

He sings along with the recording of "Amazing Grace." This feels good, and he sees in Olivia's face that it is. He is one step closer today to losing his job, now that the council has outlined what the new Safe and Sorrow office will look like, so he sings a little louder than he normally would. He is singing for Jonathan Henley. Jonathan was sixty-three years old, lived at 29 Fanshawe Crescent, alone in a garden flat where he'd been for twenty-two years. Notice of the death came on the day that Ed's foot ached so badly in the joints where his arthritis flared that it was difficult to put the foot down on the floor when he got out of bed. He cursed that pain, despised it so. By the time he reached work the pain had lessened, but he remembers it now, remembers it with gratitude as he sings for Jonathan who has no pain. The man's flat from the outside looked fine enough, but inside—oh man. The place was littered with newspapers as though Jonathan had kept every edition of the *Times*, the *Sunday Times*, the *Times Literary Supplement*—a whole lotta *times* for Jon—that he'd read since he moved in. The paint was peeling off walls and the banister; books filled their cases and lay piled high on the floors. The man had some fine learning. According to the neighbour who stood at the door while Ed did his work, Jonathan's learning was the thing that kept him apart from his neighbours, kept him to himself. "A friendly enough man," said the woman whose alluvial voice gave Ed goosebumps, "but we always thought he didn't like to talk, only liked to think, so we didn't really try—when he was away we assumed it was with family. How wrong we can be sometimes." The woman was in her fifties and trim, and she looked to him for more talk, but Ed silently noted the pain in his foot, thanked her, and left with plans to return with the removals team. Why for rass' sake was he always running away? He's seen a few women over the years, had sex if he could get it, but whenever there's a woman who seems like she could actually know him: not a chance. Surely Catherine is waiting for him to come home.

Jonathan Henley will be buried, not cremated, so Ed has had to arrange the pallbearers and hearse to drive the few yards to the communal grave—a half dozen in this one already. He and Olivia follow the hearse towards the far east corner of Rippleside Cemetery. Olivia is quiet, contemplating, and Ed is hush-hush in the spell of this young woman.

The coffin is lowered, the priest says his words of dust, of ashes, and just like that it starts to rain.

"Jonathan might like this," Olivia says.

Ed looks at his puzzle of a daughter. "Why do you say that?"

"I don't know, you never know—some people like rain." And he sees now. She doesn't care what it is that they know about Jonathan, as long as they have wondered, for even one moment, what he might have been like.

And the man with his face in the Mazaruni River, his arms splayed, and his legs floating like dry branches? The least Ed could have done was stop long enough to wonder.

At the A13, after the funeral, Olivia is calm, and even though there is so much they will never get back, there is something better between them, the way intentions are more solid than dreams.

"And the job?" Olivia asks after their tea has arrived.

He doesn't want to worry her, but a shake of his head has her bobbing again. "It's fine, fine . . . I know how to find work," he says to reassure her.

"You need to invite them to one of these—I'll talk to Robin again," she says, and her voice is macaw-pitch, her breath quick.

He looks up at her. "You think I'm a joke, right?"

"What? No . . . " And she sits forward in the brown vinyl chair. A clang comes from the kitchen. Ed listens for the comforting bright hiss of something frying, but he can't hear a sound.

"I think it's time you and Catherine talked," Olivia says. This is not what he's been angling for; still, his shoulders rise.

"Is that what she wants?" Ed says, trying to shush the hope from his voice.

"Yeah," she says, and oh man, oh man.

"Good-good. That's good," says Ed.

"I will set that up then."

And now it is he who is bobbing, and the sounds of the A13 turn buzzy, and it's all he can do not to stand up and pull her across the table to him. Silly rasshole. He calms himself.

"Well," he says.

She gathers up the things around her, puts them in her satchel.

KATRIN

Each of Robin's voicemail messages tastes like sand. She cannot understand how this is so, because she has never experienced the taste of words before now. From working at Epicure her taste has become more sensitive. She knows the taste of every ingredient in the chocolate hazelnut ganache. And she knows how they make gianduja curls for the top.

In Robin's message he tells her that they must talk, that he loves her, that they will find a way to help her mother. Maybe his colleague will let Beata stay in her home for very little, or in exchange for some housework because his colleague's children have grown up and many rooms have been left free. Perhaps there will be room for both Beata and Katrin. There are arrangements that can be made. But in the days since she last saw him, her back turned towards the door as he left, her eyes on the dirty dishes from their dinner in the sink, she has not heard what she has wanted in his voice. There is no sound of changing his mind about Emma in his voice.

She is so stupid.

"Katrin, you are dreaming," Alejandro says over her shoulder. "You must make coffee while you dream." Epicure is busy, but she cannot concentrate or remember the orders or make enough coffee.

"Al, I am tired, will you take over for me, just a minute?"

Alejandro stares at her like she has sworn at him. "Tired?" His face has no sympathy. "Maybe you should sleep not shag on the nights before work." He uses his elbow to push her a little to the side, and he opens a bag of espresso. Katrin hates him. But just for one minute until she remembers that he is on her side.

"I'm very sorry," she says and takes the bag from him and continues her job. "I'm sorry." She looks at him and nods, to make certain he believes her. He leaves the counter to serve a customer.

Not all landlords will stop two people living in a bedsit. If she takes the flat in Walthamstow she will need another job along with Epicure to pay the rent. Or her mother must find a job as soon as she arrives. If they move even farther away from the centre the travel will be expensive and she will still need more money. She could take more work from Claire. She could work at the new Epicure in Soho. Katrin washes her hands. The buzz against her thigh tells her there is a text message. She has forgotten to leave her phone in the back room with her coat. She reaches into her pocket.

You don't have to respond, but I wanted you to know I'm thinking about you constantly, and that I am holding you in my heart.

No, don't hold me in your heart, Katrin wants to tell him. Don't think about me. She reads the message again and wonders why he does not say that he will tell Emma that he loves Katrin who will be living with him. It is because Emma demands to be primary with the father of her child, and Katrin has for a long time—with her father, mother, lovers, Ania—been secondary in her own life. This thought brings the weight of a boulder onto her chest.

"For fuck's sake, this is basic . . . you are not on a break, we are busy. What are you playing at?" Claire's voice has made the boulder move from chest to stomach. Claire has money in her hands. Rolls of notes and bags of coins that she is bringing to the till where she has stopped to find Katrin staring at her phone. Katrin who has no words again. This has all been coming. All the hours of working with Claire have been coming to this when she will feel the smallest she has felt in her life and it will be her own fault. "Al is taking all the tables; you are checking your phone—is there any part of this picture that I shouldn't fire your arse over?"

Katrin's eyes fall closed for only one second but she would like to keep them closed. She turns to face Claire. "I'm having trouble now. It will not last; it is just for now," she tells her.

Claire shakes her head and turns towards the cash register. She pours the coins from the bag. She flips open the trap for the notes and fills tens and twenties in the slots. Her face does not change. Katrin has stood up to the snake and there is a small twinge of pleasure in her chest. She is learning how to be in England.

—

Robin has sent two more texts by the time she wakes the next day. These make her weak because he has said things that only they know the meaning of. He has repeated their secrets and their words of love in the night and the words of songs they have sung together. These texts are not helping. They confuse how she feels with what she must do. She must take the flat in Walthamstow today and she must ask Claire for hours at Epicure Soho. And she must not think in the second person. She must think with I in every thought. I have remembered to do everything for this week, she says to herself, and there is toilet paper, dish soap and milk in the fridge.

It is grey but warm outside. It will be Easter soon. On the 38 bus there are no schoolchildren today. Next week will be the days of Crucifixion and Resurrection. Beata will be on her knees at church and not thinking about London, so that is good. Beata loves the Holy St. Mary church in Gdansk as much as she loves her daughter, so this week Mary will look after her.

"It will be dead today," Alejandro says when Katrin arrives at Epicure. Claire is not yet in, and this feels like a bad omen.

"There are reasons to thank Christ," Katrin says and he gives her a thumb up. She loves Alejandro when they are like this. "And maybe Claire is one of the dead," she adds but feels guilty; she doesn't mean this.

"She's at the Soho branch. She'll be in later."

The landlord from Walthamstow needs to know by noon if she will take his tiny flat for seventy pounds more per week than she is paying now. Katrin's phone is in the back room and Claire is not. The regular cappuccino-and-Danish man is in the front seat; a young mother and her daughter have ordered tea and hot chocolate from Alejandro. This is her chance. She goes to the back room.

Her handbag is not organized. This is the next thing that needs attention. Her phone is difficult to find at the bottom of it. She sees another text from Robin: *Please don't treat me like this.* This stabs her heart. She doesn't mean to hurt him. She will call him on her break. The landlord's number is her last dialled so she will call him now.

"Katrin." Claire's voice is over Katrin's shoulder and the blood is cold in Katrin's arms. She turns around to see that Claire has no snake in her throat. Claire does not look angry. Claire looks like she is happy, and this is the worst look so far that Katrin has seen.

"I thought you were in Soho," she says.

"And so you could piss around."

No, she wants to say, no, please.

"Please get back to work," Claire says, and the quiet calm tone makes the flesh inside Katrin's cheek feel like it has been bitten.

ROBIN

At least there's no sun today, despite the warm weather. Pathetic fallacy. And if it rains, so much the better. A jet flies low above and the noise is comforting. Kurosawa would use the noise and the pending rain. He would begin this scene with a long, wide-angled exposition—water, concrete, a lid of clouds—and then move to the contracted theatrical space to focus on the unknown woman. Robin looks around him, and, of course, there she is. Bayo is sitting at her spot behind the library, writing furiously in a notebook. Her hair has come undone from its clips and some of her extensions hang loose from her head as though she's been clawed at. He makes himself small, afraid that movement will alert her. Has he begun to fail his most needy students, now? Who else has Bayo complained to? Formaldehyde. Timber. Mannequin. Puncture. Words that are nowhere near a poem. He misses Katrin so much he can barely breathe.

Bayo is mad; he is not. God, surely not. He has had no word from Katrin in four days. One more hour like this, this clawing from inside and he and Bayo might as well make a life of it together.

He takes out his phone and checks it again. Maybe the texts haven't gone through. They don't; the network fucks up.

Are you okay? Please ring me.

He sends it. He could ring her if he wanted. So, why doesn't he? Nothing is fixed yet; he doesn't want to mislead her.

Firefly. Butter. Pig's breath.

He dials. "Hi, hi. How are you doing? Just checking in," he says to Emma's voice on the other end of the line. "I thought maybe we should have dinner."

—

From behind, Emma is sexy, her hips, the curve of her shoulder: great proportions. The mother of his child. A surge of hope. He can do this. Maybe they can be a family. He watches Emma walk around his flat as though she's never been before, and a tinge of resentment surfaces when she stands at his bedroom door, sizing it up, wondering where the cot will go, where her clothes will go—those heavy hiking boots she wears when she trudges across the Lizard Peninsula to Kynance Cove, where just above the rocks at the highest point the choughs fledge and fly.

"I've made dinner," he says and when she turns around he goes cold. She's cross, put off; he clearly doesn't have enough space. "Something healthy," he says.

The chicken stir-fry over rice is his best meal. Emma sits down. Afterimage: Katrin laughing until she can't stand up, tears rolling, when he'd tried to do a Polish accent and it came out Indian.

"I'd forgotten that you're a good cook," Emma says.

"You're much better," he says. He can do this. They are good to one another, always polite, always friends.

"What will you do for Easter?" she asks. She wants him to go with her to Cornwall, maybe to his parents', to start this little family thing off with a good holiday.

"Don't know. Lots to think about. You?" There's a silence as Emma touches her ear.

"I'm sorry," she says. She has blue eyes that have always looked bigger than they really are, because her head is small, her black hair a frame. Audrey Tatou. Emma is a broad, stocky Amélie.

"I don't know what you're sorry for, but you don't need to be," he says. He can do this. His mother and father talk like this. His mother and father have been married for almost forty years.

"It's a lot of pressure on you, I know." See, she's kind. "But it's an adventure." This is not helpful. He doesn't want an adventure with her.

"My interview is day after tomorrow," he says because he wants her to know that if he doesn't get the job they're done for—they won't even be able to afford this place let alone a place for when she moves out. And what about her work? Will she go back to being a dental hygienist? Wasn't that what she was going to do in Truro before all this happened? Pays well. Recession-proof. People's teeth are always dirty.

"You're not good at interviews, are you," she says. And this is how the forty years will go?

—

He hugs her goodnight at his door and tells her that it was great to see her, that they are doing well, that this is all going to be fine. And when he closes the door his stomach hurts so badly that he has to sit straight down on the floor. He remembers the chance-operation poetic strategy. He will rise from the floor only when his clock says 23:11.

FRANCINE

When people say heads will roll, they don't really mean that. What they mean is heads will drop. Eyes will dart to the floor as you pass your colleagues in the corridor. Doors will stay closed during lunchtime breaks as everyone decides to eat at their desks. There will be no water-cooler chatter. Francine is sure something is going down today.

She walks past Lawrence's office but stops, turns and knocks on his door.

"Hi," she says, as she opens it without waiting for an invitation.

"Hi." Wary; cold, even.

"Just saying hi, really."

"Great."

"Is there something going on today?" She had vowed never to do this again, didn't want him to have anything to hold over her.

His face suggests that he knows she's breaking her own vow.

"No, not particularly, not today, but next week, before Easter break," he says and seems nearly to smile, which makes her feel sick.

"Okay then, thanks—sorry to bother you," she says, and closes the door.

The hallway smells of fear. She returns to her office and closes her door, clicks on Guardian Soulmates. She types in ReallyYouandMe, and her password: Isoam.

CharlesNW8 has sent her a message:

I like your cheeks. They look like they hold a lot of love. Have a look at mine and let's meet up.

You're a fatface but so am I is what this message is really saying, but when she checks Charles's profile she's shocked. He's young-looking, maybe in his thirties, but his profile says forty-five. Handsome, with a smile that reminds her of John Clarke's, but a little less crooked.

This is a ruse. If this is really Charles then there's something wrong with him, or he's cheating and has put up an old photo. She wants to punch that face.

She picks up the phone and dials.

"It's me," is all she says, not even wondering if Patricia will recognize her voice. "Want to see a movie?"

—

"I'm pretty sure I'm going to be made redundant," Francine says, within seconds of Patricia arriving.

"What? How do you know that?" She puts a hand on Francine's arm. Francine doesn't move from under it, but feels queasy.

She turns and starts to walk towards the Prince Charles Cinema. The sky is big and boozy, the moon like a fat, squat egg over the buildings in Soho. Patricia catches up to her and keeps looking over, examining Francine's face.

As they sit in the cinema Francine regrets that she's chosen the film this time, and that it's a silent film, the one she missed after it won an Oscar. She's nervous about breathing too loudly. The opera was at least something to hide behind.

"You know, Francine," Patricia says. Francine turns towards her and feels a warmth in Patricia's croissant breath.

"There's a veil . . . "

A veil? She looks up at the curtain over the screen that is parting. Yep, guess that could be a veil, bit thick . . .

" . . . between us and death, most of the time."

Oh. She feels like burping, but she holds it back because Patricia's trying to say something and how is it that this woman is both far away and close up at the same time? Too far. Too close.

"But when we witness it, or when someone we love dies . . . "

It's like Patricia is on the inside of her brain and not beside her in this cinema where the lights go down and the screen comes alive like daybreak.

" . . . that veil drops away . . . and we see it, and it's . . . " Music starts. Strings. Horns. "Frightening," Patricia whispers the last word.

Francine tries not to breathe too loudly.

—

The film has had its light-hearted effect. She stays silent, but she is dancing inside like the actors in the last scene, and she's making silent plans to lose weight and to dance on the outside too. This is good. And here is Patricia beside her on the tube, just letting her sit with the silence.

"What you said before the film," Francine says, finally. Patricia turns towards her. "About the veil."

Patricia nods.

"That's for kids . . . that's the kind of thing you say to a child."

"Well—" Patricia starts.

"It is, and I get you, sure, but it's not true. Not now. I know, I feel it. There's no veil, and there never will be again." There's relief, and nothing else to say.

Patricia looks around the tube carriage, back at Francine and gives her a smile that Francine doesn't get the meaning of.

"The film was good," Francine says.

"Yes, it really was. Charming."

"I never get it when English people say charming, if they mean it was kind of creepy or not. In the States charming isn't always a good thing."

"It's a good thing," Patricia says. "You're charming too."

Francine squirms. "Then I understand the word even less now," she says.

COLD BLUE STEEL

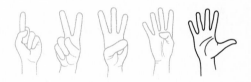

OLIVIA

"Please," slips from Olivia's lips, but Catherine is still asleep. Olivia slides her legs alongside her mother's and feels how hot Catherine's skin is. Her mother is hot a lot these days—throws the duvet off violently in the morning, tugs off jumpers and scarves like they are strangling her. Catherine won't admit that it's the menopause, and Olivia sometimes feels embarrassed watching the sweat pour down her mother's forehead, but there's no doubt there's something going on. "I don't want the summer to come," Catherine said to her last week, "The summer will kill me." But Olivia doesn't want the summer for completely different reasons: her dissertation project will have to be finished before that; she will still be a virgin; and, worse, she will have had the conversation she's about to tackle with her sweating mum. "Mistakes," she whispers, but it is intentional. "Mistakes, Mum . . . everybody makes 'em." She presses her face into her mother's back and rubs her cheek along the moist skin, smelling Catherine's tanginess and stale Calvin Klein, Obsession. "Mum," she says again, into the skin, "Mum," and hears the catch in her own throat.

Catherine turns over gently. "Baby, what is it?"

"I've found my dad." Right.

Catherine's jolting shoulder is almost like a punch to Olivia's jaw. "Ow," she says, and lifts her head. "Ow!"

Catherine sits up and takes Olivia's head in her hands. "Sorry, baby, sorry . . . What are you talking about?"

Olivia rubs her chin, and bloody hell she could just haul off on one at Catherine right now, but she has to handle this carefully; she can't blow it.

"Wood. I've met him; we've met. Again." She looks into Catherine's face to see the effect.

"Where?"

"At the council office, where he works."

"And what were you doing there?"

She should have rehearsed this, should have made him the knight coming to the rescue, should have known her mother would need it to be mighty-like.

"My project. I was doing research; he was there." Simple.

"You remembered him?" Catherine is sitting up straight now, the duvet pulled up around her like she's suddenly cold.

"Not exactly," Olivia says and takes hold of the duvet where Catherine is clutching it and slides closer, slipping down beneath the cover, her head resting on Catherine's forearm. "I figured it out."

Olivia runs her tongue along the roof of her mouth and feels the canker where she burned herself on a microwaved pizza pocket. She uses her tongue to count the teeth along the upper row and to steady her breathing. There's no talking about Wood. No seeing, no hearing from. She's broken all the rules. She waits inside their breath, which is now in tandem. Catherine's skin is not powdery now, but more like steel, hardened but hot, like the hot-water pipe. "Mummy," she says to soften things, but nothing yields in Catherine's adamant arm.

"What have you done?" Catherine says.

Olivia sits up. "I haven't done anything. We talk, he's helping me with my project—"

"He's doing what?"

"My research . . . he's giving me information." But it's hot as shite under this duvet and Olivia kicks it off now. "We talk. And he wants to meet up with you."

Catherine leaps out of bed and puts on the blue Scottie-dog dressing gown that the twelve-year-old Olivia gave her for Christmas, which she still wears, faithfully, every day.

"You don't know what you've got yourself into," Catherine says.

"I do so."

"No, you don't . . . you really don't. Why didn't you tell me about this before?"

Olivia gets up and is standing beside Catherine, but Catherine doesn't want to be standing at all; she wants to be getting out of here. She closes the bedroom door so that there's no chance her mother will leave.

"I knew you had your shite with it all, that's why," Olivia says. Catherine begins to pace.

"You just have no right—"

"Excuse me?" Now it's so fucking hot in here. Olivia's voice makes Catherine stand still. "*You* have no right to keep me from him." Olivia is amazed by her own swagging. "For years you lied to me; you told me you didn't know where he was—"

"I didn't!"

"But you made it sound like he was in Afghanistan or some shite like that, not like he was just around the fucking corner, Catherine."

Her tongue goes back to her teeth, this time the bottom row: three, four, five. Catherine's green Kat Slater eyes get smaller as her breath gets quicker, and she's like a kettle on boil; she takes off her fleecy Scottie-dog dressing gown and it falls to the floor, leaving her all fleshy in her nightie.

"Edward is not your dad," Catherine says.

Olivia laughs because this is what Catherine has been trying to get at for all these years, this fact that if a dad is a dad he would actually be there, raising you, and not off somewhere else with maybe a whole other family or maybe not even knowing that every morning you wake up and it hurts in your stomach because he's gone. Catherine has been trying to drive this point home, gently, since Olivia was thirteen, but it's not going to work now. There is biology. End of.

"Catherine, all your shite about a man not being a father if he's not around—what, like Granddad is such a shining example?"

"You're not his . . . you're someone else's." Catherine's eyes are wide now, gone all glassy-like.

And it takes a few more taps of the teeth with her tongue before Olivia actually hears what it was that Catherine said. Like there is a lip-synch problem in this movie and the sound comes after the movement of the mouth. Catherine steps closer to Olivia and puts her arms around her. And everything is there in her skin. Not powdery. No longer hot. There's only one sensation, like cold blue steel.

ROBIN

He arrives at the door of Epicure and sees her standing at the counter beside Alejandro as though in an afterglow—of sex, or jokes, or just spring air. He hesitates, then enters; Katrin sees him, is jolted out of her reverie, rushes towards him.

"I can't talk now," she says, blocking his way, and a bolt of shame passes through him. "I'm sorry," she says. "Just not now." Oh God, what a fool he is.

"When?" Now she will pity him; he will see it on her face.

"Come," she says and takes his arm.

Her hand. Her hair. The perfect rhythm of the way they walk beside one another. She tugs him harder, then moves slightly ahead.

"I love you," she says. But she's crying. He pulls her sleeve.

"And I love you," he says, but she doesn't stop. It hasn't been enough to make her stop, and he scrambles to find what will be. "Where are we going?"

She keeps walking quickly, but slows in front of a furniture shop. She stops to stare through the glass. Eames chairs, Cornell desks, Mondrian coffee tables. This is the kind of home he'd make for her. How did he get to this place where furniture tortures him?

"What will you do?"

He doesn't understand. He follows her eyes to a white Eames chair. Then he realizes.

"I can't do anything. Not yet. I promise I will, though, after the baby is born."

Katrin moves off from the shop window to the next one. Within her, though, she's not budging. Her deliberateness is set in gear. The thing you love someone for is the same thing that will kill you in the end. The next shop has clothing. He wants furniture: a loft; he will build her a loft in his flat. This will work, if he gets the job. When the baby . . .

"You can't do anything yet," she says and nods. "You tell me when you can," and thank God, she has given him some reprieve. There is possibility here, even if he knows of no way to manage it. Possibility and madness are not the same.

KATRIN

Epicure is quiet, the sun has come out, and something has changed today in London. The feeling of wanting Robin is in her chest, her stomach, her arms, her legs, and between them. There is not a part of her that does not miss him. The day is too slow. She will apologize for hurting him with her silence.

"Claire says we can clean the freezer because it is so slow today." Alejandro has come out from the back room and he stands beside her at the counter. Like her he does not want to do this work. They stare out into the sunlight and Katrin notices particles darting between them. She wants to tell him how frightened she is about Claire's calm face in the last two days, and how she has lost the flat in Walthamstow, but she does not want to pierce this moment.

But suddenly it is pierced, and he is there.

"I can't talk now," she says to Robin and hurries to the door of the shop to stop him from coming in. His smile disappears. "I'm sorry. Just not now."

"When?" His face looks like she has hit him.

She cannot stop her throat from being tight, her tears from rolling. "Come," she says, and she leaves the shop and takes his

arm to pull him with her. "I love you," she says beneath the rolling tears. And she is stupid for letting him see that she is weak.

"And I love you," Robin says, and tries to stop her from
walking fast, but she keeps going. "Where are we going?"

She does not have a destination.

They pass the furniture shop with a chair that is one piece
of moulded fibreglass, the arms curving out from the seat like
wings of a gull. She has wished she could buy this chair for
months, but now this wish is pointless.

"What will you do?" she asks.

He looks puzzled for a moment. "I can't do anything. Not
yet. I promise I will, though, after the baby is born."

She stops in front of the next shop that has shoes and vintage clothing. There is a hat that has embroidery that would
make it camouflage among butterflies. It is difficult to breathe
now on Upper Street. It is difficult to breath anywhere in this
England. There is nothing here that makes her free.

"You can't do anything, yet," she says, nodding, and she
hears how so quickly she has forgotten to live in the first person.
"You will tell me when you can," she adds, but she is really
saying, I was wrong. She has been doing English all wrong.

She turns around and heads back to Epicure. Robin follows
her, but at the door she tells him he cannot enter or she will be
in trouble. "Later," she tells him. But as soon as she walks
through the door and sees Claire she knows about where she will
be later. Orange blossom marmalade, bittersweet chocolate flur-
ries, sweetened cream-cheese frosting—these she knows in the
present participle: spreading, stirring, pouring, baking, working.
The verbs are in the continuous form, but too they are verbs of
movement and position. Katrin sees in Claire's face what she

must do. She walks to the back room, collects her coat and bag and makes a signal to Alejandro that she will call him. She is steady as she walks through the coffee shop and out the door.

She is Katrin from Gdansk again, because to be from nowhere is impossible. "I" . . . she says, as she walks to the 38 bus, "I," to remind herself that this is correct . . . I am coming home, *mamunia*. I will not make you worry.

FRANCINE

The next time Francine is outside of Ryan's house it's 7 p.m. and darkness is more than an hour away, spring having come, the clocks moved forward, making the day feel like it's got some heft.

"Hey." She waves out of the open window of her car. "Hey." More friendly the second time. Spring. She's wary of feeling happy just yet.

Francine and Ryan drive with the windows down.

"Rajit gets sentenced soon . . . Thursday—they might . . . "

"They might?" She looks over, fast and stern. This is not the way a young man should be thinking. A young man should have more resilience than Ryan has been showing in wanting another man to suffer. Thursday is also when she'll know if she's sacked or not.

"Then we'll see," Ryan says.

"See what?"

He puts his hood up, like on a colder day. "Just see . . . " Anger like mud. She sits back and concentrates on the road.

"So, nearly finished your term? An Easter break coming . . . " she says as she decides to take a different route. She heads towards Finchley Road.

"Yep, yep." He's nodding inside his hoodie. "Where are we going?"

"No idea," she says but is thinking of maybe driving up and around Hampstead Heath. She wants the smell of spring.

"What, we on a date now?"

She laughs.

He smiles.

She would never have made a kid as good as Ryan.

OLIVIA

A coat, some makeup, a twenty-quid note. She rushes down the stairs with everything she needs, and what she needs most is to get out of here. The television is blaring with *Deal or No Deal* and there is TV drum rolling and TV telephone ringing and her head is going to bust open if she has to hear another second of it.

"Livi!" Eric shouts from the sitting room. Christ no. She pokes her head in the door of the sitting room. The contestant has said "No deal," and there's loud applause.

"Idiot!" Granddad says to the contestant.

"Which way you headed?" Eric asks her.

Way far away, but she merely shrugs.

"Pick us up a Chinese for tea, will ya? Dad . . . give her dosh," Eric says. And there's a one-, two-, three-second wait while Noel Edmonds says we'll find out after this break, and Olivia turns, runs back up the stairs and fetches her satchel. Running back down the stairs she's not-soon-enough out of there.

—

"I want to party," she says, and Jaz's face lights up like Olivia is her very own brand new baby.

"Well-sick!" Jasmine squeals and launches into how her Grenada DJ hubz is doing a gig in that basement on Romford Road and they will go there tonight. Jaz is talking at a wicked speed and asking her what they should wear but Olivia doesn't want to talk, or think, for fuck's sake. She just wants to be out.

Jasmine goes out to pick up things she says she needs, and Olivia circles Jasmine's bed for nearly an hour before it takes her down, and she falls asleep there. Two hours later when Jaz returns she can't remember where she is or why, but she's told that it's late enough to start getting ready.

She puts makeup around her eyes, following the outline of her lids with charcoal liner, slowly, trying not to poke herself in the eye, 'cause she's not used to this shite that most girls do on a daily basis. But this shading, this bandit mask, feels right because: fuck.

"You look hot," Jaz says when Olivia appears in the hallway ready to go, and Olivia wants to scratch Jasmine's eyes out. "Here . . . " Jaz adds, and hands Olivia a small white capsule. Oh.

"Meow meow," Jaz says, "my treat."

Olivia knows that Jaz is new to this, that she tried "MDMA-zing" once last year which made her in love with her media studies buddies for a whole week but that Mcat is cheap and nearly the same and easy as shite to get and why not. Why not?

"Not sure," Olivia says, but takes the pill and slips it into her coat pocket. "Let's get going." Her body is already humming, thumping, twitching, and she needs to dance.

—

The dubstep is in her chest. And she is strapped up like a suicide bomber with this bass beat between her breasts. She bounces on the spot, then moves through the bodies. Jaz is chomping on her teeth like there's something she should be eating but can't find, and she smells like fish. Jas is in meow-meow heaven and has her hands all over the boy wearing the wife-beater who smells less like fish and more like a dead whale. Olivia has the meow meow in her hand and could take it now if she wanted, could take it and touch the dead whale, touch herself, touch the sky, because there's nowhere else to touch when everything is a lie.

"Errybody hands up, errybody hands up . . . "

She does as she's told by the thumping singer in the speakers, fisting her right hand with the meow meow, the left hand open like a hallelujah and errybody hands up, errybody hands up, she bops to the centre of the dance floor.

An arm comes from behind her and wraps around her waist. The whale smell comes too, and she looks over her shoulder, around his smooth sculpted arm, to where Jaz is standing, waving, all gift-giving and full of promises, having sent the cornrows dude in the wife-beater over to her.

The bomb strapped to Olivia's chest beats harder as the music gets louder, speeds up, and *jump, jump ya, jump, come on na*, and the whale dude has his other hand on her arse and it's like he's propping her up from tummy to bum, like he's trying to hold her all in, the way she's doing too, so she lets go a little and they jump like they are told to, and then move over to the wall, and he holds her in some more and then puts her back to the wall, and she opens her eyes and his face is right there, all sweaty and lippy, his bulgy eyes closed, his hands moving over her hips and bum now, but her hands are still in the air, one clutching the meow meow, so she lowers this one and opens her palm, pokes his shoulder with her fingers, his eyes open and move fast-like to the capsule in her hand, and his smile is bright white, and the bomb at her chest ticks louder while she fingers the capsule and holds it up, knocks on his big white teeth to be let into the tongue that is as dark as a plum, a thick-wide disc that laps up the capsule like a starving mollusc, and while he's swallowing he is pressing his chest into hers and moving his hands between her legs and farther up, up, his hand, just there, is still, like the second before a bomb goes off, then she moves, just an inch forward, which says sure, yes, and he goes to the top of her jeans and down with his whole big hand, flicking away the top of her pants and passing through the bush, all matted with sweat, and then his finger makes a j and up he goes, and the other one too, both way up and she is barely breathing, and now that he has swallowed the pill the purple tongue presses her lips and she opens up and the mollusc dives in, but it does not taste good, does not feel good, but the breathing and the fingers and the oh way up higher in her than is possible and there's nowhere she can go now, nowhere that isn't into the dynamite strapped to her chest. . . .

But still no.

Olivia turns her head, shoving the whale dude's mouth out of the way. She pushes on his chest and grabs his arm, lifting with all her might to drag his hand out of her pants. He is strong, doesn't let her, but she pushes him, lifts her knee and presses him back with it. He takes his hand back, smells his fingers, licks them, and she ducks under his arm and hauls her arse out of the basement without her coat, into the iron-orange wind on Romford Road.

—

When she opens her eyes the next morning to the sound of a knock, she looks to her left and she is in the bed alone. Jasmine isn't home. When Jasmine's mum opens the door she closes her eyes again and deep-breathes so that she won't have to tell her that she has no fucking idea where her daughter is. The door closes with a creak, or maybe a cry.

She checks her phone. There are text messages, but none from Jasmine.

Again you disappear. SU demonstration Fri. Will you meet me?
Nasar

There's a fire in her face and she wants to aim it at him and set him and everyone else alight so that they burn, burn, burn. The whole world should fuck off right about now.

Stop contacting me. I will never meet you. Leave me alone.
That ought to do it.

A similar one goes to her mother who is oh so worried she doesn't know what to do. Well, should have thought about what to do at the beginning of all the fucking lies.

Jaz, where the fuck are you? Can I live at yours for a while?

She throws her phone to the bottom of the bed and curls up under the duvet that is not hers, in the bed that is not hers, in the house with a mother that is not hers, in the city where she is nothing.

When she wakes up again Jasmine is sleeping beside her, smelling from Mcat, bloody hell, like Billingsgate market. She gets up, puts on Unkle's "Sunday Song," loud as shite because she knows Jasmine won't hear it and that her mum will be at church.

She stands at the foot of Jasmine's bed and feels that thing like dynamite in her chest again, as Unkle sing *You can be so imaginary, nobody knows or seems to see, I've reason enough to keep from you, the consequences I can't undo.*

It's one of those moments when someone like Robin would say she has choices, would tell her she could make something of it or she could let it all take her down. Fuck, she could burn them all, him too.

The next tune is "Only the Lonely." Dub version. She rushes to the iPod deck and switches off the player. There's nothing to be done. She picks up her satchel and heads out, with a remaining shred of gratitude for the university library that is open 24/7.

FRANCINE

It's like being in a damn projector, that's it. As the tube leaves
Baker Street station, she nearly has it, is on the brink of figuring
it out—this thing that is going on with the smells, with the veins
and bones behind people's skin: the suited guy's hand on the top
rail; the skinny leather-pants woman shaking her foot up and
down and around as she chews gum; the seventy-year-old
woman that no one has given their seat to, Francine included,
because she feels fat and pinned sitting, as the carriage lurches
along the Bakerloo line towards home. This way of seeing things
is like being the projector itself, like life has a movie and she's
showing it. All these people and their bodies: celluloid. And
when life checks out, when it clicks off, it stays in other places,
like in her hand, like in her finger. Like in her jaw. Sayonara!

She doesn't leave the tube at her normal stop. She stays to
watch a woman with a small makeup mirror putting on her mascara, and she wonders how the woman hasn't poked herself in the
eye. The woman stops, having found a zit, which she squeezes, and
Francine will never get over the things people do on the tube not
knowing or caring if anyone watches. Two more stops and
Francine gets off at Willesden Junction. Outside she walks quickly

because she knows there is a window between six and seven that might work: Rajit's wife will be busy making supper, and Rajit will answer the door, will talk to her, and she will . . . what?

—

Flowers—big puffy hydrangea. Blue flowers are only a little bit ridiculous. They say something strong. She holds these behind her back.

"What do you want with us?" Rajit's wife says in the doorway, the door wide open, not as an invitation, more like a gesture of defeat: take all of this now; you want it too? Francine looks through to the kitchen and sees Rajit at the stove. She got this all wrong.

"I just wanted to give you my support," she says but holds the flowers by her side, tilted down to the steps; blue is ridiculous.

"Support? You are a funny lady," Rajit's wife says. "You want to support us. He has no licence to go to his job every day. You will support us now?" She doesn't quite laugh but very nearly. Francine sees Rajit put down a large ladle. He turns and shuffles towards the front door. He looks old, his hair matted, and still in his pyjamas like a ward patient.

"Who is this?" he asks his wife.

"She came before, remember?" his wife says.

Francine has never seen a less dangerous-looking man.

"I was there," she says.

Rajit looks accused, not at all what she meant.

"I was right behind you." What an idiot. Rajit starts to turn and walk away. Mrs. Mahadeo comes closer like she's going to hit her.

"He's a very proud man, Miss," Rajit's wife whispers as she bends towards her. The woman's thin shoulder touches hers, and

Francine wants to have been more proud in her life. *Don't ever spit, baby.* Her mother had been proud, but it has bypassed her.

"I know the sentencing is soon—Thursday, right?" she says, and Rajit turns back towards her. "I just wanted to wish you . . ." What is it that you wish a guy who might go to jail? " . . . fairness." But that's as stupid as the blue flowers.

Rajit stares at her and in his stare she sees legs, arms, a crushed face, a broken helmet: the recurring content of his thoughts—and these comfort her for being like her own, and for a split second they dissolve together in the transporter, beamed up by Scotty.

"I'm sorry," she says and turns, only hoping that they don't despise her.

ROBIN

There are three on the hiring panel; he sits before them like a felon in front of a parole board: the dean, the head of health sciences as the external, and his line manager, Richard, who looks sheepish. Has he told them about the Bayo business, and will they take into account her complaint? To have passed her because she has paid fees, because she will carry debt, because she is a young person who needs to be encouraged: is this what the world demands of him now?

"Robin, welcome. Do you have any questions about the process or the post before we begin?" The dean has opened the meeting and it's too late to back out now.

"No, no thank you," he says, clearing his mind of everything but what he rehearsed: the stinging, precise rhetoric of form over function; the knife-edge of reason over intuition. If he stays in the place he can trust—the place where minutiae create kingdoms, where the facts he possesses can be trained onto the subject of film like a dazzler in the green electromagnetic spectrum—if he can have no after- or future-images, he will get through this.

The interview commences and he tells them about his research, about the notion that contemporary independent cinema can be analyzed alongside avant-garde poetry by interrogating the idea that all motion produces space, produces the time-image, and the time-image presents movement as a multiplicity of relations. Cinema, like poetry, wants to create the finite that restores the infinite.

He finishes and realizes he has barely taken a breath. He launches back in. "And these are the same principles I apply to teaching, that this teaching in turn feeds back, via student response, to concepts and ideas, making an interplay between theory and practice that is crucial in contemporary culture." Each week he is renewed by his interaction with the students; the results he has helped them to achieve in their coursework confirm this crucial exchange. Since his arrival at Thames Gateway University, over twenty of his students have achieved first-class honours degrees. He takes a second breath and looks at the faces of his parole board. He can read nothing, but he has done all he can.

The interview ends after he tactfully answers questions about how he would approach teaching larger groups of students. Richard thanks him for his cooperation in this round of restructuring and assures him of their intention to be among the finest film departments in London. Afterimage: the white shadow of bones like tiny pins, translucent fingernails, baby fingers.

—

He has had a dreamless, undisturbed night. No images, sounds, sensations of any sort. Outside: sun for Easter weekend. Friday is a holiday, he has finished classes for this week, and all he has to do now is wait. Christ.

He orders an espresso from a young man, twenty-two at best, whose hair has been cut in a number two, his stud earrings tiny diamante, making a trophy of the shape of his head. If he doesn't get the job, Robin will get a number two. He will not go as far as the earring, but the hair will have to go.

This café has nothing on Epicure, a few streets up Upper Street. But it's safe here, while he has nothing constructive to say to Katrin. His hand wants her. His mouth hallucinates her taste. He is like a man away at war, deprived of everything that feels like home.

His phone rings. Richard. He doesn't even bother to take a breath, like you're supposed to do on the verge of bad news.

"Richard." Robin is calm. He asked a barber for a number two, years ago, when he thought he would fail his PhD viva, but the barber told him to be optimistic and come back only if he had. He listens to Richard's voice at a remove, as though Richard, or he—one of them—is under water and the other is above it. The way Richard tells him that he has the job makes Robin feel like he's sinking—a backwards elation that he wasn't expecting. The job allows him the responsibility he must take on in any case. There's no turning back.

"We wanted to invest in your position as an early career researcher," Richard says. Robin knows enough about the finances of the university and budget cuts to translate this as, *You're the cheapest of the lot.*

"Thank you, Richard. Yes. Have a good holiday," he says and hangs up.

He pays for his coffee and walks up Upper Street. He takes out his phone, to call Emma, but rings off, and continues north. By the time he's at the door of Epicure, the sun is so hot on his forehead that he is seeing spots before his eyes. He will tell her that with the job he can give Emma money to live elsewhere with the baby. They will find a solution for her mother. Aren't all solutions as obvious as the feeling of this sun?

He doesn't see her at first, but never mind, she must be in the back. He sits at a table near the counter, not the window, ready to resist if she asks him to leave. He doesn't want to disrupt, just to tell her there is hope.

Alejandro comes to his table. He's not as tall as he remembers him and this is another good moment in the day. He pushes his glasses up higher on his nose.

"Is Katrin here?"

"No, she's not," Alejandro says.

The man has sideburns but seems harmless, so what has Robin been all in a knot about? "Ah, I was hoping—I thought her day off was Sunday."

"She's not here any more," Alejandro says, and his eyes show some sort of compassion. Robin senses a throbbing in his shin.

"Since when?" It was only a little over a week ago that he was here. They walked; she said *you tell me when.*

"Last week," Alejandro says. Too many thoughts to have them here. He thanks the man, stands up and leaves the café.

The 38 bus takes forever to bring him to Katrin's bedsit. He rings the buzzer. Again. One last time. She might have found another job. He didn't even think to ask. Fool.

FRANCINE

Thursdays smell like pickles. Francine takes her sweet time to walk from the parking lot through the atrium, past Starbucks, the student union shop, the main reception, out the door to the university square, across the square with a little wave at the river, then to the Watson Building, past the Costa's, up the lift, slow, slow, slow, no rush on this day that will be her last. If they give her a few months' notice will she bother coming in again at all? Nah, a few long weeks of sleeping in and eating chocolate until she smells of it is more likely.

"Hello, Simon," she says when the elevator opens and he moves towards her, looking like the marked man he is, depleted and thinner thanks to the shingles.

"Francine," he says, nodding. Simon is the kind of guy you could stand in the elevator with and not notice.

The day ticks over as she sorts out things on her desk, in the shelves, in her files. Years of files to clean out. Sayonara. She starts a pile for shredding; she will destroy each and every report so that no one can follow the trail of six years of her not giving a shit, of her pushing papers around for the real academics, of sitting on her butt growing fat on slice after slice of cheap pizza. What is the sound of one hand clapping? It's a riddle she learned in eighth grade from Mr. Sullivan when they studied World Religions. The smell of melting snow in spring, earth and dog shit rising from beneath it. Nail polish on the nails she'd bitten down far below her finger's soft pads. Ivory soap wafting up from the crook of her arm as she slouched at her classroom desk, listening to Mr. Sullivan but staring at Trice Hopkins' chin. She's not until now understood the answer to the riddle, which is "yes." Yes, she says, yes, to nothing, to all of this nothing, to the fact that living on air was never a possibility; the airless creases in Dario's twisted trouser legs. Nothing.

Yes.

Towards 5 p.m. her stomach rumbles, not with hunger, not even with fear. There's a light knock at her door. Lawrence is there, looking as pale as she feels.

"We're in the clear," he says, his face expressionless.

Larry, you're a fat ass, she thinks, and has not taken in his words. Larry, Larry, you need to get off your fat ass.

"All of us?" she finally says, her stomach churning.

"All of us," he says, but without a smile, as though he regrets that this is the news he has for her. When he closes the door she is aware that the curdling in her stomach has not subsided, that her stomach is, in fact, a little disappointed about the outcome of the day.

—

Spittle on the windshield is not something she's taking personally tonight. No, it doesn't all happen to her. Someone got fired and she didn't. Someone teaching history or a non-viable foreign language, or maybe even anthropology. She didn't wait for Lawrence to give her names. And now Ryan is running towards her car, hoodie up through the rain. He opens the door and throws himself into the passenger seat like cargo into a hull. He is jittery, can't settle.

"He got thirty-six days plus community service for the rest . . . lost his licence permanently." He says it all through his teeth, hot spittle hissing.

"His family will suffer," she says.

He looks at her and snorts, shakes his head. Looks back at his hands, where he's picked at the cuticles around his nails. He shakes his head again but doesn't say anything yet.

"You shouldn't have left the scene before giving all your evidence," is what finally comes out. There's a scalding, like steam, on her skin. His fingers picking, picking.

"You couldn't have saved him," she says. He shakes his head again.

"You need to leave me alone now," he says to the dashboard, not daring to turn his head. His hand reaches for the door handle.

What is the sound of one hand clapping?

She drives down Salusbury Road past the mosque. The sky mewls. The rain in Spain falls mainly on the plane. On the plain? She has never known which. She pulls over in front of the Sainsbury's, parks, goes in.

The self-service check-out voice tells her to take her items and thanks her. The flowers are shabby and predictable, but she is pleased with them. Tulips and freesia: two bunches. She walks up Salusbury Road in the spitting rain; the smell of wet asphalt is like cake. She crosses the road to the middle, waits for a north-bound lorry to pass and heads towards the other side, where dried bunches of roses, lilies, and a few fresh tulips hang from a rope around the oak tree a few inches from where Dario's head lay face down. She wonders who it is that keeps replenishing this shrine, but likes the fact that they've both thought of tulips. She slides the freesia in the string ring and stands back to examine their effect. Just right. She walks to the other side of the tree where there are no bouquets. She pulls on the string to slide in the tulips.

"These are from Rajit," she says.

ED

Catherine never liked a pub. Nor any other public places to eat or drink; she did all her drinking and eating in their tiny house in Bow. And things don't change in all of the years you think it tek to change a woman. The thought of her was in his head like paper close to fire, day in and out since Olivia put it there, causing him to do sit-ups and push-ups in his flat, stopping the grog for two weeks. Then Catherine called him. She wanted things in broad daylight, where everything is real and true, she said. So they are in Parsloes park, on a bench like old people in the afternoon and this is exactly how he used to imagine them—sitting and watching people walk past, knowing Olivia was good and in school. Except that now in front of them is a wall with a painting of a head like a mad hatter, grey streak in black hair, and letters that spell something about the mad-ass graffiti artist who made it with a can of paint. Above it is another drawing—a green man, the Incredible Hulk, busting out of his clothes. Not romantic, but not dull either.

Catherine looks old for a woman not yet fifty, but he's not looking there, he's looking into her eyes that are not looking at him, and he's trying to find the tiny Marilyn Monroe in her and to get those years back. She has talked, breathless-like, filling in every silence with something that means nothing. She always did that, always the one to guide him towards the feelings they were both having, and it seems today, according to her talk of nothing—about the work she does, the place she lives, and the state of things now that things are tight all round—he thinks that the feelings she is having have something to do with money. But, true-true, the looks of the pudding is not the taste.

"Olivia is coming up good," he says, to give them something they can share, but Catherine's face goes sour and he is sorry he said it because he can't take any credit for that.

"You helping with her project?" Catherine is holding back now, he can tell.

"As much as I can, of course."

She stands and begins to walk; he leaps up to follow her. "I know you sent money," she says. So she is admitting now that she opened the envelopes before marking them Return to Sender. "Whose money was that?" she asks.

Jesus.

"My money; I worked hard for it," he says. She stops and looks at him. "I wanted Olivia to grow up good, to have everything she needed."

Catherine tosses her head back, turns and walks faster; they pass the playground at a pace before she stops again and looks at him.

"You never knew what you needed, didn't know whether to be here or there, always wanting things to be different," she says.

How to mash-up a heart is easy. "You do any better?"

She starts to walk again, slowly, as they reach the tall trees near the end of the park. "My dad was sure you were involved with Geoffrey."

"Of course he was," because Catherine's father is an ignorant rass and they both know it.

"So was he right?"

"No, no, he wasn't right." But there is no way of telling the story that doesn't make him look bad somehow. "I wasn't involved in anything that Geoffrey did," he says, and this seems to calm her if not convince her. And then he is vex. "You just went along with what your dad thought?"

Catherine squints and keeps walking. He knows this is the thing that will bruk them up, right here, once again, but he has no choice. "Why wouldn't you let me see you?"

"I couldn't trust you any more," she says—hard-hard, like she is holding stone in her teeth.

"You didn't even give me a chance, not a one," he says.

"It wouldn't have been good for Olivia."

"I'm her father."

There's a look on her face like she's sucking a tamarind. Catherine turns to him beneath the branches of the smallest of the oaks in the row. "No," she says.

He looks in her face, the Marilyn Monroe eyes and pout that have gone droopy with age and probably too much drink, there with her father and brother in front of the television. He waits for her to continue.

"No, you're not."

There is a bird making a racket above them in the oak tree. A cawing like it has been set on fire and it's trapped among the leaves that each catch-a-fire, and it's like the whole tree is going to burn down. He looks up at the cawing but can't see the bird. What he can see is the place she lived, the flat on Romford Road where she told him she was pregnant.

"She looks like me." The fire in the tree is hissing. Catherine shuffles her feet.

"You're much better looking than he was," she says.

And now he knows. The man before him, the one from St. Kitts; the one whose photo he saw in her purse: wide-faced, big hands, for so. The one who, three weeks into Ed's courting of Catherine like she was the last queen of England, was going back to St. Kitts and asked to see her one last time.

When a couple months later she said she was pregnant it wasn't with a thrill in her voice the way a woman expecting a baby should be. It was him who was chuffed, looking around Catherine's flat, declaring it was unfit for bringing up a child, and securing them a council house.

"Catherine." The sound of her name is flat and treacherous. *You knew all this time?* But that is just a waste of words, because of course she knew. A mother knows these things.

"What about Olivia?" he says.

Catherine eases herself down to sit on the grass. "She knows now."

"Since when?"

"A couple weeks."

The last time he saw her was at Jonathan Henley's funeral where she watched Ed sing "Amazing Grace" like a fool.

Christ. The damn bird keeps cawing like a rass. A mad good-fa-nothin' bird. Not tiyoooh, yooh-yoooh of a toucan; not yeeh, yeeeh of a kiskadee. This bird is caw-caw like it sick.

"You're the one she remembers—to her you are her father," Catherine says.

What does someone remember from four years old? His legs are boneless beneath him and he slips down to the grass beside her, not to sitting, just perched on one knee like a man proposing to a tree.

He's nobody's father.

Saltfish, tamarind balls, metagee: he doesn't need to remember the taste of these now, or to rhyme them off for Olivia. His mother's bangle in the top drawer of his dresser—her pulling it over her hand and wrist the last time he saw her on the steps of her sister's house in Rose Hall Town: this too can wait. His auntie Margaret has children who pay attention to mum, but for twenty-two years she has wanted to see her granddaughter. For eighteen years she has been sending small gifts for her, the gold bangle the most precious. Every Guyanese girl must have a bangle, and most fitting if the bangle is from the grandmother whose middle name the child will bear her entire life. Olivia.

Niggeritus, backoo, obeyah, piknee: he need not mention these. If you eat labba and drink creek water you will return to Guyana. None of this matters now.

Catherine does not move or say a word. Sitting, kneeling, the two of them under the tree on fire. He's surprised by how quickly it seems that the light has gone dimmer and there is a pain in his knee. He gets up and Catherine does the same. They walk together, slowly, to the exit of the park. She wants to say something, he can tell, but no, please don't. He catches her eye and then turns to walk away to the bus.

OLIVIA

Good Friday, flip the bird to you, Jesus, and all she needs is more Maltesers, more coffee from one of those chains, she doesn't mind which, 'cos principles and politics and parental units are the fuck-up of the tiny bit of herself that once thought she had something significant, special, banging, to be sharing and making a difference with, but all that's holy in this weekend is the fact that the library is still open. She is the fuck-you-I'm-going-to-crack-it-and-make-something-of-herself Olivia who never did a single thing but look out for everyone else, never had a thought that was solely her own and never did like she's doing now which is writing with her head trained on the page like it is in a brace, and writing a word at a time, building to a sentence, not looking further than a sentence or thinking about the whole of the sum of the sentences; she's writing one word like it's one foot in front of the other, out, out, out of here.

Another ping from the mobile at the bottom of her satchel. These are regular-like now, one every few hours. Pleading. From Jaz. From Catherine. But nothing from Nasar, the most obedient of the lot. She pulls her phone from the satchel.

I saw Wood. Told him everything. Please come home now.

Her heart goes all dented for Wood but not for Catherine, because a mother who lies to you your whole life will have to do a whole lot more than ask please. She holds tight onto herself in that clench she has perfected. In four thousand more words, one after the other, she will examine legislation that needs to go beyond current rights issues: beyond the disposal of bodies; beyond crimes committed against dead bodies in which there is a tangle of competing rights pitting survivors against the deceased, or the deceased against the police or the powers of the state; beyond cases of harvesting sperm from a corpse; beyond the definition of sex with a dead body as rape; beyond the anatomical gift act that regulates organ donation and follows the wishes of the deceased unless the family vetoes them and gets the last word. And if she gets beyond all these, she will have arrived at something resembling an original idea. There is a case to be made for rights that take into account a proper goodbye.

ROBIN

His side hurts, his calf, his right hand, and there's a feeling in his ear like someone is twisting the tip. He stands up. If he stays perfectly still he can feel his insides churning, his body's organs at work as though against one another. He lies back down on the bed. The ceiling of Robin's bedroom has a brown stain left over from a leak of many years ago, a stain he's not got round to painting over. He will have to do that, soon, before Emma moves in, before things get crammed with baby paraphernalia, before he forgets that these small things make a difference to a life, that aesthetics are important. These are the kinds of things that people with children forget. The stain looks like the figure of a giraffe. Perhaps he should keep it.

He has been lying on his back now for over twelve hours, the light on throughout the night while he dozed and woke, not sleeping deeply enough, not having changed out of his clothes.

Emma is thrilled with the news of his job. She is planning on bringing him an Easter Sunday lunch to celebrate, to share as a family.

The fact that he waited outside Katrin's bedsit for an hour until he realized how futile that was, the fact that he returned to

Epicure and Alejandro was able to confirm that she had not left for another job, that Alejandro had received a few texts from her about the possibility of leaving London but nothing more, the fact that Robin's calls to her phone were answered by the woman who tells you that the number has not been recognized, the fact of Katrin as only an afterimage: his head is somewhere else entirely from his legs, feet, fingernails, groin, heart. The only thing to do is to keep staring at the giraffe.

He looks at the clock and waits until 23:11 before he closes his eyes again.

—

Emma's Easter lunch is roast lamb, potatoes and green beans. She is gentle, careful, trying to help him feel better because he's told her he is ill, has some sort of Asian flu probably, some ghastly thing from his students, not well at all.

"Any old excuse not to wash up," she said at first, but she must have then taken seriously the anguish in his face, because now she's clearing up and making the flat comfortable for him. This will be his life. Surely not a bad thing.

"Maybe we should go to Cornwall—you could use a break, and you have two weeks before teaching starts again. The sea, some walking, check in on your folks," she suggests. But he would be too tempted to slip down one of those cliffs. Too tempted to tell his folks that he doesn't love this woman and that they should not go thinking it's all just one big happy family now—that it's not as simple as that. He will look after his child. He will. He will love, provide for, play with, challenge, educate and be a good, honest role model. But before he can do that he needs to drag all the pieces of himself together in one spot, to pull in his insides, to gather up his fingers and the strands of his hair. Together.

He goes back to bed when Emma leaves. The giraffe holds its head up high as Robin's body litters the room. Deleuze: The shadow escapes from the body like an animal we had been sheltering . . . It is not the slumber of reason that engenders monsters, but vigilant and insomniac rationality.

What kind of success is it to have saved himself a job where he does nothing but think? He sits, picks up the journal on his bedside table: L=A=N=G=U=A=G=E. He flips through, but then tosses it aside. He lies back down and stares again at the ceiling. He tries to focus on the feeling of being a dad, but nothing comes but terror. Fact is, fear might just create a new stain. Deleuze: If you're trapped in the dream of the Other, you're fucked.

He picks up the list tucked into the journal. On it are Bernadette Mayer's suggestions for poetry experiments:

- Write the same poem over and over again, in different forms, until you are weary. Another experiment: Set yourself the task of writing for four hours at a time, perhaps once, twice or seven times a week. Don't stop until hunger and/or fatigue take over. At the very least, always set aside a four-hour period once a month in which to write. This is always possible and will result in one book of poems or prose writing for each year. Then we begin to know something.
- Attempt as a writer to win the Nobel Prize in science by finding out how thought becomes language, or does not.
- Take a traditional text like the pledge of allegiance to the flag. For every noun, replace it with one that is seventh or

ninth down from the original one in the dictionary. For instance, the word "honesty" would be replaced by "honey dew melon." Investigate what happens; different dictionaries will produce different results.

None of these is as structured as chance-operation. He looks at the clock, watches it until 23:11. The first book of poetry he takes from his shelf is *White Egrets.*

"The chess men are rigid on their chess board." Okay, line one. He turns out the light and tries to sleep.

ED AND ROBIN

The stapler is his—he must remember to take it. They give you rass-hole staplers in the council and this one he bought himself, top of the line. Sammy steals it at least once a day, but it's Ed's.

"This place," Sammy says as he opens the office for the day. "This place," again, and Ed isn't sure if Sammy means the Safe and Sorrow office or if he's talking about the local authority, or London, or the whole damn world. It doesn't matter, because all of them feel like a head-shaking mess to Sammy today, and this you can see in the man's shoulders, which have gone hunch-up. But what's to be hunch-up for? When water throw away ah ground yuh can't pick am up.

"You know, it's not me they've booted out only because they'd have to give me more severance, don't you? Longer-term service, uninterrupted. You know that, right?" Sammy says. They both look over at Ralph, who looks straight ahead, filling out of a form on his computer.

Poor Sammy is feeling sad, but this shaking-head is the only way he knows to show it. He hasn't looked Ed in the eye since they heard the news.

"Sammy," Ed says, calm fa so. He pauses so that Sammy will stop and turn around, but he doesn't, just keeps tidying up, putting paper in the shredder. "Sammy, I'm fine, you hear?" And Sammy does hear, but that doesn't make him stop tidying, and Ed can tell from how Sammy sits down at this desk that his heart is mash-up. Ed will remember to get Sammy a raisin Danish on his break.

He's not the first one in, but Robin is standing at the door of the Safe and Sorrow office as soon as Ed opens it. He knows him only by the glasses that look bigger on the man's face now.

"You cut off all your hair!" Ed says, in a tease, but in fact Robin looks better this way, more grown-up, dignified-like. He doesn't bother to take Robin to the staff room. Sammy and Ralph can overhear anything they want at this point.

"How's Olivia's project going then?" he asks. "Haven't seen her since before Easter. She tried to reach me, but I've been busy-busy," he tells Robin because when guilt is so big, lies come fast and easy. He will ring her back, he will, but what to say? Almost-dad. Not good enough.

"I would like to contribute, to her project, your funerals," Robin says.

"Doesn't matter, not now," Ed says.

"Oh," Robin says, yet sees nothing like sadness in Ed's face. Only some small trace of Olivia. "I'm sorry," he says. He touches his pocket and feels the crunch of the paper there, the ridiculous, irrelevant game of the past fourteen days.

Wood's face opens up to a smile. "Sorry? What you have to be sorry for?" The man's accent is strong today. Robin nods.

"I thought I would try, in any case—Olivia's idea, it might bring some good," he says.

"Well, it might, but who knows when the next one will be—we can't predict these things. Maybe Sammy will work with you." Ed looks over at his friend, who is listening but making a show of ignoring the whole damn scene, probably wondering what the rass is going on over here. These two men like surra and durra on the stage, both wishing they could do a little something, both just sorry-sorry to one another. Olivia missing in between them. The St. Kitts man must have been something. Who gave the girl her sense of right and wrong? Is that something you are born with?

They sit in silence until it becomes uncomfortable. Robin pulls the piece of paper out of his pocket, unfolding it. He reads over it, quickly. Crap, not a poem, but deliberate, like lightning. He gives it to Wood, who takes it but doesn't look at it. There's a gritty irritation in Robin's eyes, as though sand is caught on the underside of his eyelid. His eyes water and he wipes them. In cinema a flash burn is named after the effect of snow blindness, which is akin to a sunburn of the cornea. But a flash-burn effect is too obvious, too simple for now.

Wood holds the piece of paper, still just looking at him. Robin imagines Wood at the head of a coffin, reading his plagiarized nonsense.

"Well, it was good to meet you," he says.

"And you," Ed says. Robin stands up and shakes his hand. This man is something good, true-true.

Then Robin has the opposite of an afterimage: a time image that produces space, the finite restoring the infinite; it's the house where Katrin's grandmother grew up, beside the river, and his finger on the tiny buzzer alerts its occupants to a visitor. Fact is, Gdansk is only a city. Gdansk cannot be that big.

OLIVIA AND ED

"An examination of civil rights in death," Olivia says, and keeps her knee from moving. Holds it there, stone-like, 'cos this is how it's going to be from now on, steady, like steel, but knowing, like silk. She will not be tricked again by Catherine or anyone else. "My supervisor said I needed something historical, not practical—it's not practice-based research," she says. Ed nods, but maybe he's disappointed that she abandoned the lonely dead. She hasn't, really, it's only the appearance of stone there in her leg; there's no stillness in her heart.

The A13 feels different. Same emptiness, same salt, pepper and brown sauce, but today it looks sparkly bright, as though Mary has been scrubbing and buffing and picking out the grime with a cotton-tipped swab.

"Sounds good," Ed says, and man, oh man, the girl is clever-for-so, but where once he thought he had something to do with it, now he feels like a rasshole fool. There's no one here but Mary to see him cry if it comes to that.

"It was possible all on account of you," she says, and it's true, even if it was for all the wrong reasons. Catherine is the lifetime liar, and Olivia is taking her sweet time to talk to her mother again, but Wood—Wood is solid fam.

She's humouring him, of course, he thinks, because he is laughable, lonely, nearly dead himself. He takes a sip of his tea and sneaks a quick look at the evidence of her face, and maybe there is a trace of the St. Kitts man there in the wideness, when all along he thought it was like Auntie Margaret's face.

While Ed is staring at her Olivia knows there's stuff for him to get used to, expectations he has to stop having, so she lets him. She lets his eyes wander over her ears, her nose, her chin, like he's looking to see if maybe Catherine was wrong after all. Olivia hasn't even wondered what the other bloke might have looked like, doesn't want to know, doesn't want to have another face or another voice in her head to haunt her. Once she thought she would ask Ed to sing the song again, of the brown girl in the ring, but, hell, no. She doesn't want any more incantations or ghosts.

"But I still want to do the project with you—it's still right, still good," she says. With her dissertation finished, she's confident of a 2.1, at least, and if she doesn't get a first, well, she'll still become a lawyer, will still train further, will still make enough to move out—alone—but there's no giving up; this she accepts. The questions change. Who will _____ these people? Fill in the blank. Living with Catherine, Nan, Granddad and Eric won't be as bad, for a while, if she knows at least this much about herself.

"Look, Olivia," Ed says, and meets her eye. There is no denying that she is beautiful and of course she is nothing like Geoffrey. He pulls apart the paper napkin that came with his tea. "The man Geoffrey killed . . . " the napkin looks like snowflakes . . . "I wanted to say . . . " and there's a tinkle-like sound from Mary's bracelets as she wipes the table next to them . . . "I arrived at the spot where Geoffrey killed him—minutes too late—and he was there, his face in the river. He was dead, I was sure of it, but I could have done something, maybe. I could have called someone; I could have turned him over. I could even have said something like I was sorry, but I didn't. I did nothing. I watched Geoffrey run through the bush and I didn't tell anyone what I saw. I went back to the camp farther down river and I pretended I saw nothing, and no one asked me, and no one expected me to know, so I kept it to myself. I had gone to find Geoffrey, to give him the money he needed, to make sure he wouldn't get into trouble, and found a whole lot worse." He looks back at her. Olivia has questions in her face the way some women have desire. She nods. "It's what I thought you did for family, for a brother."

"You thought?" she says.

"I don't know, now. I don't think so, no," Ed says. The real story was so much easier than he had imagined for so long.

"So, you'll let me know when the next one is?" Olivia says, and for a second he thinks she's referring to Geoffrey, before he realizes.

"I might not have a funeral again before I go—you can't plan these things. I have only three months."

"It would be a good thing if you got none in three months, wouldn't it?" she says. Olivia is mash-up for anyone's heart. "But if you do, you'll tell me, right?"

"Yes, I will," Ed says.

"We could go to the museum again. Or I was thinking, I've always wanted to go to the Carnival."

"Oh?" She's never jump-up, never played Mas or ever wind-up and fete so. He nods, and his heart is doing a j'ouvert jump-up of its own. "I was doing some research, too—there's a Guyanese poet . . . it might be good."

"Oh?" Same intonation as his, but she is not mocking him.

"Death must not find us thinking that we die."

"That's good!" she says with a flourish. They both pick up their teacups at the same time. They sip.

"Wood," she says, and she sees where the word has landed in how his shoulders relax. This man was the only one who ever picked her up and held her.

FRANCINE

At the door to Ronnie Scott's Patricia doesn't look unhappy, doesn't look like a woman whose whole department has been shut down—"Who needs a degree in anthropology when you could get one in marketing?" Patricia said flatly to Francine on the phone. It was Francine's idea to come out tonight. "It's fine," Patricia says to her as they walk up the stairs to the salsa room.

"What will you do?" Francine says.

"Never write a book again," Patricia says, and Francine is surprised by her equanimity, not believing that she could be as fine as she professes. Upstairs Francine checks their coats, gets them a drink and then the feeling of being in the transporter is back.

Diaphanous men in their twenties: African, Latino, tight jeans. Very tight jeans. Their skin is translucent in Francine's X-ray vision.

There is a dark Latino dancing salsa with a tiny woman with straight, brown hair whose short flounce skirt splays like a sail when he turns her. The man's arms are as sculpted as an Oscar trophy.

Patricia raises her glass and sips from a straw. Francine looks at the pad of lines on the skin of Patricia's knuckles, there like ancient footprints or dinosaur knees. They are the oldest women in the room. There are one or two middle-aged men, but the rest are in their twenties or thirties, not English. How is it that Patricia has no self-consciousness here?

"You look good," Patricia shouts over the horns, conga drums, the singer and his repeated *galenga, galenga, galenga*. But Francine is sure she looks like shit and that to see through her you'd have to penetrate her puffy, ricotta-cheese cheeks. But maybe Patricia has seen through her all along.

The instructor turns down the music and she notices for the first time that the men here are checking them both out. When she looks through them, she sees them in a sandbox: dump trucks and spades and diapers full of poo hanging down from their backsides. If she looks harder, she sees them fifty years in the future: their skin loose and iguana-neck-like, their butts gone soft and droopy; their penises bulbous but flopping. What is the sound of one hand clapping?

"Line up, line up. Girls on one side, boys on the other—but some of you will be acting the part of boys," says the instructor, who is taking into account that the females outnumber the males. Francine does as she's told and is face to face with the Latino with the Oscar-trophy arms, who couldn't be older than thirty.

"Now face your partner—girls, stretch out your arms; and boys, take her waist. Girls, hand on shoulders."

He starts the music again and shouts instructions at them while doing the moves himself, his hand on his tummy, his hips swinging side to side. He does the steps, shouts the ins and outs, the hand holding, the spinning, and Francine follows along with trophy man without a foot wrong. She looks up at him, sees him smiling at her, and he pulls her close, suddenly: "Manuel," he says in her ear. She looks down at her feet. His hot breath on her cheek makes her nervous and she misses a step. When he releases her she looks up and says, quietly, "Francine," but he's not looking at her any more and will never know her name.

"Now change—cha cha!" the instructor shouts and Manuel moves her forward and back, one-two-three. She searches for Patricia and sees her with one of the middle-aged men. She's not smiling, but not unhappy either as she concentrates on her steps.

"Rum makes me stupid," Francine says to Patricia in passing, after they are instructed to switch partners. They dance for hours, and the beat will not give up. When she stops for a rest, Manuel takes the rum and Coke from her hand, places it down on the table and leads her again to the dance floor.

"You are good," he says, after he twirls her as the music changes, goes slow and thumpy. He brings her in close, and, yep, there it is, his hand on her giant ass like a butcher with a prime cut. She holds her breath. "You are very sexy," he says in her ear. This is not happening. She says nothing. He pushes her back and holds her at arm's length, looking her up and down.

She laughs, which he seems to like, and he pulls her close again and gives her a peck on her cheek that feels nearly like a lick. A tingle at her neck, along her arm, to the tips of her fingers and she squeezes his hand. Oh shit. She didn't mean to do that. She is the opposite of a thirteen-year old, but feels exactly the same. Maybe the thing that love comes with is seasons. She sees Patricia smiling proudly at her from the side of the room.

They close the place, are the last ones out, even after Manuel and the women he gravitated towards at the end of the night, who are young but do not have Francine's life raft of a butt, of which she is a tiny bit proud.

"Let's get something to eat," Patricia says, and out they head and turn onto Old Compton Street, where Francine smells urine and is convinced she hears bones clacking. She stops and stands on the spot to watch. The black cast-steel bollard, the warped brick of the corner building, the corrugated iron that covers the shop window: she is small and soft beside these.

"That was special, no?" Patricia says, coming close.

Francine tries to smell her but the familiar butter and lavender are lost amongst the piss and beer on the pavement. Iron, rust, fried onions, exhaust fumes, tobacco. She smiles but doesn't answer, doesn't say heck, yeah Patty! Because she's wondering how much a landscape gardening programme might cost her, wondering if she'll make more than minimum wage in any future job, and she doesn't want Patricia to look at her with horror when she tells her that she's quitting her job in QA and going to tell Larry he's fat. She doesn't want to worry Patricia or for her to think it's false solidarity in the face of her redundancy. Instead, she leans in towards Dancefloor Patty and kisses her on the lips, and holds her mouth there. Patricia doesn't pull back, not first in any case, and when Francine is again aware of how she feels, well, she's certain it's only a hot flash.

OLIVIA

Oi. She flicks away the wasp on her wrist. It's hot even in the thick-as-paint shade of the yew tree outside the crematorium at the Rippleside Cemetery. Holy, holy, holy, like a beat girl poet, 'cos Olivia is now down with ceremonies as though they are the new #Demo. Though there's no knowing the religion of Diyanat Bayar, who Ed thinks is Turkish, or maybe Armenian, which would change things, the service is about making praise, even though it's not in the chapel. Diyanat's UK passport might even have been stolen, forged, and so the truth is that no one knows a thing about this body that is about to be burned and disposed of. The twenty-seven-year-old Diyanat, if that is his name, has no family in the UK. The Turkish consulate is busy with Turkish nationals, the coroner told Ed, and haven't been able to trace anyone yet. The coroner who registered the death also told Ed that Diyanat has a tattoo on his arm of an anchor, but there's no link to Diyanat being a sailor, because Diyanat's last job was in the bakery where he'd been hired only a few months ago. Holy, holy, holy.

Olivia watches as Ed arranges the bouquet of lilies on the top of the cardboard casket. This is his last funeral. Ed wanted her to be here, saying he had something to show her, something that he thought would make her happy, and something that was on account of her.

When Olivia was still researching her dissertation, way back in May, which was the last time it was hot like this and the last time she saw Ed, she read about three people of the same family discovered dead by the police in their apartment in the northern district of Tokyo. Electricity and gas had been cut off; there was no food in the house and just a few one-yen coins on the table. The grotesquely thin bodies belonged to a couple in their sixties and their son in his thirties, and they had all died of starvation. The management property reported getting no rent, and the newspaper said that the family had asked a neighbour for help. The neighbour told them to go on welfare, which they didn't do, on account of losing face. The report went on to say how lonely deaths are increasing in Japan. In the winter two sisters in their forties were found dead in their freezing apartment on snowbound Hokkaido.

"Thank you for coming," Ed says to Olivia, as she is the only mourner in attendance. The funeral director and his assistant stand off to the side, looking like they're daydreaming about the cold pint they'll have as soon as this is finished.

"We are here to pay our last respects to Diyanat Bayar, who was too young to be leaving us, really," Ed says and then looks down at the casket. The breeze around them is soft and she feels gooseflesh rise on her arms despite the heat.

Ed looks older. Not so much in wrinkles or greying or geezer-like stuff, but just in the way his mouth falls when at rest. Right. She will not worry; she is working on this part of herself in relation to everyone else. He will find another job. Just look at him. Wood is strong, worthy, a man with a good head. He takes a piece of paper out his pocket and unfolds it, catching her eye with a look that says: *This is it, here, now.*

"I would like to read something for Diyanat—something that was written by a friend of ours, a while back. He gave it to me and asked me to read it the next time I had the opportunity, and this is that opportunity, so please allow me," Ed says, and gives her a nod.

Olivia feels the gooseflesh grow and spread up towards her neck.

Ed looks down at the paper and begins.

"The chessmen are rigid on their chess board,
I can hear little clicks inside my dream,
Auntie stands by the kettle, looking at the kettle,
If I were a cinnamon peeler,
That strength, mother: dug out. Hammered, chained.
What can I say about the storms?
An eagle does not know who he is,
Who modelled your head of terracotta?
Chalk and beaches. The winter sea,
I wonder at your witchcraft
One morning Don Miguel got out of bed,
Let us go then, you and I,
Not a tent of blue but a peak of gold,
No getting up from the bed in this grand hotel."

Ed looks up proudly at her. But Olivia doesn't think she caught it right. There's nothing she understands about the poem and what it means. She wants him to read it again, to take his time, because what is Robin saying here?

The funeral director and his assistant make their way to the casket, looking annoyed, as though their time is being wasted in this boiling July heat for this man and his daughter to work out some puzzle between them. They wheel the casket towards the back door of the crematorium and Ed watches as Diyanat takes his leave. Olivia leaves the shade of the yew, headed towards Ed, practising her one-foot-in-front-of-the-other strategy. Since her last exams she's been calmer, been spending days sleeping when she wants to, nights with Jaz who is single once more, and she is slowly starting to allow Catherine to talk to her again. She has a paid internship with the Citizens Advice Bureau starting in August and she's had the time not to feel panicked.

"What did you think?" Ed says.

"Yes, yes," she says. "I'd like to hear it again."

Ed holds the page up to her. "You take it," he says.

"No, it's yours," she says and pushes his hand back.

There'll be no more use for this poem, she knows, but she's afraid to read it for herself now. And maybe she doesn't need to.

"I should get going," she says. She doesn't want to go to the A13 today; she wants to stay out in the sun.

"Okay," Ed says, and she has to resist the dented feeling in her chest. Wood is proper nang. Wood is going to be all right. This is not where she's from, but this is more like who she is.

She kisses his cheek and stands back, turns and walks towards the gates of the cemetery. The sun is wicked and makes the back of her neck ping like there's a message for her. If Nasar still has the same number, it will be in her phone.

Right.

ACKNOWLEDGEMENTS

This book was possible thanks to the insight and inspiration I gained from my students and colleagues; the quiet writing space generously provided by friends; and the generous feedback from special readers. My thanks to—among other students, too many to be named here—Danielle Jawando, Samantha Dodd, Jo Berouche, Joe Caesar, James Moore, Annette Kamara, Sandra Majchrowska, Erica Masserano and Naida Redgrave, who inspired the fighting spirit of the students in this novel.

Thanks to my colleagues at the University of East London for their support, resilience, and good spirits during difficult times: particularly to Stephen Maddison, Marianne Wells, Kate Hodgkin, and especially to Tim Atkins for poetry, humour, and Zen. I am grateful to the University of East London for research support and leave that enabled me to finish this book.

Thanks to the green mamba for Ned Time, to Andrew Ruhemann and Jennifer Nadel for Paris, to Mike Perry for Ffynnonofi, and to the Morris family for kindness and Wood. I'm indebted to Marko Jobst and David Friend for crucial feedback on early drafts; to Fides Krucker for writing companionship, banana bread, and voice insight; and to Stephanie Young for being there, reading fast, and knowing what a first draft is. Eternal gratitude to John Berger for his wisdom and generosity.

Thanks to Andrew Kidd for belief, rigour, telepathy; to Anne Collins for courage, enthusiasm and invaluable support; and to the kind people at Random House Canada for making this book happen.

"I'm the pen your lover writes with" is from a poem by Bernadette Mayer; her poetry experiments inspired Robin's poem, which is formed by the first lines of the following poems:

Derek Walcott, "White Egrets"; Anne Carson, "The Glass Essay"; Jo Shapcott, "Somewhat Unravelled"; Michael Ondaatje, "The Cinnamon Peeler's Wife"; Anne Carson, "That Strength in Decreation"; Dionne Brand, "Ossuary IX"; Al Purdy, "Man Without a Country"; Ted Hughes, "The Earthenware Head"; Anne Michaels, "Fontanelles"; Daniel Wideman, "Glass Eater"; Don Paterson, "Two Trees"; T. S. Eliot, "The Love Song of J. Alfred Prufrock"; Seamus Heaney, "Death of a Painter"; and Carol Anne Duffy, "Cuba."

Quotations from Gilles Deleuze are from *Capitalism and Schizophrenia: Anti-Oedipus* (1972) and *A Thousand Plateaus* (1980).

TESSA McWATT is the author of five previous novels and *There's No Place Like...* , a novella for young adults. Her second novel, *Dragons Cry*, was shortlisted for the City of Toronto Book Awards and the Governor General Literary Awards. Her other novels include *This Body*, *Step Closer*, and *Vital Signs*, which was nominated for the 2012 OCM Bocas Prize for Caribbean Literature. She teaches creative writing at the University of East London where she developed the BA and MA in Creative Writing and founded the UEL Writing Centre.